MOUNTAINS OF GILEAD

MOUNTAINS
OF GILEAD

a novel by JESSE
HILL FORD

An Atlantic Monthly Press Book

LITTLE, BROWN AND COMPANY

BOSTON 🌱 TORONTO

ATLANTIC–LITTLE, BROWN BOOKS
ARE PUBLISHED BY
LITTLE, BROWN AND COMPANY
IN ASSOCIATION WITH
THE ATLANTIC MONTHLY PRESS

Published simultaneously in Canada
by Little, Brown & Company (Canada) Limited

PRINTED IN THE UNITED STATES OF AMERICA

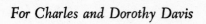

For Charles and Dorothy Davis

My son? and what's a son? A thing begot
Within a pair of minutes — thereabout;
A lump bred up in darkness, and doth serve
To ballast these light creatures we call women;
And, at nine months' end, creeps forth to light.
What is there yet in a son,
To make a father dote, rave, or run mad?

— Thomas Kyd
The Spanish Tragedie, 1587

BOOK ONE

1

DOCTOR Ocie Pentecost heard a band playing "The Saint Louis Blues." It would be one of the high school bands in town for the strawberry festival. The band was probably over on the asphalt playground of the elementary school, warming up for the parade. When he entered the corridor of the hospital he could no longer hear the band. Sister Margaret Angelica was writing a medical report at her station desk outside the delivery room. She got up and hurried down the corridor towards him, her starched uniform rustling as she came, her face pale and drawn. The hospital was understaffed and the strain of long hours showed in Sister Angelica's face. It was the month's end, and the babies, like unpaid bills, were coming due all in a rush.

"Thank heavens, I thought you wouldn't make it in time," she said.

"How are the pains?" Doctor Ocie asked.

"You'll have just time to scrub."

Inside the delivery room a woman was howling, a monotonous, hopeless sound.

"Is that my patient yelling?" Doctor Ocie asked.

"No, that's the dentist's wife. It's Mrs. Burkette, Doctor Fielder's patient. She's about two hours away."

Ocie nodded and pushed through the door to the doctors' dressing room, slinging off his coat and coming out of his shirt with one smooth movement. He slipped into a scrub suit, then went into the scrub room where he moved the brush vigorously over his hands and arms, smelling the astringent soap. There would be just time to catch the baby. Just time.

When he had scrubbed he pushed through the swinging steel door and realized then that Mrs. Burkette, who was still howling, had *been* howling all the while. The sound annoyed him.

He found his own patient sweating and groaning quietly and gritting her teeth while a nurse wiped her forehead. The monotonous yells of the other woman continued without pause. He was about to check his own patient's degree of dilation when the infant's head appeared. The nurse at his elbow handed him the scissors and he split the balloon-tight vaginal flesh with short, quick snips, and with the episiotomy done the baby came on easily. Doctor Ocie caught him, the infant cried spontaneously, and the nurse took him from Doctor Ocie's hands, a raring healthy male that would go a good seven pounds, the doctor estimated. A nurse's aid handed him the tray of threaded needles and he began suturing the episiotomy.

Thank God she isn't a patient of mine, he thought, as the other woman continued to yell. He knew the type. Her mother had probably warned her about the terrors of childbirth. Her mother had told her how mothers suffered, and now, even though this was her third child, it would not come without a lot of howling from Mrs. Burkette.

She was Doctor Fielder's patient, and Fielder was the youngest physician in Somerton, so young he seemed almost callow, and yet Ocie himself had once been Somerton's youngest physician. Now he was its oldest. The years go by, the doctor thought. Yes, the years went by and one day you woke up and someone had died during the night, and suddenly you realized you were the oldest physician in town. If a man lived long enough he could expect something of the sort.

The nurse said the baby weighed seven pounds. Doctor Ocie tied off the last stitch and shucked off his bloody gloves. There was no need in trying to talk to his patient now. She was resting. He could see it in her eyes that she was resting and that she was comfortable now, comfortable and proud. "A fine boy," he said, patting her shoulder. It was her fifth child, and Ocie had delivered them all, from the very first. The bond between them was strong. Her hand gave his arm a grip of thanks and she nodded.

Ocie found her husband, Rankin Morgan, waiting in the hall. Ocie had delivered *him*. And there the fellow stood, strapping and sun-burned, with the broad face and the strong teeth, the huge arms and the slightly curled, sand-colored hair of the whole Morgan clan. Rankin's big hand enveloped Ocie's and Rankin grinned shyly.

"You got another boy," Ocie said.

"The nurse just told me."

Ocie clapped him on the shoulder. "Seven pounds."

"He'll grow, I reckon," Rankin said. "When can I see him?"

"Wait in Katherine's room. The nurse will bring him up when he's clean. Then you can say hello to the mama and the baby both."

Rankin once again grinned sheepishly and turned away with a wave of his hand, heading for the obstetrical corridor. He disappeared around the corner and Ocie went back to the scrub room to change into his street clothes. Fielder was there, scrubbing. "Ever hear so much noise out of one woman before?" he asked.

"She's loud," Ocie agreed.

"She's a ring-tail tooter. I don't see why she doesn't get hoarse. I'm gonna give her a shot and see if I can't bring that baby on a little faster."

Ocie nodded. He could remember only one other patient who had howled like Mrs. Burkette was howling, a patient of his, long ago. One of his *first* patients, in fact, he realized, back when he delivered babies at his clinic, long before the hospital was built. He had finally given his patient ether to shut her up, and the baby had been scrawny and cyanotic at birth, almost dead in fact. Ocie had been afraid it would not cry, but at last it had begun to draw air into its narrow lungs, and finally it had begun to cry and the mother had come out from under her anesthetic and vomited and screamed for water and vomited again. Her trouble was that she had thought the thing inside her was a tumor, and for months she had told no one about what was happening. She had been close to the menopause and had confused her pregnancy with the onset of that herald of a woman's sunset years. Ocie smiled, thinking of how young and how frightened he had been, and of what a stormy patient the woman had been. They had called her Madam Shafer, although her real name was Octavia. And Madam had been a ring-tail tooter herself, while she lived. But Madam Shafer had died quite a few years back, before the miracle drugs, of pneumonia.

"Well," Fielder said. "I'll see you."

"All right," Ocie replied. Fielder was short and stoop-shouldered. His intern's pallor had not yet been worn away, and just now he had most of the problem patients. Ocie watched the door to the delivery room close after the young doctor, and he went out into the corridor. Sister Angelica waved to him as he went by her desk. A doctor started with the problem patients and he ended up with patients like the Morgans, a whole clan, all farmers and all descended from early settlers in West Tennessee. When *they* chose a doctor he waited on them all, and they had chosen Ocie. It was a thing to be proud of, a large practice, good patients who loved and trusted you. And yet, as he thought about the Morgan clan and the other families he served, the other babies he had delivered, Ocie thought too about his own retirement from practice. He didn't give it *much* thought, for there were four more babies due, all probably to be born during the night or on the day following. Babies came that way, in flocks. But Ocie thought: Maybe in two years I'll retire and go live in Florida.

Maybe in two years. Babies came and years went. Years ticked swiftly away. He left by the doctors' entrance, got in his car, and drove away from the low, flat hospital building.

In order to make his house call he had to turn right on Mount Olive Road and then swing back into Main Street on the outskirts of Somerton, all in order to avoid the traffic jams caused by the strawberry festival which was in progress. The festival brought thirty thousand people into a town built to hold eight thousand, causing a yearly nuisance; yet it helped trade, encouraged the farmers, and gave the committees in charge something to haggle over. Because of the haggling Ocie had carefully steered clear of any involvement with the running of the strawberry festival, just as now, he skirted the jammed downtown sections of Somerton in order to make his house call on Gabe French, Sr. Gabe Senior was a wheelchair invalid and something of a nuisance himself, living as he did, holed up in a single room of his capacious house, almost barricaded in the room, it seemed, with a Negro man to wait on him, never leaving the room, much less the house. No matter how sick he got, Gabe Senior refused to go to the hospital. Ocie turned his car into the driveway, took his treatment bag out of the back seat, and walked past the massive oak tree that shaded the side entrance to the enormous old clapboard house. He crossed the screened porch and went down the high-ceilinged hallway to Gabe Senior's room. He found Gabe's daughter-in-law, Betty Morgan, sitting with him.

"I'm better," Gabe Senior said when he saw Ocie, speaking before Ocie could even say "Hello." Gabe Senior sat in his wheelchair with an old red quilt tucked about his legs. As usual he was immaculate, close-shaven, wearing a white stiff collar shirt and a maroon silk tie. The French menfolk were nearly all handsome and their womenfolk were, nearly all

of them, pretty. Gabe Senior was another example in a long
line of nice-looking Frenches. Ocie stuck a fever thermometer
in Gabe Senior's mouth and turned to Betty Morgan. "You
just got another nephew," he said to her.

"Well, I guess I better take her a present," she said reluctantly. Ocie's patient with the new baby was Betty Morgan's sister-in-law.

Gabe Senior pulled the thermometer out of his mouth.
"Going to Gratt Shafer's wedding? Eh, Doc?" he asked.

"No," said Ocie. "Four babies due."

"Well, I sent Gratt a cup and saucer," Gabe Senior said.
"What did you send him?"

"I sent him a silver pitcher."

"But you ain't going to Memphis?"

"No."

"If I weren't in this wheelchair I'd go," Gabe Senior said.
"I always liked weddings, all except my own."

"Now, Papa," Betty Morgan said. She put her hand gently
on his arm. They tried to keep Gabe Senior's mind off of
his wife, for he could fly into a rage just thinking about
Mother French. And yet, most of what had happened was
Gabe Senior's own fault. He had brought the crippling accident on himself.

Since his accident years ago Gabe Senior had not spoken to
Mother French. They shared the same house, but they rarely
saw each other. It was a case of pure hatred between them.

Gabe subsided. "I'd go if I could," he said, putting the
thermometer back in his mouth. But it was no sooner under
his tongue than he took it out again. "Tom McCutcheon's
mad as hell. I guess you knew that."

"Well, he's got no call to be," Ocie said shortly.

"I don't know that *I* blame him," Gabe Senior said. "I suppose I'd feel about the same way Tom McCutcheon does if Gratt Shafer jilted a daughter of mine."

Gabe Senior was taking sides because he had an unmarried daughter himself. His daughter, Mattie French, was also a friend of Patsy Jo McCutcheon's, the girl Gabe Senior believed Gratt Shafer was jilting. The friendship between Mattie French and Patsy Jo was what you might expect, for both were about the same age, past thirty, and both now feared they were going to be old maids. It would be useless, Ocie knew, to argue with Gabe Senior, so he remained quiet as long as he could.

"But is Gratt *really* jilting her?" Betty Morgan asked.

"No," Ocie said. "He isn't. He's taking the best way out of a bad situation, a situation that would never have gotten any better. He told me that much himself."

"But *Tom McCutcheon* don't exactly tell it that way," Gabe Senior said, waving the thermometer. "McCutcheon don't quite tell it all that sweet and simple."

"McCutcheon's a blowhard."

"McCutcheon tells it another way entirely," Gabe Senior persisted. "And I wouldn't go so far to call Tom McCutcheon a blowhard. The McCutcheons have been in Sligo County for a long, *long* time." What Gabe Senior really meant was that it was unseemly for Ocie to side with Gratt Shafer, a second generation resident of the county, against someone with as old and as good a name as Thomas Gideon McCutcheon. In terms of the county's history, Gratt Shafer was a johnny-come-lately. And, of course, were Ocie himself not a doctor, *he* would be a *nobody*, for Ocie had migrated to West Tennessee from the middle section of the state. To Gabe Senior, the fact that McCutcheons had been in the county longer than Shafers was an unshakable, irrefutable, solid-rock argument. "You better think about that, Doc, before you go calling Tom McCutcheon a blowhard," Gabe Senior went on, issuing a reprimand. For in Somerton, as Ocie knew, the *old* families were *always* right. Ocie nodded, accepting Gabe Senior's argument. It was the easiest way. "Well," said Ocie, "I see what you mean."

"Sure you do," Gabe Senior said, a bit mollified. "There's something wrong about all of this, something awful, something terribly wrong." He put the thermometer back in his mouth, and this time he let it stay there, even when Betty Morgan sided with Ocie, taking Gratt Shafer's side, against Patsy Jo McCutcheon. "Patsy Jo ought to be horse-whipped," Betty Morgan said. But Gabe Senior let the thermometer stay where it was, between his compressed lips. He only frowned at Betty Morgan and they were all three quiet then until Ocie took the thermometer out of Gabe Senior's mouth. "You don't have any fever," Ocie said.

"I told you I was better, didn't I?"

Betty Morgan French sold children's encyclopedia sets house to house, among other things. The strawberry festival got people out of pocket, and even if she could find a prospect at home during festival time, it was doubtful that she could close a sale, for everything had a way of being put off until after the festival. The festival created a slump for Betty Morgan right at the beginning of June each year, and there was nothing she could do about it.

Now she had to get a present for Rankin's baby and take it up to the hospital. She stayed with Gabe Senior another ten minutes after Ocie left. Then she prepared to leave too. "Well, I got to go, Papa," she said. She had planned to spend most of the day with Gabe Senior. It was like her to feel that she owed it to the old man because he was her husband's father, because he was Gabe Junior's father, and because he was an invalid. But now, they both knew, she wouldn't be back that day. Her own people, the Morgans, would want her now. The Morgans would want her to brag over the new baby boy Rankin had fathered. They would be waiting up at the hospital this evening, waiting for the whole family to show up and hug Katherine, the baby's mother, and add a present to the pile of presents in her room. Then, when the hospital babies were shown, they would expect Betty Morgan to be there, in front of the long glass window in the hallway, waiting when the curtain was drawn back and the new Morgan was put on display. And she *would* be there. It didn't matter that nobody could tell anything about a baby so newborn, especially by looking through a window at him. If you were a Morgan you would be there and you would say: "He's a Morgan all right. Look at him waving those arms!" And someone would wave back at the baby. "He's waving to his kinfolks," someone else would say. And soon they would all be waving *hello* to the new Morgan. But it had been the same when Betty Morgan's own two sons had been born. The Morgans had done the same for Gabe Senior's grandchildren, and so he could not really begrudge Betty Morgan's departure — regret it, yes; begrudge it, never. She bent to kiss Gabe Senior's cheek. "I'm sorry, Papa," she said. But Gabe Senior waved her off. "You better git on up to that hospital," he said, trying not to let his disappointment show. For from now until Mattie French came home for a few minutes at suppertime, there would be no one for Gabe Senior to talk to except the Negro man who looked after him. But sometimes he and the Negro played checkers, and if the Negro let him win, Gabe Senior could pass an afternoon very pleasantly.

"Good-by," she said. But he only grunted and rapped on the wall with his cane to summon the Negro. "Henty!" he bellowed. "Oh, Henty?"

Betty Morgan met Henty in the hallway, running for Gabe Senior's room. Henty was a convicted murderer, a dark, wise Negro of fifty or so. He was paroled to Gabe Senior, and his keeping out of prison now depended on Gabe Senior's good will towards him. "Morning, ma'am," said Henty as he passed. Betty Morgan nodded to him. Poor devil, she thought. For Henty had traded one prison for another.

She stepped out of the house and pulled the door shut behind her. The old house had been cool, and now she felt the sun glaring on her through the trees as she turned up the sidewalk. She had a long hot walk ahead of her. But she was used to walking. She made her living walking from house to house carrying her sample kits, and from years of walking she had learned to associate the houses she passed with the people who lived in them. In a sense, the people finally came to look like the houses, and the houses to look like the people. You saw a house, you thought of a person; you saw a person and imaged on your mind was the place he lived.

Two blocks up she passed the Shafer house, where Gratt Shafer, who was marrying a rich Memphis honest-to-God debutante, lived. An old Negro, Bojack Markam, kept house for Gratt Shafer, an old-fashioned type Negro who cooked and washed dishes and mopped the kitchen, waxed the automobile, mowed the yard, tended a little garden and raised chickens out behind the house. And like every house she called on, there was trouble connected with knocking on the front door, the trouble at the Shafer house being that Gratt Shafer would not buy anything if *he* were there, and if the Negro were there alone, *he* wouldn't have any money — or at least he would *say* he hadn't any, and from then on he would pretend he was deaf if she tried to ask him questions about *when* he might have some money. It was disheartening to call on the Shafer house, so she rarely tried the place anymore. For no, you could never depend on getting any money out of an old-fashioned Negro anyway. With an old-fashioned Negro like Bojack, his employer simply wrote him out a check when he went to the grocery. Then Bojack kept what was left until he ran out of money. Then when he was out he asked for more and his boss wrote him out another check. In truth, a Negro like Bojack wouldn't know what wages were even if he bumped into them on the street. But, well, Betty Morgan comforted herself, there aren't too darn many Bojacks left in this world.

Had she turned left at Main Street, instead of turning right, toward the center of town, she would have passed the McCutcheon house. As it was, she glanced up that way at the old house on a solitary knoll overlooking North Main. Unlike the wide-windowed Shafer place, the McCutcheon house was tallish, with narrow, mean-looking windows. The house was not boxy and square and comfortable like a home should be.

In the same way, the people living in the house, had an uncomfortable look. Patsy Jo had the haunted face of a beautiful young woman who lies awake nights and dreads the next day ahead of her, who dreads her whole life away. And her father, Tom McCutcheon, seemed himself to brood like the narrow windows. Betty Morgan always felt his brooding stare as she passed the place. Getting to that house, there was a long walk to the porch, between the two old magnolia trees, and, going there, Betty Morgan always felt that someone inside must be looking, watching each step of her approach. Then when she knocked *he* came to the door, sometimes shaven and clean, neatly dressed and gentlemanly, but sometimes, too, unshaven and gruff, dressed in old, mud-stained clothes, smelling of sourness and whiskey and bad dreams that will not go away, holding a roll-your-own cigarette in his yellowed fingers. If Tom McCutcheon were dressed up Betty Morgan felt free to go inside. On such occasions he might buy some shaving lotion for himself, or some cold cream for Patsy Jo, or a box of spices for the kitchen. But when he came to the door unshaven, Betty Morgan merely excused herself, and felt, or *thought* she felt the pressure of his eyes watching her leave. The McCutcheon house could be a shivery place to call on all right, and the McCutcheons themselves were proud and noble and queer, all combined. Patsy Jo and her father were the last members of the proud, queer old family. Unlike the Morgans, there had never been a great many McCutcheons. The McCutcheons had not been ones to have a lot of babies; Tom himself was an only child. Now the line ended with Patsy Jo. The end of a line well respected, because the McCutcheons, though few, had always been big landowners. Their land had made them rich, and for a long time, what they had lacked in numbers they had made up for in prosperity, until the present generation, that is. For Tom McCutcheon was certainly not as well off as his father and grandfather before him had been. He didn't have the outgoing swagger she had learned to expect of a truly rich man. For no, Tom McCutcheon was cold and withdrawn and had a vicious, quick temper.

The crowds got thicker the closer she walked to the center of town. The popcorn and candy vendors were yelling and the curbs were crowding up with folks waiting for the afternoon parade to begin. It made the longest time in the sun that year for the most of them, so that the trademark of the festival to her was red, sun-burned faces, the most of them strange faces. But that *was* the face of the festival, a strange face. The vendors came from the south, following the carnivals north from Florida again now that winter was over. The vendors plied the crowds with giant balloons and plastic raincoats (if it clouded up to rain) and twenty-five cent sunglasses and monkeys fashioned from dyed rabbit's fur. The carnival itself was hired from out of state somewhere, contributing to the alien voices and the unfamiliar sights and smells and sounds. Betty Morgan never felt quite safe up town during the festival. In fact, deep down, she hated it.

The store where Mattie French worked was on the second

block of the business district. It was a jewelry store, and Betty Morgan went in and found Mattie all alone in the store.

"You shouldn't be here by yourself, not during festival time!" Betty Morgan said.

Mattie, a pretty blonde, with bright fair skin, smiled. "In Somerton? Betty Morgan, honey, nothing ever happens in Somerton. What are you doing up town? Is anything wrong, dear?"

"It frightens me to see you alone. If I had been a man I could have grabbed you before you knew what I was up to — you've got to be careful, Mattie." But it was no use. Mattie wouldn't believe anything could happen. She couldn't see the danger, and Betty Morgan gave up trying to convince her. "Rankin and Katherine's baby came," she said.

Mattie took a silver cup out of the drawer under the fine china display and gift-wrapped it. Betty Morgan paid a dollar down and promised she would pay a dollar each week until the cup was paid for. It would take eight weeks to pay for the gift for Rankin's baby. Mattie made out the sales ticket and Betty Morgan signed for the cup. Outside, the parade had begun. A high school band went yawping down the street. It was playing "The Saint Louis Blues" in march tempo, and one part of the band was out of tune just a bit with another part. The sound went wheezing past and then broke off as the drum majorette's whistle shrilled. The drums took up the beat then, carrying the band safely away, its horns silent.

Patsy Jo McCutcheon stood alone in the crowd and thought: Alone, always alone.

It was like living on an island in a sea somewhere, where ships never passed: you had to keep believing a ship would pass some day and take you back home, back to the world. That was life for her in Somerton, that was life when what you had built your dream on was out of your life. She felt like a balloon that had been blown up for a long time and led to expect that full feeling way of things, that light feeling, had stretched to become used to it and now she was like that same balloon punctured, feeling all wrinkled, all flat, with the snap gone out of her and nothing where the air or whatever it was that filled her as long as she had Gratt Shafer, where that had been was now nothing.

Whereas before, Somerton was a town, her home town, and the people in it were happy people you could look at and smile to think about how well they were doing, now, with Gratt gone, the town was an island and the people might as well all have been goats for all she cared. Their eyes had the same dumb brilliancy, she noticed, as a goat's eyes. They stood looking at the parade and chewing peanuts and pop corn and grazing on cotton candy. Just a herd of citizens.

A herd. When Gabe Senior French was younger and was going to Washington pretty often to call on his congressman he always had a standing order at the hotel where he stayed that went: "This is Gabe Senior French and I want you to fix this order up right away. That'll be for tonight, yes. I want a suite of rooms, a case of whiskey, and a herd of whores . . ."

What would people think if they saw her smiling now at the edge of the parade when Gratt Shafer was getting married the very next day? She wondered. Yet she could feel how it

was, how it *had been* at the lake, the hidden, faraway lake
in July with clay banks rising red to the grass above it, and
the grass reaching trees beyond, not the waterside willows,
but the deep green oaks, and above the oaks lay the blue sky
and the buzzards . . . or sometimes one lone crow would be
seen when she looked up, passing across the sky, and down
from her knees down to her toes, where her feet stood sunk
in the mud on the lake's bottom, the down-under part would
be cold, and from her knees up to where her hair just reached
the water at the shoulders, all hot, like a warm bath; and
Gratt coming after her now, and she knowing he will try to
do *it* in the water, to have his way there and she laughing, the
effort hurting her belly as it did always when she laughed or
tried even to breathe deeply while deep in the water that
way.

"What if somebody came and saw us?" she asked.

"What if somebody came and saw us what?" Gratt Shafer
said. The sun, his eyes blue, and the rest of him brown where
the sun hit him, and because he was just nineteen she could
see the pimples that had not quite faded from his skin. Not
too many, not too noticeable, but there. They had been worse
when he was seventeen. When he was twenty-one they
would be gone and the hair on his chest would have reached
out. Now it was just a little round nest of hair, hollowed
there. She pulled it.

"What if somebody came and saw us swimming in the lake,
without swimming suits — naked," she said. She looked about
fearfully.

That shook him a little, scared even him, so he walked out

on the bank and looked around. The thing was that the lake was in a field that had to be crossed, and if you looked around every now and then you could be reasonably sure nobody was coming. It wasn't a place used very much. Just a little lake with no good fish in it to speak of and one bank worn down where cattle came to water, the other banks straight. A mud bottom and all around the lake a field full of flowers and grasshoppers and bug noises when she was still a minute and listened. He came back, so lithe and sure.

"Nobody's coming."

"Still they might."

"Come out on the bank."

So she went out of the water and tried to stand on the rock at the bank's edge and wash all the mud off before she stepped out on the reddish sand. It was no use. When she reached the towel her feet were muddy anyway. The mud on the lake bottom was black, and on the banks red. The sand was red and she lay back on the blanket spread beneath the willow tree and felt the wind coming a little cool from across the field. But when she was dry the wind would come hot again and she would then go back in the lake. But now, at least, the wind was coming cool, but Gratt wasn't. He was heating up. Now his lips touched her mouth. Then she looked down at him, down kissing her breasts.

He was like the gauge on a pressure cooker. If she didn't keep her eye right on him he would suddenly be standing over in the part marked *"Danger!"* He was nearly that way now. He was always worse out of the water, for something about her coming out of the water seemed to set off whatever chain of things that went on inside and outside of him, whatever it was, that made him get *that* way, *stay* that way, it seemed.

"I told you you can't do that," she said. "I told you no." It took a push from her.

"But . . ."

"Anything but that." It was the last rule, her last one unbroken.

Then he was on her. She bit his shoulder and slapped at him as he pulled away, but he caught her wrist. And now they were looking at each other.

"You little bitch," he said.

"Did you think I'm fooling you, Gratt?"

He rubbed his shoulder, rubbing her teeth marks. Then he became gentle and rubbed her leg, knee and thigh. He whispered her name. "Patsy Jo." The whisper went through her.

"Go look. See if anybody's coming," she said.

He went again to the top of the little rise, through the grass, and came back.

"Nobody," he said. He kissed her. "Look," he said. "Just let me . . . just . . ."

But she said, "No." She twisted away.

"Patsy Jo." He was still whispering and she opened her eyes and looked at the willow leaves, at the silvery underneath of them. His hands and his lips. Something tugged inside her now. Someday she must say, "Yes."

"No," she said. He sat up, wilting a little.

"You damned little teaser!" He spat into the grass.

She went over with him the history of all that had developed between them. It was a matter of one step at a time, beginning with holding her hand. Then he kissed her, and the kiss got complicated, and that was all right. Because for a while that satisfied him. But next he wanted to feel where her breasts were, through her blouse, and then he wanted to put his hand between the halter and her breast. Then he had to remove the halter entirely and kiss her nipples. If she would only let him do that — *just once*, he had said. But *once* she did something there was no stopping it thereafter. "The trouble is, I love you," she said. "That's the trouble."

"Just let me," he said. "Just look . . ."

"I *feel*, I don't have to look."

"You're ruining my health. I can't sleep. Look, I respect you."

"Then leave me alone."

"You don't want it?" He looked at her craftily, hopeful again.

"I *do* want it. I want it from my husband *after* I'm married, that's all."

"How do you know you'll ever get married." He came closer.

"*Somebody* will want it that bad, I know somebody will. It's all I've got, it's all *any* girl has, and after that's gone you can't bring it back. You said if I'd come in swimming with you just once — well, we've been swimming this way all summer, Gratt. And there *has* to be a stopping place."

"Why? What will it hurt? Don't you *want* it?"

"You said if I'd take my clothes off and swim with you, you promised not to beg any more, not to beg for anything else. Isn't seeing me enough? Why did you promise? What are your promises worth?"

"I . . . I didn't know how it would be then, before now,

I thought this *would* be enough. Look, all I want is to put . . ."

"Don't say it. Don't ask me. Just get the hell out of my life. Don't you have other girls that will? Get one of them, one of those whores you date, and bring her out here and when you and she do it you can pretend it's me. Pretend you're screwing me."

"You don't mean that. You don't mean what you're saying. It's different with us. It's different, because I love you. If you love somebody it's not like a whore, it's always different. Different as daylight and dark, different as summer and winter."

"Is it different, Gratt?"

"I swear it is."

"Do you really love me?"

"You know . . . you know I do."

"And when we're married this is how it'll be? This is how being married is, just us this way . . ."

"But there's the rest of it."

"I can't, we can't do that part, not yet, not till we marry."

"But what about the years before we marry, what about all that time?" He was in despair. She could see it, could even see in her mind those years of waiting. They were killing him. "I can't ask you to wait all those years. We might have changed by then. We might have grown up some way and found out we weren't really supposed to marry. What then?"

"I know it," she said. The same question bothered her. *The future,* and yet here and now he was beside her, on and over her like the breeze and the willow shade. Beneath her she sweated on the blanket. She was dry now. She shivered a little and rolled away from him, getting to her feet. He reached for her, but his hand only brushed her ankle and she went back into the water. Going into the water helped. It brought her back to her senses; it made the world once more crisp and sure. It was the cold mud about her ankles and the green water. It was pulling up her knee and seeing it submerged there, hugging her knee, her own flesh against her breasts like a baby, seeing how smooth and brown she was under the water. She swam away, to where the depth was over her head and then swam back and came out, her hair now plastered to her shoulders and water running in rivulets down over her breasts, over the flat swell of her belly, dripping in the red sand beside her feet, the warm sand.

When. He watched her come out of the water. "How can you go on living all your life for *someday*, thinking you'll be married *someday?*"

She took her hair in her hands, squeezing it to get the water out. The water made her hair coarse, and at the beauty parlor, when Madge washed it, she would say, "Patsy Jo, dear! Why don't you wear a bathing cap, honey? If you could just see how them old minerals in that water you swim in is clotting this shampoo! My, if you could just *see* it!"

But she liked the feel of her hair trailing behind her in the water, and the feel of his eyes, she liked that feeling too; there was something so complimentary in the way Gratt Shafer watched her, something to make her shiver.

"Someday I *will* be married," she said.

"And until then you'll go right on teasing, teasing a guy until he can't stand it. Is that it?"

"And *my* husband will know he's getting the real thing. I'll screw him until I can see the whites of his eyes." She stretched and looked where the trees touched the sky. "I'm going to have a good life, and not you nor anybody else is going to mess me up, Gratt Shafer. Nobody but a selfish short-sighted son of a bitch would want it from a girl until he had married her. So guess what that makes you?" She looked at him. He lay on his side in the hot, reddish sand. He was biting a straw of grass. The hair on his legs was reddish gold, the legs themselves brown and muscular, the feet bony and strong. She had been curious about him at first, curious to see what he would look like without clothes.

"I like an honest girl. I like to know where I stand . . ." he began.

"Like those roadhouse sluts you . . . you screw all the time?" She broke in.

"Let me have my say, will you please?" He looked up at her now, his eyes serene. *Teasing,* she thought. *Teasing.*

"Okay, my little man," she said. "You're like all the rest of them. You have to prove something don't you? And the only way you can is to go whorehopping. Hunting season closes and then its open season on whores."

"I think you're jealous. I was just going to say I like my women honest. I don't like them to act one way and talk another."

It was always the same. It was the grand argument, and Gratt Shafer was no different from the rest of them in West Tennesee, all over the world for that matter. He could prove that she must yield, could prove it by the sun and the moon, the stars, the bees, flowers, simple arithmetic, songs, movies, books, jokes — he even had Bible quotations on his side. That was what learning one Bible verse a day from five years old onward accomplished for some of Southern manhood, the crafty ones. They became so familiar with the Scriptures in that learning that they could give a dozen or more quotations and examples from the Bible which, when you put them all together, spelled only one thing. If a girl *did* she was after all only going by what the Bible said girls did, she was only being honest, she was only doing what it was there inside of her and *wanting* to do anyway. This was the telling blow, this use of herself against herself. Furthermore other girls did it — they *all* did but kept it a secret from each other. Gratt Shafer wouldn't tell, he would keep quiet and they could play their own little private game just like the rest of the world, and no one ever would be the wiser. If she didn't do it she was dumb or warped.

"Why don't you be honest with yourself? Who are you trying to fool?" he said.

He stood up now and took her in his arms.

"Why do you have to do me this way?" she asked. "Don't you have any respect? How long can I hold out? Gratt? Don't you see?" But there was no sense pleading with him.

"I love you," he said.

"Look, I don't want to get pregnant. What if I got pregnant?"

"You don't have anything to worry about. I've explained all that a million times, haven't I?"

"I . . . I'm sorry. No. My answer is no."

"Are you afraid? Don't you love me?"

"You know I love you, Gratt. I love you, but I hate you

too. You're such a . . . such a bastard. Such a lowdown, sweet, little bastard."

"Lie down on the sand. It's warm."

"No, I better swim."

But she was kneeling and then she lay back and saw the pale, blinding sky and closed her eyes to the brassy light of the sun. She opened them and saw his eyes and kissed him, thinking: Is it going to be now? Is it going to be now?

She didn't know herself. The sand was warm. Some days it was too hot to lie on, but today the sand was just pleasantly warm.

"It feels good doesn't it?"

"It's warm." She felt a strange, pricklish sensation. It swept over her skin. He kissed. *Like wind on the water,* she thought.

"Turtles lay their eggs in sand and the sun's heat makes them hatch out," he said. "I've seen the tracks. You can tell turtle tracks because you can see where the turtle's tail dragged along."

"I'm still afraid someone might come."

"They'd have to come across the field."

"You'd better take a look."

"I just did," he said. "There's nobody."

"Love," she said. "Gratt?"

"Yes."

"I love you, Gratt." And she thought: I will love him now and he won't forget it. It will be so good he will never forget. Never, never forget.

Never. There was another band coming now, in bright blue uniforms. The music struck up and Patsy Jo held back the urge to cry, but the tears still came. It was the effect of the music, blaring past, and the bright uniforms, the young faces of the band members, the pale ivory legs of the majorettes, and the rattle and snap of the drums. Gratt Shafer wasn't coming back. She knew the music, it was "The Washington Post March." Gratt Shafer was gone, he didn't exist for her any more. He might as well be dead. It was a good band and the trombones were playing well. Instead of marching on, the band marked time and the music swung into the bridge of the melody. The crowd was applauding and whistling. It was a championship band all right. And Gratt Shafer was getting married the next day. He was gone and summer was here again, it was strawberry festival time, and her man, Gratt Shafer, was gone. The music said it all, the way music will. Gone from her. It said it over and over until she was there in the crowd crying like her heart would break while the people around her clapped their hands and whistled. She tried to hold it back, to think of something else, but she couldn't. The sounds couldn't be shut out, and then it came to her that when you are in love any tune you hear is a love song, even "The Washington Post March" or "Anchors Aweigh," even "Old Zip Coon" on a banjo can tear your heart out when you're in love and when the one you love is not there, when he will *never* be there. Never. God, God, what a long time it would be, longer than memory, longer than dust, longer than the whole world. That was what *never* meant. *Never any more.*

She was gasping into her handkerchief. She backed through the crowd and leaned against the front wall of the drugstore. Nobody noticed. They were wrapped up in the parade. And finally the band stopped playing a minute and the drums took over and the majorette's whistle blew a couple of times and the band took off up the street, breaking into the "Marine Hymn" now. But the pause had at least given her time to gather herself together, and she started up the sidewalk, not going home, not going anywhere. Just walking, just walking and not wanting to see anyone, thanking the crowd for that much privacy, for the fact that no one paid any attention to her. She kept walking and wanting something. She probably wanted to be dead, Patsy Jo McCutcheon decided.

Toonker Burkette recognized the tune, "The Marine Hymn." The band was passing down Main Street in front of his office. Toonker's patient heard the band too and he rolled his eyes. The patient was a farmer with a mouth full of rotten teeth. He lay back in the chair with his mouth propped open, his breath emitting the sweetish odor of the tobacco chewer, an odor not really unpleasant. Toonker got a firm hold on the molar, the one that had been aching. But when he pulled only a part of the tooth came out. The rest had broken off, so Toonker tried again and this time got the rest of the tooth. He gave the farmer a roll of gauze to bite down on, helped him out of the chair, and stepped into the next cubicle where a patient was already sprawled out, waiting. She was a big country woman with straight hair the color of ruined hay. She had her mouth open and was pointing to a tooth. No, she wouldn't take any deadening. Toonker got a hold on the tooth and yanked it out. Then she pointed to a lower jaw tooth and he got that one too. Each time he pulled a tooth she grunted. The sound reminded him of an old horse. It seemed to come from deep inside her swollen, gut-packed abdomen. This was what the strawberry festival brought him, the extractions. The people who had never had a filling in a tooth, much less an inlay. The festival brought them in, they saw the shingle hanging in front of the office, or someone at the seed store sent them over to him. There was no art to it, but there was one consolation — an extraction was fast work and he got *cash* for pulling a tooth. You yanked, you had your money. And later perhaps he could make dentures for these same people, when they got tired of trying to gum their food. The woman bit down on gauze roll and stepped out to pay Toonker's receptionist. Toonker switched back to the first cubicle and another patient, a farmer. All that remained of the first man was the smell of his tobacco-scented breath. Toonker had just fastened his forceps on the farmer's tooth when the telephone rang. It was the hospital, so Toonker took the call. Doctor Fielder told him his wife had just had a baby girl. Mother and baby were doing well. "Fine," said Toonker. "I can't get away just now to come see her."

"She understands," Fielder said. "I guess you're pretty busy."

"Honest to God," Toonker said. "I'm covered up. My arm's tired. My back's killing me."

Fielder laughed and Toonker hung up the phone and turned back to his work.

The band had stopped playing and moved on up the street, but the drums were still beating out the time and Toonker held the song in his head, "The Marine Hymn." He worked with a sort of rhythm now, thinking what crazy bastards Marines were. Gratt Shafer had been a Marine and had never recovered from his experience. The Marine Corps had left a mark on him. Nothing you could see, but a mark just the same. You felt the mark.

Fielder had said the baby weighed eight pounds and three ounces. Such a fat baby, Toonker thought. My wife, he thought. He tried hard to keep his thoughts from wandering. Fielder had said she and the baby were all right. She wouldn't know he was there even if he could get away now and go to the hospital. She would be all doped up, drugged. But he couldn't get away. He wanted to feel guilty, he wanted to feel sorry for her, but there was a band on the march down Main Street. It played "The Marine Hymn," and in spite of himself Toonker imagined a hundred horns coming in on it loud and full, the notes belting out and hitting a man where he lived. Two things he wished on days like this: one, that the country people would not pause and try to pass the time of day with him; two, that the county agents, those loafing, over-paid asses, would get with a couple of home demonstration experts and comb the highways and gulleys and hedgerows of Sligo County promoting the use of underarm deodorants. And the baby came, he thought. He remembered that he had figured the child would be born just about on the day of Gratt Shafer's wedding. Gratt Shafer's wedding was tomorrow. Once again he tried to think of his own wife, lying up in the hospital, but somehow the only thing that came into his head was the memory of his mother's admonition not to marry the girl in the first place. Well, he would get to the hospital as soon as possible.

Tomorrow he would go to Memphis to the wedding. He would go alone. He had already been to some of the parties given for Gratt and his bride-to-be, and he had attended those alone too, on account of his wife's advanced pregnancy. He enjoyed getting down to Memphis and consorting with the big rich people, the friends of the girl Gratt Shafer was marrying. Of course there had been one pretty embarrassing moment. (He winced, remembering it.) The stag party Camack Patterson had given for Gratt, the stag party was the occasion, and Toonker had enjoyed the party immensely, for it had meant getting inside Patterson's enormous house. Patterson was a Memphis boy Gratt had made friends with at college. He was one of those fashion-plate-type rich boys and when you saw him you knew right away where it was Gratt had learned to dress and act and talk the way he did. You knew it was Patterson who had changed Gratt over from a Sligo County hick to the kind of fellow who could fit right into the best society. Patterson had been Shafer's fraternity brother at Vanderbilt, and they had roomed together four years, by which time not even an expert, Toonker figured, could have told Shafer apart from a city-bred millionaire. It was the sort of luck some people had. Gratt Shafer was just lucky, Toonker thought, wincing again as he remembered the stag party, remembering Patterson's house, where the party had been held. The house was a real show place, and Patterson, who was naturally to be Gratt's best man, had taken pains to introduce Toonker to a number of the big shots there. Toonker had made a mental note of their names and faces, using his memory system. Every time he met a person for the first time he focused his attention on the stranger's ugliest feature. Sometimes it was the nose, or a mole, a scar or a blemish. The job was especially easy if the feature were baldness. Much of the time it was the mouth or the teeth, for mouths, Toonker had observed, spoiled more human looks than any other single feature. In lucky instances the person might walk with a cane, wear a hearing aid, have a missing finger, or a withered hand. Anyway, Toonker always noted the ugly feature and paired it up with the person's name. It helped him the most when meeting big shots, for even if they *were* rich, they had *their* drawbacks too. He had used the system at Camack Patterson's party, making mental notes so he would be able to speak to the big shots by name when he saw them again at the next party. But the trouble was that he was thinking so hard he drank a little too much of Patterson's very old and expensive Scotch whiskey (it was being served in any amount, all you wanted) and the next thing Toonker knew he was wandering in the formal garden out behind the house, and the last thing he remembered was stopping to look down at a large, goggle-eyed goldfish, and then vomiting into the pool. He had simply made an ass out of himself. But at least people had remembered *him*, after that. It wasn't every day, after all, that a dentist from a place as small as Somerton, Tennessee, went to Memphis and shot his lunch into the de luxe fish pool behind *Camack Patterson's* house. Well, *mansion* was a better word, because you couldn't call anything as elegant as Solitude a *house* and really do it justice.

Well, and tomorrow was the big show, Gratt Shafer marrying the debutante, Eleanor Fite! Dimly he remembered a story or a movie which seemed to fit this case, was it *The Princess and the Pauper?* he wondered. Anyway, Shafer had fallen into it for sure, he mused. The Fites were rich big shots.

And, of course, Toonker thought, because this was Somerton, there had to be some hick trying to embarrass the whole town at such a big moment. Because *he* was a McCutcheon, old Tom McCutcheon had to show off his ugly temper because Gratt Shafer was lucky enough to marry a Memphis heiress instead of having to settle for old Tom's daughter, Patsy Jo.

Only thinking back, back to the old days in high school, Gratt Shafer had seemed the last guy one might suspect would make that kind of success in life. "The very last guy in the world," Toonker said to himself, wiping his hands as the patient leaned over and spat blood into the little rill of water gurgling in the waste sink beside him. "Now look," Toonker said aloud, to the patient. "We need to get all those teeth out, understand? You're going to need dentures."

"False teeth?" the man said with a look of horror. "How much it *that* gonna cost?"

"Why worry about the cost when your health is at stake?" Toonker countered. "Teeth are your health, aren't they?"

"Well, I don't know. I thought your health was how you feel. You feel good, then you got health, something like that."

"If you don't have teeth you can't chew. If you can't chew you can't eat. If you can't eat then your health will go bad."

"Well, my daddy, he never had any teeth. He just eat mashed potatoes and gravy and milk and he got on okay till he died. Course he was a little thin."

"Let's set up your appointments now."

"Naw, naw . . . tell you what. I'll come back and then you can set up them appointments. I'll be back in after the cotton season, how's that?"

Toonker tried to reason with him. The teeth were for his own good. The plates could be made for him next month — in July. "That way you can pay me after you sell your cotton."

And besides, but Toonker didn't say it, when the year got past cotton season there was Christmas and after Christmas it would be 1951, so if the plates were going to be made and paid for this year the work would have to be done before the end of September.

"Well," said the patient, trying to talk around the gauze rolls in his mouth, making a buzzing sound. "Well, I *might* think about it." And then he ducked out.

Another band was coming. Toonker was tempted to go out to the sidewalk and watch it pass, but there was another patient already waiting. With a sigh he walked into the treatment room. "Which one, ma'am?" he asked patiently, grabbing up the forceps.

"The Marine Hymn." Standing on the corner, Gratt Shafer watched the parade. He was a block from home, from the old house, and nine years away from the memories, the painful reminders the tune contained for him.

The knot in his stomach made him turn and walk back to the high lawn behind him. Seated beneath a maple tree on the grass, he had a view of the scene passing in the street, the bands, the floats, a troop of riders representing the Somerton Saddle Club. The knot in his stomach remained and he tried to get a hold on himself, to fight back the unreasoning waves of panic. The horse troop passed and a company of National Guardsmen marched past behind a drum and bugle corps.

It was nine years since he had marched to the strains of "The Marine Hymn." The regiment had assembled that morning at 0900 in front of the 1st Battalion's billet. It was November 28, 1941. The U. S. Fourth Marine Regiment was pulling out of Shanghai, China. Second Lieutenant Gratt Shafer could hear the crowds, for they were already formed up along the line of march, 40,000 yelling, flag-waving Chinese waiting to tell the Americans good-by. It was like standing outside the world's biggest football stadium and hearing a touchdown. The regiment formed up behind its band and the march began,

Good-by to the billet area, eyes front —

Turning now into Bubbling Well Road and the music going up ahead, the drums proud, the regiment alive, in motion, and somewhere beyond, the crowd of cheering Chinese. The music swelled up above the cheers now and then, the drums penetrated always, and now . . . the turn into Nanking Road. Their column was heading for the Bund, for the President Line's dock and the crowd pressed in so close you could hear and feel and see that they knew the regiment was going off to war. It was a scent in the air like blood, it was a beautiful, strange smell.

The band carried them all the way. They marched to the dock. As they boarded the power lighter and slipped down stream to the *Harrison*, swinging on her anchor in the current, the band kept playing.

Good-by to the Garden Bridge, to Soochow Creek. Good-by.

The Chinese were on the river banks now, still yelling, still cheering like maniacs. It was the damndest send-off in the whole damned history of the whole dying world, it was an entire nation of people saying good-by to the last hope they had before the curtain fell on act three in China, and was raised up on Act I of World War II. The Marines knew it. And the Chinese knew it.

Good-by to the world's greatest bordello, to the House of a Thousand Pleasures.

The marines stayed at the ship's rails, waving to the Chinese on the river bank. They yelled themselves hoarse, and finally the band formed up on the promenade deck at 1400 and played "The Star-Spangled Banner." That's when a good many China service veterans wept, and told a whole city, told Shanghai, told China, *so long forever*. She had mothered them. It was the terrible, awful end of an entire tradition, and it crushed something inside of Gratt Shafer, until his throat couldn't bear it. He found himself holding the salute and crying when the band stopped and the *Harrison* weighed anchor. They steamed down the Whangpoo River. And the band quit. That was when the silence fell, when the Chinese on the bank quit yelling.

When the ship cleared the Whangpoo and hit the lazy roll of the China Sea the Marines broke out machine guns. They trained the guns on fly-overs of Japanese planes. *The planes*. It was a dumb show. The Jap planes appeared and the

Marines manned the guns, but there was no gunfire. On the
first of December, 1941, they disembarked — in the Philli-
pines.

On April 9 following, in that jungle spring on Bataan
Peninsula, in 1942, he walked out of the jungle onto the road
leading from Mariveles. The ammo dumps at the base were
still smoldering. The fuel storage tanks were afire. Black smoke
boiled into the distant sky. Gratt Shafer was hungry, a little
feverish, and sick. He had not slept in two days, and what
remained of his makeshift platoon, of the few Filipinos, the
few stranded naval personnel who had never handled a rifle
before, the Army Air Force men, and finally the smattering of
Marines who had made up the combat cadre for Bataan's
hastily assembled makeshift army, were scattered now. The
narrow dirt road was a winding trail of mud in the rainy
season. But it was dry season when he walked out of the
jungle, and the road was dusty. A motor pool unit had stopped
their trucks where he emerged, and dismounted. They had
stacked their arms and the mechanics and truck drivers were
squatting or lying down. Gratt Shafer thought:

It is now each man for himself.

An army private approached him. "Lieutenant?"

"Yes," he answered. "Yes?" he repeated, feeling weary and
sick.

"When are the Japs coming?" The private was worried.

"How should I know?" Gratt Shafer said.

"How do we act when they come?" The private spoke
softly.

"Keep your mouth shut. Stay still and keep quiet."

The soldier looked at him. "You hungry? You look sorta hungry, sir."

Gratt Shafer nodded. Then he threw down his rifle and the forty-five pistol he had carried. He kept his canteen. He took out his wallet. The soldier came back with some canned fish and a can of pork and beans. Without saying anything he opened the cans and took Gratt Shafer's canteen and filled it at the little spring. When he came back Gratt Shafer had laid the pictures out, two snapshots of Patsy Jo McCutcheon. Between bites of fish and beans Gratt took off his lieutenant's bars, his Vanderbilt class ring (class of '39). He looked at the pictures one last time. He would keep nothing but the canteen which the private handed him now.

"We may need water. You have to think about these things," the private said. He looked down at the pictures. "That your girl?" he asked.

Gratt Shafer nodded. "She used to be."

"A Dear John case, huh?" The private was sympathetic. "I had the same thing happen to me."

"It wasn't exactly a Dear John," Gratt said. He wanted to tell the man about Patsy Jo McCutcheon. It was the first time he had been willing to talk about her at all, and the reason was, he realized, that it no longer made any difference. They were going to be captured. They had put down their arms. The enemy was coming because the Marines had not been able to stop him. His mouth went dry and his saliva wouldn't come right when he chewed. He kept trying to get his mind off the notion that in a little while they would be prisoners. It was strange to be dead-tired, but not sleepy; filthy, but too scared to walk down to the creek and bathe. Fright whipped through him in waves.

Even though he hadn't told any of the Marines stationed with him in Shanghai, even though none of them had known anything about Patsy Jo McCutcheon other than that he carried two pictures of her in his wallet, still he found himself talking about her now to a man he had just met, a man whose name he did not even know.

He was talking about her now even though his main reason for joining up in the first place (so he had told himself at the time) had been so that he *wouldn't* have to talk to anyone about Patsy Jo. Requesting foreign duty had been an excuse to get so far away from Somerton that no one could pierce the shell of his inner thoughts. Until now he had believed the scar tissues in which his memories of her lay buried were so thickened and so tough as to be impenetrable. Until now he had kept all thoughts of her pushed away into a deep cove of privacy. He had suffered alone. But now he was blabbing away to the man beside him.

"I meant to marry her, but . . . but I had to get through school first."

The other man dropped to his knees, admiring the pictures. "She's real pretty — easy on the eyes," he said.

"But I guess I wouldn't be interested in a wife, not now," Gratt Shafer said. His heart began pounding with fear.

"Oh, me neither," the other man said. "You take me, I was married one time. It was enough for me. Never no more." He looked at the pictures again. "So this was your girl."

"She *was*, yes."

"And you was going to marry her."

"Yes, only I had to get out of college. That took four years. Then I went home and gave her a ring that had belonged to my mother."

"You come close, didn't you."

Gratt Shafer nodded. "But a buddy of mine stopped me and after that I never knew whether to thank him or hate him."

"You mean he told you she was . . . well that's a damn woman," the other man said. "Every last one of them is a bitch. And so you joined the Marine Corps to forget about her."

"Well . . . well to tell the truth, maybe I gave *her* a bad deal. I don't know. You see I put the wedding off — I mean as far as I knew she wasn't going out with other guys or anything — not *then* anyway. But you see something had happened while I was in college. But anyway my friend talked me out of it. My friend talked me out of marrying her, and after that she started to take up with other guys. Or anyway, I *thought* that was when. Maybe I *pushed* her into it, I don't know. It's hard to tell, looking back."

"You did right not to marry her, buddy," said the other man. "Your friend advised you right."

"You think so," Gratt said. "You really think so?" He was not able to bring his thoughts into order. His hands trembled as he picked up the pictures one after the other.

"Oh, yeah. Hell, yeah. You don't want to blame yourself," said the other man.

Gratt put the pictures down and threw the empty bean can away. Then he wiped his spoon on his trouser leg. "The whole trouble was me, probably. It didn't seem like I could live with her or without her. So I kept seeing her once in a while and I got jealous of the others. I got so jealous it made me sick and I would sometimes . . . you might not believe this."

"I know what you mean, fellow," said the other man. "I been through it."

"Sometimes I'd crouch in the hedge beside her porch and wait for the other guy to bring her home. I even took a pistol once, and sat there while it rained. Maybe I was going to shoot the guy she was out with, maybe I was going to shoot her. Anyway he brought her home finally, and I watched. I sat in the hedge and watched another guy play house with her up on the porch, and I just sat there and let the rain fall on me."

"You didn't shoot him? Well, I guess I would've shot him. Maybe both of them. Didn't you say nothing?"

"I didn't open my mouth. I just sat there until it was all over, listened and watched — this girl I loved and another man."

"Well, it does make you sick. Take on the other hand, though. If you had married her she might've turned out the same way."

"He came down the porch steps afterwards, wiping her lipstick off on his handkerchief. He passed so close — I couldn't have missed."

"It must've been a big temptation," the other man said.

"That was when I found out that you just don't shoot another man down — not like that you don't."

"Well, everybody ain't like you though. Take me . . ."

"You just don't do it," Gratt Shafer said. "I had no claim on her."

"Oh, I know. I know what you mean. I know what a bitch is, okay."

"I just remember these things. I never told anybody before."

"But it's good to have something like that off a man's chest," said the other man. "Some things can just get too heavy to tote around all bottled up inside." He tapped his chest with a broad, dusty finger. The name stenciled over the pocket of his fatigues read: "Pfc. Perkins."

"I said something to her about it and she just let me have the working girl's protection, right across the mouth."

"I must have slapped her off that porch if she'd have hit me," Perkins said.

"Not me, though. And then some time after that, I don't know when, this friend of mine . . ."

"This same buddy?"

"No, another fellow — he told me she was putting out, well I knew it of course. But then he told me *when* she had started. It was after what happened while I was still in college . . . she had gotten in a family way."

"Oh, I see it better now," said Perkins.

"She got that way and I got it fixed up — an operation, you know. But when this other guy told me how *long* it had been going on I saw red, and so when he told me I hit him — broke his collar bone, because when I socked the swing went wild and he went down and his glasses fell off. I must have gone crazy. I just stood over him, he was an old friend, and I watched him lying there on the ground, my hand swelling, him holding his shoulder. He got up and just said to believe it or not, and I picked up his glasses for him and took him to the hospital."

"You didn't have no business hitting him, but then it can make a man lose his temper."

"It had gone far enough. Too far. I had to get away," Gratt Shafer said. He took a sip of water and screwed the cap back on the canteen. "I couldn't take any more."

"So that was the end of it."

"Oh, not quite. She wrote me a few letters while I was in Shanghai, and I wrote her some."

The other man nodded. He was older and smaller than Gratt, with the large competent hands of a mechanic. He pointed to the nearest of the stalled convoy trucks. "I drove that rig there," he said. "Last night we evacuated the motor pool. I guess it was you guys we heard up the line firing. Firing and falling back, firing and falling back. Then the firing quit and we heard the Jap tanks, you know how they squeak. So we knew it wasn't our tanks and we lit a fire with everything that would burn and took off. All I grabbed was some grub." He paused. "You had a good-looking woman," he said. "It's too damn bad about her."

"Thanks," Gratt Shafer said. He unfolded his handkerchief on the ground and put the pictures in it, then his wallet, wrist watch, class ring, his money. Even money was worthless now. *Especially* money. And yet he remembered a man, a civilian assigned to his outfit, a man from Manila. The civilian had been in charge of a whole suitcase of money, not a small suitcase but a big suitcase that taxed the man's strength merely to pick it up. It was all the money from a bank in Manila and the man was trying to get the money out before the Japs captured it. It had been a hell of a thing, rather comic, to see a man so worried, so taxed with responsibility when all was lost and death was so close on his heels.

"What's your name?" said the other man.

"Gratt Shafer."

"I'm Lennie Perkins," the other said. "And I wish I was back in Alabama right now." He gave a nervous laugh, a dry, flat sound that said he too was afraid.

Gratt Shafer tied the corners of the handkerchief together.

"What are you doing with your stuff?" Lennie Perkins asked.

"Throwing it away. You better do the same."

Gratt picked the handkerchief up and got to his feet. He hurled the bundle into the brush thinking: *Out of sight, out of mind.*

"Why did you do that?" Perkins asked.

"Just to be safe. When they come after us they'll search us. They'll take everything we have anyway, so why give them any satisfaction?"

Lennie Perkins nodded and began emptying his pockets. There was a picture of his mother which he showed to Gratt, a bent gray woman beside an unpainted house; a picture of a horse he had loved. "This was Pete, my horse," Lennie Perkins said. "A smart son of a bitch, if I do say so, sir." He paused. "And here was my girl. The bitch I married." He was kneeling on the ground with his possessions spread out before him in the dust. He picked up the picture of the gray-haired woman and kissed it. "My maw," he said, without shame. Then, quickly, he tied his few mementos in his handkerchief, but instead of throwing it, as Gratt Shafer had done, he walked back into the jungle, and returned a few moments later, empty-handed. "That's done," he said sadly.

They took up what food he had then, and when their pockets were full Perkins gave the rest away to anyone who would take it. Nobody seemed to be hungry for worrying. And in a few minutes they heard the first tank. It came around a bend in the road, with Japanese soldiers riding on the outside of it, and the American officers, Gratt Shafer included, warned the other men to stand perfectly still and be perfectly quiet, and that was what they did, while the tank came squeaking down the road and stopped beside the pile of discarded rifles. The tank stopped and the soldiers jumped off and took some weapons from the pile for souvenirs. They paid no attention to the Americans, but went gravely about the business of getting a souvenir or two. Their uniforms were dusty and they looked tired. Then they climbed back on the tank and it moved away up the road. There was another tank then, followed by a third tank which was loaded with a bunch of rowdies in clean uniforms. The rowdies passed among the Americans and took watches and rings and blankets. When they climbed back on the tank one of the Japs spotted a blanket he had not noticed before, in an American soldier's pack, so he called the man over to him, jerked away the blanket, and then kicked the G.I. in the face and sent him sprawling. The hurt man sat up, holding his nose, while the rowdies laughed and the tank moved. It moved then, following the others while the stunned man sat just where he was, his nose bleeding.

Gratt Shafer wondered where the tanks were going. He

found out when all the prisoners were marched along the winding road to Bataan Air Field. For when they finally reached the field the tanks were already there, forming a circle. The field was a mass of prisoners, standing in ranks by the thousands, some wounded, some starved-looking, all standing in the hot sun. The Jap crews manning the tanks had their guns trained on the prisoners, and it passed through Gratt Shafer's mind that *this was it — the end*. He expected the tanks to start firing any second.

This numb expectation raised the hackles behind his neck and stiffened his back. His group fell into formation by ranks. And it came to him then that if the tanks opened fire from the circle, they would be firing *at one another,* and he wondered if the Japs would think of that, and decided that probably they wouldn't, or that even if they *did* think of it they would still fire into the ranks of the prisoners. A man's only chance would be to try to hit the ground when he saw the first puff of smoke from the barrel of the first tank gun; then, even before he heard the sound of the firing he would have to hit the ground and play dead. And he might have to play dead all day, lying there on Bataan Air Field, trying to lie perfectly still while the officers went up and down with pistols making sure nobody was *playing* dead.

Making sure. They'll shoot us, he thought.

From where he stood he could see one of the tanks, and he kept looking at its gun.

"They *can't* kill us," a voice nearby said hopefully. "It's against the rules." When the tanks moved aside the prisoners who had not been bayoneted for having Japanese money or souvenirs in their possession, marched away from the bodies of the dead, the bodies of foolish comrades who had not emptied their pockets. They marched all that night, almost without stopping, and sunrise found them still on the march. Those who could not keep up were shot immediately.

Marching behind him, Lennie Perkins passed the word to Gratt Shafer:

"You get the word, Lieutenant?"

"What?"

"About the hospital ships?"

"What about them?"

"The guy behind me just passed the word. They got two hospital ships out in Manila Bay. They're being painted white with big red crosses on them."

"What for?"

"For *us*. They're going to ship us to Venezuela for a prisoner exchange. Venezuela is neutral."

Gratt Shafer, in spite of his own suspicion that the rumor was false, passed the word on to the man ahead of him. And in spite of himself, he began to believe in the two white ships. His imagination fed on the image of them. All about him the weary, marching prisoners talked about the ships. Everybody had heard of prisoners being exchanged. It was the sane thing to do. *The sane thing.*

He kept remembering the two white ships, so real to him — the two white ships resting there in Manila Bay. By the time the death march was over, when they had buried their companions by the hundreds at Camp O'Donnell, and later at Cabanatuan, on the prison farm where, like the others, he worked in the fields from dawn until dusk, working barefooted; and, in the rainy season, planting rice, moving in platoons across the rice paddies, while the rain fell, standing close to the wire used to space the planting, holding the rice plants and thrusting them down into the warm mud, he remembered the ships. He remembered the white ships when he was shipped out to Japan, he and the healthier ones, for slave labor in the coal mines. The white painted ships became a private joke, a nightmare joke that haunted him afterwards in the coal mines at Omuta. He thought of those rescue ships bitterly when a mine cave-in killed Lennie Perkins. The ships that never materialized were like all of a man's dreams that never come true, like the sum and total of all a man's disillusionments. They were phantom shapes, ghosts which could keep a man moving through life, forever propelled by false hopes.

Sometimes when the winter snows banked up outside the prison compound buildings in which they slept, in the last hours of the night, before they were awakened for another long day of slavery in the mines, he dreamed of the ships. In the dream, he and the other prisoner, he and Lennie Perkins, especially, would be marching towards the dock and somewhere a band would be playing "The Marine Hymn" and Gratt and Lennie would be prisoners one instant and men of the Fourth Marine Regiment the next. They would be prisoners, heading for the hospital ships to be taken to South America for the exchange of prisoners, and suddenly they would realize together that they were mistaken, for instead of Manila Bay before them it would be the Whangpoo River. They were marching down Nanking Road again and the crowds were cheering. But as they stood on the dock they saw, in Gratt Shafer's dream, they saw, with failing hearts, that the ships had already raised their anchors and were slipping away. The gigantic red crosses emblazoned on their sides were already receding into the distance. It was a cruel dream, and a cruel awakening came when the Japanese guards came hiking through the barracks shouting: "Speedo! Speedo!"

The sum and total of his disillusionments formed a knot in his belly, a knot that stayed there in his innards until the prisoners were liberated in 1945. To merely remember Japan wrenched his imagination and caused a ghastly unearthing, a dismemberment of things, as if a bomb had dropped into a graveyard. The memory presented to him just that horror, of things unearthed — things better forgotten, for all the good mourning over them would do. Those memories, all of them, were better put away, like the dead, for eternity.

"Like the dead," Gratt Shafer told himself aloud. The high school band was past him now, the parade was continuing, but he had no heart for it. He looked at his watch. It was time Camack Patterson were in Somerton. He went down the terrace to the sidewalk, still shaken. It did him no good to think about Patsy Jo McCutcheon. For Patsy Jo was a light that failed, and yet the lump, the knot she had caused, remained. At the corner he saw Camack Patterson's automobile parked at the curb in front of his house. It gave him strength, just seeing his friend's car. It brought the world back in focus again, and once again Gratt knew where he was going. He started up the sidewalk towards home. *There has to be,* he thought, *another chance at life. Just because you lose at it one time, that's no sign the show is over.* He was not quite so young as he had been the day his regiment had marched out into Bubbling Springs Road, but walking now he felt a return of some of that old hope and pride. Eleanor Fite was in Memphis, waiting, and once he got there, once he got *there,* once he got to *Memphis,* things would be all right. They had to be. He had come too far, down too many crooked roads, for things *not* to be right this time around.

He tried not to think about Patsy Jo McCutcheon. He centered his thoughts instead on that day — nine years ago now, almost — when he had marched down to the docks in Shanghai. Regardless of everything that had followed that day, he still remembered it for a proud moment. He had felt like a man *that* day, like a part of something that was more important than himself. There were, after all, he thought, far worse things to be than a patriot.

2

GRATT SHAFER's mother thought at first that the child inside of her was a tumor. She ignored what was growing there in her belly as long as she dared. But when she could hold in her distress no longer, the news got out in Somerton: Madam Shafer had a tumor! She was in her forties and her husband, Doc, tried to make people believe he was only seventy. When the "tumor" showed up they had been married ten years. That was in 1915.

The tumor spoiled everything for Madam. She went to bed and wouldn't see anyone, not even Doctor Ocie Pentecost. She drew the shades in her room and wept in the semidarkness. She thought she was dying and her whole life passed before her eyes like a circus parade. There was her Kentucky childhood, her Eastern finishing school education, her first marriage (it had been childless) to a young physician on the medical faculty at Vanderbilt University. She recalled her happy years in Nashville as a faculty wife, ending with her young husband's death, and her subsequent marriage to Adam Shafer, a Doctor of Philosophy and a man just then ready to retire as Head of the Anthropology Department. Admitting to sixty-five years at the time, Doc retired when she married him. As Madam's rejected suitors told it he was a lot older than any sixty, and had to be propped up for the wedding ceremony, didn't in fact even know what day it was! They said it was a moot question whether Madam should have married *it* or turned *it* over to the Department of Anatomy. But Doc's story was he had a bad cold on his wedding day and was already all doped up when some of his faculty cronies came over bringing some spirituous liquors. They had proceeded to get him corned so bad he couldn't hit the campus with his hat. In that condition, he had stood up for the ceremony.

But it was, anyway, called a May and January affair and was talked about all over Nashville, Tennessee, in the academic circles, which were many and large, then as now. But it would have been more fair to have called the marriage an August and January, or maybe even a September and January affair, because Madam, as some of the jealous faculty wives were not slow to say, was not exactly a spring chicken. Madam herself, they said, was on the *verge* of ripe.

"Madam" was her nickname. Her maiden name had been Octavia Ashmore. Before her first husband died she met Doc Shafer and she soon found out that Doc was a "character." He was a blustery old man, a native of Wisconsin who didn't give a hoot for the Southern "sacred cows" and went around conversationally de-horning them. His impious attacks on Southern History and Southern Traditions and Southern Ideals had earned him the eternal hatred of certain professional Southerners, and by all rights, these attitudes of Doc's should have repelled Madam, but somehow they didn't. They didn't, even though old Doc just the same as scrawled public toilet obscenities on the temple walls of Southern and South worship. This alone should have culled him out of the running as a suitor for Madam's hand, if his age alone hadn't sufficed. But no, for reasons she could not later explain, nothing had culled Doc out, not even what she discovered about him at the last moment. What she found out at the last moment was that Doc had been involved in a pretty awful scandal at Yale University. It had cost him his job at Yale. She discovered that while at Yale Doc had been either in on, or at best an unwitting party to a hoax. It seemed that certain skull fragments were represented as very early American human, and later turned out to be parts of a modern African ape. (The ape had died of fever when the traveling circus it belonged to played New Haven.)

But Madam married Doc anyway and helped Doc fulfill his dream. He had dreamed of excavating a certain group of Indian mounds. And that's how Doc and Madam came to Somerton, Tennessee in the first place, for just south of town were forty truncated cones of earth, each one about three hundred feet high, and the whole bunch good for nothing — if you happened to be a farmer (a good many of Madam's people had been farmers) — forty mounds rearing up on an otherwise perfectly good plot of rich bottom land two miles south of town.

Until Doc appeared in Somerton the mounds had been considered a nuisance by every white man, beginning with the first one who broke the ground about them with his ox teams. After all, even Madam could see that the mounds converted acres of valuable flat bottom land into small worthless hills.

The early settlers in the territory, then Western North Caro-
lina, bitterly named the mounds "Indian mountains," and
finally in the hot, dry August of 1842 the Reverend Bartholomew Luther Meeks came to Sligo County to hold a two-
weeks protracted camp meeting in a field not far from the
mounds. Brother Meeks was a Bible-slapping renegade Presby-
terian whose trail into the West was marked by a string of
deserted wives reaching all the way to the city of Baltimore
and truthfully, Brother Meeks was a man of considerable
charm. On the second day of the Sligo County meeting he
told the gathered multitude that he had seen a vision in
which the Lord said He would return in 1843 on August
seventh, at the seventh hour of the morning to ". . . a wild
and mystic place in the West where forty mountains, made of
man, rise out of the earth." Whereupon, said good Bartholomew Luther Meeks he had straightway sold his goods, and
taking up The Book had come riding west, seeking that
mystic place the Lord was going to show him. It had taken
ten years (and, though he didn't mention it, fourteen wives)
to reach those mountains. And thereupon, all of a sudden, he
gave a wild whoop (it was said of him, Brother Meeks, that
his voice went through a man like a nail). "This here, my
flock," the preacher shrieked, "is the place, and them yonder
air the Mountains of Gilead!" With that, about a score fell
down with the jerks and a dozen more started babbling the
unknown tongue. The astounded Prophet of Religion so enjoyed his success that he remained in the county nearly twelve
months to the day, preaching his famous "Mountains of
Gilead" sermon, predicting the Second Coming, watching the
Sligo Countians jerk and moan, listening as they cried out and

fainted before a sudden vision of the heavenly advent flashing past their glazing eyes. The Reverend Brother Meeks took his fifteenth wife in Somerton, a Miss Polly America French, and prospered mightily. But a mere three days short of the seventh hour of the seventh day of August, 1843, when he had predicted the Second Coming, the Reverend Bartholomew L. Meeks struck out on a fast horse for Arkansas, alone. He left Polly America to weep for a year before she remarried. He left the camp meeting ground to be plowed up and sown. He left all, except the ignominy he had visited upon the French family and the name he had given the Indian Mountains, to be forgotten.

"Mounds?" the farmer says a hundred years later, peering suspiciously at the stranger. And then, "You must mean the Mountains of Gilead. You come all *that* way just to see *them?* Well," reluctantly now, "you go yonderway into town and turn to your right, that's south on Seventeenth. Now about two miles out you'll run right along aside of them things, a-pooching up out of the bottom like big old frog warts."

The Mountains of Gilead brought Doc and Madam Shafer to Somerton, because the mounds had captured Doc's scholarly imagination. From the first time he heard of them they exerted a pull on him. Living near them had to be the final remedy. For Doc had to be where he could explore their secrets. And so, bringing his bride, Doc moved out of the midstate, out of the Middle Tennessee blue grass country and into the western third of Tennessee with its swampy forests of cypress and pin oak, its roughness, its flat cotton and corn fields, and its rolling meadows of harsh pastureland. In the cold months Doc saw the raw winds come whistling over the levees from the Mississippi River bottoms sixty miles west, and in the early spring he watched the clouds slide along overhead sometimes in a long solid shelf that moved swiftly east for days on end. Such a wind was unseasonably warm. It stirred an uneasiness in his blood. For he knew the wind was curling up from the Gulf of Mexico and he knew it was spoiling for a clash. When that wind blew the tornadoes came and came nearly always at night, while people were sleeping.

Because Madam Shafer missed the cultural stimulus of Nashville, she founded a theatrical group in Somerton called the Thespians. She even wrote a play which the Thespians produced and in which she played the lead. But that was before her "tumor" developed. The "tumor" robbed the Thespians of her leadership and without her the theatrical society began withering and finally perished. She and Doc turned their attentions to their child, loving him, giving him too much of everything. He had model railroads and swings, ponies and seesaws, guns and boxing gloves, bicycles, anything you could imagine. It was because they were old enough to be his grandparents. He was an unexpected gift and for this reason they doted on him. And somehow he survived all this and emerged pretty much unspoiled. He grew into a fair, even-tempered child, well-behaved in school, and inclined to spend long summer days reading under a shade tree or, sometimes, helping sort and clean the artifacts Doc brought home from the Indian mountains.

Doc did everything with a flair. Each morning he left for the mounds driving his old truck. Doc struck off down Main Street with Bojack Markam, his Negro, riding beside him, Doc's white beard fluttering in the wind. The truck roared and clattered. Windows flew open and dogs barked when Doc passed, for he drove the old truck as though it were a chariot and as though he were an Egyptian Lord, pursuing gazelles.

As a little child Gratt Shafer romped with his dog through the vacant fields. When he was older he and his friend, Toonker Burkette, swam in the river in the springtime, riding their bicycles out the highway past the Mountains of Gilead and pushing through a cotton field and then a mile along the railroad embankment to the bridge where "the place" was. They caught turtles and kept them in wash tubs in the backyard. They killed bluejays with Toonker's .22 rifle, and one summer they spent entire days hurling hatchets and knives at a particular oak tree in a grove not far from Gratt's house. Gratt read the Tarzan books, made bows and arrows, and camped out all night on the river bank with Toonker. They built a radio, and rigged up a private telephone between their houses. They lived nine days in a two-story tree house built in Gratt's backyard. And one summer evening Gratt came home late taking his supper (Madam would leave it in the oven for him to keep it warm) out to the back steps to eat it and talk to the Negro. Bojack lived in the carriage house and did chores about the place when he was not helping Doc during the day. Bojack sometimes had news on happenings among the colored folks.

"Say, Gratt."

"Yeah?" He sat down on the steps by the old man and started eating.

"Hear about the woman killed yestiddy?"

"*Killed!* Naw." He looked up at Bojack, in surprise.

"Sure was. She was thirty-seven. A boy eighteen shawt her and then turnt the gun on his own self. But the boy, he ain't died, yet."

"The boy ain't?"

"Naw. It was a thirty-two owl head pistol what he used."

"Don't eighteen sound mighty young to be shooting folks, Bojack?"

"Man, what you saying? Ain't that what a woman thirty-seven get? Fooling around wid a child like that? I knowed that boy and he weren't full grown. And she was hugging him up, making love at him, and him so young. So first thang she know here he come at her wid old thirty-two owl head.

" 'Lawsy, lover. Boy what you *got* there?' she say. 'Put dat thang up. What you doing?'

"And he say: 'I gonner let you down, for you two-timen on me.'

" 'Lawsy, O please, O lover, O sweet Lawsy.'

"And then why next thang she know old owl head done barked at her and let her down. *Down,* what I mean.

" 'Hug dat up in your arms,' he say. Then he tune up to cry and turn old owl to his own chest and commenced to shoot his own self, whimpering like a dog. But he still living."

"You seen her, Bojack?"

"Yeah. I went by up to the L. B. Jones Funeral Parlor."

"How did she look?"

"Just nice and pretty as you please. She *was* a pretty woman."

"Bojack?"

"Huh?"

"You ever — hug up to her?"

"Oh, I reckon I is, maybe twice or three times, something like that amount. But it been a great while ago, back before you was born, sonny boy."

Gratt Shafer traded a pocket knife with four blades for a harmonica (they called them French harps), and later, because he couldn't play it, he sold it to Bojack for a quarter. Bojack could make it sound like a train chuffing off across the bottoms late at night. He could make it sound like a cotton field in the afternoon when the pickers begin to drag their heavy sacks wearily, and he could play First Monday, the first Monday of each month, when the traders came to Somerton carrying gourds and driving mules and leading hounds leashed on binder twine. He could make the French harp sound like the auctioneer and the man who sold roasted peanuts and boiled peanuts, and the First Monday hounds getting into a fight; he could play the gourds rattling and the mules standing patiently all day to be traded. One other thing he could play was the strawberry festival. He played the festival better than almost anything else because he liked the festival better than the other things. He got the sound of parades and the feel of cotton candy, and the sight of Starkey Poe going up in the big red ascension balloon to jump out with his parachute. It was the festival that made Somerton (to Gratt Shafer's way of thinking) the best town in West Tennessee for a boy to grow up in. Old Bojack could play the festival so Gratt Shafer, listening, saw how hot it was and how the crowds stirred along the sidewalks, and how the bands marching past in the street always made him cry. Band music did him that way because it was so loud and pretty. But Bojack couldn't play a *tune* on the French harp. He only played *things*. He would put the French harp to his mouth and cup his big squarish hands artfully about it and, resting on the back porch steps while a midsummer's sunset faded slowly to its last apex at the horizon's edge, he would close his eyes, and softly begin to play.

Gratt's favorite teacher at the high school was Professor Sims, the Latin teacher.

Gratt was reading Caesar when Doc died, and when he got to Virgil, Madam came down with pneumonia. She had suffered with a bad heart for years, and she didn't last long. For a long time after her death the boy felt dissevered from other people, from schoolmates who had parents living and from adults, older people who had children. Recovering from his sorrow, missing his mother, dreaming of her, waking again and again to realize she was really and eternally gone, he felt at last like an object set adrift at sea, unpossessed, belonging nowhere in particular. The bank became Gratt Shafer's guardian and Bojack moved out of his room in the carriage house, formerly the harness room, and made his quarters in a small corner room off the kitchen. Living in the house proper, Bojack could better look out for the boy's raising. Gratt Shafer was sixteen when Madam died, and living thus, alone in the house with Bojack Markam, he passed two troubling years.

For one thing Patsy Jo was pretty, maybe a little leggy when he first took notice of her, maybe not quite filled out, coltish in the way a colt can give the suggestion of being more bones than flesh, but the makings of beautiful woman-hood were all there, in the white skin and the hair dark as a crow's wing, in the quick flash of her eyes, the shape of her face, molded about high cheekbones, and the husk in her voice. The way she talked led a boy on, led him on to thinking she had seen more of the world than she really had seen, so that the beginning was slow and in a way funny, a way he could never explain because she got to him before he really knew it, perhaps because he was just seventeen himself. It was young, but you married young if you didn't go to college; you married and bred and died young. It was a tradition.

She had a way of laughing, and would say: "I want to die young and leave a beautiful corpse." It was more something a man would say, a young rakehellion, a flush-faced corn whiskey-drinking bastard like the ones that cracked up their jalopies and had a young funeral when the car and the body had been found, where both went through the bridge into the Forked Deer River, the speculation being whether or not the young man was already dead "whenever the car hit the water," or whether he drowned, and whether or not it was true that if you kept your head you could get out of a car in the water that way and live. There were those who claimed to know people who had gone off a river bridge in a car and made it out alive, but you never met one walking around in 1935, not one that you could really believe. So it was something he would have expected out of a man, which showed she had a man's knack of looking at things and perhaps explained why she got along with men better than women. She had a few girl friends, but she was the kind every guy will break his neck to date. She created a certain excitement in a man. It came off her almost as though it were something you could smell, and she knew about it, because if you tried something that went too far to suit her she would unwind the working girl's protection and leave her fingerprints outlined in red on a guy's cheek. On the second date she gave Gratt Shafer a nosebleed and after that he was cautious. And, yes, he tried to give her up. He thought right then about not calling her for the third date. But all he did was think about it, for the very next week he called her again and it was the same way, the thing, whatever it was, making him want her worse than anything or anyone he had ever imagined before, but she knew what she was doing. She was already wise. She was not one of the dumb ones who don't know what they've got, that what they are sitting on is a lien on the world which can be cashed in at whatever price they are willing to set, who didn't know the American Protestant Doctrine, or at least couldn't put it into words the way Patsy Jo McCutcheon could. *You* could have never thought of it, much less said it. But Patsy Jo thought of it, knew it, understood it, and said it from time to time.

"Let me tell you, Gratt," she would say sweetly. "I'm not trying to be ugly."

And he would say: "Yes, I know you're not trying to be." Then the spring wind would stir whatever scent there is about the night when the car window is down and the car itself is out in a pasture where the lights of traffic moving along the highway are about half a mile off, so that if by mistake or on purpose one of them even should turn off the road and start across the pasture you would have half-a-mile's warning, which was plenty. It gave the girls a feeling of safety to know they had that long to disengage, half a mile, which was why he always chose the spot. Only it didn't work with Patsy Jo.

"I'm not trying to be ugly," she would say, "but there is a rule. And the rule is that you either sit on it or sell it, and I'm not ready to sell it no matter how tired I get sitting on it, even if I have to wait five more years to get married. Now do you see, Gratt?"

And with it coming at him cold, that way, he had to agree. In fact he admired her, in an off-brand sort of way. It was one thing to be smart that way, and another to put your smart into practice. For the world worked with him against her, to make her.

To make her. And he would say: "Then why date me at all? Because this is a blind alley."

And she would say: "Suit yourself."

After he had taken her home he would drive slowly out the Memphis highway, carrying that same sense of her presence with him, its excitement. He could imagine she was still beside him and he would talk to her then boldly, telling her he loved her, telling her some day he would marry her, after he had gotten out of law school, because he was going to study law. (He never, finally, did study law, but back then it sounded good.) And in his mind he would hear her answers, feel her head against his shoulder, where she had never laid it, and slowly he would unpeel her clothes . . .

The place he usually wound up, on those evenings, had a string of lights, dim and multicolored, stretched about outside it like Christmas decorations, and he would pull the car off the highway and wait for the lights to go out. And when the last drunk had finally staggered out and wobbled away in his car, the lights *would* go out and the waitress or barmaid or what-have-you would come briskly out carrying her purse. He would lean over and open the door of the Packard (it had been his Mother's when she died) and with this new, tired companion, he would find a log road somewhere and go through a monotonous routine with her, a few drinks and a long argument and finally her submission, more often than not a reluctant meaningless thing on her part, a weariness with it, and him, and life, an emotion that would enter him no sooner and no later than the exact instant his moment was come and gone. *Come and gone.* Then *her* feeling would enter *him*, as though it were water, that feeling, and he a sponge. He would soak up instantly all the self-disgust he could hold, and panting now, the ghost of his excitement leaving him at last, he would now notice the greasy hair net, the pencil-thin eyebrows that were so stylish with all of her kind, and the gray, rubbery flesh. And she, now feeling re-laxed, feeling home-free for having *that* part of the date over — the unpleasant part — would suddenly get giggly and gay and glad to be off work and sitting in a Packard where she could play the radio and hum off-key and kiss him tenderly on the ear, go, in fact, through the entire routine of endearing caresses that, done fifteen minutes before, would have made what *he* had just experienced something more than a self-dis-gusted shock. So that it was as if the disgust in passing into him had, at the same time, passed out of her. And he was now the one disgusted, who wanted secretly to push her away as she lay tenderly on his shoulder, smelling a little of onion and cheap permanent wave solution, and of an indefinite something, at once antiseptic and evil, reminding him that he had just trod a path traveled many times over by men of all conditions and descriptions, some of whom were now dead or now asleep or now traveling far over the world, those others having in common with him the single fact that they too had entered this thing now leaning against him, this craven, this debauched, this love-starved, half-human creation of a thousand perversities dreamed up in the dim-lit minds of cigar-puffing drunkards. It was to his credit that he never slapped her. It was to his credit that he even escorted her to her door, and sometimes even drove twenty miles to a town where they had an all-night restaurant, and bought her breakfast. And he never lied to her, except to change his name, for he had been told once that you never gave such women your real name. And he never gave her a present.

One quarrel was with the way in which Gratt Shafer lived, the ambitionless, aimlessness of his life, as though he were waiting for something to happen, something which would wake him up to his responsibilities, the trouble being that what he waited for would never happen. Time would pass him by and he would never wake up and be a man.

Four years in college didn't help, four years during which he lived in Nashville most of the time, managing nevertheless to effect Patsy Jo's pregnancy, aimlessly again, as though he were, as she told him he was, a living, breathing menace to the world, a bomb walking around, waiting to explode, a poison, a disease. That was how she put it to him. For no, no, she didn't want to marry an accident going somewhere to happen. And a fatherless child was not something she wanted to add to her father's, Tom McCutcheon's, troubles. So she had an abortion and tried hard after that to fall in love with someone else. What she wanted was a man who was going to be a truck driver or a psychiatrist or a counter man in an all-night restaurant or a teacher or a bootlegger — anything, it didn't matter, as long as he was going to be something she could count on, for a man who is going to be something, as she put it, can be counted on to stay with you and stand by you through thick and thin. And she didn't care if it had to be thin for the most part instead of thick. For money was not the major consideration. Gratt Shafer had *that*, he had money all right enough, and wads of it, left him by his old lady. She had left him her money and none of her cunning, there was the trouble. She had carried him inside of her and dropped him like a calf and let him grow up without absorbing one ounce of whatever it was that had made *her* people smart enough to amass a fortune in timber and coal and what-have-you. Not that it was such a hell of a big fortune, for it wasn't. But it was enough so that Patsy Jo could have lived the rest of her life comfortably, without having to worry about where the next meal was coming from or how she would educate the kids — their kids, Gratt Shafer's and hers.

But the money alone wasn't enough. She had to have someone she could count on, and she couldn't count on Gratt Shafer. She told him that much over and over. He was a big, broad-shouldered, bland-looking man, young-looking, always that —yes, that was part of his deceit too — looking young, and not even lazy, not even that to excuse him, for he had all the energy anyone could ask for, all the strength and force was there, except that whatever it was he was waiting for, the right time, the right moment, the right opportunity, just never happened. If he got anything out of college, it was perhaps a somewhat wider view of the world, and the wider view showed him, apparently, the same thing the more narrow view in Somerton had shown him, absolutely nothing. He took up drinking in college, so that she had believed for a time that he would be an alcoholic, and that liquor was finally what he had been looking for, waiting for, but that hadn't been it either. Liquor hadn't been it any more than college had been it, or the shock of getting your girl pregnant, or of seeing her off trying to fall in love with other men — none of it seemed to affect him very deeply, which would have made him a true ass in spirit, instead of what he really was, just an honest bomb, a well-meaning, destructive, good-natured bastard of a son of a bitch who went off to Vanderbilt and weathered all the courses they had there, graduated in the middle upper third in his class, with a Bachelor of Arts in Business. What kind of business the world would be guessing until he died, for he never offered to enter a business. Not that he didn't have chances to, not that he wasn't approached by plenty of West Tennessee people who needed a little capital, a silent partner, but no, not Gratt Shafer. He could have been a millionaire by just sitting around on his bottom and watching the world go by, but that didn't suit him either. He wasn't interested, didn't care, couldn't bother to listen, so that finally she decided that he had gotten everything from his father, the old man himself, the old dude she hardly remembered except for having heard people talk about how queer Doc Shafer was, how lopsided. For that was it, Gratt Shafer's father had been interested in only one thing, if what was said about him could be counted on for the gospel, *he* was interested in the Mountains of Gilead and the rest of the world could go to hell.

So what Gratt Shafer was cut out to be was a college professor like his father had been, only the faculty at Vanderbilt had not been able to convince Gratt of it, had not been able to keep him even long enough to get a Master of Arts degree. Even the M.A. would have helped, for it would have given her the excuse that he was a disappointed "brain." Then maybe she could have married him and worried him into getting a Ph.D. She would have been in business herself then, with something she could have and hold and halfway depend upon. And one day he would have then discovered his *own* Mountains of Gilead, or whatever the hell it was a man with any brains discovered outside of himself and fell in love with, he would have discovered it and she could have relaxed.

Except that it didn't turn out that way either. Except that as far as Gratt Shafer was concerned there were no Mountains of Gilead in his life, nor even in sight. He just drove home on Sunday afternoon with his diploma, bringing a Memphis friend, or a college friend, anyway a friend he had made at college, the only thing he got out of it except a diploma, this Camack Patterson, who even then had a way of looking like he smelled something when he met someone he considered beneath him, a way he looked when he met Patsy Jo, a way he had looked, probably (Gratt hadn't been looking) when he caught his first glimpse of Somerton and realized that this was where *his* friend hailed from — the only friend *he* had made in four years at Vanderbilt.

Anyway Gratt had come home that Sunday evening in

June, in 1937, and when Monday morning dawned he was no nearer to a job, to respectability, to the love of anything or the aspiration towards anything, than he had been shortly after his seventeenth birthday, when she, Patsy Jo McCutcheon, had had the first date with him. He was just home, and that was all that could be said for him . . . that he had gone away and he had returned.

That was when she faltered for the first time, when it hit her how hopeless he was. She had just about been the rounds — a Missouri woman's college, two years; two years of bridge in the afternoon, of parties with somebody's visiting bachelor nephew or cousin at her elbow, something that walked and talked and sometimes even made a faltering pass at her, or even returned to Somerton bringing candy, something that occasionally sent flowers, but nothing in the end that she could wholeheartedly give herself to for life, nothing real in the way of a man.

So she went to work in the Factory-to-You Store. That was the next step, to keep her hands from shaking, to admit outwardly a little of what was happening, to admit that she was not getting younger and that time was not passing any slower, that she had to do something which would show that *she* at least had some sense, even if Gratt Shafer didn't. Working helped, it propped her up inside by making her dead-tired physically, by getting her store-grimy, by letting her worry about Herman Gold's problems, by, in effect, marrying a dry goods ready-to-wear business where working your guts out was just sufficient, where the work was there every morning like it had been the morning before, and the one before that, where a girl suffered properly for the hangover she couldn't afford, where she worked until she was so tired it didn't matter that there was nothing in the bed that night — she slept anyway. The Factory-to-You Store was the next step for her.

But not for Gratt Shafer. He had a comforter, however, a comforter in Camack Patterson, who could see nothing wrong in Gratt's being idle without being lazy, drinking without being a damned drunk, in his waiting for that which, by then, she was so sure would not come, that she no longer gave it any serious thought. Gratt Shafer was doomed, and if she didn't get on *her* horse, she was doomed too. She didn't want to be part of his doom, to be in on his destruction. So she began to struggle. He would go to bed with her, he did that all right, but not with any idea of exploiting her, no, she couldn't even blame him *there*. Still, she put the pressure on, without really having any hope, and finally he proposed. He proposed in a way that told her theirs would be a union without issue, a marriage merely in the sense that they would live in the same house, and then was when she knew, felt, sensed, yes had it fallen on her like a regular landslide that having him *propose* was about the hollowest victory she had ever won from him, that getting his mother's ring from him had been like taking candy from a baby, no, worse even than that, because the baby didn't care, that was the terrible part. The baby didn't care.

What she had done, and she told him so, was to enter into his pact with destruction, with doom, with whatever it was. She did it by asking him over and over again when he was going to grow up, to which he replied that he didn't know, no one had told him, and further, he halfway didn't give a damn, since the world had worn him out too, had worn him clean down to a nub of himself. He had been thinking a good bit about his father, lately, he said at the time. He had been wondering why he, Gratt Shafer, had been born at all. He had been wondering if it would not have been a lot easier on everyone concerned if the thing inside his mother had really been a tumor after all.

But of course she loved him and couldn't say anything one way or the other to him, for that is what her love had become by then, a hopeless, sinking silence, in which she gave herself, sometimes, on impulse, to another man. She gave herself not wanting to be mean or vulgar or low, but wanting to find out if Gratt Shafer really and truly was what she believed him to be, if he really was the only one, and if it really was true that there *could* be in this life any such thing as love. But the other man, when she gave herself, brought back the truth of love, that love *was* real, that another man never would replace Gratt Shafer, that *he* was really the first and the last, the Alpha and the Omega — this was what it told her, with another man. This was how she got her balance when the whole world began to spin under her feet, when she felt that the earth would be bound now to swallow her up, for with another man it was different. It really tore her up. The punishment afterwards was the only lovely part, the lovely part being that she could suffer then, at last, for having been untrue to Gratt Shafer when she owed him nothing of the sort, nothing of the kind, not even the time of day. Yet there, and only there, was a lovely lot of suffering to be had, and now and then she had to have it, if only to find her footing again.

It was what happened to her, that slow spinning sensation, when Gratt Shafer proposed. So after the abortion she took the other men and always woke up the next morning feeling awful, suffering, crying, fondling the ring. And then one evening she learned that Gratt Shafer had gone away. It was an unlikely thing for him to do. But when she learned of its truth she was relieved. She even began to hope something had happened, something that might free him from the husk, the cocoon of himself, and set him off soaring and free.

And that was the world, in that it always gave you what you had asked for when the time was too late, giving you what you wanted after the part of you that had wanted it had grown so tired, wanting, that the final possession meant nothing. You wanted to be grown up and to have breasts, but when the pain of waiting and the pain of growing were over, the joy which the sudden granting of the wish would have given you was crisp, dead as an old leaf. He was gone. The old leaves filled her heart and finally set it to hurting, to aching. That had to be her luck, to fall for someone like Gratt Shafer, to fall so very hard and never again, really, to come off of her knees, to spend the rest of her life crawling because she couldn't have all of him, because part of him was gone eternally wandering, never to return. That had to be her luck, so that she could finally even envy the girl who married the guy who turned out to be a drunk, who lost his business and beat her, who finally lay helpless while she worked and raised the children and nursed him — even that could be a life. She could even envy Betty Morgan French going house-to-house, coming home to Gabe Junior and his infantile whims. But at least Betty Morgan had him all, all there was left of Gabe French, Jr. She had his children.

It turned out that Gratt Shafer had joined the Marine Corps! The news gave her heart a flutter. When he was reported missing and the months passed, she could finally believe he was dead, and a feeling of calm possessed her. At least if he were dead, he had died *for* something. And no matter what else, as the days passed, she felt that he was hers now, and he was a chapter of her life ended. She preferred him that way in the end, *dead*. It broke her heart, she cried. But the calm sureness that this, then, was the answer, gave her a great deal of comfort, so much that when Gratt Shafer came home alive, she felt tricked. It was the first time that she had hated him, but she did hate him then. She hated him for coming back, for being fifty pounds underweight, for having the disguise of respectability cloaked about him, something he hadn't won and didn't deserve, for underneath, inwardly, he was still, she knew, just the same.

Perhaps the thing to have done then was marry him. To move in immediately and take over, to force the issue he had dodged. But she wasn't built that way. She wasn't built that way and he hadn't changed, so she gave him the ring back and gave herself to him Sundays, and when she couldn't stand it any longer she cheated on him a little and sometimes imagined that she was going crazy, which was, as she could best recall, when her father began to take notice and to be concerned. It was after Gratt Shafer's return when things still didn't get any better, when their affairs, hers and Gratt's, still didn't move any closer to a settlement, that Tom McCutcheon waked up to a few things, or at least if he didn't really wake up *entirely*, at least began to *suspect*.

Maybe the fact that he was getting old had something to

do with it, and perhaps his instinct told him everything was all wrong. But at any rate he began to fret, to look for who was to blame, to wonder if she, Patsy Jo, were whoring around, and to begin trying to grasp what was, perhaps, totally beyond his powers in the first place, to grasp and somehow to understand what was wrong and what must be done now to make things right.

She had warned Gratt. She had told him that the old man was getting riled up. She had lived in the same house with him all her life, and that was long enough to be sure when something was bothering her father. Except that Gratt had no more capacity for understanding her father than her father himself had for understanding whose fault it was in the first place that she was not already married, if not to Gratt Shafer, then to someone else.

For all the old man could see was that she was thirty-four and getting to look sort of hard and used. If she were going to have babies she would have to hurry, and if she didn't have babies then he had somehow failed to provide for her. If that happened, then he had been failing all along where he thought he was succeeding. And so, for a while he blamed it on his wife, Patsy Jo's mother. He blamed her for having left him with a child to raise, especially a girl child. (It was beyond his comprehension to imagine that he could have failed to raise a son properly, but a girl, a girl was a different matter.) So that whatever there was in Patsy Jo's father that was like Goliath began to rouse itself, and even though he had been somewhat withdrawn and dark, somewhat violent-*looking* for as long as she could remember him, what was happening inside of him now gave her pause. He was rousing himself to some conscious act, some calculated alteration of the world, which, lately, he had discovered was about to go all wrong.

And by this time Camack Patterson had driven his *own* victory home, hollow though it was. By this time he had taken the aimless, dangerous, well-meaning, but hopelessly lost Gratt Shafer to Memphis often enough to convince himself, Camack Patterson, that all Gratt Shafer lacked was to be removed from Somerton, to have a rich wife, and truly, to live in Society. It was all extremely logical on Camack Patterson's part, for a rich wife and Society were exactly what he himself needed. Society and a rich wife were, in truth, the mountains Camack Patterson had been pointed to all his life. So he, Camack, arranged the wedding.

It snowed that Saturday and Camack drove to Somerton over bad roads, bringing Florence Bradford with him. Patsy Jo had asked him to bring his own partner and Florence had seemed a good choice. She was young and dumpy and sweet. She was full of foolish small talk. The words seemed to roll out of Florence like the melodies that come from a player piano. All you had to do was change rolls occasionally and Florence tinkled on and on with a sort of brilliance, with an inane and brittle pattern, like the narrow place in a brook. There was no need to think around Florence, in fact, there was no point in it. She took charge.

"*Patsy Jo*," said Florence. "That's sort of a mouthful."

Camack drove carefully. He had left Memphis early to make sure they got there on time. "Now who is he, again?"

said Florence. It was time to change her roll. She was staring
vacantly at the snow, pushing at her red curly hair.

"My friend," Camack said. "Gratt Shafer. He's a very fine
guy."

"And not married," said Florence. You could almost hear
the new roll click in place. "Well, a girl has to ask why. Except no one would ever have to ask you, Camack. You married a law office. Are you taking me up here for him to look
over? That's how you men operate, like slave traders. Now
isn't it? All right, then I want to see him. You think there's a
chance or you wouldn't be taking me all this distance. Why
don't you bring him to Memphis? Take Mohammed to the
mountain, I say. These hidden friends of yours Camack, these
hidden mysterious friends! I can hardly wait . . ."

Patsy Jo had Florence for a bridge partner and Patsy Jo
was tired. She had tried to smooth away the signs of strain
that showed in her face, spending half an hour at it before
her guests arrived, working at the uncharacteristic rumple of
her black hair and the lines about her deep brown eyes, the
lines reaching into her handsome face. But she couldn't hide
it all. For after all, she had been clerking all day long in the
Factory-to-You, the store owned by Herman Gold, the indus-
trious Jew from Indianapolis who had migrated to Somerton
after the war. In the spring the work wasn't so bad. But the
closer Christmas came the harder things always got for the
clerks at the Factory-to-You, for Herman depended on a big
volume of business during the Christmas season. She was tired
and she looked at Florence and thought Florence was about
what Camack Patterson could be counted on to bring. "A

little society gash," thought Patsy Jo. Florence was winding up all *the make* she could muster and trying to put it on Gratt. Patsy Jo felt it in her legs, a numb fright or anger in them, when Florence spoke to Gratt or looked at him. Now Patsy Jo was sorry she had asked Camack, but it was being sorry too late, which is the worst way, and she tried to keep her disappointment from showing. She tried to concentrate on the game. But little Florence was also a lousy partner. She was not a bridge player. She was just a dangerously innocent-looking little debutante gash who was playing the man market. Having Florence in the living room made a bull in your china cupboard look like a flea in a cotton warehouse, by comparison. For Florence was sex and money, with vocal chords, and she was saying to Gratt Shafer: "Look at *me*." Gratt was looking. He didn't have any better sense than to look, and Camack was enjoying it.

Patsy Jo found her smile coming a little too quickly. She shuffled the cards with an angry rip. And when it was her time to deal she dealt too rapidly, cursing inside, for she was giving herself away. She was letting Florence have the satisfaction of *knowing*. Florence would know she was upset. Between hands Patsy Jo tried tactfully to coach warm-eyed little Florence. But Florence ignored her suggestions and rattled on about the Junior League. Florence played out of turn and out of suit and said how charming Somerton was with its dirty streets and buckled sidewalks and its quaint little rundown houses. "I must have been through Somerton a thousand *times*," said Florence. "But you know, I never knew it? And when Camack said he was taking me to Somerton I said: 'Where the hell is *that*, dear?' Wasn't I *crazy* not to know where Somerton was? Why, Patsy, I don't really think it's bad here. In fact it's kind of cute to be out in the country this way, now and then, you know? It is my turn? Is that your queen or mine? I bet I've been through here a thousand *times* and never once knew it."

Not only that, but Florence bid five spades when she meant to say five clubs and she trumped Patsy Jo's ace twice. She kept dropping her cards and letting the men scramble for them. "You'll have to pardon me," Florence would say. And, "Patsy, honey, did we go down *again?*"

And Camack, playing as usual for blood, sprang at the chance to run up a score. He was never quite so overbearing and obnoxious as when he was winning. Patsy Jo said so, aloud. And trying to help Florence at the end of their third disastrous rubber, Patsy Jo said, "Florence, honey, third hand always plays high. You see?"

"Always," said Camack, raising one eyebrow officiously. "Indeed?"

Patsy Jo said the rule was a good one.

"A dangerous maxim: 'Third hand always plays high,'" Camack said, biting off the words.

Distressed, Florence tried to smooth things over with her sweet voice, "But, Camack, if *that's* the way they play in Somerton!"

"Good bridge is good bridge everywhere, *even* here," Patsy Jo said. And, turning to Camack, "Will you keep quiet while I tell her a few things."

"Not if you tell her wrong things," said Camack testily. "I couldn't sit idly by and watch you do her a disservice. I *can't* let you tell her *wrong* things."

"Please, *please!*" Florence said, a little mortified, shifting her little self uncomfortably. Her glance wavered uncertainly between Patsy Jo and Camack. Finally Florence turned to Gratt Shafer. *Do something, stop them!* her pleading look seemed to say. But Gratt Shafer, as innocently as he could, ignored her. And in the next instant Patsy Jo uncoiled, slapping Camack Patterson savagely on the cheek. Standing suddenly, his face furiously red, Camack threw his cards at her face. They fluttered to the rug.

"Get out," Patsy Jo said hoarsely. "Get out. Get out. *Get out!*"

She and Camack stood facing each other, both nearly overcome with anger, both trembling. But Florence had soon stampeded into her furs and wrenched open the front door. She stood there, hysterically bleating, "Camack! It's snowing. Come on!" as if the snow coming down outside were the entire cause of her alarm.

The cold wind and the raw smell of snow rolled together into the room. Gratt Shafer stayed neutral, sitting where he was. Pausing with his overcoat flung over his arm and his hat in his hand, Camack turned with a trembling, ironic little bow, the gesture of the man who wishes to say aloud, "There, you see, I *told* you so" and he said aloud, "Good night!" And the door slammed after him. Camack and little Florence were gone, and a final gust of cold wind filtered out of the air, curling about their ankles, making the stern, angular drawing room of the McCutcheon house seem all the more unfriendly. Patsy Jo thought how the house must be peering out upon East Main Street after Camack and Florence from its high, breadloaf-shaped knoll. She thought what a thin, high Victorian house it was with its narrow windows. Those windows looked out sourly between the large magnolia trees which seemed to glare at the night. She heard Camack's car doors slam shut. Still standing just as she was when she had hit Camack, she said, "The nervy little bastard."

"I'll go," Gratt Shafer said. "It's too damned bad. I'm sorry the evening had to end this way. Camack was rude."

"Don't go, Gratt," she said. "If you leave it will only be worse. I don't want to be alone. Oh, I don't know what got into me. It was as though a flash of light streaked through my mind. The next thing I knew I hit him. I slapped hell out of him, and I'm *glad*. I'm glad my fingers hurt."

"You know I won't go unless you want me to."

"Gratt, he's poisoned your mind. Now you'll just leave and never see me again. Because he *has* poisoned your mind, hasn't he? Admit it! That nasty little nest-fouling bastard. He's poisoned your mind. Isn't that why you want to get away, to leave me now?"

"If I went home now you might feel better in the morning, that's all. He was rude. Still I don't see why you slapped him. What did slapping him prove?"

"That I'm human! It proved that my heart beats. It proved that I'm so *damned* sick and tired. Oh, Gratt, it proved lots of things. Well, go on then. Go home! I acted like a bitch, embarrassed you in front of your mighty millionaire friends. I mortified your innards. But that's your trouble, Gratt. You're like a slimy little land snail — it takes just a pinch of salt, like tonight, and you start shriveling inside. I've sprinkled salt on snails and seen them curl and die, and now . . . you're shriveling. Well, what was I supposed to do, kiss Camack Patterson's feet?"

"I said he was rude."

"Wipe his nose?"

"I said . . ."

"You *said!* You're always *saying.* It's your long suit. But when I think he deliberately brought along that stupid, infantile little bitch! He *knew* Florence couldn't play bridge. He knew she'd create a scene. He wanted it!"

"I don't think he wanted it. Tonight just happened. And besides, now it's over. You and Camack just don't get along; it's a . . . a clash of personalities." He sighed.

She sat down across the bridge table from him, biting her lower lip. "Deliberately," she said. "Oh, don't be naïve, Gratt. You're too sweet. Camack takes advantage of you." She paused. And then, "Gratt?"

"What?"

"Are we still the same, do you feel the same about me?"

"The same," he said.

"I didn't mean those things I said. I was mad, that's all."

"I understand," he said.

In the following awkward silence they heard her father, old man McCutcheon. Somewhere in the back of the house the old man was coughing. Gratt had heard that cough when he first started dating her (seventeen years ago, but seventeen years didn't seem like such an awfully long time once seventeen years had ticked away, perhaps in this case, she thought, because at the time he started dating her neither of them had any idea it would last seventeen years); but when Gratt had first started taking her out he had thought the old man had tuberculosis. Later on she told him it wasn't tuberculosis. It was a chronic allergy that kept her father coughing all winter, from November to March, and made him wheeze through the warm months. Her father had simply never gotten acclimated to the world. Some people never did. Patsy Jo waited. But then she had been waiting for seventeen years. Couldn't Gratt see it was beginning to wear on her? Habit, she thought, the world is all a habit; I'm one habit and Camack's another habit, and Gratt himself, maybe he's a habit too.

But now was the end of something. Her senses were churning with the realization. It came to her as an uneasiness. Her slap had been more than just hitting Camack's cheek. It was her declaration. The end, and a declaration. She was still breathing rapidly. The old man coughed again.

"Camack, it's Camack," she said, almost whispering. "He's tried to ruin our lives. He keeps trying and I keep hating him. I've never hated anyone like I hate Camack Patterson, do you realize that?"

"I know," he said quietly.

"But you don't hate him."

"No," Gratt said. "Are we going to start all over again on Camack? Because if we are . . ." He didn't finish.

And finally she said, "Let's turn the lights out and watch the snow." And going to one of the narrow windows she drew aside the lace curtain.

He switched off the two end lamps flanking the Victorian love seat and stood beside her at the window, looking out. The snow was coming thickly down in the yard and in the street, a cold, dim, bluish white. And beyond the street she saw the lamps above East Main, circular blots of yellow, like dying suns, muffled with halos, fading in a series to gradual darkness in the near-white distance. She slipped her arms slowly about him, beneath his coat. She was shivering a little. "I hope he wrecks driving back and breaks his mean little neck. I hope he never gets home to Memphis alive," she said, pressing close to him, her face turned to the window where the snow swirled a little coming down. He turned to her and she began to sob. She shuddered.

"I could kill him — I could *kill him,*" she whispered.

They heard the old man, coughing wretchedly now, the sound muffled by the walls that separated them. The old bastard has a long wait till spring, she thought.

The spring following was 1949. Camack Patterson, still nursing his wounded pride, shifted his strategy.

Gratt met him on the first Wednesday in April in the lobby of the Peabody Hotel, having driven down to Memphis from Somerton expressly to have lunch with him. As they crossed the broad lobby toward the dim little bar where they ordinarily had a bourbon and soda before eating, Camack took Gratt's arm.

"I think there's a painting here," Camack was saying. "Yes, it's still there. I was going to say if it hadn't been sold already you should have it. It would fit that spot over the mantel in your den."

By "den" Camack meant the room that had been Doc Shafer's study, a mahogany-paneled room crowded, for as long as he had known Gratt, with glass display cases containing relics from Somerton mounds. There were the usual beads, bones, clay pots; the weapons of flint and the symbols of life, death, and fertility. Doc's study had smelled like a museum, having a certain inoffensive odor of ancient decay. And the room had looked like a museum alcove, with each object in it precisely numbered and labeled with stiff yellowed cards, hand-printed in India ink.

At Camack's suggestion Gratt had finally given the den's entire contents to Southwestern University which had set up the cases in an empty hallway. Gratt had also given the University the picture which had hung above the mantelpiece, a photograph of Doc Shafer and his Negro assistant, Bojack Markam. They resembled two miners on safari, wearing wrap leggings and mining caps, their faces smeared with sweat and clay. Between them they held the jawboneless skull of a mound-builder. And a white ink legend across the picture's lower edge read, simply: "Mound #17, July 21, 1918."

"Yes, here it is," Camack said, steering Gratt Shafer toward one of the large pillars which held up the lobby ceiling. The painting was part of an exhibit hung at the hotel by the Memphis Art League. Framed in wormy chestnut, it was an oil, representing a group of small sailing vessels, apparently Dutch, resting idly on a dull bluish sea, either at dawn or sunset. In the left foreground, obstructing the bilious sky, a pair of fishermen worked in a convenient, well-nigh opaque fog with what appeared to be lines, nets, or perhaps even oars. The painting was entitled "The Fishers" and was priced $200.00.

"But I couldn't pay that much!" Gratt said, smiling pleasantly. Suddenly Camack released his arm and with a subtle gesture, a nudge, caused him to look at a blonde young woman standing about twenty feet away, beside the fountain pool in the center of the hotel lobby.

"My cousin Eleanor. Do you know her?" Camack asked.

"No. Who is she again?"

"Eleanor Fite, my second cousin."

Eleanor Fite stood by the Italian marble fountain pensively staring at five mallard ducks whose occasional quacks expressed discontent with life in the lobby pool. She shooed a sleepy-looking drake off the fountain's edge into the water. The duck swam dejectedly away, ruffling its feathers.

"Come on," said Camack. "I'll introduce you."

"Hello." Eleanor hardly looked at Gratt Shafer. Rudely she directed conversation entirely to Camack and seemed, in a cruel way, to enjoy making Gratt Shafer feel like an outsider. Her dress was bright blue silk, a gay motley of blues, like a mixture of cornflower blossoms, oceans, ice and skies. She carried a purse and wore small, high-heeled shoes of the same material. She was a slim, exquisitely finished, lovely girl. She could set senses drifting with her smooth, youthful voice. You felt how the words broke out of her in a fashionable, pleasing disconnection of thoughts. Camack listened to only part of what she said. "I love these little ducks," Eleanor said. "I'm meeting a friend. People from the Delta — the Peabody is the only place they can find . . . we were in Miami . . ." She was beautiful, finished and tantalizing.

Would she have lunch with them? Camack asked.

How nice of him to ask her, she said. But, she reminded him, she was meeting her friend.

And finally she said good-by, smiling at Gratt Shafer in a quick, perfunctory way, as though she might never see him again, as though he were a small creature fenced out of her world. Her smile was a quick kindness, a fine careless gesture, Camack thought, like a peanut tossed to a monkey, with never a look back to see if the animal had picked it up from his sawdust floor and were cracking the shell. He tugged Gratt away, sensing that Shafer felt a little piqued, in a sense bruised inside, but Gratt would know, nevertheless, that this, precisely, was the way Eleanor Fite had intended for him to feel. She had struck down his guard before it could be raised. Camack sensed it. Her cunning left Gratt a little astonished. She had waked him and planted a seed of incompletion in his belly. They continued toward the little cocktail bar. Over their drinks, in the cool twilight of the place, Camack said Eleanor was still in her twenties. She had graduated from an Eastern school and afterwards had spent a good bit of time in Europe. "Getting it out of her system," was Camack's way of putting it. By "*it*" he meant the urge for being alone, the urge for freedom and lovers, for swimming naked in the Mediterranean and staying tight on champagne while mandolins frittered away at melodies until dawn drowned them in the surf. Now she was home, and ready to marry.

"Who's the lucky guy?" Gratt Shafer asked.

"Who? Oh, nobody yet. I just meant she's sitting on ready, that's all." Camack watched him closely, Gratt dropped his gaze.

"I see," Gratt Shafer said. He swirled the single swallow remaining in his drink and gulped it down.

After lunch they strolled down to Front Street and watched the Mississippi, how the wind made ripples on it, riding upstream on the expanse of yellow water which marked the division of a continent, the river before them silent in the sunlight, glazing beneath an April sky, and behind them Memphis, thriving with sound. It was a favorite sight for Camack.

"Why don't we have a few hands of bridge some evening at my place?" Camack said, watching the river. "You and Eleanor might enjoy . . . like each other."

"Yes," Gratt Shafer said, looking at the wind ripples, sweeping upstream like a flight of birds skimming over a grain field, "I think I like her already. She reminds me of the spring."

The spring. He remembered Patsy Jo McCutcheon bare-footed and riding in the car beside him and the road passing between green fields where the newborn calves lay in the grass sleeping. Spring was, he thought, how long ago?

And he had said: "I love you."

And she: "If you love me I can stand it. I can have the baby right down in the public square and nothing matters, not as long as you love me. Or if you say so I'll go to Memphis and have the operation, and you don't even have to go along because I don't want to ruin your life. Being pregnant isn't the end of the world any more than the first time you go to bed with a man is the world's end, but there is something that can make you believe either one of them is the end of everything. That's when he doesn't love you. Why should I ruin your life, Gratt? I don't want to ruin it."

And he had thought: *How beautiful.* (*How beautiful as nothing else ever could be, to know that what was inside her there was both of them.*) But he did not say it.

For just then they had passed over the long bridge and up the road beside the creek. In those days, as a college sophomore, he had been something of a dreamer, and so he had waved his hand at the spot and told her someday he would have a house there and he would have the creek damned up to make a lake that would spread over the bottom and on the rise (pointing where the corn was just barely sprouting and beyond it where the high oaks were just greening) he would build a house.

It had calmed her even though she was afraid of that thing in her belly. She didn't want to be left alone. But now his spring vacation was over and he would be going back to the University.

"I feel better now," she had said. His plans for the house gave her something to fasten her attention on and gave him a chance to look at her and covertly to think how beautiful she was. Then she wore her black hair long. "When will you be going back?"

"Tomorrow."

"God," she said, "how will I stand it?"

He told her he had to get ready for his examinations. To tell her about the fraternity dance and the other girl — the one Camack Patterson had gotten him a date with — would have spoiled the moment, the whole beauty of it. He began just then to see that he was living two lives, even while he was talking about the fictitious exams and she, as though she had already known even then how it must finally end, had begun to cry. He told himself that if he were living two lives (and he was) they were at least both his own. He was within his rights!

The abortionist, he found, was a charming impostor in charge of a small private hospital. His black hair was a little silvered at the temples. He had a large plain mouth and big masculine hands. In society he was looked upon as a saint and a saviour, and Gratt Shafer felt a deeper gratitude toward him than he could express.

"Almost anything can be taken care of with a little finesse," the abortionist said. He stroked his mustache gently, unconscious of the movement.

"I thought this was the end of the world," Gratt Shafer said.

"Of course you did," the abortionist said warmly, "but then it wasn't."

"How can I thank you, how can I tell you what this means to me — to her?"

"You mustn't try. Your friend had a tumor, we'll say. I removed it for her — nothing more." The abortionist blushed shyly and averted his great brown eyes. Gratt Shafer was standing with him in the little hospital corridor. The sun outside slanted into the clean brick wall and scattered in the blooming forsythia shrubs below the window.

"I'll always be grateful," Gratt Shafer said. They shook hands.

"It's been a pleasure," the abortionist said, "to know you both."

A tumor, we'll say. He hadn't seriously thought of his mother for some time, of Madam, but the abortionist recalled her to mind. He was too small to understand what Madam meant when she told him she thought he had been a tumor and he had asked her what a tumor was. "A lump, something bad that grows."

"Am I something bad? Did you think I was? Am I something bad?"

"No, you're something good. Mama was glad when she found out you were you and not a tumor."

"But why did you think I was a tumor."

"Because your mama was old, she didn't expect God to send you to her. She thought she had gotten too old."

"Did Doc think I was a tumor?"

"No, your father thought you were a baby boy and he was right."

Madam was preserving strawberries and the kitchen was hot with the smell of them boiling in sugar. He watched the scalded fruit jars being filled. He looked in at the berries while the preserves cooled. In a little while she would put the paraffin on top and it would turn white and seal the preserves. The berries were red, like blood. *Like tumors,* he thought, for he still didn't know what a tumor looked like. Perhaps it was like a poison berry, something wild that you could not eat. And a child was like a strawberry, something sweet. But just looking you couldn't be sure whether it was a tumor or a child God was sending down. Maybe you saw it *on the way,* at a distance. Doc and Madam saw it coming and Madam said: "Well, I'll declare, here comes a tumor." But Doc said: "No, Madam. You're wrong. It's a baby boy. I can see it plain. God's bringing us a baby boy."

When he got old enough to know *how* she had made the mistake and *why,* Madam was already dead and he didn't give it a second thought. In fact he had rarely thought much about it at all until the abortionist had already said what he had, and turned away after their final handshake. Then when the abortionist was gone Gratt Shafer had gone to the window in the hospital hallway and looked out at the forsythia blooms, resting his hands on the sill until his giddiness passed away.

Leading two lives had sapped Gratt Shafer of his courage, so much so that although he stayed close by the hospital while Patsy Jo McCutcheon was confined there, he had not dared ask if Tom McCutcheon knew. It was only when they were on the road late that evening and nearly back to Somerton that he had dared. And she said: "No. Daddy's out of touch with reality. Instead of living he's moldering — in the past, in a world I can't reach. I almost wish Daddy did suspect something, but he doesn't suspect at all. He loved my mother and . . . it's finally eroded his sanity away."

"But what did you tell him?"

"That I was going to Memphis to visit friends. He just grunted. He hardly took his eye off the page."

"It's all right. We've got time back again now."

"Yes," she said a little bitterly, "we've got time back again. But it looked so small and disappointed."

"What?"

"That little disappointed thing he took out of me." Wretchedly she began to sob. "I hadn't felt anything until I saw it. Until then it was nothing."

"Please don't think about it," he said.

But she began beating her breasts. "Murder! Oh God! it was murder. We're murderers, Gratt!"

"You can't look at it that way," he said unsurely. His voice came weak and high-pitched. "Calm down a little."

"No right," she sobbed, "we've no right . . . no one has."

"But it wasn't a person. It hadn't been born." He took one hand from the steering wheel and laid it on her arm. She snatched it away. A tumor, he thought.

"Oh it *was!*" she shrieked. "My baby! It *was*. My baby! God."

The car lurched. He almost lost control as it swerved from the pavement into the gravelly shoulder. Little stones thrashed under the fenders. He turned the car back onto the highway and for an instant the headlights swept an impenetrable thicket of tree trunks beyond the road's embankment. For the swamp lay on either side of them. They were passing through the long bottoms where trees and seeping bogwater drowned the night. Off the banks on either side death lay in all the expanse of its wet dark mystery. Her sobs were muffled now in the wind. It rushed through the window beside him, smelling of mud, moss, and drowned leaves.

"Please," he said.

"No, I hate you," she said. "I hate you and I hate him. I hate the whole damned world."

"We'll go away somewhere."

"No," she said. "Never."

"I'll take you away."

"No!"

"We'll go away."

"No. It's too foul! It's too late. We've done it — my baby, to my baby!" Her voice broke in a strange low whine. And then: "Murdered," she said softly, a sudden tenderness in her voice, "my baby's murdered."

After a while the road rose out of the bottoms. The new crescent moon shed a thin light in the sky and rose for a short distance ahead of them. Then with the next curve it swung out of sight. Patsy Jo McCutcheon was silent.

"You said you could go through anything if . . ."

"That's what I thought," she broke in. "But that was before I knew. I guess you'll always think wrong before you know."

"But if you hadn't seen it . . ."

"No," she said. "I *had* to see it. You don't understand, Gratt. Maybe you never will. Maybe it's beyond a man."

"I love you," he said.

"Don't lie to me. I don't want to hear it."

"But I love you."

"Just don't say it. Don't say anything. Just — for God's dear sake — don't say anything else. Just let me be alone. Alone!"

She'll get over it, he had thought. Then and there he promised himself to have her up to the University for a week end and to hell with Camack Patterson. *I'll make it up to her,* he thought. *Even if she's not right for me, still I love her. I'll make this up to her somehow.* And in his own baffled way he had believed that he could.

It was late when they reached Somerton but the light from the iron lamp was visible in the living room when he stopped the car by the curb in front of the old house. He switched off the lights and offered a halfhearted caress but she drew away from him. He got out of the car and carried her suitcase to the porch. She walked ahead of him, small and alone, drawn into herself. She turned at the porch, taking the suitcase. In the dim light only the careworn shadows of her eyes were visible. "Thank you," she said. She turned away. "Good night."

"Good night," he said softly. She opened the screen door and went inside.

He had turned and was going back down the walk. He heard her voice and then Tom McCutcheon's. The words were indistinct, matter-of-fact. But he turned about, drawn back by the sounds (drawn like an insect to the light), and tiptoed softly up the porch steps. Standing in the shadows beside the window he could see the yellow shade of Tom McCutcheon's iron floor lamp. McCutcheon sat beneath it, a book in his lap. Patsy Jo had put the suitcase down on the rug. She stood half-facing him.

"So you got back all right," Tom McCutcheon said. "Have a nice time?" He spoke wearily.

"Yes. I enjoyed getting away, even for a few days. We played bridge most of the time."

"Your friends had some nice bridge parties for you?"

"One right after another. Evelyn has lots of nice friends."

"You'll have to ask Evelyn to visit you sometime," he said. "She must think a lot of you."

"I intend to have her up sometime."

"You have a lot of nice friends, Patsy. I'm glad of that. I want you to have a good time. I want you to be happy. Are you?"

"Yes."

"You're looking more like your mother everyday. I said as

much to Starkey Poe. He didn't know your mother. 'If you want to know what Adelicia looked like just look at Patricia Josephine,' I told him. 'She looks more like her mother every-day,' I said. Your mother was a beauty." Tom McCutcheon took off his glasses and held them against the book. The light made a harsh shadow against his cheek in its black unshaven stubble of beard.

She picked up the suitcase. "Well, good night."

"Patsy?"

"What?" She turned back. Her face was haggard.

Little night beetles thumped the window screen beside Gratt Shafer and moths walked upon it with fluttering wings.

"Why don't you sit down a minute and talk to me? It seems like we never talk any more."

"I'm tired," she said.

"It won't hurt you to talk just a minute will it?" His voice was pleading and lonely. She left the suitcase on the rug in almost the same place and sat down on the sofa, near his chair. The light and shadow contoured her figure, imminent in her tight green dress. Gratt Shafer had a glimpse of her legs, like soft ivory, as she crossed them.

"You been crying?" Tom McCutcheon asked, his voice suddenly awake, as though he saw her for the first time.

"They were smoking in the car on the way up. An ash flew in my eye," she murmured. The lie came quick, smooth as a snake.

"They should be more careful," Tom McCutcheon said. "For a minute I thought something was wrong."

"No, an ash from Jane's cigarette. That's all." Her voice was distant, bored, unresisting.

"Jane, eh? She brought you home?" He groped in confusion at the name.

"She was on her way to Nashville."

"Why didn't you invite her in — she could have spent the night. I've never met Jane, have I?"

"No."

"Why didn't you ask her in?"

"I . . . she was in a hurry. Besides, I couldn't ask her to stay the night, not on such short notice."

"Ashamed for her to meet your daddy?"

"Please don't start that."

"I'm accustomed to polite company, you know. I've been ostracized here, of course. But the McCutcheon name still stands for something."

"I said please . . ."

"If you're ashamed of your daddy go on and say it, say you're ashamed." He paused to roll and light a cigarette.

"You know I'm not ashamed of you," she said after a while, in the same dead tone.

"Sure," he continued. He flicked an ash nervously into the crowded ash tray on the littered table at his elbow. "I need a shave and these clothes aren't decent, I'll grant you that much."

"Do we have to start this?"

"Let me make my point, if you please! My point is I *could* shave this beard off. I've got nice clothes back there in my closet — decent clothes I could put on. All *you* had to do was phone me before you left Memphis and I could have been ready to receive company."

"It's no use," she said. "This isn't getting anywhere."

"But why, Patsy? Why didn't you just pick up the telephone? I wouldn't mind a long distance call, you know that." The old blowhard! Gratt Shafer thought.

She looked at the old man hotly. "That's a laugh. The very time I called would be the time you'd be off in the bottoms with Starkey Poe. Or here, maybe sober, maybe drinking. You'd be with him, running coons, or gone three days in the mountains on a bear drive. Now just *when* was the last time you looked decent? Or can you remember?"

"I'll grant you my solace is hunting today," he said loftily, "but there was a time. I went to good schools . . ."

"The past! It's always the past with you. This is now. It's *today*. Do you hear?" She was brutal.

"You don't have to raise your voice."

"But you don't listen, Daddy. You don't hear me."

"Never underestimate the past, that's all I say. You're ashamed of me, aren't you?"

"Yes! I'm ashamed of you. I'm ashamed of you and I'm ashamed of me!"

"My girl, my little girl. You're all I have, everything *I* have to live for."

"Please, don't. Daddy, it's me I'm ashamed of . . ." She suddenly broke and began to cry.

"I had to raise you all by myself," he went on, his voice angry, as though he were talking to himself. "I'm not worthy to touch one hair on your head. But I tried, tried to be worthy of my little girl. But then your mother left me, left us both. It was up to me alone then. But it's not enough to look at your life and say 'I tried.' Not enough." He sighed. "Failed," he said.

She caught hold of herself and dried her eyes, wiping her face brusquely. "No, Daddy," she said in a level voice, "you're not a failure."

He shook his head wearily.

"You haven't failed me," she said mechanically. "You've been everything a father should be. We're both tired right now, just tired, that's all."

"I do all I can," he said. A bit of ash tumbled from the cigarette and broke on his shirt front. The beetles drummed at the screen. "Do you ever hear from Gratt Shafer?"

"No, Daddy. I've told you before, that's over with. I haven't seen him . . . for months."

(Again the lie came smoothly, with just the right hesitation!)

Tom McCutcheon nodded. "Then that's all over," he said.

Gratt Shafer put out his hand to support himself against the porch wall. *She lies so well I could almost believe it,* he thought. And thought: *Damn!* Thinking in amazement now, amazed at the way she humored the old man, at the way she coddled his queer temperament. He wanted to leave but instead he stayed on, frightened by what she was capable of, almost enraged by it. Damn! He closed his eyes for an instant and clenched his teeth.

Even from the porch Gratt Shafer saw the ruin in her face. She was hardly recognizable. And as he watched she bit her lower lip and her eyes closed briefly. *Of me,* he thought, she's thinking of me. He was sick of watching them.

"You never did really care for him, did you?" McCutcheon said.

"No, Daddy," she murmured, looking down, twisting her hands in her lap.

"I know. You're waiting for that little doctor or some lawyer."

"Yes, Daddy," she murmured wearily, closing her eyes. "If you don't mind, I'm sleepy."

"Of course. Well, I'm glad my baby girl's happy. Here, kiss me good night."

She stood up and leaned over, kissing him on the cheek. Then she turned and took up the suitcase and went swiftly into the hallway.

"Good night," said Tom McCutcheon in a low voice. "Good night my little girl." He stumped out the ragged cigarette butt and sighed. For a time he sat very still, staring at the rug, wide-eyed, sunk in his thoughts. His white forehead shone under the glare of the reading lamp, snowy pale in contrast to his black eyebrows and his dark thick hair.

Finally he took up the steel-rimmed glasses from the book in his lap, slipped them on, and began to read. Gratt Shafer turned away then and went silently down the steps. Before starting the engine he sat in the car a few minutes. He kept thinking of her face, he kept thinking of what she had become, and it was his fault. I did it, he thought. His mouth grew thick with anguish. He gripped the steering wheel and wept, jerking forward like a spastic.

3

TWO months after their first meeting Gratt Shafer started seeing Eleanor Fite alone. Eleanor was cool and reluctant. Eleanor was calculating. She put him on his best behavior and kept him there. And in the fall of 1949 they became serious and the winter came and passed and it was 1950. Gratt Shafer was going to marry her! The news hit Somerton like a surprise.

The announcement was in Sunday's Memphis newspaper and Patsy Jo discovered it, standing in her fur-trimmed mules, her hair still rolled up, while outdoors a feeling of rain was threatening. She read it and cursed, *God damn!* under her breath. She read the announcement over twice more and God damned twice again. It was not yet six A.M., and she had been lying in her bedroom, already awake when the rolled-up newspaper hit the wooden front porch.

She took it back where her father was eating breakfast. "Gratt's going to marry that rotten Memphis bitch," she said quietly and put the announcement down in front of him. The page carried a sedate picture of Eleanor Fite.

And he said: "Well, well." He was wheezing. Thunder was starting to roll outside, off a little way in the distance, north. A storm was driving in, and now he looked up at her. The narrow, high-vaulted breakfast room always made him seem bigger. He sat with his legs under the oak table, wearing two day's growth of beard and his white shirt had the collar off of it. In the kitchen the Negress was frying sausage and humming, not loud, but just loud enough. And the first rush of rain swept down outside. "And you'll let him do this to me," Patsy Jo said. "Won't you?"

His sunken eyes stayed motionless. "How could I stop him?" he said. "What did you ever lead him to expect?"

The thunder was drudging again off in the distance, like the sound of heavy furniture being moved in another room. Then lightning clicked outside and the crashing roar thumped down, a thunderclap just above them, rattling plates in the corner cupboard beside her. There had been that instant's pause after the flash when her shoulders tensed.

"Expect! I expect nothing from you," she said. "For years he's been going to marry me. Now it comes out in the paper he's not."

"Don't lie to me, Patsy!" he said. The sunken eyes flickered with sudden heat.

"But you don't give a rat's tail," she said. "Hell, no."

"You never said he promised you. Now think straight, because if he did . . ."

"Well, he did. He promised me right in there on his damned knees. He gave his damned word." She pointed to the front room.

"Courting a little, now that's one thing, but now a promise, that's another thing, *entirely*. I'd have to talk to him about any *promise* he might be breaking." His voice went high; quavering in anger. He went a little yellow, like a corpse.

"You don't care!" she said. "Why put on? Gratt asked me to marry him and then said he wanted it kept secret till next fall. A damned *secret! Now* look!"

"Think hard!" he said. "You're *sure?*"

She didn't answer. She turned away instead, lowering her face into her palms.

And she heard him hiss: "Oh, no. He won't do this, not to *mine. By God!* I'll kill him!"

"You won't!" She was choking with it.

"I'll kill him first!" He shouted, pounding his fist down on the table. The Negress stopped humming.

Patsy Jo let herself start crying. "God," she said aloud. "God!"

"There, there now," he said. "I'll make it all right. I'll kill the suck-egg son of a bitch!"

She was crying too hard to see anything. "You won't," she said. "Oh, go on, kill him! But you won't though. You won't!"

"I'll kill him" he said. "I *will*," he said quietly. "Shafer grabbed the wrong cat by the tail. The wrong cat, by God."

She had done all she could. She wiped her eyes and looked out the window. It was just light enough now to see the rain and it had set in and was driving steadily against the dark ground.

She was too shocked and tired, tired of the whole affair, to feel then just what it was the old man intended, too shocked to feel it, much less to worry about it.

But later, when there was time for second thoughts, a

vague terror shot through her, and she had to lie down until it passed away. There was something going on inside her father, something she did not want to admit, something she did not want to think about too clearly. There was not time for thinking just then anyway. For she was busy, busy hating Gratt Shafer and wishing he were dead, or that she herself had never been born. Either way she was miserable, and there seemed no earthly end to what she would have to endure now. "How will it be Christmas?" she wondered. "How will it be to be stood up forever?" It gave her a funny feeling.

It reminded her of another funny feeling that had struck her once long before in connection with Gratt. It came about one day when they were younger, in the spring of the year when they were both eighteen, on a Sunday, when he had taken her out to the Mountains of Gilead for a picnic. It wasn't much of a place to go, being within sight of town as it was. There were better places. There were the woods out at the Wolfe Creek Pike and there was the old tumbled-down church and graveyard off the highway north of town. Both of those were good places, easy to get to because you could drive your car right up to where you wanted to eat practically. But the Mountains of Gilead were different. You had to park your car out on the road there south of town where everybody that passed by would see it and recognize it. And if they knew a girl was out with a boy and they saw the car at a place like that, it would let them know the girl was off way out across a thousand yards of cotton patch amongst the mounds, hidden in those Indian-made mountains amongst the trees that were just then greening. From the top of one you could see for miles all around you. So they would figure the girl and boy were up to something to take so many pains making sure no one could slip up on them. They would figure she and Gratt were out there in the Mountains of Gilead doing they-knew-what, and for that reason she didn't want to go there with him. And besides she didn't want to do all that walking over plowed ground. Even when you reached the Mountains of Gilead, where were you? Nowhere. And she had tried to talk Gratt out of the notion, but he was firm. He even went so far as to get his old house servant to pack the lunch basket. It gave her a funny feeling, all right. When she and Gratt were halfway across the cotton patch a carload of boys rolled by Gratt's car back on the road. They stopped and blew the horn and whistled. *They* knew. She hated Gratt for making her come with him. "There, are you satisfied?" she said.

It didn't seem to bother him. He shrugged his shoulders. "My father's life work was out here. If I can't show my girl, whom can I show?" She made a sign with her finger.

But when they climbed to the top of the biggest of the Indian mountains, the whole wide land seemed spread out at her feet and there was a breeze cooling her forehead. She saw Somerton rolled out flat to her left and the tilled land rolling out to the right to where it finally hit the cypress forest. There was a little creek that meandered in behind the Mountains of Gilead and then wandered away off toward the river bottoms curving in from the southeast. Being there was like discovering she owned the whole world. She didn't care any more how many people drove past on the road and recognized Gratt's car. When he told her that the Indians had built the mountain one basket of dirt at a time she only glanced at him and facing into the breeze again, feeling it lift her hair, she said, "I don't care how much digging and how many baskets of dirt it took to make this place. I don't care how many years they spent doing it. I don't care, Gratt, because it was all worth it, every last basketful."

He went on explaining his father's theories to her in his quiet, detached voice. The Mountains of Gilead were part of a walled city that had flourished ten thousand years before. Its inhabitants, the mound builders, were sun worshipers among other things, and they had practiced human sacrifice and cannibalism. Their mounds had several purposes. They were used as places to sacrifice victims to the sun. If the enemy stormed over the walls the population could withdraw to the summit of the mounds and defend themselves from those superior heights. Inside the mounds they built chambers to hold the skulls of their sacrificial victims. The mound builders were good farmers and soldiers and according to Doc Shafer's theory, they were the ancestors of the Toltecs who migrated to Mexico and started the Aztec civilization. They had left their city and journeyed far to the southwest, to a flourishing promised land. At first a few went and came back, telling what they had found. Then others packed up and began the long hike. Soon the city was so depopulated that savage nomadic tribes began to attack them, laying the city to siege and throwing down its walls. Finally all of the mound builders either left for the journey to Mexico or were destroyed. This was the story Gratt had grown up with but had, for the most part, kept to himself.

"I learned not to talk about these Indian mountains," he told her. "I found out no one in Somerton feels like I do about them." Gratt stopped talking and Patsy Jo looked at him again, getting a shivery feeling from the distant glow, the glitter in his eyes. Then she saw what was different about him, she saw why he was different from the other people she knew. It was this thing he *felt,* this thing which no one else in Somerton appreciated. It made the Mountains of Gilead his. No one else could claim them, no one else had time to love anything made ten thousand years ago. "I love this place, Gratt. You've made me love these old Indian mountains. Talk all you want to!" she cried. "Because I don't care, you hear? Honey, I don't care because I've seen what it's like up here and you're right, it's different from what I thought it would be." He was the first one to show her that something beyond herself could be wonderful.

And now he had shown her how the victim must have felt when they tied her to the altar and yanked out her heart just to make it rain. And sometimes after she had driven by his house she would turn south and drive past the mounds. Looking at them always brought that funny feeling back.

4

O NCE *a year Starkey Poe was the most important man in Somerton, Sligo County, Tennessee, the man Bojack Markam played about on his harmonica, the man everyone knew and watched once a year — Starkey Poe.*

And he was a wool hat sight, what the colored folks call a cracker (speaking with contempt) saying he eats white ham (salt pork). A rabbit runner, with the accent on the "runner"; a dirt-dobbing, clay-eating, shady-faced pore white, who like as not howled at the moon now and then; the sort of fellow that don't give a hang no way, but he's quiet about it, just as he was when the county tax assessor came out after him to pay us and offered as how seeing he didn't have no money no ways why mebbe he could work it out — work out his taxes? Yes, mebbe, if he had the guts for it, for they was looking for a feller who could ride a balloon up, a sort of crowd-gatherer for the strawberry festival, a new idea the fruit packers had got up, anyway to go up in it and then jump out with this parrychute. Like a umbrella, you know. Yes, Starkey

Poe knew. But still he was wary, maybe running rabbits or something had wised him up — where was the hitch? Well, they did have this other white fellow who was professional but it seemed the parrychute didn't open for him over in Arkansas at the air field where he was performing (Poor bastard.) But then they had got a balloon and knew where they thought they could borry a parrychute and if he did it this time why it would pay up his back taxes. And if he didn't? Why then they'd just have to auction off his land from the courthouse steps, that's all, right out from under him. But now then say he did jump, then he could have the job every year and it would pay his taxes and give him a little something extry, like maybe enough to buy his tobacco and cigarette papers and fishhooks. Anyway it was the tax assessor's job to find somebody.

Shore. What did he have to lose, trying hit onct? For Starkey Poe was a young fellow then. The balloon then was the kind you build a fire under. (Gratt Shafer remembered how the old balloon turned bottom upwards after the man jumped out, and came down after the parachutist, smoking in a slow, lazy drift.) But the new one, the 1950 model, uses helium and has a valve that lets the gas out of it after the parachutist jumps. But the new valve sometimes is slow and sometimes the balloon and basket will drift quite a ways, with the fire department following it, outside of town. Like once it lit in the Forked Deer River and a bunch of field hands that orta been in the berry fields but was catfishing instead saw it come down and figgered it was Jesus or somebody big like that coming back, and threw their poles in the river and lit out for the nearest church like they will go for the storm cellar when it thunders, and one old uncle who couldn't walk was left behind, and with his eyes all dim mistook the fire chief for God, and his firemen for Moses and some of the other outstanding prophets, and then damn near found his legs enough to go in the river getting out of their way, would have gone in only they caught him and tried to explain, only he was a little deaf too, and kept on shouting and singing and still wouldn't believe it wasn't really Jesus out there on the water even after they had toted him pack-saddle all the way up the bank to opposite of where the balloon was resting, out there hung on a snag. The ground was so mucky they had to get two teams of mules to drag out the balloon and gondola. And the repairs cost the strawberry packers three hundred dollars (they could've paid Starkey Poe six years on that amount) and they threw in a hearing aid for the old uncle, maybe so they could explain to him, or maybe so they could hush him up.

But that first time Starkey Poe was fairly a young man and Gratt Shafer was just eight years old and hanging onto Doc Shafer's hand when they cut the balloon loose out at the horse show grounds and it soared up a good ways. And then from beneath the basket came a drift of smoke, a sort of puff, and the parachute billowed and Doc said the young man had intestinal fortitude amounting to guts because the man at the Jackson Airport where they borrowed the parachute at the last minute said he wasn't guaranteeing it to work as it had been left there by a barnstormer two years before and had been rained on he thought — well, the fact was he wasn't sure and wasn't guaranteeing what was in the pack, maybe the barnstormer's lunch or his dirty laundry if he didn't think no

more of the parachute than to leave it behind. And well, just
tell him to strap himself in it, maybe you could use a little
binder twine where that latch or buckle or whatever is gone
there. And tell him to count five or something, or if he can't
count (well if he's going to jump with this he probably
can't count) so tell him to feel all the fingers on one hand,
one at a time, and then take this thing and pull it. Then if
the cloth don't come right out why to shake it — the cloth —
out, to pay it out sort of like fishing line tell him, and if it
don't open then why to shake the ropes a little bit to get the
air in it. Then if it don't split, which it might do by then,
why he orta be all right. Oh, yeah, and if it wasn't enough
he had to do already, give him a fifty-pound sack of flour to
open and carry down with him and shake out as it leaves a
nice little marker trail so's the crowd, your rubberneckers,
can see him; I mean that flour gives it a hell of a big extra
jolt. But if he's jumping at noon — say, I guess you fellows
better hurry — what I mean, he might leave without no
parachute if he's like you say, and then mebbe he'd be better
off. Anyway, I ain't taking no responsibility for it opening or
not . . .

Anyway open it did and it came down just fine, only broke
his left ankle a little, so he hobbled over and took the fifty
dollars and held it almost five minutes before the tax assessor
took it back and gave him his receipt which Starkey Poe
folded up and stuck under the band of his hat, which somehow, he still had, and it looking like something he had found
in the creek after a high flood. The assessor asked him if he
was game for the next year, to which he is supposed to have
said, "I reckon."

On the last bridge before town Starkey Poe stopped, tasting the dry roof of his mouth and smelling the fecundity of young corn which stood in long rows across the bottom, toward the Mountains of Gilead. He paused a moment and then stepped on across the old bridge, stopping again, on the other side, by the river embankment, and looking down, (through thickets of purpling pokeberry shoots, through a sanctuary of gnats reveling in the cool, rotting shadows) he saw the water itself and the loaf of sand at its edge. But he decided not to climb down for a drink. He turned away toward town. For there was a water fountain beside the Peoples and Farmers Bank of Somerton. He could wait.

He resumed his swinging stride, holding the rolled-up suit of red flannels under his arm. Looking at the Indian Mountains always reminded him of hunting among them with Tom McCutcheon. He thought of McCutcheon's little beagles selling out after a hill rabbit, bringing the rabbit around the foot of one of the Indian Mountains, taking him clean up one side and down another sometimes, until the rabbit finally passed McCutcheon or himself and tumbled dead. For Starkey and Tom rarely missed, and with his shotgun still smoking Starkey would grab up the little animal and slit its belly, slinging out the guts before he tied the carcass to his belt. On a cold day the red and purple insides would raise a frost of little steam. Next, McCutcheon's little beagle hounds would be off again, tails high, noses snuffing the ground and directly the dogs would yell and finally settle down to a steady yodel as they carried another rabbit along in front of them, bringing him slowly back to where the hunters waited.

Looking at the Mountains of Gilead, deep in the bottoms to the right of the long narrow road, Starkey Poe wondered what McCutcheon could want with him. There would be time to go by and see the old man before going to the horse show grounds. The commercial fisherman who had come to the door of Starkey Poe's cabin shortly before daylight had given no explanation *why*. He had said, "Tom McCutcheon said he needs to see you — bad." And then the man had turned away, going on down the hill to the river while Starkey Poe stood wondering. The smell of fish lingered and the outboard motor coughed one time before it caught. It had given one quick snort and then the fisherman had roared away to run his trot lines and barrel nets. It had all been quick, less than a quarter of an hour since the first sound of the outboard had reached Starkey Poe, lying in his bunk waiting for daylight. The way the boat was skimming it had to be a market fisherman, for it came on full throttle. But then opposite the cabin it had stopped all at once and a paddle hit the bottom of the boat. When that sound went echoing over the water Starkey had gotten up and hauled on his overalls and gone barefooted to the door. The chickens roosting under the cabin had begun to cluck and the dog, already whining, began to bark and then hushed back to whining when Starkey spoke to him. "Anybody home!" the fisherman hollered.

"Howdy," Starkey Poe replied.

"Breakfast on the fire yit?" The man came closer, bringing the fish smell.

"I was a-waiting for daylight," Starkey Poe said.

"The hell you was. I bet you been a-lying up dreaming while I done already caught a hunnert pound of fish. I already done a day's work before you waked up."

"Well, I'm sorry the pore sich as you must rise so early. We rich fellers sleeps till daylight. Or ain't you heered?" The dog was growling.

"Will that son of a bitch bite?"

"He would yesterday. I reckon he still does."

"That figgers okay," said the fisherman. "I brung you some word from a friend."

"Well, much obliged," Starkey had said, "and stay to breakfast."

But the man wouldn't be persuaded. He had given the message and left.

"Tom McCutcheon said he needs to see you — bad."

As he crossed the railroad and passed the Negro cemetery where the pavement took up and the road became Seventeenth Avenue, he heard the bands playing up on Main Street. "Well, soon I'll know," he thought. He looked up at the sun. It was late, but there would be time to see McCutcheon before he reported to the horse show grounds and climbed into the balloon. The jump was set for after the parade.

In the next block the sidewalk took up and Starkey Poe looked at each house as he passed it, looking to see the people or glimpsing their wash hanging out behind in the sunlit backyards; he looked at the little square houses and put out his hand to brush the occasional picket fence. He passed the green-painted grocery which had first been a hog pen and next a barn and now was finally a neighborhood store with tin BC and 666 signs nailed on its sides, and big blue Ex-Lax thermometers hung on both door frames. Cutting left at the store, he went down by a row of diners, and then past the beer and pool hall. He met the first of the crowds there, mostly old drunks, too sick or too busy to walk up and watch the parade. He crossed Fourteenth at the combined bus station and cab stand and went from there on up to Main. People were milling around the water fountain and he had to wait his turn. Standing back, he saw two men come out of the bank. The larger one, he saw, was Gratt Shafer. Taking his turn, Starkey Poe leaned down to drink. He took a little water in his hand to freshen his face, and then, wiping his mouth with his faded old blue bandanna, he set out up Main Street for McCutcheon's house, passing behind the crowd lined up on the curbs. The floats with pretty girls riding on them were passing now, and some of the crowd cheered and some clapped their hands. It was always a long parade.

Tom McCutcheon answered the door himself, holding his shaving brush. Half his face was already lathered. Starkey followed him back to his bedroom, taking off his old felt hat, feeling the coolness of the high-ceilinged house as it dried the sweat about his temples.

"Just shaving," McCutcheon said. He pulled a big chair away from the wall and put it beside his bed table. "You can sit there," he said, turning around to the mirror over his dressing stand. "I was wondering if you got my message."

"I did," said Starkey Poe. It was always a wonder to see the stuff McCutcheon laid out to do anything. Rather than sit down, Starkey stood so he could see. There were little folded cloths. There was a china shaving mug. There was a tricornered pan of scalding water. There was the bright pearl-handled razor that McCutcheon took out of its case and stropped on the strap hanging on the wall at his elbow. And something else, something else crowded the marble top of the dressing stand — a shiny old brass-mounted horse pistol. Starkey knew then what he smelled. It was the Hoppe's Number 9 Solvent McCutcheon always used when he cleaned his guns.

"Have a chair," McCutcheon said, pointing with the razor.

"I was just a-looking at your soap mug."

Starkey sat down. The slightly alien scent of the old revolver made him uneasy. "It's nice, kindly blue like a gal's eyes, ain't it?"

"It reminds me of a pale sky," McCutcheon said. "My mother bought it for me when I started shaving." He drew the razor down his cheek and wiped it clean on a scrap of paper.

"I'll bet you wouldn't take nothing in this world for having sich as that, something give to you because they thought so much of you. You been lucky. You know that, Tom?" But McCutcheon chose to ignore him. He watched McCutcheon's hands, scraping the lather away, wiping the blade on the bits of paper which were laid aside. "'I'm due at the horse grounds in a little." He shifted the rolled up long underwear, making certain it was rolled tight. He held the roll in his lap. The smell of the gun solvent reminded him of the pistol again and suddenly it came to him that this was the same cap and ball revolver McCutcheon had shown him once years ago. "My father's," Tom had said, taking the gun from its wooden case. There was a case which held the loading implements and the cleaning tools, the powder, balls and caps. The gun on the dressing stand would be the same one that he had seen before, the same perfectly oiled, perfectly preserved old pistol. *"My father's,"* he had said.

"What are they saying about me?" McCutcheon asked.

"Who?" Starkey Poe said. He put the underwear and his hat on the dark waxed floor. "I haven't heered anything. But then I wouldn't, out there to myself. Is that why you wanted to see me? Is that it, Tom?"

"In thinking about somebody I could tell this to I realized you were the only living man I could trust, Starkey. I lay awake last night and it was like you feel after bad whiskey, when you want to puke, and you just lie there hoping you won't have to, and then you get up, thinking you will, but when you go outside the fresh air sends your gorge back down. That's how my life is now. But I have to, I have to do it."

"Do what?"

"Kill a man," McCutcheon said, wiping the blade.

"Kill who?" Starkey Poe said.

"Gratt Shafer."

"But ain't he Doc Shafer's boy?"

"Exactly. I promised him this morning. He has my word on it."

"Godamighty! *Why?*"

"A matter of principle, pride, honor. Because he broke his word to Patsy Jo. Promised to marry her, deceived her. And now he's marrying somebody else."

"Tom, talk sense. This here is *today*. Nineteen-hunnert-

and-fifty, or was when I opened up my eyes this morning. It don't operate thataway no more, and if I know it, then anybody ought to. You need me to talk you out of it — ain't I right?"

"No. I just need to know how to do it, how to kill him. Maybe I need you to help me catch him when I decide how it has to be done."

"Couldn't you argue Gratt Shafer out of it. Hell fire, did you *tell* him?"

"Well, I tried, but you can't reason with a simple little bastard like Gratt Shafer. You might as well reason with a cow's turd. Yes, I told him how it was, how it had to be. I told him I wouldn't kill him unless he *made* me do it. I tried to be nice and even went so far as to go over and call on him in his own house when I could have phoned him twice as easy."

"And what did he say for hisself?"

"He just said 'You go to hell,' says Mr. Shafer. He laughed and then I laughed and I says 'if that's your final word.' And he says, 'Yes, Mr. McCutcheon. It is. It's my final word. You can't scare me.' And I says, 'But it wasn't my aim to *scare* you, Mr. Shafer. If you marry anyone else after promising yourself to my daughter, then I'll just have to kill you.' And I had to smile because I could see he didn't believe I *would* kill him. And he smiled because he still thought I was trying to scare him. No, Starkey, it wasn't like trying to talk to a cow turd. I take that back. It was like trying to talk to that *wall* yonder. It was like *his* ears weren't *built* to hear what I was saying. And he laughed and then he says, 'I suppose it wouldn't help any to say I never promised your daughter.' And I says, 'No, Mr. Shafer. It wouldn't. Because then I'd have to call you a liar and I don't like to have to call a man a liar under his own roof. I'd rather do that outside because it's unseemly to break up nice furniture like this.' He smiled again. 'So you think you're that much man, Mr. McCutcheon?' he says. And I says, 'Well, I could break *your* neck, Mr. Shafer.' And he says, 'Well, maybe you could. But now that would be against the law, wouldn't it, if you broke my neck?' And I gave it right back to him. I says, 'No more against the law than a breach of your promise to my daughter, not to mention what else she may have consented to because she thought you were going to marry her.' And he says, 'Then let's go to court. Don't you intend to be law-abiding, Mr. McCutcheon?' And I says, 'Mr. Shafer, the law must sometimes stand aside. My daughter made a mistake, yes. She mistook you for a gentleman and you turned out to be an infernal son of a bitch. But that's no reason for her shame to be dragged into public. That would be like a gentleman suing a man for assault and battery when the proper course is to look the man up and beat the hell out of him personally. This isn't something you take into the public courts if you happen to be gentlefolk.' He smiled again. 'Oh, *gentlefolk,*' he says, 'and *gentlefolk* just march out and say they'll kill you. Is that right, Mr. McCutcheon?' He was cool and calm and I could never tell what he was thinking, not in a thousand years. 'Do you intend to go through with this marriage, Mr. Shafer?' I asked him. And he said yes he did, that I could have learned that much from the newspaper, or did I read the newspaper, or was the newspaper too common for gentlefolk to read, he wanted to know. Just like that. And I said yes, I read the newspaper, but that extenuating circumstances sometimes made sensible men change their plans, even if their plans had already been in the newspaper. Then just what was I proposing he do, he wanted to know. And I told him he would have to marry Patsy Jo if he married anybody, because he had promised himself and had not been released from his promise. Did I want my daughter marrying such a son of a bitch as him, he wanted to know. And I says, 'Well, I don't relish the idea, now that you bring it up, but I can't choose for my daughter.' Says he, 'No, all you do is enforce her choice once it's made, isn't that it?' And I says, 'Well, that's pretty close. In a way that's pretty close. Now am I going to have to kill you or not?' And with that he took me by the arm. 'Now I told you once you could go to hell,' he says, 'and I'm in a hurry. So just get on out before I have to do something I'd be sorry about afterwards.' He went with me to the door and in the hall there was another man about his age, a stranger. They were in a hurry to go somewhere, so I left. The last thing I said was, 'Remember, I warned you.' And the last thing I heard was him laughing and the other man laughing with him." McCutcheon dipped a clean cloth in the pan of hot water and began wiping his face.

"Then he don't believe you," Starkey Poe said.

"No," said McCutcheon. "I don't think he does. But I can't help it. I warned him. So it's a case of what I have to do now, a case of what I *must* do. But I wonder if I ought to let him get out of Somerton before I do it. What would you do?"

"Why, Tom, I guess I'd drink me a pint of whiskey and six ounces of paregoric and go off somewhere and lie down for about three days. Then if I felt like you do when I woke up

I'd have to do the same again until either I plumb died of paregoric and whiskey or the notion soaked out of me." Starkey Poe shook his head, clasping and unclasping his hands.

McCutcheon folded up the razor and put it back in its case. "What I meant," he said, "was that it might not be *fair* to kill him now. You see, he's got a chance to change his mind any time between now and tomorrow afternoon when he walks up to the altar in Memphis. I don't really have any right — any *call* to kill him until after he says 'I do,' with another woman."

Starkey Poe stood up. "Tom," he said, "now you give me that pistol there." He put forth his hand, palm up. "Give it here and I'll get rid of it. It's about to get you in trouble. Ain't it about to, Tom?"

"Do you know, I've never had any use for that old pistol until now? It's almost funny, how I've kept it all these years." He picked up the pistol, looking at it, weighing it in his hand.

"Give it here, Tom. I'm asking you, *please*."

"My father thought the world of it, always practicing with it. I guess you could call it his prize possession, and never in all his life did *he* shoot a man. He was always *ready* to do it, but he never *did*, you see? And when he died and left it to me it seemed like, well, like something useless. But still it was his, so I kept it. And from the time he died to this day, do you know I've never taken it out and fired it — not one time? See? Look how clean it is? Clean as a hound's tooth! Clean as a whistle!"

"Tom!"

"Now, by God, the time has come to use it! Now I know

why he gave it to me. Do you *know* what you're asking for when you ask for this gun, Starkey? What would you do with it?"

"Drop it in the river where it belongs at!" Starkey Poe said. He reached for the pistol but McCutcheon drew it back, out of reach. Starkey turned away from him slowly and stooped down to the floor for his hat and the roll of underwear. "I'll go," he said quietly.

"I thought you'd see *my* side of it, Starkey. Was I wrong?"

"Oh, he's put it to you. He done you good and proper, Tom. But when it comes down to laying him out . . ."

"You're *afraid*. Your guts go back on you and you can't see what he did when Patsy Jo, my own daughter, got to that hot age. And they all get there, you know that? Maybe if you had a daughter of your own and let's say you raised her all by yourself, then you could see."

"I might, I guess."

"She reaches that age and it gets so she wants it bad. Her teats ache. But Gratt Shafer — does *he* give a hoot in hell? Well does he? You know he doesn't, Starkey. All he wants is what any man would want if he didn't have any decency about him. So he works on her. Kissing and putting his hand where she has to take it off, and putting his hand back — *always putting it back*. And what is he thinking? *Love*, is that what? Does he mean to marry her? Why, hell, all he's thinking is that if he can satisfy that hard headlong nerve of his, then nothing else matters. 'Tell her anything, *anything*,' he thinks. And the night comes when he strips her down to her waist, because she loves him. See how mean he is? But

that's just how the Gratt Shafers are. And while he works on
her, don't you think she suffers? Good God! She suffers all
the way, with what I taught her pulling one way and that
soft, that mucous something under her belly, putting up the
softest argument she's ever heard. It begs her. And it keeps
on begging even after she's dressed and her teats are dry again
from his saliva. It keeps pleading with her after Gratt Shafer's
given up *that time.* And when she's in bed alone and she
can't sleep, don't you know she starts wondering? She won-
ders why God gave her that thing, if it had to cause her all
this trouble. And now you wouldn't kill him?"

Starkey had turned again. McCutcheon was wheezing. His
breath came in little growls. He trembled. Still holding the
pistol, he suddenly sat down, going all the way down to the
floor and leaning back wearily against the wall. "Tom?" Mc-
Cutcheon looked up strangely. "You okay, Tom?" Starkey
Poe said.

"Just . . . just tired, I guess," McCutcheon said.

"You look pale, Tom."

"Just dizzy. Thinking about Shafer makes me dizzy. All
these years and I never looked what was going on in the
face. And I knew just as well what was happening, how that
mean little bastard was moving on her, little by little, night
by night. And finally he was having his *way* with her. And I
knew it. To hell with her and me and decency, he was
having his *way.* And the more she loved him the more tire-
some the thing got, where he was concerned. Shafer wasn't
looking for love. And what did I do about it?" McCutcheon
shook his head wearily. "And he says, 'You go to hell,' and I
laughed and he laughed."

"I'm due at the show grounds, Tom. Are you okay?"

"I saw her toughen. I saw her get that hard look. You see her heart always breaking or mending. He kept quitting her and coming back until she looked used — like a whore."

"Could I get you something afore I leave? You look whipped out."

"You go on. Leave."

"I could call you a doctor."

"No. Just promise me. Promise you won't tell anybody?"

"You have my word on it, Tom."

McCutcheon was breathing easier. Slowly he gathered his legs under him and stood up, going past Starkey Poe over to the bed. He turned and lay down on it, holding the pistol in his right hand and propping it on his chest. He lay staring at the ceiling. Starkey Poe left him lying there and slammed the front door, returning to the street. He had eight blocks to walk.

5

THE program had been an hour away, then half an hour, and soon now, the program would begin. The drums rattled, then "Dixie" ripped out and drifted away. Then came "America the Beautiful" with the trombones sliding; and next "The Yellow Rose of Texas" rippling above the snare drums like horses prancing sideways. "The Washington Post March" followed, and finally came "The Stars and Stripes Forever," bouncing above the tubas.

The balloon was the center of it all, bound like a captive between two upright posts which were planted in the midst of the horse show grounds. Counting the basket and gondola, the balloon measured sixty feet high. It tugged at its ropes like a live thing. The gas bag was round as a spider's abdomen and smooth as a gourd. With its sandbags empty the rig could lift a brace of oxen.

The high school bands marched back and forth on the field. The Discusville band had sixty pieces and its uniforms were yellow with a green stripe on the britches and green piping on the cuffs. The Piketown band had come all the way from Western Kentucky and it had red uniforms with gold braid. The biggest truck from the Somerton Fire Hall rolled on the ground now, its engine roaring, its bell clanging. The fire chief drove. The truck stopped and he stepped down. The chief wore a shiny stiff cap like a railroad conductor's and he was soon joined by the mayor, who drove up in his blue Chevrolet and parked it beside the fire truck. The mayor and the chief mounted the bandstand together.

Sitting beside Mattie French in the grandstand, Patsy Jo shaded her eyes. The balloon was due to go up in a little while. The bands were trampling up the dust. Waiting for the moment of the ascension got just a little annoying.

"I get sick of all this corn," said Mattie pleasantly.

The Mayor grabbed the microphone and the bands all stopped marching and playing. "Friends and neighbors, ladies and gentlemen, home folks and visitors to our fair city," said the mayor. "Welcome!"

The mayor was a country boy who had never quite gotten all the cow crap from between his toes. He loved a crowd and he loved a microphone and one day when the boys up in Nashville said he was ready, he would run for governor and probably make it because the crowds loved him right back.

"God has give us a beautiful day today . . ." the mayor went on, pointing at heaven. He was leading into the introduction of one of the local preachers who would say a long-winded prayer, praying for more industry, more jobs, more people, more money. It was the merchant's dream, a Somerton surrounded by smoke stacks and whistles, full of people carrying lunch pails and jostling against each other to pile into the stores. The mayor wanted the long rows of factory dwellings and air that smelled like cinders and chemicals. Instead of eight thousand he wanted *eight hundred* thousand people. Progress predicated in terms of the payroll, that was the mayor. He hated Labor and promised Michigan industrialists that laborers in Somerton would work longer and harder and cheaper because they loved Somerton and wanted to see Somerton grow. Laborers in Somerton hated Labor just like the mayor hated it. People in Somerton were more interested in jobs than they were in money and to prove it they would buy land and build buildings and float bonds to attract industry. They did all these things publicly, and with a flourish. And privately, the city fathers, the mayor included, met in secret sessions with the northern industrial chieftains. For the idea was to keep ruthless speculators from buying the land needed by the factory, buying it that is, before the city councilmen or *their* relatives got it.

Somehow, seated in the grandstand by Mattie, Patsy Jo could not get Gratt Shafer out of her mind. And she had come with Mattie to get her mind off of him. But it hadn't worked. It had worked the other way and she was worse off than she had been back at the Factory-to-You Store. It had been a mistake to ask for time off to come see the balloon go up and Starkey Poe come down. It had been a mistake because she wasn't any better off out in the hot broiling sun hearing but not listening to the mayor's magnified voice twanging like a loose guitar string, because what she saw instead was Gratt Shafer — that face of his and what went with it, the dreamy purr of his voice rushing along beneath his eyes, beneath the vision he had back then of the Law with a capital L. For he planned to be the best lawyer in the

South and he was going to take her. "And I'll take you with me." The two of them against the world. That had been how she imagined it. For when he began to talk and dream all at the same time, making his plans as he went, she had begun dreaming too. But now the dream was over. The big waking up had happened.

"What did I imagine?" she thought. "Did I see him about to swing low in a chariot? Or maybe poling up the south fork of the Forked Deer River braving the wastes dumped in it? Maybe I saw him on a barge with a gang of Ethiopians poling it."

And I'll take you with me. He had taken her all right. Wednesday nights after youth fellowship. Out of the church and into his big car, it tooling over the road with him driving and the headlights sweeping the pike ahead and after he hit college, his expansiveness, the quaint little pine board tourist courts, cabins really, with a cute naked light bulb in the ceiling (unfrosted and naked as a streetlight, like the one on the corner where you used to play when you were a kid, where you watched the bats swooping in after the bugs, watching in between your bouts at hopscotch), a room complete with moths pinging the light and the few casual cockroaches cruising the walls, an insect Highway Patrol with feelers waving. And the bed that sagged in a certain place where all the weight had been put too many times before and the walls fine and thin for overhearing talk in the next room when Gratt went out for ice, the sound coming through the walls like something on the other side of the curtain, so you knew they heard *you* when *they* were quiet and while you lay wondering what they had heard you listened.

And Gratt Shafer would be in Memphis today for the wedding rehearsal and then tomorrow he would marry just like everybody knew he would, just like everybody knew all along. Like Mattie and the mayor up there gripping the microphone and Toonker Burkette back in his office yanking out teeth, like they all knew he would. Just like the balloon would go up and you could sit all day and wish it would spring a leak or blow to hell up and burn and nothing like that would happen. Or you could hope the parachute wouldn't open just so you could say you saw it not open, not because you meant any harm to Starkey Poe in his suit of red underwear, but mainly because you were tired of being an old maid — a thing which cannot admit when it thinks it might be pregnant, but must stand the dizzy feeling all alone and go on like everything is all right instead of being able to say to somebody in a normal voice: "I think I'm pregnant." You could wish that. Or you could wish your daddy would really do it — kill Gratt Shafer like he said when you all the time, all along, could feel the nerve draining out of him like air out of a punctured tire when you are on a muddy road alone and it is raining and at night. So you sit in the car and listen to the air run out and listen to the rain and see the mud in front of the headlights, waiting for you, for your new spectator pumps, waiting for you to squat by yourself out there in your tight skirt, crying and afraid and trying to get that damned son-of-a-bitch tire off, because that is being an old maid too, if you happen to drive a car, it is changing the tire yourself in the night, and in the mud and the rain, hating to get out in it but afraid to stay and afraid to try to walk out for help. And every sound that might be the rain also might be the man who thinks after he has raped you he has to beat your brains out with a tire tool so you won't tell, a combination like ham and eggs, *rape her and kill her,* and that is being an old maid too. It is not having his baby nestled warm and fat against your breast and it is not having somebody that really gives a damn whether some tramp cracks your skull. And most of all it is not having the only man you could love, whether he drives a bread truck or delivers the mail or checks the berry crates down at the sheds, or owns seventeen oil wells and six diamond mines, for if you *are* anybody what he *is* or *does* makes no difference if he is the *one.* He can even be a mild-voiced little-town guy with big-town ideas and level gray eyes and a heart even Houdini couldn't figure out, how it is unlocked. And he can be on the way to Memphis, your Gratt Shafer can, and you discover you can stay alive and hate him and love him and want him even if it means you want him — *really want him* — dead. Because if you can't then nobody else can either, nobody else can have him. For you don't share him, not even with God. If it is love, you don't.

And I'll take you with me. Even if that's all the promise he ever gave or ever will give, the giving of it once was enough and you believed it then and you will always believe it, even when it is finally the only thing in the world you have left to believe, and the whole world is telling you that *one* was a lie. Even when he is on the way to Memphis you will still have the promise resting inside you like a gift, and it is he inside of you. And in a way the promise works out true, for whether he wants you or not, you go with him in your heart. You feel him every mile further away. You feel where

he is and what he sees, and at night you feel when he is asleep
or with the other woman, the one that never could love him
the way you do, the one who got him because she didn't
particularly give a damn whether she got him or didn't. And
you know you will always wonder all of your life whether it
was because you wanted him so bad that you didn't get him,
and you can feel nearly sorry enough to cry when you think
of that other guy, the chump who begged you to marry him,
the one with the plastered hair and the car he couldn't afford
and the too-shiny shoes. You think: "Did he feel that way
about me?" It comes to you that probably he did feel that
way to let you use him like you did when you couldn't have
Gratt Shafer; that he must have since he was there like the
radio for you to turn on or snap off when you got tired of
him, that other guy. It dawns on you that instead of a lump
to fill the seat across the bridge table from you, he was a man,
and that because Gratt Shafer was making you miserable, you
were passing it down to him, to Gratt Shafer's substitute, that
other guy. And you wonder if that is why the little man lost
his job and his car and stayed drunk about a year before he
straightened out and moved to St. Louis, where he got to be
a big unhappy success. You wonder if he looks at his wife now
and thinks of you. You wonder about the Christmas card with
no name on it, and it comes to you that maybe it would have
been better to have made somebody else happy if you couldn't
be happy yourself, to give somebody else the one they wanted
— to give them you.

"Damn the world," she thought. She looked out at the
corn field, the great green deep acres of it rolled out like the
sea in the field beyond the whitewashed fence bordering the

grounds. The mayor envisioned factories there. Homes and factories and schools and a big wide federal highway, instead of peaceful corn to rest your eyes on while you tried to rest your heart, while you tried not to look at the balloon and the bandstand and the uniforms and the flash of the instruments. The bands were impatient, but they were the only ones. The others, the ones in the stands, were spellbound, for hearing the mayor was for them like listening to a symphony was for sophisticated folks in New York City. It was like being in the concert hall in the afternoon and hearing the piano virtuoso rehearsing. He was good and they knew that what he was doing for them he would do all over the United States some day. So they stayed quiet and hung not on what he said but on how he said it, not listening exactly, but rather, *feeling*. If a man was good, if he was going to be governor, you felt it and you wanted him to go on forever. You were sorry when he finished talking because while he was up there you were someone else and the world was something else too. It was a place full of courage and hope and you were part of it. You laughed and then your chest swelled and you felt you could cry for a little bit, and then a feeling hit you like a chill in your stomach and the goose bumps rippled along your arm. He hit the theme about dying to defend your country, and you were ready to do it right then, without a second thought. While he talked you wouldn't trade being a West Tennessee farmer for being anything else in the whole damned world, no matter if it hadn't, in six weeks, rained enough to wet a rat's ass.

She glanced at the man nodding beside her, a man with weather cracks furrowed into his lean cheeks, with powdery pale eyes reflecting all the droughts he had seen, reflecting the sky and the drought which must follow now in August — yes, with eyes predicting the drought and here it was only June, only festival time again and thoughts of Gratt Shafer would not leave her. "I should have stayed at the store," she thought.

Back at the Factory-to-You with the other old maids, back there she was the youngest clerk and she was thirty-four, which made her young enough to resent the usual ideal working conditions, like the unventilated toilet with the door you had to hold shut while you sat down. There was no lock because Herman didn't allow a lock. A lock on the toilet would encourage malingering and primping. The toilet hadn't had a sincere scrubbing in years and there were things written on the walls of the little boxed-in place because you couldn't keep the public out — entirely. She could not count the times Herman had rapped on the door, just a couple of bangs that shook the whole damned closet and might, someday, break away the pipe connections from the wall. The two little bangs meant that he was getting impatient to have a crowd of customers waited on and that if he had to he would jerk open the door and drag out, by the opposite door handle which she would be clutching, whichever-the-hell clerk it was who thought she could waste so much store time on the pot.

And the hours were six-thirty in the morning until eleven at night on Saturdays and during sales, and there were no chairs and you couldn't smoke and the cooling was overhead fans and there was no porter or janitor. The girls and Herman did it all, even moving the heavy crates and the sweeping out, and when they weren't using the toilet they unscrewed the light bulb to save electricity and were careful not to tear the wrapping paper too long.

Your customer like as not had hair which looked like something that had been caught in a buzz saw, a face like ripe strawberries, and a body like balls of dough. She was a massive something who let you wait until your feet were stinging, while flies dodged through the doors, from outside and then back out again. It might be the only dress left in her size, the one she was fingering, and you explained it was popular here, and didn't say it was called an oversize in Memphis.

This here dress she was wearing, she would say, she made it herself. And you saw it was the color of snuff and was like a tent with arm holes, so you put her attention back on the dress she held in her hands while she shook her head and made that puttering sound with her lips. And you waited. You maybe looked at her hat if she was wearing one, and if she was it was probably green and was stuck on her head like something accidentally but securely caught in her hair after the buzz saw finished with it. And abaft the crown was a thing you decided must have once been a feather before something stripped it. Anyway it was an erect something with a prickly-looking brown stem and you looked back at her hands and said something else, while her fingers fractured the patterns in the material and her head swayed, setting the fossil feather in motion. And at last the hands decided. The parched "Okay" came out of her lips which began puttering again and then stopped, like an engine out of gas.

Patsy Jo had sold the dress, hoisting the blousy mass to put it in a small box. Before she had it wrapped Mattie had come in to ask if she didn't want to go watch Starkey Poe go up in the balloon. Herman hadn't liked it, but he agreed for her to go anyway. He knew about Gratt Shafer like everyone else, and maybe he had thought going would help her. So he nodded and Patsy Jo cranked the cash register, ringing up the sale before she went out with Mattie. They went to Templeton's drugstore first, pushing up to the counter for a Coke, lucky to get two seats with all the festival crowd, and Patsy Jo sat sipping a Coke and cooling off and feeling better because Templeton's was air-conditioned. The thing about Mattie French was that even though she sat beside you in the drugstore wearing her white dress and fluffing her blonde hair, talking and trying to comfort you, you still got the feeling she was enjoying herself a little. You felt she was a little bit like somebody standing around an automobile accident where there is somebody pinned alive under the car and you can hear them groaning and look in and see them lying all bloody-faced behind the smashed windshield. And you are the person pinned inside the wreck, that's what you are to Mattie. "I know how you feel," Mattie said. "You need to get your mind off of him."

And Patsy Jo thought: "To forget feeling like a goat has butted you between the legs," but she stayed quiet with the straw in her lips and looked down into the glass, at the Coke draining out of the ice, while under her arms the sweat dried out and the cold hit the roof of her mouth and then dropped down inside her, into her vitals.

"It's about time," Mattie said beside her. "It's about time for him to cast off."

"Thar, he's gittin in the basket yonder," said the farmer.

The mayor was through with his speech and the fire chief was helping Starkey Poe into the basket. The drums started beating. Mattie reached for Patsy Jo's knee and gripped it tightly. The fire chief handed up the sack of flour and Starkey Poe took it and put it down inside the basket. He was climbing around now, checking the ropes one last time, looking like a devil in his suit of red underwear, a devil wearing black brogan shoes to hide his cloven feet and a shapeless felt hat to cover his horns. Now he climbed down and the mayor and the fire chief both lifted the parachute and harness and buckled Starkey Poe into it. The drums were thumping a little faster, just a very little bit faster, and Starkey Poe climbed into the balloon. He waved his hand and the ropes fell away. The balloon shot upward, free of the posts, the last long mooring rope swaying under it as the balloon and the gondola and the man dropped away upward into the sky.

At first he saw only the bands, saw only the movement of the drummer boys. Then the instruments came up and the music started. He gripped the sides of the basket and next saw the grandstand dropping away under him and finally the streets beyond it and the people piling out of their cars and pointing up while the whole town spread out under him and then as quickly, began to draw in tight with the roads ribboning in now and the river glinting in the distance and the band going faintly under him.

He had learned that each time was just as hard as the first time and he was thinking how it was that way when he opened the release valve and heard the gas hissing out. He swung himself over the rim of the basket and let himself down on the rope, seeing the land under him sway a little. He was nearly to the end when he remembered the sack of flour, and he waited a second until his arms stopped aching and then went slowly back up the rope, back up and into the basket again, skinning his face on the side of it. But he got the flour sack and ripped it open and held it in his teeth, tasting the pasty cloth, and he went back over the side on the rope and saw that the balloon had stopped rising, or at least looked like it had, like it was hovering. His jaws aching, he let himself down to the rope's end the second time and hung there until he was too tired to hold on any longer. And then he dropped, rolling over and over with the sky now above and now below him and the flour rushing out of the bag, blinding his eyes for an instant. He grabbed the ring at his chest and gave it a quick jerk. The harness bit into his crotch. The empty flour sack fell beneath him in a lazy spiral. He grabbed the shrouds and pulled up to take the strain off the harness. He rode in the shadow of the parachute's canopy, high and thistle-like above the expectant land, descending.

The flour was like a still column of frost in the blue sky and the parachute blossomed like a flower beneath it. Mattie's hand still gripped her knee and Patsy Jo looked steadily at the parachute as it came on quickly down, low enough finally so she could see the bright red figure beneath it. But it was drifting outward, away from the grounds and it was soon plain that he would land in the cornfield. People were already breaking out of the stands and racing that way, going over the whitewashed fence. The parachute landed and for an instant the white spread of it was visible above the corn. Then it was sucked out of sight.

The fire truck started, and the bands which had stopped playing now, marched aside. The siren began to wail as the red engine started away. The balloon was falling now, falling to the west, and the truck screamed off after it. They stood up. The show was over. The stands were clearing. The mayor had driven off in his blue Chevrolet and the musicians had unbuttoned their tunics and were straggling off the field.

And Patsy Jo knew that summer had come again.

"Do you know what I wish?" Mattie French said.

"What?" Patsy Jo could hear the siren plainly as the truck wended its way into the country. They had wrecked the fire truck once, chasing the balloon. She couldn't remember just when, but she had been a little girl when it happened. She turned to Mattie.

"It's silly," Mattie said. "It's silly as hell, but sometimes I wish Starkey Poe would break his neck. But he never will. He'll be doing it when I hit the menopause."

"What made you say that?" Patsy Jo stepped down a row and Mattie followed her.

"I'm morbid today," Mattie said close behind her, as they passed out of the entrance between the stands. "That damned siren gives me a chill."

It was far away now and getting farther all the time, but still Patsy Jo could hear it, and she could feel the other thing, like an ache in her bones. She could feel *him*, that he was somewhere now, somewhere far off. "I'll drown it, I'll drink it to death," she thought. *And I'll take you with me.* "Yes," she thought, "you son of a bitch, you lovely, wonderful bastard. You took me all right. You took me." It made her a little blind for a moment, a little ill. She wanted to scream but she held it in and it passed. If you waited long enough almost anything would pass. They got to Mattie's car and started back up town, past the Negro funeral parlor. The Negro undertaker, L. B. Jones, was on the stoop. He had probably watched the balloon from there. Now he watched the traffic go by in the street. He was a dignified figure, wearing a dark suit and gold-rimmed glasses.

BOOK TWO

6

GRATT SHAFER did not know what time it was. He knew only the familiar but rare sensation which nearly always followed a bout of drinking and love-making, followed by a light sleep. He awoke from that, and for an instant, until he had recognized the dim fragrance of Camack Patterson's guest room, did not know where he was.

Then knowing, remembering, he resigned himself to the confusion and the unrest of the knowledge and the memory, in the same instant envisioning the house where he lay, separated by a deep lawn from the street in which automobiles could be heard passing in the darkness three hundred yards away, passing the deep lawn, passing the lights on the stone gateposts, passing then away into silence where the street curved into downtown Memphis, leaving its path between the wooded park and the row of estates, making that final curve which carried the automobiles into Union Avenue and on towards the Mississippi River.

Gratt Shafer and Eleanor Fite, seeming to him now like strange and separate people, separate in some way from himself, had taken two glasses and two bottles of champagne and had left the party which followed their wedding rehearsal, crossing the lighted patio and then the dew-wet lawn at the edge of the golf fairways, leaving the clubhouse to contain the rehearsal party, leaving its peculiar sea-like cacophony of voices, underlain by chords from the dance orchestra. They had come away here to Solitude, entering through the kitchen and climbing the service stairs to Gratt's room above the porte-cochere, those two strange people, glad to be alone at last, he, Gratt Shafer, and she, Eleanor, who stirred beside him now as he lowered his arms.

No mistaking it, tomorrow he would marry her, tonight he lay with her, and it was as though even this were part of Camack Patterson's planned initiation of him, lifting him in some way out of Somerton forever, and into the more sophisticated world, into the companionship of this more sophisticated woman. And even though no one said it, the least of anyone's worry at the moment was whether Gratt Shafer and Eleanor Fite were in love. Love might follow marriage, or it might not, but love in the end was nothing you could lay your finger on, unlike money, nothing you could dunk your finger in, unlike a good champagne, chilled almost to ice. Love was even less explainable than laughter, and less dependable, for you could be sure that a laugh now and then would cheer you up, and you could be sure that with time enough and money enough a life could be passed away pleasantly enough, and no, perhaps it could not be *lived,* but the time could be passed. But nothing in connection with *love* could be that sure, so why let yourself in for it? To love was only to open yourself up to be hurt, to suffer. Love was to be made, not endured. Gratt knew he had to believe this.

Eleanor's head moved against his shoulder. She was awake too, and though beside him, seemed locked also in her separate world, the world of blue polar ice, the arctic colors that had seemed such a part of her since the first glimpse he had had of her in the lobby of the hotel. All the distance was still there, the same distance between them, as though not in ten thousand years would he grasp the realness of her, even though he should live, and care, that long.

He had appeared at the right time, well recommended, and she had accepted him. The engagement was announced, the invitations sent out, the entire mechanism for religious and legal union between these two set in motion, while she remained as cold, almost, and as distant and strange as the picture which appeared in the Sunday Society section, the picture of Eleanor Fite, daughter of Mr. and Mrs. Fletcher Fite of Memphis. The bride-to-be was a graduate of and a member of and the granddaughter of, and the groom was from Somerton, and was a graduate of and had been a member of, and there would be a Southern wedding trip after which the couple would be at home in their Carrington Place apartment, in Memphis. The newspaper had handled it all so nicely, never mentioning the fact that the groom-to-be had or did not have a business or profession, saying nothing about the Death March, the Marine Corps, nothing about the war, or Patsy Jo McCutcheon. It did mention the groom's parents, the late Doctor and Mrs. Adam Shafer, and his grandparents, whom he had never known.

In a sense the newspaper account had been a definition of

happiness, one definition anyway. The newspaper never said in such cases whether a marriage had grown out of desperation or boredom, long acquaintanceship or brief lust, convenience, or, as in his own case, for there not having been any *logical* way he could think of to avoid it. In a very real sense he had obligated himself to this woman beside him now. He had seen her frequently, talked to her parents, and with Camack Patterson's help had made himself acceptable to her friends and the friends of her family, that entire circle which one drawing room could contain, the inner set in the Mid-South's cotton town, which now regaled itself at the Country Club at his expense, rejoicing more for a series of excuses to entertain and bestow gifts, than from any *feeling,* as in a more primitive society, as in, for example, Somerton, that here were two young people setting out to have and raise children, to fulfill a preordained purpose in life — none of that here. No weeping old ladies, no groaning organ, no sighs, no local tenor bursting his heart on "Ah, Sweet Mystery of Life!" No mystery here, in fact. And the Memphis police would not dare paint the groom's automobile nor tie old shoes and tin cans to it, just as surely as they would not neglect this rite in Somerton, the police in Somerton being what they were, being good as the next man, being essentially people and secondarily police. In no sense was Gratt Shafer heading into a country marriage where everyone is sure this is the single time, the big moment, for both the bride and groom. Not that true, enduring love couldn't happen in Memphis. No, he didn't believe *that* either, lying beside a woman he hardly knew, depending on it that he would get to know her a little better as time went on and she slept across from him in her bed in the room on Carrington Place which they would share. But he didn't love her. Nothing like it. It was even pleasant to think about, to know that because he didn't love her he was emotionally unbound, free to be himself, the only trouble being that he had not and probably would not, not in ten thousand years had he possessed that much time, get to know himself well enough to enjoy any such freedom. What was it? The freedom of spirit? The freedom of *being* — was there some secret that put God back up in heaven and made Christ divine, which made faith something more than accepting that which one did not believe, simply because of *seemliness,* simply because an orderly society demanded it? Or did he torture himself unnecessarily attempting to know, to fathom, to see even dimly one single truth, one unshakable, everlasting verity concerning the human heart — just one, Lord. Just one single flash of lightning, one peal of thunder, one *sign* to let a poor bastard know You've only been on a vacation for two thousand years, but that really You are still there, and really, that You really *are* coming back, no matter how much we may hate to think of Your returning, no matter how awful it would be to have to choose between heaven and hell, between being bored to death or burned to death, throughout all eternity.

"Gratt?" she said, crashing into his thoughts.

"Yes?"

"Then you aren't asleep."

"No, dear."

"I was just thinking, there is so much I'd like to tell you. I feel the words trying . . . trying to push out of me some-time. But they never come out. I don't have anything to hide from you, Gratt."

"I know," he said.

"I shouldn't want to hide anything, I don't think. You know I've had other men."

"Yes. But we needn't be clinical."

"Clinical?"

"A doctor could examine you and determine that."

"Could he. What a nasty thought. It's a nasty-minded in-vasion of a woman's privacy."

Had he expected Eleanor Fite to be virginal? He wondered. He decided, no he hadn't; hadn't expected, hadn't cared. For in her *own* terms, the terms of *her* world which he had accepted as his now, by merely asking for her hand in mar-riage — in terms of *that* world the question of virginity *was* childish, and yet, *she* had brought it up. She had brought it up, he decided, because she realized how narrow was the world he had abandoned to become her consort in this world which Camack Patterson was sure must be the grandest one of all.

She had a great many mysterious silences in her, sides to her that he felt he would, perhaps, never entirely understand. Perhaps it was tantamount to a seventh veil, a shell or shield which presented her to the world as she was, as she really was, utterly cold and beautiful.

Tomorrow he would marry her.

"Kiss me," she commanded. Her flesh, her hair, and the bone beneath were different in the darkness, for without see-ing her, as now, she seemed larger, almost gross compared to the mental image, the memory he held in his mind from the moment of their first meeting, of the lobby pool and the ducks and the blue print dress. Then, at home, on the patio with her mother, she had been wearing shorts, white shorts and a white blouse, no make-up, and it struck him then how much younger she was than he, how almost like a schoolgirl she looked. She was reserved and shy, but excited, for by then he had taken to calling for her at regular intervals and it was already settled, except for his putting it into words, that he would ask her to marry him.

There was no need asking what sort of child Eleanor had been. Mrs. Fite furnished all that information, not exactly as though she were explaining the pedigree of a pure-blooded dog, but it was something, he thought, on that order. Then of course it was true that he had not grown up in Memphis and that he had not known Eleanor from childhood. Mildred Fite told him about her own family and about Fletcher Fite's family, how the family connections ran, what Fletcher Fite's business interests were. It was an interesting story that continued through afternoons, through cocktails and dinner, a long and leisurely sales talk that let him know Eleanor had been protected insofar as possible from early and hasty affairs of the heart. She had all the right accomplishments too, such as playing the piano a little, playing tennis and golf and bridge a little, but not singing, for she had no voice, nor swimming very much, for she would sun-burn easily. And other than her family and her accomplishments there were her friends and her family's friends, and Mildred Fite patiently explained everything in relation to Eleanor. It was almost a mother's ritual, a breaking of the social hymen which had put Eleanor beyond the reach of just *anyone*. Some of it had been embarrassing. He had been a little saddened to see motion pictures of her as a child, to feel how much in the house was centered about her, how central to everything her happiness was, and how certainly they were giving her to a man who did not love her, to a man she probably didn't love, and all out of an idolatrous trust in life without pain or emotion, without thought, almost. Now it was time to marry. Later she must have children. Then Fletcher and Mildred would build her a house nearby their own and enjoy the children. There seemed an age for everything, a time schedule into which he, Gratt Shafer, now found himself fitted, a way of life which asked nothing more nor less than to be left alone, to perpetuate itself with dynastic regularity, a sleeping happiness, at best. A life of graham crackers and milk, this was what he was destined to accept and savor. It worried him, and yet, Camack Patterson had told him he must not worry. Gratt Shafer must not think he must only *accept* and *agree,* yield to the good life, the best there was. Lying beside Eleanor Fite in the darkness, he was not so sure. It was as though he had betrayed something, as though he had sold a part of himself unwillingly and were grieving for its return. It was not so much Somerton or his boyhood or the seasons of the year, not so much the good people, those old folks who had been parents to him in kindness, after his own parents died — the inspiring schoolteacher, the football coach who believed in him, men like Ocie Pentecost, the physician, who had taken a pride in him, who was capable of unjealously rejoicing in his manhood, in everything in him that was kind, strong, intelligent, and worthy of a young man — it *was* this, and yet it was none of this.

Perhaps the emptiness in his chest, the sense of loss, perhaps this was only the death rattle of sentimentality and homesickness. Perhaps, as Camack Patterson believed, this marriage to Eleanor Fite would be the making of him, would show him his direction in life, and its purpose. But what of Eleanor, was it fair to her?

As it was *he* was acting on faith, if faith were, after all, the acceptance of that which one could not believe. For inside him the feeling was all wrong, it was, in the end, that feeling which troubled him, which set him wondering who did to whom the greatest injustice, he to Eleanor, or she to him. Or were either of them to blame for accepting the laid-down pattern, for doing what was expected of them, simply because it *was*?

The greatest injustice was done to Eleanor Fite, he decided. For she had a good right to more in a man than he could offer, to much more than a *never-was* school pal, resurrected for her out of Somerton, Tennessee, by Cousin Camack, from something very like a living grave. This marriage must be a come-down for her, but then she had character, after all. Eleanor had what let a person accept the second best in life without complaint; yes, *character*, which was, when you boiled it down, nothing more nor less than real talent for suffering in silence.

There was nothing so banal as sexual emancipation connected with what they did while the automobiles continued whispering past, making that barely audible squeal of tires as they swung past the corner, around the curve, and into Union

Street headed west, to the river. Nor was the sublimity of love there, in what went, even though it went rather automatically, to the satisfaction of them both, for he would be certain not to let her down, and she would make sure she did not fail him — there was the whole definition, the essence of compatibility. As she freely admitted, *she* had never been in love, and without admitting it he could only proceed now in the shadow of the fear that once upon a time, perhaps, *he* had been, that *once*, after all, might be God's limit for any man. If so, his time, his chance, his moment, were each one past and gone — over with without his ever knowing.

He got up at last and groped for the champagne, the remaining bottle. Finding it at last, faintly cool, damp from sweating against the night, he untwisted the little teat of wire, now laying the cork's wire harness aside with the torn fragment of heavy foil, and pressing inward now against the cork with his thumbs, rotating the bottle slowly as the cork rose. Lifted by the rhythmic pressure, taking now an impetus of its own, the cork popped at last, shooting away in the darkness. The wine foamed. It spilled on his bare legs and dripped at his feet.

At the sound of the cork, popping away, Eleanor Fite turned on the lamp and sat expectantly in the midst of the old French bed, naked, her legs crossed. She smiled then, holding out her glass to him.

They drank all of it and then dressed. He wrapped the empty wine bottles in the paper dry-cleaning sack that had contained his clothes for the wedding, making a bundle which he carried downstairs when they left, dropping them in the large trash can just off the kitchen, on the back porch.

"There," Eleanor said. "That was neat. Who cares if we have headaches tomorrow?"

"You won't have a headache, will you?" he asked.

"Oh, yes," she said. "I always do."

He opened the car door for her, closing it after her, seeing, as he passed behind the car going to the driver's side, that daylight was just breaking. He drove her home hurriedly and entered the entrance hall behind her. They embraced.

"Good night, sweet," she said. He watched her start wearily for the stairs and then turned to go home. Outside the birds had awakened. It shamed him somehow, feeling so weary and inadequate, so faint and pale at the precise hour when the rest of the world seemed to be rousing up with such vigor and protest. It was a beaten sensation which followed him all the way back to Camack Patterson's, where he undressed again and lay on the bed, weary and nervous, unable to sleep for a long time, until past sun-up. The smell of her hair on the pillow disgusted him now, the scent was alien to his spirit, different and wrong. It came to him then, that this time, after all, he was the whore.

7

ELEANOR FITE rose out of her bath water in response to her mother's urgent thumping and her muffled cry of warning at the bathroom door. Eleanor would be late for her wedding. This was what Mother was trying to say with the sharp, staccato raps. Mother was assaulting the door for the third time. The pink tile, frosted by the steam from Eleanor's body, echoed with the noise. The sounds made her want to scream, but then, she had a headache and couldn't.

She had gotten up out of bed at noon at Mother's insistence, conscious even before she got up, of a painful champagne headache. At breakfast (orange juice, black coffee, one poached egg, one half-slice of dry whole wheat toast) she felt a cold touch of nausea similar to something she could remember having felt once before. The previous time she had feared she might be pregnant. This time she only moaned a little. By talking at breakfast about the day being the happiest in Eleanor's life, Mother showed great promise of making it Eleanor's unhappiest day. Indeed, once or twice Eleanor Fite's weakened inner self ventured that the day might prove to be her last. And Cousin Emma, who had been up for hours, walked in with that sickening freshness of demeanor which, Eleanor Fite knew, could only be induced next day from Emma's having gotten thoroughly drunk early the night before, and having as a result, staggered to bed early and slept soundly and well. Cousin Emma's remarks had been skillfully designed to insinuate that Eleanor had behaved improperly the night before this *happiest* day of her life. Although at no time did Emma come right out and say so plainly, Emma had, by her indelicate tone of voice, her knowing looks and mannerisms, implied that Eleanor Fite and Gratt Shafer had engaged in sexual intercourse! Eleanor had been weakly outraged by Emma's attack. But a faintly uttered "Aw, go to hell!" was the strongest protest she could muster for her defense. This little parry had been overheard and met by Mother (who had not the least inkling of the conversation's bloody undercurrent) with a shocked: "Eleanor!"

And now Mother pounded on the door. Eleanor Fite dried herself with a soft pink towel and examined her breasts in the full mirror. She turned and looked at her figure from the rear; the dimpled sun-tanned back, the white-pink buttocks, the nice legs. She loosed her hair from the white shower cap that had confined it. Finding everything in order, she powdered herself with a fluffy powder puff, and wearing the pink towel like a sarong, walked into the sunny, the pink, the air-conditioned brightness of her bedroom where Mother, Cousin Emma, and two Negro maids awaited her in a tizzy of nervous excitement. (Something borrowed: dear dead Grandmother's bracelet; something blue: a faded old garter that had been someone's; and something had to be sewn at the last minute.) Eleanor stood in her bra and half slip while Mother brushed her hair and shouted to the Negress, Annie Bell, who hurried after needles and thread. Then both Negresses bit thread and flashed needles. They went at the dress furiously — a tuck here, a pleat there, while Eleanor recalled that until now, it had been agreed that the dress was more than a mere dress, so perfectly did it fit. For yes, until now it had been a dream, as the newspaper said an *ensemble* of cultured pearls (how many oysters sacrificed?), a *symphonic arrangement* of imported lace, of silk that cost thousands of little worms their lives; and, oh, hell — all the fruition of the gown maker's craft. But, vicious frock, it had waited until this last instant to show its flaws. And Mother had made the "discovery" just in time. It was Mother who had first discovered the unpleasant truth, a truth which thereupon became instantly apparent to everyone — *the gown did not exactly fit*. And they dressed Eleanor for the second time that hour. Finally Mother stood back and wept a little. Slender Annie Belle brought a small glass of brandy which Mother tossed off neat, murmuring that she was still a little weak!

Eleanor Fite sat down to put on her make-up. "Just a little lipstick," Mother said. Easy on the make-up, dear. Remember, too much takes away the bride's virginal look. I read that somewhere."

"Yes," said Cousin Emma slyly, "the bride must look as virginal as she can."

"On this day of all days . . ." Mother murmured. Mother's mind, like the heart of a troubador, was disposed to wander when excited; her thoughts were like meandering butterflies over a meadow of daisies through which the fickle troubador must pass. Stimulus fluttered everywhere.

"Oh, Emma," said Mother, her voice great with charity, "*how* could we have gotten along without you?" Her mind jumped the track. "And isn't it a coincidence that Gratt Shafer's own little Somerton has its own celebration, so like our Cotton Carnival? Think of it, a strawberry festival!" Again she shifted: "Eleanor, easy on the make-up, dear, on this of all days . . ."

And Mother sighed, she sighed again, as though in all the world there were not air enough to feed the passions hungering in her blood *this* day. Mother began to hum a waltz.

Eleanor could express her own feeling no other way than with a barely audible little "Ugh!"

Two green pills had only dulled her headache. Now the pain came when she moved her head or took a deep breath. And thus the luxury of a sigh such as Mother's was for Eleanor out of the question. And finally, with lipstick, rouge, powder — all applied over base make-up cream — she let her hands drop in her lap and tried to sit perfectly still, and was miserable. *Until.*

Until, at last, Father came in all dressed in his frock coat, his slenderizing cutaway, wearing the striped trousers that made him seem taller. And of course he reminded Mother of a funeral director. (Mother said so, but said it sweetly.) And he carried his tall hat and his black cane with the gold head and his face had a smooth subdued, dignified expression, as though Father alone had been privileged to inspect a master plan which, beyond question, insured the success of the entire day's venture. Cousin Emma appreciated him in his attire, and said aloud that *he* looked wonderful. And he rewarded her with a kiss, a burst of affectionate gallantry which Eleanor noted in the reflection of her glass.

Mother now wore her second glass of brandy in relaxed lines about her mouth. Father checked his watch against the little French clock on the mantelpiece and found time progressing to his virtual satisfaction. Cousin Emma, farther off, deep in the mirror's left, lifted the little rust-colored Teddy bear from Eleanor's pillow, offering idle profanation to Eleanor's childhood with that smirking movement, done with the naked boldness of one who believes herself to be unseen. Above everything the silence told them all at once that everyone, even Eleanor Fite — blonde suffering girl in the mirror's foreground — was ready. The moment lay upon them, all.

In the mirror Eleanor saw why Mother would finally and quietly weep at the ceremony, in the church itself. For what had always been most abstract must now for Mother become most real; must, now in a little while. Still, Eleanor saw how Mother's thoughts went wandering while there was yet time. She was like a child about to go on a journey, who will use up the last instant romping in the old familiar surroundings and finally burst into tears when the moment for departure finally arrives. And what are those tears drawn from? She wondered. They were certainly caused by the interruption of the child's pleasure, but there was also the child's premonition of homesickness in them, for every place that must be left is home, she thought and the heart must remake its home again, and over again. Hope is in going a journey, but homesickness must go along too.

Mother asked, "What time is it? Fletcher, dear?"

"It's nearly time," Father said evasively, like a doctor answering someone who lies mortally sick.

"How much time have we?" Mother asked, a certain strain showing in her voice.

"Time is short," Father said, exaggerating, for it was actually early. "We'd better leave if everyone is ready."

They helped Eleanor downstairs with her train and out to the car. Father sat up front with the chauffeur. Eleanor sat in the back seat between Cousin Emma and Mother, and thought how silly they were to leave for the church so soon.

As the car began to move, Mother relaxed a little. And finally she began to talk gaily. The phrase that came to her lips more than any other was ". . . the happiest day of your life." It came out over and over again.

Feeling a little thick in her dress, Eleanor Fite listened to the talking and quietly held back her fatigue.

And just then the church chimes began ringing, coming forth with clear silvery sounds, measuring in stately numbers a hymn which none of them recognized, but which pleased Fletcher Fite enormously, for he had given the carillon to St. George's church in memory of his mother.

"Our chimes!" he said happily, turning around on his seat beside the chauffeur to face the others in the back seat.

"How beautiful, how sweet," said Cousin Emma in a dutiful little voice, for she had not heard them before.

"Fletcher gave them in memory of his mother," Mother

began. It was one of the stories she told over and over. They had heard it many times.

"Yes," Cousin Emma interrupted, "I know."

"When his mother died Fletcher was heartsick," Mildred Fite continued, determined to tell the tale anyway. For in a way she herself was the story's heroine. It had been Mother who suggested that her husband give the carillon as a memorial.

Eleanor sighed, trying to shut out the wearying details of Mother's story. At the same time she tried to make some sense out of the chiming notes.

"I should *know* what the chimes play at my own wedding," she thought. And then she wondered if the chimes were being played for her wedding or if they were simply played at that hour of the evening everyday. She was annoyed a little not to know, but she decided it wouldn't be worth all the bother of asking about it.

8

TOM McCUTCHEON recognized the hymn that the carillon's bells played, and once across the street he paused to listen to the sounds from the lofty Gothic belfry drifting out above the walls of brown stone, which had, on their lower reaches, long tentacles of green ivy vines, hanging upward like ropes floating aloft from undersea. The hymn bridged the years. His mother had sat at the organ and he kneeling below her skirts had pumped the pedals, gripping them with his small hands, listening to her clear voice — for the hymn was her favorite one:

> Wake, awake, for night is flying:
> The watchmen on the heights are crying,
> Awake, Jerusalem, arise!
> Midnight's solemn hour is tolling,
> Her chariot wheels are nearer rolling,
> He comes; prepare, ye virgins wise.

The notes struck his breast like a poniard and for a moment he turned his face away from the church, for it had been a long time since he was thus reminded, a long, long time ago.

He wished he were back again, beneath the organ, smelling his mother's skirts. Yes, he had loved her. He had pumped the organ until his arms were tired; they ached, but still he pumped on, and still heard the slow clear voice:

> Rise up, with willing feet
> Go forth, the Bridegroom meet:
>> Alleluia!
> Bear through the night
> Your well-trimmed light,
> Speed forth to join the marriage rite.

The last note rang and faded in his mind. He lowered his eyes and methodically composed the lie of the churchyard, the low stone wall that flanked it, and the low ridge that rose behind it into thick woods. The wall was not so high that he could not leap it, and once in the woods they would never find him. Without dogs they never would.

The massive church lay in a park-like field, a field trimmed and green, planted with puffy maple trees. Golden bars of light from the waning sun speared through the foliage. The tended formality of the churchyard began at the street curb and abruptly ended at the wall bordering it. For the rear wall was like a dam. It held back a great tangling chaos of undergrowth which poured its verdure down the ridge behind.

Inside the church just by the door, he was met by a lean, officious little man who at once gave off a hostile vibration. Plainly, this man was in charge, and just as plainly he welcomed not at all the sight of a strange face so early. He was like a museum guard who takes his duties too seriously, who believes he must be gruff. McCutcheon at once consigned to the little man all the vices of the world's petty officialdom which, though scantily paid in coin of the realm, feels itself amply rewarded by its authority freely to insult anyone whom his petty Omnipotence feels has broken or even *bent* a rule. Plainly, the commandment McCutcheon violated was: "Thou shalt not come too early."

"Yes, sir?" the little man said in a snappy voice, which conveyed low regard for the creature addressed.

"The Fite wedding?" McCutcheon said.

"Not until five-thirty! The ushers aren't even here," the little man said, with a banal stare. "I'm only the *florist*," he went on, making little effort to disguise his synthetic self-deprecation. By intimating his unimportance he plainly hoped to appear essential. "Good," McCutcheon said. "This, then, is the right church. I'm Mister Smith." He spoke in a level voice, removing his hat and putting out his hand.

"Lynch is mine," said the other, taking Mr. Smith's hand with a reluctance which suddenly accelerated to an abrupt grip and a quick vibration of the arm. Apparently seeing that a distasteful encounter could not be avoided, the little man tried to have it over as quickly as possible.

"Awfully early, Mr. Smith," the florist said, withdrawing his hand.

"The Fites are old friends," McCutcheon said.

The florist plainly did not believe him. Apparently, though, he was used to impostors. "Are you seated in the ribbons?" he said.

"No. That's why I came early."

"Uh-huh," Mr. Lynch said. "Well." He continued staring.

"I can find my seat."

"Suit yourself. Ushers are due in the next hour. Just don't sit in the reserved pews."

"No," said McCutcheon, going past him into the nave. He sat down in a pew on the left side of the aisle, nearly halfway to the altar. A moment later Mr. Lynch supervised the laying of the aisle cloth by two colored porters in stiff white cotton coats.

9

THE chimes played one last hymn and Tom McCutcheon alternately listened to the notes and looked about him at the interior of the church. It was both deep and high, with a ceiling supported by arches of stone. The nave was lit by lamps and chandeliers which, although electric, imitated the glow of candles and dim oil lamps. Although the church was comparatively a new one, having been built in 1947, great pains had been taken to give the interior an appearance of age, so as to make one feel the bones of a saint might lie buried somewhere beneath its floor. Like paste jewelry or imitation antique furniture, McCutcheon found the effect both a little offensive and a little amusing. He was thinking about the relation of sentiment to the intrinsic value of things, when a new hymn from the carillon chimed familiarly:

> God of our fathers, known of old,
> Lord of our far-flung battle line,
> Beneath whose awful hand we hold
> Dominion over palm and pine —
> Lord God of hosts, be with us yet,
> Lest we forget — lest we forget!

Bells, ringing from an invisible chamber — he could imagine that impersonal musician pulling the wooden handles, ringing the chimes and at the same time thinking with one part of his mind about something else. Automatically putting in the pauses, the musician would count the measures as the notes were struck, but because he was a human being, the poor man's problems would prevent his listening to the magnificent music being made by his own hands. Others, in a radius of miles, would pause to listen, drawing in the marvelous purity of the sounds. To them the chimes would convey God's promise of life just as those listeners witnessed the promise of evening, as the day prepared to end, with a stilling of the breeze and a final stretch of the sun into its sunset. Those others who heard the chimes would rejoice at the sounds, while in his little chamber, the musician would take advantage of this brief moment's privacy to calculate his debts or think about his wife or his mistress, or his lack of either. His thoughts would be nibbling at him all in concert. As comforter the musician could not have comfort; a Saviour cannot save himself from Crucifixion. The limitation of man: that he can know truth only when he acts it out, yet he cannot always *recognize* truth in the act, nor can he hold the truth once the act is complete. And so with the act's end, beauty ends, and truth ceases and man is left only his torments. His torments return to their nibbling like mice, those torments, which, temporarily frightened, like mice, temporarily cease their gnawing.

The chimes tolled, the world went on, the musician died and was replaced, and someone whom the musician could not see had the words formed for him: *Lest we forget!*

Forget? Forget the gun in your hand, now out of its waist, experimentally hiding under the black hat? The cross of gold on the altar? The image of Saint George in the high window to the left, with his milky features held fast in panes of lead, his horse shying, his lance driven downward at a slant into the scaly dragon's breast, but by the appearance of the dragon's claw, which clutches the lance, there is no way to know whether the dying beast is thrusting the knight's point away or pulling it down deeper into its vitals? Forget riding the bus eighty miles and walking fifteen blocks in order to kill a man? Forget why you must kill him?

His thoughts ran on unhampered. With each pure stroke of the chimes, with each passing of a minute into the vacuous, filtering, powdery past: it was obvious to him that the reason he must kill Gratt Shafer was in some way imprisoned in the gun itself, like a lamp's genie, like the sentiment which is inseparable from something truly old. His reason was the invisible, spiritual manifestation — an object — a pistol, yes! exactly. Reason was an instrument, the instrument was a gun. He had to use it to carry to the end that act for which both he and it had been made, for the use by one man (himself), to kill another (Gratt Shafer). But this was not all, for the gun was not just any gun. The gun was his legacy. It was God's clearest proof of a legacy in violence. And he thought (holding the gun): "My father fired the pistol at snags in the river; my father circled about a stump and emptied the pistol into its rotting wood; my father died and left his pistol to me. It is my legacy, and faced with that which neither judgment nor good sense nor oblivious drinking nor all the moments of truth to be had and known in my encompassed lifetime; nor any act of love, love-sacred or love-profane — when faced with that which none of these can heal or assuage, then all the arguments of the world are insufficient against the final act, which is removal of the Specter. And there is no place to turn other than legacy of your blood, for you are tamed, and the heart, the heart is purblind. And the specter — the *specter* is yourself!"

The warning, the pounding of his heart, and the dizziness that followed, warned him that he was having a seizure. He fought back the sense of panic, trying not to lose his composure. He decided he must think of something, anything, anything, even the beginning of the seizures themselves, yes, he would think of that . . .

Tom McCutcheon's seizures had started when Gratt Shafer's wedding plans were announced in the Memphis paper. The first spell had hit him in the afternoon of the day Patsy Jo had shown him the announcement at breakfast. He had made it to the bed that time and had lain staring at the ceiling. But then the rain had been falling. It had been falling steadily and he had listened to the sound of water and he fell asleep, and when he woke an hour later he was all right.

The pattern was always the same. It began with thinking about Gratt Shafer and the wrong he had done Patsy Jo. Next McCutcheon reminded himself of his own ignorant negligence. It was like being woven into a net. His face would start to feel warm and for a time he could run over details with a degree of factual calm. But in the end his feeling would run away with him. His hands would begin sweating. His stomach would suddenly cramp. He would hear himself wheezing and the floor would tilt with him uncertainly, as it had when he was a child, as it had when he would spin around deliberately with his arms extended, turning around and around while his mother played the parlor organ and he hummed the melody, humming until his legs tripped themselves and he fell down to the rug and was "drunk." To be "drunk" then was to lie on the rug and watch it tilt under his belly, was to smell the dust of his mother's parlor rug and hear the organ, and to feel the room rock under his bare knees.

And later, when he was grown up, "drunk" was the rattle and snap of dice and the smell of a poker hand held to your nose, was a horse ridden to a lather and dead between your legs, and was a woman and the next morning when you didn't know her, when the room, the bed, the washstand, and even the face in the mirror were a little strange; "drunk" then was everything a little strange and uneasy in your belly, like the thirst after you had slept, like someone laughing in another room and you said: "This is not me — is it?"

He was an only child and his mother had eagerly financed his adventures — his wild oats. His mother's first husband had left her well fixed and the one she took when the first one died, Tom's father, had doubled her fortune. But Tom's father too had passed away before Mother did. And in the end she was left with young Tom and she loved him as only a mother can when the child is all she has in the world to love. She left him money and she left him memories.

First the house. But it was not a white-columned colonial mansion. It was a big squarish two-story place with a floor plan like a T, with wings projecting across the front and a single long section extending rearward and finally connecting to the kitchen (which had once been a separate building) by a covered porch. And the house was not one of those that had been planned and built all at once. It was, rather, one of those old home places that had evolved, beginning with a rough log structure. Of the outer planking, much had been nailed over hewn timbers, hiding the old pegged and notched construction, covering old timbers like an education was supposed to cover up and hide the natural man. Mother's organ, her linens, the family silver, some of which had survived burial during the Civil War, and Mother's china. But he could remember nothing which could make anyone call the place luxurious. The furniture was all plain, built stoutly to serve its purpose for generations.

From the stout split-rail fence snaked about the lawn to the big fireplaces of field stone, the house was just an old Southern country place. Tom's father, Luther, let three favorite hounds sleep by the hearth on cold nights. The animals would doze comfortably while Luther McCutcheon sipped a hot toddy and read a Sir Walter Scott novel, pausing now and then to read a passage aloud to Tom's mother, who sat working her embroidery. Now and then a hound would "jump a rabbit" before the fire. His long legs would twitch and he would whine in his sleep. If the dream woke him he would raise his head and gaze at Tom with intense yellow eyes, his long ears pricked out like broken fans. Then, lulled by the pleasant seething of the logs and the murmurous tone of Luther McCutcheon's voice reading the Waverley Novel, the dog would settle his jowls once more to the warm hearth, and closing his eyes, would sigh off to sleep.

When Luther died the hounds were turned out of the house and the Waverley Novels gathered dust on the shelf. But little else about the place changed. Mother took over the management and Tom had no worries. His debts were always paid for him and he found his mother always proud — of how tall he stood, of how splendidly he dressed and rode, of how handsome he was.

And Tom repaid her by marrying beneath himself. And, as he often thought afterwards, at least partly out of spite, Mother herself had died just over a year after his marriage. And not a month later the old house caught fire. Luther had caused a covered passageway to be built between the kitchen and the house and the fire proved him, posthumously, to have been a fool. For the fire had started in the kitchen and the blaze had crossed on the connecting porch as on a fuse. The old place had exploded in flames and in its place were left a few chimneys standing like stone trees, and a T-shaped mound of ashes.

Plainly, whoever had built the kitchen separate from the house had known what they were doing. And plainly the connecting porch, neatly latticed, white painted, and planted alongside with flowering shrubs, with rose vines, jonquil bulbs, bridal wreath, and sweet pea; the connecting porch and all the beauty beside it, had been an act of foolishness. (If you went back, even now, in early spring, the volunteer jonquils — *Narcissus jonquilla* — so sweet and foolish and yellow, would lead you to where the covered porch had stood, would lead you there like grave markers.)

The fire was bad, but Tom and his bride, Miss Adelicia, took it as no great calamity. Indeed, rather than rebuild the old place, they took the fire for a sign that they should move twelve miles into Somerton. "Things" were going on there, and twelve miles was too far to live away from "things." Besides, they reasoned, their holdings could be managed just as well from town, and much more conveniently than *in situ*. (The term had stuck in his memory, and since it was Latin it seemed to give his decision more weight, as though somehow the authoritative wisdom of the Ancient Roman Empire stood back of it.) *In situ,* exactly! That was to say, "on the place itself." They would move to town. There was no one living to disagree.

Remembering, he sighed. He then remembered the blue shaving mug of French china, *arbiter elegantiarum* among the other implements on his dressing table, for it had been a gift from his mother. And she was now dead thirty-five years. And the pistol, *lex talonis,* to remind him of Luther, his father, *paterfamilias.* The mug had about it the smell of morning and Maytime, whereas the pistol smelled of brass and eternity.

Both were items saved from the fire, the fire which had precipitated his decision to move into Somerton. He could recall no one who was more eager to encourage him to move than the Cravens, and no one who agreed with him more fully that *in situ* management was a brand of foolishness. The Craven brothers were nephews of his mother's first husband and they agreed with him that living on the farm was old-fashioned. Tom had pitied them, for poor Nathan and Robert had fallen smack on their butts, covering their backsides with the dust of hard times. They were pore-mouthed shirt-sleeve country storekeepers. Or so he had imagined, until the old house burned. But the ashes were hardly cool before Nathan and Robert Craven appeared, Nathan with his red turkey-like neck and his eyes still and brown as liver, his body thin as a frame of tomato sticks. And with him Robert, a human talking machine shaped like a watermelon half, his back wide and straight, his front all curve and belly, and his head bald as a squash. Hard times had not muffled *him*, and Robert talked, the words coming out like water from an ever-flowing spring. His red, berry-colored tongue popped in and out between his lips, and he spoke with absolute authority on every subject. Robert Craven knew the world and the weather and the democrats, the boll weevil, the adultery gossip, the almanac and the distances to places like Mississippi, Alabama, Kentucky and Georgia. This last he knew because when he got able, he was planning a right smart of travels. Nathan and Robert came offering to advance Tom the money to build his house in town.

And Tom was so pleased he put up some timber land as collateral and borrowed not only enough cash to build the house, but enough to furnish it too. And the next year was a crop failure as well as the next after that. In the end Nathan and Robert wound up with a good deal of the original Mc-Cutcheon land. It was only when his wife left him that Tom stopped gambling his estate away. What land there was left when Adelicia walked out on him, he had kept. From that point on he kept the land and the land had kept him. And without knowing why, he had kept the pistol, now resting in his hand. But now he knew what the pistol was for. He knew what his father, what Luther hadn't really known. He knew what Luther really didn't ever realize. He remembered how Luther prided himself on being able to shoot snags in the river, how he raised the pistol up to "crack down" with it. The report of the gun would rip out over the water, splinters would explode from the snag and whirl slowly away with the drift, and the pungent plume of smoke would ride the air an instant before it melted on the breeze. Luther was careful to instruct Tom, showing him how to load the pistol, how the caps were fitted on the nipple-like appendages at the back of each cylinder. And when he was in the woods Luther sometimes suddenly drew the pistol, whirling about quickly to empty it into a dead stump. He fired each shot with cold deliberation. And later, before putting it away, Luther always cleaned the gun, using the implements in its wooden case.

The seizure passed. Tom McCutcheon's dizziness was gone.

He remembered the organ, the smell of Mother's skirts, the clear sound of her voice as she sang.

And then she lay dying and he on the bed with her in spirit dying also; each object in the room where she lay filled him with inexpressible grief and made him cry inwardly:

"My mother cannot be dying, for there is her little jewelry chest on her dresser where I remember it from childhood, for I remember that smell of her face powder which always lingered about it! My mother cannot be dying, for there stands her bed and I have lain under it hiding from her, loving her, wanting to be near without her knowledge; and thus I have seen the hem of her petticoat, and her feet, and have heard her humming as she dressed herself, thinking she was all alone in her room; and I loved her in my secret heart of hearts, lying so quiet in my hiding place and being so content with her nearness, such that had I reached out my hand I could have touched her dear foot. Ah, no, Mother cannot be dying. And I am not this grown and married man and that cannot be my wife at her bedside. The woman at her bedside is . . . is, yes! a cousin who came to see Mother once when she was sick; once long ago, and I am small and my mother cannot be dying because there is my dead Grandpa Tommy's picture upon the wall where it has always hung, the picture showing my grandfather then so young, with such fine mustaches and such broad shoulders (I did not know him then but Mother herself said he was a straight six feet four, and so handsome; and killed a man once for insulting him and never lost a night's sleep over it afterwards, for such was the nature of my father's father) and my Grandpa Tommy had such pale and penetrating eyes — see how he stares, even now; I must look away from that picture!"

MOTHER: Tom, son, my feet are cold.

MCCUTCHEON: (*Taking her cold foot beneath the covers, gripping it in his hands*) Is that better, Mother? Eh?

ADELICIA: I'll get a warming pan. (*Leaves*)

MOTHER: (*Weakly*) No, it's all right. Tom can rub my feet. I'm feeling better . . . oh, where is she? Where's your wife gone to?

MCCUTCHEON: Gone for a warming pan.

MOTHER: Oh, I don't want a warming pan, but she doesn't understand, does she?

MCCUTCHEON: (*Angrily*) No, Mother. I wish . . . If she could only sit down for a minute! She's worrying you. You're worrying more about her than you are about yourself.

MOTHER: But she's trying to help. I know how she feels. She feels left out — helpless. I felt that way when your father, Luther, was with *his* mother. (*Pauses*) Has Luther . . . Your father, is he here yet? Did I hear his horse? Have you sent for him?

MCCUTCHEON: Mother, he's been dead nine years. You're not thinking straight.

MOTHER: But I thought you sent for him . . . Oh, yes. My senses are drifting, Tom. I thought I heard his horse on the drive; it was so plain. Do you remember how you used to run out and search through his pockets, the deep ones in his frock coat, in the tails of it, to see what little surprise he had brought you from town?

ADELICIA: (*Entering with warming pan, her cheeks red and flushed with exertion, her manner firm and officious as people will become around the sick to whom they are strangers.*) Here, let's put your feet on this! (*Raises the covers.*)

MCCUTCHEON: She doesn't need it. I'm rubbing her feet.

ADELICIA: Of course she needs it. See, I got fresh live coals from the kitchen. See?

MCCUTCHEON: (*Angrily*) Can't you understand? She doesn't want it!

MOTHER: *Tom,* of course I want the warming pan. What's come over you? Must you shout at your wife, your own flesh and blood?

MCCUTCHEON: I'm sorry, Mother.

MOTHER: Apologize to Adelicia.

MCCUTCHEON: I'm sorry. Please forgive me.

ADELICIA: What is there to forgive? You just flew off the handle. (*She adjusts the covers.*) There, now, isn't that better?

MOTHER: (*Artificially*) Oh, much better, dear Adelicia! You'll take good care of her, promise me you will, Tom?"

MCCUTCHEON: I promise.

MOTHER: Be sweet to her for my sake?

MCCUTCHEON: I will.

MOTHER: Oh, dear Tom. Hold my hand.

ADELICIA: Take mine, Mother.

MOTHER: My dearest, yes. Tom, can you take the other one? That's better. Now I have my *two* children! Oh, Tom, I hate to leave you alone. I'm going; oh, going!

MCCUTCHEON: I'm here.

MOTHER: (*Fretfully*) I can't understand what's keeping your father. It's not like him to be late. He has his faults. Perhaps he drinks overmuch of late, but lack of punctuality! That was *never* a trait of his. Your father has always been on time. A little given to wild schemes, yes, but never the man to be late. Oh. Have I been dreaming again?

ADELICIA: Why, no, Mother.

MCCUTCHEON: Why, yes, you have.

MOTHER: Tom, I want you to write some things down — some things you must not forget.

MCCUTCHEON: There'll be plenty of time for that.

MOTHER: Now, Tom. If you please. Now.

ADELICIA: I'll stay with her while you get something to write with. (*She speaks as though only he and she were present, impersonally brisk.*)

MOTHER: My pen and stationery, fetch them from the secretary.

(*Mother cannot be dying, for there is her secretary, her old desk, folded closed in the corner by the window, and the high chair is there by it where she sat and kept her accounts and where she sat when she wrote to me while I was at Harvard, writing me every single day, writing to know how I fared the cold winters in Boston admonishing me to mind my raising, to remember who I was. Writing to tell me how the spring had already come at home, that the floods had carried off a bridge, that the peach trees had put out earlier than ever she could remember, writing:* "We did not have a backward Spring and the creeks hereabouts are booming." *She folded down this very shelf and took this very ink pot, and paused now and then to look through that very window. No, my mother cannot be dying.*)

MOTHER: Tom?

MCCUTCHEON: I'm here.

MOTHER: Take this down.

MCCUTCHEON: I'm ready.

MOTHER: First the land. The land must come first. (*Speaking slowly*) Always. No farmer succeeds who sells his land. No matter how profitable it seems at the time, land never brings its worth. Your business is to acquire land and cultivate it. When you think of selling it is time to go out and buy. When you think of buying, it is time to hold your money and wait, for the natural inclinations run to the opposite of wisdom; it is natural to wish to buy when all the others are striving to buy, instead of when they are striving to sell. Second: the people. Know your tenants by name. Remember always, *they* are the land's children. Like the land they will not work for you if they are neglected. Never give them money for supplies, always insist that they charge to your name everything they must buy to farm with. Giving them cash money is leading them into temptation. Now, have you got that?

MCCUTCHEON: Yes, I have it.

MOTHER: Now then, finally, yourself. Be as good as your word. Deal civilly with other men. But never humble yourself. Defend your honor and your name, Tom. And don't be a borrower or a lender. Observe temperance in all things. Tell the truth if it takes the hide. Don't bring suit against a man for personal injury or assault, for such a course can never reflect on you honorably. Read your Bible, and fear God. Never forget an obligation to a friend, always remember to repay every favor done for you. Neglecting a friend, forgetting a favor — these always bring grief. Above all stand by your convictions; hear advice politely, but keep your own counsel. The world is full of fools who are quick to advise and slow to accept the responsibility for what they advise. Pay your gambling debts promptly, these are obligations made upon your honor and are as binding on a gentleman as any contract made according to law. And when you are tempted to any dishonorable act, remember your name. Remember me.

Lest we forget?

How could he have forgotten her? He thought: "How could I have forgotten my mother?"

And inwardly:

(*My mother cannot be dead, for there is her house still*

standing; and the trees about the old carriage drive are just turning, and there her late roses are just budding yonder on the arbor.)

It only came to him that she was gone and that he was irrevocably grown into a man and that he was himself married now to Adelicia when the plantation bell began tolling. It brought him galloping out of the woods toward the column of smoke which, even from horseback, in the instant that he reined up and whirled, turning from the direction of the hounds and the fox, he knew. He saw the lofting column of smoke rise black above the distant trees and knew that it was the house — *her house.*

He brought the whip down into the horse's side and clutched home the spurs. His own agony leapt down the ridge a pace with that of the horse; and him thinking: *Mother, my mother is dead!*

Down the hill and through the creek, shallow and icy cold, toward the wild tolling, laying on the whip and cursing the horse, he went: *Mother, my mother is dead:* and finally he cut through the woods lot and the pasture, clearing the old slave wall and finally the gray weathered rail fence; then, through the bare trees, then, seeing it all too plainly, feeling inside himself the explosion of flames. A Negro had the plantation bell rope and hung on it like a jumping jack until the house was clean down but for the chimneys and the steps and the old limestone foundation wall, clean down and glowing gray and red and yellow-orange. He thought: *My mother is dead.*

The bell stopped.

And then he believed it.

And he went through the things saved from the fire: A pair of conch shells Mother brought home from her first wedding trip; Adelicia's little sewing basket; the pink lamp that had been on the organ; Mother's strong box; the papers from her secretary, some of her silver, linens, quilts, and china; and of his father, nothing but the pistol in its case; of his own, a few clothes and trinkets. And finally the blue shaving mug of French china, a gift from his mother; the chain, the watch, the Phi Beta Kappa key, the knife.

He put the gun back inside his coat, thrusting it into his waist beneath his vest. The chain, the watch, the knife, the Phi Beta Kappa key, the adornments of the vest, the last item a gentleman puts on in the morning unless he is carrying a pistol. The pistol must always be put on last, behind the time-piece, the gold knife, the chain and the key which attests either to a first-class mind, or a certain type of determination or sometimes both of these combined. But above, beyond this, there was more; the key represented the time it took to build a fortune in the West — so that the beginning which finally brought about the attachment of the key to the chain (his mother had given him the chain) went back to 1827, the same year that the boundaries of Sligo County were laid off, the year his great-grandfather came on the land with his family and commenced in the woods and had to build from the stump up. The key started at the stump.

Tom McCutcheon's grandfather, Grandpa Tommy, was ninety in 1905, and could "whup" his grandson when he saw the lad needed it, hale enough at ninety to do this for a lad of ten even though his "close up" memory failed him so that he would not uncommonly lose his pipe from one day to the next and fret until he found it. But his "way back" memory was clear and having at last found the pipe he would cut a twist from his hunk of tobacco and huddle in the chimney corner in the big kitchen separate from the house, the pipe so old and gummy that it growled, glowing and growling when it was lit, the smoke rising furiously and the old man kicking logs into the fire with his boots until the flames were high enough to suit him. The fire would crackle and his pipe would growl, and he would say to Tom, who roasted chestnuts and apples on the hearth:

"Eh, boy? You, Tom? My daddy came into this territory when I was going on thirteen, eh? Just so he did, and we commenced in the woods and had to build from the stump, so we did. We had a pretty place and in the spring I remember how the grass begins to grow green. It grows as high as a man's head. And stock of all kinds is in fine order. Without any feed at all hogs is fat a-foraging on acorns. But I don't know if that country back then, this country, would have suited you or not, Tom. It was pretty as now, but in a different way; different for being tough. But my daddy came west because unimproved land was low and sold for two dollars per acre up as high as five, and he bought one hundred sixty acres for three hundred and fifty dollars and we bought a fine lot of hogs and did fine business with them, eh?

"And my daddy had a fine horse, a horse such as they had not seen in this country before, by name of Duke, and we did a fine business with him for the making of young Dukes. Before too many years the fastest horses in this territory owed Duke for what he passed on to them, and I had my own mare

and from her my own colt the *very next spring* after one following, eh? Daddy often said as how it was much better than
anything to the east, for here I recall as everything in the eating line was cheap, with corn forty cents a bushel that year
and for long after that year, plenty of deer and turkey in any
amount. I can see that first summer now if I close my eyes,
how wet and warm and all the creeks were booming by April,
for *it was not a backward spring that year*. Just so it was, Tom.

"And the first year we broke fifty acres and quit, for our cattle got tired. We had three old and seven young steers — five
yoke, and oh, by June the sod corn looked fine and little
Polly was walking about and my daddy often said that his
youngest son, Willy, was the fairest child in all the West.

"Says Daddy: 'He has never been whipped yet, Willy
ain't: and if he lives a little while longer without it he never
will get it. By the powers, with his spirit Willy will soon defend himself.' For that was how my daddy indulged his little
Willy boy.

"Your Uncle Will was that one who rode with General
Forrest and drowned December 27, 1863 while swimming his
horse across the Wolf River. They sent word to Somerton he
was dead and a friend took his body into town where my
daddy went to get his drowned boy, his Willy boy, drove into
town in a wagon to get him and heard how Willy was part
of a party sent ahead to secure the bridge at LaFayette, for
Forrest was taking out the companies that had been raised in
this territory on the sly, after the Yankees had passed through
and were even then holed up at Fort Pillow — the country
was fenced in by the Yankee cavalry — but Forrest come in
to take out the men they had raised for companies and take

them out he did. So they said about forty Yankees was guarding the bridge and Willy and some others was to swim their horses across from above and get in behind them so as to bag the whole crowd. Only in the crossing, somehow Willy lost his breath in the cold water, and somehow sank, and even though they pulled him out and done all they could, he was drowned. At any rate the bridge was took and the Yankees captured, but I remember hearing Daddy always say how awful much it hurt him to drive a team into town after his dead soldier boy Willy, his dead boy with his hair froze to his head and his clothes on his body stiff with ice. Your Uncle Willy, that was, the fairest child in all the West."

Thinking of Willy always made the old man pause, cough, reload his pipe and look at the fire for a while. Then the pipe would begin to growl again. For the spell would not last forever. It lasted only those instants when the recollection came suddenly clear and sweet and as painful to Grandpa Tommy as it ever was when it was fresh.

And then: "Do you know, that second year, 1828, we sold our bacon for five cents a pound, in the summer, and in the fall we got twenty-five cents a bushel for our corn? And Tom, why, Tom, cattle was in such demand they brought twenty-five dollars a yoke! It was the prettiest fall that year I ever saw, warm and pretty so much that in the last of November the leaves — I can see now if I close my eyes — how it's the last of November and the leaves is yet green. And word came there was to be a railroad from Nashville to the Western Boundary of this State. I was a friend of the railroad, but Daddy said, over and again: 'I hope it will not come.'

"But come it did, eh, Tom?

"The next year little Frances was born, and my mother thought her the prettiest for her fair skin and red hair and black eyes. And next Emit was born, and he was dark like yourself, dark skin and black eyes."

The old man had lived it the whole way through, lived it so that he remembered when bacon went to seven cents a pound and oxen to forty dollars a yoke. Sheep went to a dollar fifty a head and although the family had no money they had (after five years) twenty-five cows and calves, and in seven years had eight hundred acres of land with two hundred forty in corn, fifty in wheat, eighty in oats, and a peach orchard that was "mighty full" that seventh year and three hundred fifty apple trees beginning to bear. And the railroad did come through their farm.

And on the twenty-sixth of November, 1840, after thirteen years of labor, by which time Tommy who was the oldest was twenty-five, old enough to be gone on a trip west to look at the Arkansas girls, old enough to marry one to bring home — in that year and that month and on that day his daddy fell off the house and broke his leg. Tommy got his mother's letter while he was in Green County, Arkansas visiting "connections" there and looking over the Arkansas gals, and his mother wrote:

"Your father fell off the house on the twenty-sixth of November and broke his leg and had it cut off on the fourth of December and died the seventh of this month."

(Her letter was dated December 15, 1840.) And she continued:

"He had no fear of after death but had a great wish to stay with me and the children and to have seen you one last time. My mind is not comforted enough at this time to give you much satisfaction, dear Tommy. He made his will and left the property all to me and begged for me to educate the children. We had other bad luck this year, Tommy. We lost two Negroes, one dying and the other run away or stolen. I received your letter of the thirteenth of this month in the midst of a great storm and destruction of mind. Sister Betsy is dead and Ben McCutcheon has married again. I pray you, my dear son, come home."

And home Tommy McCutcheon went, taking with him an Arkansas gal who was the prettiest in the whole country, just as Duke had once been the fastest horse, just so the gal he took home was ever after that something to brag on. Tommy McCutcheon, for whom Thomas Gideon McCutcheon was named, who lived and saw and remembered it all and hunkered down about the kitchen fire and took his morning dram and spat at the burning logs and sucked at his pipe, making it growl, sometimes shucked a hot chestnut and put it in his mouth shifting it about, as he said, like an old horse trying to make his last two teeth hit together, and remembered how his second son came while the first child, his little son Daniel, was lying a corpse in the house. "For we had all had scarlet fever and when little Daniel was just recovered he came down with croup. And, oh, Tom, my Arkansas gal lay upstairs in childbed with hot rags packed on her belly." And Tommy's mother, who was not well either had tried to attend to them all and Grandpa Tommy told how he had gone back and forth between the two rooms, feeling his heart about to burst with the strain, feeling himself torn by the struggle between life about to begin in one chamber and life about to end in another. And the second child came ". . . when my little son Daniel was lying a corpse in the house, for he could not live past twenty-four hours once the croup had set in with him, for that's how it was, Tom."

There was much more that Grandpa Tommy recalled. There was the war, the confiscation of the land afterwards, a trip to Washington, an interview with President Andrew Johnson who had written him a pardon which later was revoked by the Secretary of War; and finally there was a second pardon for Grandpa Tommy, the land was saved, and the Reconstruction somehow weathered through. But the war's most vivid memory for him was that of the ragged, hungry soldiers of the Confederacy who came by on the road, stayed a while and worked for their meals. They stayed until, like a far-traveling dog whose family has left him or lost him while going west, until like such a dog they had strength again to take the road south for the long return to their land, where somehow they must begin over again. And in that hour the whole South was to Grandpa Tommy's mind like Jeff Davis who, chained to a dungeon wall, awaited his execution at the hands of the Radicals, and others who felt the suffering South must be made to suffer still more, and who took the assassination of Lincoln as their excuse to begin the long punishment. Tommy McCutcheon always said afterwards of the Yanks that he could like them well enough in war. "For they fought well enough for men forced to it, and died like men; but, by the powers, they was so mean afterwards I used to wake myself up mighty near every night and say out loud: 'Remember the damned Yanks!' And I trained my head Negro, Marcus, to greet me every morning, noon, and night and say: 'Remember the Yankees, Marster Tommy!' And I would always say back, 'Yes, and may the powers damn them every one!' And it did me good the longest day that Negro lived, so it did; yes, just so it did, Tom, eh?"

What had interested Tom most, the war, the old man would rarely tell about. For he was not given to saber-rattling. Grandpa Tommy's life had commenced in the woods and had been dedicated from the very day he and his daddy set out to build from the stump in the year 1827. In going to war he had been defending what he had built, and he was more concerned to recall the year corn went to a dollar and eighty one cents a bushel and rust hit the wheat than to rejoice in any way for the fact that the great hand which now held his pipe once had taken up the sword. And he hated the Yankees more for trying to take his land after the war than he did for any shot they fired at him or any cattle their foraging officers took and slaughtered or any buildings they burned during the war. For he had commenced at the stump and marveled to see the grass spring up shoulder high and had lived each season and felt the booming of the creeks in his blood and the hard winters which followed into reluctant springs; had *felt* it as though the agony were his own and not merely the frozen earth's. And he knew the smell of oxen and the gutting sound of the plough in new ground, and could feel the exhaustion of an animal as though it were a part of himself; knew by the smell of urine and dung and ammonia and frusty roots being turned into the sunlight what size the sod corn would be, how it would please the eye in June after April following. Knew and felt, remembered and saw again in the growling of his pipe which could assume a shape between his sentences, sentences which ran on with no beginning and no end, so that the war beside this had little meaning, and was just a part of a great series of springs and summers and falls and winters. The war was in its finality little more than a time of famine and suffering which came and passed. He did not care to fathom its meaning nor question its origins. It was enough to say that speaking of what you failed at can bring little comfort. That to remember with any joy such a period of hardship to farming was in a farmer unseemly. Had he killed Yankees? Yes. But not in anger. Had he been wounded? No. But he had been wet and cold and sick, which was a deal worse sometimes than being wounded and cared for in a hospital or allowed to go home on sick leave. The war left him with stiff joints and sore bones; it cost the lives of many of his connections; Willy drowned stiff, who was his own brother and the fairest child in all the West and never had a switch laid to his limbs. Willy's death had put a great burden on Tommy's heart. Later, seeing an Army surgeon saw a Texan's leg off, Grandpa Tommy had been reminded of his own father whose leg had been broken when he fell off the house on the twenty-sixth of November, whose leg had been cut off the fourth of December, who died on the seventh of that month, three days later. These things and Brother Emit's death in a federal prison in Mobile, Emit who had dark skin and black eyes, captured and left to die alone of fever: these things impressed him more than all the battles and skirmishes or how a cannon sounds or how a dead man looks on the field. He did say it was a pity the way the horses were killed, said it hurt him to see the poor animals suffer, and put him in mind of all Duke's colts which he had nursed up and broken. "I hope I never do hear another horse scream," he often said. And Tom McCutcheon still always wanted to know from Grandpa Tommy how a man looked when he died. "How? How? Why he looks like a doornail, eh? *Dead,* that's how he looks. Think? You don't think nothing atall at the time. You know he's dead and not wounded or just senseless. How? You just know it when you see him, eh? Just so they was, a dead man. Why, Sir, he looked *dead.* Just like a doornail."

Remember the Yankees, Marster Tommy!

And so when young Tom went to Boston and entered Harvard University (Harvard College, founded 1636), *Harvard,* he still remembered the Yankees, but found to his bewilderment that *they* had forgotten the war pretty much. But Grandpa Tommy's pipe still growls in memory although he is buried, buried but not dead, for his pipe is still at home on the kitchen mantle, which is hewn from stone, and his dram glass is there. Grandpa Tommy is in the family graveyard sleeping beside his Arkansas girl and the Boston winters come and Mother fears they are cold, but *omnia vincit labor,* work overcomes all things, and Mother's son is now custodian of the family's honor. *Sicut patribus, sit Deus nobis!* As God was with our fathers, so may he be with us! And he kept the faith, and carried off the trophy and was awarded the key, the *summum bonum,* the chief good, and saw it become one with the watch and the chain and the knife of gold, the adornments of his vest, thus combining *utile dulci*, the useful with the pleasant. And so returned home, a Bachelor of Arts, to Sligo County, Tennessee, and saw that his father, Luther, was still a crack shot with his old pistol and still never tired of circling a stump with it and whanging away. Grandpa Tommy commented before he died that it was a sign of the way the world was changing when a son of his would choose to shoot his stumps rather than have them burnt and grubbed up, and he calculated that the lead Luther had pumped into the stumps and shot into the river would tax twelve yoke of oxen (were it all collected into one lump melted together) to drag it. And it came to Tom McCutcheon that perhaps his father hated stumps and shot at them with such fury because of Grandpa's memory (of how it all commenced in the woods and had to be built from the stump up) outraged him. Perhaps inside Luther somewhere very deep he knew how many oxen had burst their hearts tugging at stumps and maybe he felt the stumps mocked him because he did not war against them as Grandpa Tommy had, and so he shot them to splinters. Luther McCutcheon was not so wild and high strung as his pale-eyed father had been, as his dead father whose picture hung on the wall where Tom McCutcheon looked at it the day his mother died. For Luther McCutcheon might have shot a man dead to protect his honor but he could not have boasted truthfully afterward "that he never lost a night's sleep afterwards over it." Luther was not like Grandpa Tommy McCutcheon. He could not have killed a man and maintained a clear conscience afterwards. Luther had been more like Uncle Emit, a good child, and all his rage was vented against stumps in the woods and snags in the river, for he would not shoot wild animals either. Still he prided himself on his shooting and was given up to be the best pistol shot in West Tennessee. "And no wonder, as much time as he wastes at it," Grandpa Tommy would say, snorting a little. And he took a delight in comparing Luther's soft habits with his own, for Luther was rarely out of bed before six o'clock and commonly took a nap in the library each afternoon following dinner. And he was fond of rich cigars and brandy and spent a great while reading Sir Walter Scott's novels and discussing the excellence of their style at the dinner table. Perhaps he read so because Tommy and the Arkansas girl had pampered Luther a little as he grew up. They encouraged his withdrawn pose as a scholar, his love of clothes, his fox hunting (which he did from horseback and loved so long as the fox was not caught). His knack for languages enabled him to learn Spanish and immerse himself in Spanish novels, grand tales of the cavaliers and conquistadores, romantic tales of their loves and quarrels, of chivalry and honor, and family pride. So that the choice of Harvard for young Tom was really Luther's own, and was in a sense a reflection of his own dreams come alive in Tom's image, for Luther had not been sent to Harvard, nor anything like it. Luther had four years of academy school and two years at Marion Institute, South Alabama, a military prep school, where Grandpa Tommy had sent Luther to prepare him for a military career. But when Grandpa Tommy had gotten Luther's appointment to Annapolis, during his second year at Marion, Luther had declined it and returned home, satisfied to stay with the farm. And settled at last, he married one of the Moran girls after her first husband died, and marrying a pretty widow, marrying late by Grandpa Tommy's idea, but exactly doubling, almost to the penny and the acre, what he was worth.

"Luther don't hardly wear a shirt but once and then gives it to one of his Negroes and breaks him out a fresh brand-new one, and don't go by the Express Office but what he's got a gang of wine and liquor and what not, and cigars bought through the mail, eh?" Grandpa Tommy would say. And then his pipe would growl and stop. And: "My daddy and me come out of bed by three-thirty and had broke the neck of a day's work by six. Six is when Luther figures it's time to yawn and get up after his book if its light enough outdoors to read Mr. Walter Scott. Just so. Just so it be, eh? And many a time ain't I come out of the field and fell over a weed and laid there all night so whipped and tired that like as not the Trump of *Doom* couldn't have no more than just made me snuggle down on my weed a little more. Eh? And Luther says he has to read himself to sleep burning up oil and candles until after midnight and then so tired next day he has to bed down out in the library like a consumptive or a night-feeding varmint and pretty soon he'll start a-whickering and a-snoring; and always at about the time I would have reached the field or orchard or the barn and put my hand to something — me and my old daddy, may God bless him. Now ain't that so, son?"

"Yes, sir," Luther would say. Pleased at the comparison the old man drew, happy at the indolent picture of himself, at the picture of a rich, refined planter; Luther McCutcheon was happy to consider three generations and think of the progress, to think how Grandpa Tommy had begun at the stump, how he, Luther, read Sir Walter Scott and took naps in his library after dinner, and how his son, Tom, the third generation he liked to muse on, would someday go to Harvard.

It pleased him too when he heard the old man continue: "And I went into the west and wooed and won my Nancy Matildy who was an Arkansas gal and the prettiest in the whole territory and we filled our house with children, and Luther, our son who lived, why he waits right at home and marries a pretty widow and has one boy, Tom. Eh?" The old man speaks fondly, for Grandpa Tommy is also proud to consider the three generations.

And of young Tom: "I see the Moran blood in him, so I do," says Grandpa Tommy. "He is high strung and has got the Moran mettle, and will go in the woods and kill a buck with so many points his antlers make him look like a porkypine, and will load him across his horse's flank and ride in with him with blood fairly painted on him and I'll say Tom you look and smell like a heathen. So you do, boy. You got a touch of the lion's whelp off the Moran side, eh?"

And *Tom* McCutcheon was a grown man and had the Phi Beta Kappa key and Grandpa Tommy was buried. Tom caught the mumps and defied them all and kept on riding and hunting and the mumps went down on him and swelled his testicles the size of Christmas oranges and turned him black in the face with pain so that he clutched the bedpost and groaned like a woman in labor and cursed between his gritted teeth and the doctor said it was a rare bad run of mumps, but that Tom would recover. Recover he did. His potency was still there, like in Duke, the McCutcheon's first stud stallion, and like Duke he did a good business in his wild years, all free of charge. But the mumps could have done what scarlet fever and measles and croup and pneumonia and falling from houses and drowning and wars and old age all had failed to do. Luther felt it was his fault for putting the mumps in a position to do it, of course, because he had done just that when he did not send the widow he married, did not send Mother, to childbed every year or so, but then fewer were dying and Tom had lived through the second summer and then the third — had lived through that time when most of the short graves were made — and it began to look as though the time would soon come when there would no longer be more short graves than long ones. Luther was that far ahead of his times. But Luther feared his own error when Tom fell stricken. For when Tom's testicles swelled and when the doctor came Luther took the doctor not quite out of earshot to say:

"What concerns me is that swelling in his cods."

"Happens lots when grown men come down with them" the doctor said, meaning by *them* the *mumps,* which like *license* the doctor accepted as an innately plural word.

"Still I don't like to see his cods so swollen. Is there any danger . . . ?"

"Pain is all, likely all, very likely," the doctor said. "I give him something to ease it and some powders to make him sleep lots."

"But afterwards?" Luther said.

"Just good as ever, more than likely. I give him something for his pain, like I said. We'll follow him along," the doctor continued, using another favorite expression which somehow seemed to imply that Tom McCutcheon was on a pleasant stroll through the woods instead of lying helpless with pillows under his knees.

"Still it looks so bad."

"Looks," said the doctor firmly, "ain't important. *Is* is what counts. They *is* only the mumps." And the doctor had been right.

"I was worried," Luther said.

"Course you was. But as I say, we'll follow him along."

Thus the mumps almost did what none of the rest could do, and although he did not know it at the time, the groans that he heard in his semi-delirium, which seemed in the dream-world of the doctor's powders to be the sounds of some strange, almost dying creature, were the sounds of an entity near to dying, were the sounds of the near death-agony of the McCutcheon line. And because it had been a tough and pro-liferous line, his suffering had been great and the groans some-times rose to a shout that filled the whole house and caused Luther McCutcheon to weep secretly in the hallway, biting his lips and holding back his sobs, lurking outside Tom's room where Mother discovered him again and again and with her Moran's compassion took him back to his library. It was another testimony of his gentle nature which Mother seldom tired of telling, after the fever had seized on Luther and car-ried him off, while he lay on his bed peacefully dreaming, seeing as from a subterraneous distance the occasional unfold-ing of a Waverley Novels scene. And in those hours before his peaceful death, he calmly told those hovered about his bed in the death watch just which characters he saw, and some-thing of what they said. Both Tom and Mother understood.

—

Tom McCutcheon marveled over the great sensation of peace which whelmed over him as he sat in the silent, empty church, caught in the immersion of his memories, seeing life recount itself before him in such clarity.

Grandpa Tommy and his daddy had commenced in the woods and built from the stump. Luther McCutcheon had fired the pistol into the stump, even though it was already dead; and Tom was left with that between his legs which had no more worth than a stump for, having fathered no son, the McCutcheon line must end as it had begun, at the stump.

The part of him which had been as a Tree of Life had been almost cut to a stump during that illness when he had both felt the pain and listened to the agony and yet had not known what it was, at least not just then.

But after a time his social gentleman farming, his wild oats sowing days, ended like the sea getting flat after a storm. His passion for gaming and women died out and he found himself looking more longingly at the land, going entire weeks at a time without drinking, so that Mother knew the tempering fires of license and the toughening flagellations of debauchery had at last taken effect, had brought him forth from the initiation purged and clear-eyed. In short, Tom was just the sort of gentleman Mother had sought to create all along.

He was a tribute to her handiwork, a beautiful blending of McCutcheon and Moran, of serenity and disquietude, fire and ice, temper and temperance; pride, and yet too, she thought she saw and perhaps did see some of Luther's calm humility.

And here, she knew, was the most crucial hour in the whole

process of the making of a man, for the critical time was reached, the catalyst had been applied, and now, ere he grew too cold he must choose a wife and marry. For once past his time of pause, he might drift; perhaps into bachelorhood, or back into debauchery, which must now become degradation. He was in the wine of his manhood; the wine must soon become vinegar now unless it were put up.

Very gently, she told him it was time to marry, and afterward, while she sat playing the organ, not singing but simply playing a slow quiet hymn, he left and went outside and down below the house toward the barn, walking slowly and pensively in the warm air of early spring, toward the pink sunset sky which seemed to contain all the quiet, questing repose he suddenly had found. He went into the barn, which because of the sunset was dark inside. The pigeons cried softly, settling into the high eaves to roost and the heavy scent of hay and the soft sound of cattle breathing, the scrape of a horse against the feed trough in his stall as he searched out the last grains of his ration of corn, all came to him now with a great sense of fullness and completion. He stopped and let his hand drift over the dusty uneven barn wall, feeling the complete dry preservation of it on his fingers, feeling within the barn the vast continuation and permanence of life, and the sweet rest of all the creatures housed about him. And it seemed as though in that mystic hour he had made a discovery of the first significance. His mother's words came back to him and the strains of the hymn were inaudible except for one particular note which came to him alone above all the rest, that were beyond the ken of his hearing. The note was repeated irregularly, but because he let the clean sound enter him

when and how it would, it occasioned him no surprise nor
pain. The sound brought on a strange elatious repose to his
heart.

"*My dear Tom, it's time you took a wife.*"

The answer seemed to come from without, from beyond
his known world, to well up from a great and gentle void.
The words from the Order of Holy Communion, out of the
Book of Common Prayer, were waiting and ready to be called
forth:

"*It is meet and right so to do.*"

And on that instant he felt that all the vicissitudes were removed from his future life. He felt that all possibility for
pain and anger and jealousy had been washed away. I'm
going to be happy, he thought, with a mild sensation of surprise. And he believed it.

When he came out of the barn the air was a little cooler
than he had remembered it and the fresh manure, cleaned
just that evening out of the warm stalls, blended with the
steaming ammoniac smell of the decomposing dung heap beside the barn. The lamps were on in the house and the organ
was quiet. As he walked toward the glow of the windows
through the pinkish, darkened air, it had seemed to him that
he would live forever.

10

GRATT SHAFER
He and Camack Patterson heard the door slam from the deacon's cramped office, a monastic little cubicle off the narrow hallway behind the altar. Fletcher Fite had just stepped in briefly to say the bride was there, and had left, seeming well pleased with everything, looking very nice, very satisfied, and proper in his swallow-tailed coat, looking very calm and settled.

"What time is it?" Gratt Shafer said. Unconsciously he had come to depend on Camack Patterson for everything, letting himself drift, trying not to worry, but succeeding only when he could manage not to think about where he was and what he was doing. And he was not especially alarmed at the thought of being stared at by the hundreds who would crowd the pews. Now that the moment had arrived, or almost arrived, he had no fear of the public exposure, no worry over the wedding rings being misplaced, not one worrisome thought concerning any physical aspect of the ceremony itself. But from the instant that he and Camack Patterson had entered the deacon's barren little cell, having been shown to it by the porter in his white coat, having come into the hall's darkness after the opulent ride from Camack Patterson's house through the beautiful afternoon in Camack's gleaming, chauffered car; from the instant he entered the little cell and sat down in the hard chair and looked up at the high slotted window in the outer wall, he had felt impendingly a swamping sense of guilt. For nowhere else, as in that little room, alone with Camack Patterson, alone with three modest shelves of books, a small rough desk, and a crucifix of pewter or some baser metal on the bare stone wall; nowhere as here had he so strongly felt how wrong it was to marry a woman he did not love. Looking at the bare stone floor, at the stones upon which the deacon must kneel daily without the benefit of carpet, pad, or cushion, he felt that surely there must be punishment somewhere for what he was about to do.

Eleanor Fite

Daddy, her daddy, had come in and said the groom was in fine shape. Her head was aching again. They had the assembly room for the acolytes, the place where the candle lighters and snuffers were stored, and in the corner there was a little extra altar with a nice gold cross on it and there was a half-opened closet with choir vestments hanging inside, and everywhere there were plenty of chairs. She sat on one. She would need a rest, a stretch in a nice sanatorium — somewhere where the aspirin was free and cold cloths would be put on your head and you could sleep for about a damned year. That was how she felt, she decided. She felt ghastly. Trying to look pleasant was bad enough. Trying to look pretty increased her pain. At least Mother would have to leave before long. The bridesmaids were sitting about giggling. Thanks to Mr. Lynch, they were all here way, way early.

Next time, she thought, I'll run the hell away and marry somewhere pleasant, like Acapulco or Venice, because this is a lot of superficial bull.

The reception — maybe that was what she needed. In my condition she thought, a few drinks couldn't hurt a thing.

She tried to think of things cool and green and far away, of restful things.

11

TOM McCUTCHEON
St. George slaying the dragon, the dragon either assisting the knight or trying to thrust the lance away, and nearly an hour to wait before the music starts — "But at least," he thought, "I'm in position, and able to rest my eyes by looking at the altar." He associated the church and the theater: Church and Theater, for the Church, he knew, was the birthplace of theater, was where the lying-in had transpired, where the birth of the drama had taken place in England, old England which was just at that time about to be Merry England. In the beginning they had only been trying to inject a little flavor into holy days, but the flavor of the holy day got out of hand. The *holy day* became the *holiday* and the jugglers and acrobats had to be put out of the church and into the street. Or, at least, this was one way to consider what had happened to clear the way for Shakespeare; Balaam had to come riding into the church on his ass, cursing, getting laughs out of the communicants . . .

Randomly. Thus randomly: his thoughts wandered. Cautiously he felt for the pistol under his coat. The pistol had shape and purpose in the midst of much confusion. And whereas before (long before), it had come to him that he would live forever; it came to him now that the other person, a younger Tom McCutcheon, was in some way a separate entity from this present self, now remembered as one remembers a friend who has since been lost track of, and has become a stranger. The young stranger, himself, had found a great mysterious well-being and a great good in all of life; found it all in an instant, in a great and illogical love of life and the continuum of life as it whispered about him in a barn at dusk. The reality of what he felt had lurked that long-ago evening in the smell of fresh dung overlying the ammoniac odor of rotting manure, and then he had gone on toward the house, convinced his mother was right, sure that through himself some great good was about to be accomplished in the world, and all because his mother had said to him: *"My dear Tom, it's time you took a wife."*

The wife he took was Adelicia — Adelicia Frick.

But he took a wife without realizing the significance of that which the mumps had almost taken, without suspecting what his father, Luther, by then long dead, had feared. He took a wife but she was not like Grandpa Tommy's Arkansas girl or Luther's wise and wealthy widow; she was not the prettiest gal in the whole territory, nor was she a mature woman who could bring him not only her own property, but property garnered from a previous marriage as well, to thus double his riches to the penny and acre; but Adelicia did have beauty Grandpa Tommy would have admired, and many refinements Luther would have respected in his aspiring, bookish way.

Adelicia Frick, whom he married when she was twenty, was a woman that he felt befitted him, a woman who equaled in splendor the rest of his trophies, including the gold key from Harvard; she matched, he felt, and equaled him and served as a proper adornment to his arm just as the knife, chain and key properly adorned his vest.

But Mother did not entirely approve. No. The history of Adelicia's family told him why. As Adelicia's father, as old man Frick had told it, Tom had put together the history in his mind. Old man Frick had at last supplied the final piece of information, telling it on his deathbed, how the Frick family came to Sligo County from Northern Indiana in 1870, coming from the north while the bitterness over the lost war was still heavy down south. They came for vague reasons, most of which died with the old man, with Elmore Hans Frick. But at least one reason Elmore came was because an older brother of his mother's, an uncle, had sent word to him again and again to come south and take over his farm. The old man promised Elmore Hans a whole section of land if he would move to the South and look after him in his old age. It meant Elmore had to sell out his pitch of acreage near Indianapolis. But finally, in 1870, he did sell out lock, stock, and barrel, except for two wagons and two teams and a dappled mare in foal with a horse colt which she dropped the April following that cold winter of 1870. The Fricks struck out for the South hauling their goods in the two wagons, going through the knee-deep snow; old Elmore Hans Frick, his wife, and his young sons who were fourteen and sixteen years old, Spence, the youngest, later Adelicia's father, and Andrew Thomas.

They came for several days and finally reached Cairo, Illinois, crossing the river on the ferry there for one dollar each wagon. Paw drove Mother's wagon on the ferry first and the boys, with the dapple gray mare hitched to their wagon, drove their wagon on behind.

But when the ferryman had shoved the boat off from the bank just a little way and had started raising his sails — when the sails started up — that was when the dappled-gray mare broke loose and went over the side and seemed to sink in the first plunge like a lump of iron. But then she rose and swam by them for a distance, trying twice to come back aboard in spite of the sails which still half scared her to death. And finally she swam the rest of the distance and staggered out awkwardly beside them at the landing. She stood shivering and snorting, with the broken halter hanging from her head. When their second wagon was loaded off, the ferryman tried to buy her.

PAW FRICK: You don't want that mare. She wouldn't pull the hat off your head.

FERRYMAN: How is that?

PAW: She won't work to harness. She wouldn't pull the hat off your head. I wouldn't sell her to you, that's all.

FERRYMAN: How is she to ride?

PAW: Why like a rocking chair; smooth as sweet milk. These boys now, they ride her all time. Don't even hitch her reins when they get off; just drop the bridle and there she stands till they come back.

FERRYMAN: I'll give twenty-five dollars for her, just like she is.

PAW: The season on the foal she's carrying cost twenty-five dollars! But now if you want her, why then I'll let her go for three hundred dollars plus the season on the foal.

The ferryman said no. And they were fourteen days and nights from the farm they sold in Indiana, fourteen days and nights on the road to Paw's uncle's place in Sligo County, Tennessee; having to cross Nickajack Swamp, which at that time lay eighty miles north of Somerton and spanned fifty miles across by a pole road, but which has long since been drained and cleared for farmland.

"You could, Godamighty! You could hear a wagon a-coming on that pole road, acrost them poles laid alongside one another and thick as a man's thigh, could hear a wagon two miles off, a-thundering over it . . ."

Like the iron tires of a chariot on the Roman high road ". . . a-thundering over it. And we was one entire night camped in the midst of the Nickajack Swamp with the varmints screeching after our mules and our mare, old Lady Gray. And it was after dark next night afore we come to the edge of that bottom, but Paw Frick hung a lantern on the tongue of each wagon and we went on by dark until we come out and off the pole road by a little old cabin. The cabin folks had heard us a-coming and had *saved dinner*. We went in and eat the best meal we had sat down to since we left Indiany, and I says: 'Where have we landed at?' And the fellow who owned the little cabin says: 'Tennessee.'

"How far to Sligo County?" says Paw Frick.

"I never been, so I wouldn't know," says his host, "but this here is the road. You ain't many days out from it now.' "

It was the road to Sligo County all right, but Paw Frick's uncle had just one hundred eighty-five rough acres in place of the whole section of land he had written his nephew about. It was the natural exaggeration of the man who feels himself getting old out in the woods, having no near neighbors and wanting to be looked after. Uncle Jude's exaggeration was that of the old man who feels himself failing. Paw Frick knew when he saw the farm they had been deceived, but the Indiana farm was sold and they had no choice but to stay. That first winter they lived in a tent. They sold the mare and colt in July for three hundred and twenty-five dollars and sent twenty-five back home to Indiana to pay the owner of the stallion his season fee, and Paw Frick nor his boys neither let the grass grow under their feet, but went hard to work trading, farming, blacksmithing, bee-keeping, tree-cutting, and land-buying and finally even storekeeping, until it was plain that the Fricks had German blood in them, that determined "comer" blood that would not rest so long as there was a nickel to be turned. The Fricks were the extraordinary kind of Yankees that didn't care who called them what, didn't care how close they had to live, as long as the future held out to them something in the way of dreams and plans. It became common knowledge that any tool a Frick owned had to be kept bright as new money. And being honest, the Frick men told the man who bought the mare and her horse colt (the colt was also a dappled gray and brought his buyer one hundred and eighty-five dollars while he was still a yearling) that the mare would not pull the hat off your head. She could be ridden, *but she would not work to harness.* And he, the mare's buyer, sold her next to a logger who said the bitch would either work or he would kill her: prophetic words.

Because in August the logger harnessed her and put her on the off wheel of his wagon beside the saddle mule and when she was through kicking all she had left on her was her collar and bridle. The collar was just one item more than she was left wearing that January day at Cairo when she stood beside the ferry landing with ice freezing on her and river water draining off on the iron-colored earth, the day she showed that she would not ride a ferry either, but would first drown. Paw had been willing to let her drown after the boys, Spence and Andrew Thomas, failed twice to haul her back on board, and when twice, she came in behind the ferry and reared up on it astern, rocking it and making such awful commotion the ferryman said:

"Just leave her be boys and if she drowns, then, by the powers, I'll *pay* for her!" When the ferryman yelled that Paw Frick had signaled the boys that they must relax and just hope she *would* drown right then and there, a thing which the boys half did, since they relaxed. But since the oldest, Andrew Thomas was just sixteen and his brother, Spence, two years younger, neither could hope she *would* drown. For both boys had watched her drop colts, both had ridden her and felt the summer wind cross their faces, felt it of an evening when the air was cooler in pockets of the earth about the Indiana farm, and they rode into and out of the pockets of coolness and beside the creek willows; they had ridden her, and both, deep inside, loved her fiercely, with something of a German's fierce, clean, jealous love; it was a feeling that their German blood gave them, such, that when she came across safe, over the whole freezing distance of the Ohio River, out of Illinois and into Kentucky, they were glad and proud.

When the mare's horse colt dropped fat as a butterball in April, they were again proud; when she brought Paw three hundred twenty-five dollars, including the season fee, in July, they were proud but they also were heavy-hearted to see her go, for they loved her.

"No," the youngest, Spence Frick, who was then fourteen years old, said. "No, sir, she won't pull the hat off your head." He was damn near to crying when he told her buyer that, but he had the Frick way of hiding what went on in his heart so that it did not always well right up in his face. Spence, Adelicia's father, confessed on his deathbed in Tom McCutcheon's presence, what he and his older brother, Andrew Thomas, had done to the logger who bought the mare from her first buyer. The logger's name was Much Fentriss and he had bought her and said: "This bitch will either work or I will kill her."

Much Fentriss said it because he did not believe she would not work. He said it because she was big and northern bred and he believed the gray mare had been pampered by the Frick boys until they just *thought* she wouldn't work to harness. Besides, Much was a veteran of Shiloh and had waded water up to his behind, backing through the swamp next to the field at Shiloh until somebody had let a horse go free by getting shot plumb down off of it, and Much had somehow got his behind out of the water and into the empty saddle in time to make it away with the last bunch who fought the delaying action. (The last bunch did not count General Forrest himself who went back just to kill two more of the enemy and show the Yankees he *could* ride through their whole confounded army and make it out again whenever he felt the urge, an urge he felt at Shiloh.) And so from this, Much Fentriss had concluded he was an expert on horseflesh. He believed himself to be an expert because a wad of horseflesh and a Minié ball had saved his life. What other conclusion could Much logically draw? Not that this made Much *thankful* for horses; to the contrary, it made him contemptuous of them, contemptuous even if he would have sacrificed the entirety of his private organs, including the surrounding hair (he had no kingdom), for a horse that day and instant in the swamp just behind the field at Shiloh when a comrade obligingly got himself shot off his horse just in time and just close enough by Much to save his life. From this single miracle Much concluded that he had a superhuman power over horses, and thus when he bought the dappled gray mare, he said it: he would work her or kill her. But he *meant* to *work* her.

But Much Fentriss had misjudged the Yankee mare badly. And so he allowed several assorted white folks and Negroes to be on hand when the mare started kicking that first time. And it was not that they laughed, because not one of them *would* laugh in the presence of Mr. Much at such a time, since they all loved life. But they sat very still, nevertheless, and watched very close, like the kids when Mama spreads icing on a new-baked layer cake. They every one enjoyed every second of it, from the mare's very first kick until her very last snort when she stepped free of what remained of the harness and the wagon tongue and the saddle mule. The mule was on his knees, like he couldn't believe any more than Mr. Much that what was happening was true, because the mule also thought Much Fentriss was the All Powerful. And yet that She which Much had put in beside him had merely put her head down and begun kicking the doubletree and then the mule himself and then the harness which flew to pieces in scraps, and then the air where he had been and the doubletree and the wagon tongue until it broke in four places. Then finally she snorted and stepped out, that She, and the mule waited for Much Fentriss to take her apart and bury her. The mule, kneeling, waited for the All Powerful to begin taking her apart with tree limbs. *But he didn't.* And the mule belched and almost swooned, because his surprise, on top of his bleeding, was almost too much for him to bear. And finally the mule, in amazement, stood up and saw Much Fentriss take hold of the She's halter and lead her off.

The horse mule didn't know that what he had seen was merely Round One.

Much Fentriss didn't know it, but in Round Three the mare was going to cost him more than her price and more than the harness and gear she would and had already ruined, and the mule she had partially crippled — even more than all of it.

Much Fentriss had said only: "Well." And it was thought for a second that the Yankee mare had him then.

But after a delay and some arranging he got help (there was plenty of it standing about) and passed a trace chain around her belly and took a half hitch with it about her lower jaw and hitched her in fresh harness to a fresh wagon alongside a fresh saddle mule. The first mule he stitched up and sent back to the barn. Then he hitched a pair of mules to the trace chain leading from the mare's jaw and clucked for all three mules to *get up.*

This time the mare just quivered and set her legs and after a time her jaw gave way and her neck snapped and she died on her feet without having strained at her harness enough even to pull the hat off your head; that was in August and it was the end of Round Two.

Round Three and the end of it all came in September about three weeks later when Much Fentriss was kicked clean out of his buggy into the road bed by two loads of turkey shot which liquefied the back of his skull. The double-barreled gun was fired by young Spence Frick and had been loaded by his older brother, Andrew Thomas, who knew just about how much powder charge the old gun could stand. Thus Spence Frick at fourteen did (as he confessed later) what the entire Union Army had not been able to manage at Shiloh. He did it by crouching in a pokeberry thicket near the dusty Indian summer roadside and letting off both barrels at once. When he picked himself up the team and buggy were already going away at a gallop leaving what was left of Much behind them in the road. In the aftermath of Round Three the head Negro in Much's logging operations, a blue-gummed man named Sam Garden, was hanged for the killing. But Sam Garden was a rash, uppity, smart-lipped blue-gum anyway, and he was hanged more for these back-talking reasons than for killing Much Fentriss. Nevertheless he *was* tried fairly and found dreadfully guilty. (Much Fentriss had been Sam's protector and when blue-gum Sam Garden mounted the scaffold he showed his final contempt for everything decent by first spitting on the trap door, next putting the noose about his own impudent neck and drawing the knot up snug under his left ear, and finally calling the hangman a pore-white son of a bitch loud enough so even *ladies* in the crowd heard — this Sam Garden did all by himself.)

On his deathbed Spence Frick complacently confessed how he had squatted in the purpling pokeberry thicket, amongst the stalks, waiting patiently by the roadside in the buzzing heat of the afternoon, waiting for Much Fentriss to finish dinner and take his nap and begin his return back to the bottoms. Thus at the end of the third and final round, Much never knew what hit him or why. "He just hopped" (as his dying killer said) ". . . off that buggy seat like a sort of bird and flopped down flat in the road and his rig which was drawed by two pretty good horses, but neither one worth nowhere *near* what that gray mare was, run off with the buggy and left him lay there like the no-account bastard he was." Old Spence told Adelicia and Tom while they sat by his bed the afternoon before the following morning when he died. He lay there with his thumbs propped together above the coverlet. They received his confession in the same casual spirit that it was uttered, and thinking very little of it, kept it to themselves. "And I ain't sorry till yet I done it," Spence Frick said.

Spence Frick had ginned cotton, married well, and educated his children to a certain degree of gentility. He presented the hand of his daughter, Adelicia, to Tom McCutcheon, passing on with her the Frick vindictiveness, the Frick patience, the Frick's unerring instinct for selecting that precise point by which the buggies of the Much Fentrisses will always pass, all unsuspecting, in short, for finding the pokeberry thicket by the roadside from which an unobstructed, liquefying shot at the back of the head will always be possible. And, wisely, Spence waited till the last possible moment to

casually and indirectly tell Tom McCutcheon all of what he
had presented when, as the bride's father, he had stepped forward with Adelicia and handed her over at the preacher's
casual inquiry:

"Who giveth this woman in marriage?" In handing Adelicia
to the preacher, who in turn gave her to Tom, Spence passed
on more than the groom bargained for. Spence gave the
groom a woman who had in her the living embodiment of a
certain Yankee sense of values, an entity which Tom Mc-
Cutcheon's mother suspected, resented, and even feared perhaps. Not that Mother came right out and said it; no, because Mother was not *that* type. Still she showed Tom plainly
enough that *she* felt he had married beneath himself, for after the wedding trip, when they had settled down to live in
the house with Mother, she played the organ fretfully on occasions and sang with a voice less sweet, less content, more
nasal than he had remembered from that soft mysterious day
when he walked down to the barn and believed that only
happiness lay ahead of him. It was true, that Mother had
told him to marry; truly, he *had* married a woman of beauty
and culture and some small estate, but still (and he realized it
even at the time), Frick was a name which did not have the
solid sound it should have had. It antagonized the ear a little
like coppered silver. It sounded like a thing too recently of
Indiana. And despite its money, there was less land connected
with the name than seemed quite meet and right. But above
all, that which Mother sensed most acutely (but did not say)
was that which the bride's father had held back from the
groom until the last possible moment. But Spence Frick
proved himself honest at the end by saying: "And I ain't sorry

I done it." A Frick never forgave, never forgot, never repented. Mother had guessed it: the Fricks were good people, but they were mean.

Mother died, Spence Frick died; sooner or later everyone died and carried off their objections and shortcomings into the grave with them. For (as he later reasoned) to be alive is to object, to stand flatfooted in the path of progress, to yell and dare it to run you down. "Human-kind comes into the world objecting" thought Tom McCutcheon, "and leaves the same way, objecting still, resisting; and each casket they lower in the ground is one more protesting voice silenced, one more squeak which will be heard no more."

Mother died.

Spence Frick said: "And I ain't sorry I done it."

The house burned and Tom moved to town with Adelicia, into the gentle ferment of Somerton, which by then had survived the century's turn and boasted a small opera house and a three-story hotel. Traveling theatrical groups arrived almost each month by train and staged their one-night performances at the opera house. Thus actors and actresses occasionally brightened the hotel.

The players came, the opera house flourished, and Somerton soon had its own group of amateurs, the Thespians, a dedicated group of young, married adults. The Thespians sprang across the home parlor tea tables and into the footlights of the opera house. They put on four plays a year, installed a dramatics course in the high school, and raised the forensic arts to an all-time high in Sligo County. It was happening all over America in 1914.

Tom and Adelicia joined the Thespians and followed the

lead of the group's leading lady, a maturing beauty with a
rich, haunting voice and a great "feeling" for the stage. She
was the wife of a much older man, Doc Adam Shafer, an ag-
ing scholar who did not attract much attention. His wife,
Madam, was the live one. She it was who led the Thespians,
who even, occasionally, wrote a play herself.

More for his size and appearance than anything else, Tom
McCutcheon became a leading man. And the year the Thespians broke up (because children were being born to the
players and because the world was changing, the last Thespian
production was staged in 1916), Tom McCutcheon played
opposite Madam in *The Runaway Marriage*. The Thespians
were in their heyday. It was a daring production in which
the leading man thrice kissed the leading lady. Madam
wrote the play herself and took the lead, playing Countess
Nora, an Austrian gentlewoman; Tom McCutcheon played
Alfred, a captain in the King of Prussia's Guards, a dashing
commoner:

COUNTESS NORA: My dear Alfred!

ALFRED: (*Enters in great agitation, kneeling*) My Countess! (*Takes her hand*)

COUNTESS: Love does not respect political boundaries; love
does not understand wars; love knows only the sublimity of
two hearts which will be joined though the very heavens
should intercede.

ALFRED: Dear Countess, please say no more. We live in
separate worlds, oh my love . . .

COUNTESS: Did you say "my love?"

ALFRED: Oh, did my tongue betray my heart! Nay, forgive the tangled faults of this tongue, so snared and drugged by the unhappy circumstances of birth and duty, that it knows not, sometimes, what sentiments it speaks.

COUNTESS: Forgive? My poor, my dear Alfred, my brave knight . . .

ALFRED: Stay, Countess! Say no more. I must tell you something. Time flits, time flees away, leaving this troubled breast (*lays hand above his heart*) more desolate than are all the deserts of Africa, more cold than all the arctic plains of ice.

COUNTESS: (*Alarmed*) What are you saying?

ALFRED: The king has ordered us to war. I must rejoin my regiment. We leave . . .

COUNTESS: Ye gods! So Soon? Alfred . . .

ALFRED: I depart before dawn, and will see your face in the red sunrise above the azure Danube; I will remember your voice and hear it murmuring in the wind — oh, *dare* I speak . . . ?

COUNTESS: (*Weeping*) No. No, Alfred. You cannot leave, and this cannot be true.

ALFRED: It's better that I charge the very cannon's maw; I could not be less happy.

COUNTESS: Do you grieve because of me?

ALFRED: Remember your husband, the Count.

COUNTESS: Do you love me?

ALFRED: The very stars feel my anguish. Oh, do not ask!

COUNTESS: Do you love me: say it!

ALFRED: Nay, I'll swear it, by the heavens! Sweet Countess, zenith of my world. You do well know I love you. Love you? Is *love* word enough? But I will not lead you to dishonor. I will not . . .

COUNTESS: My gentle Alfred, rise. I have deceived you. My husband, the Count is dead.

ALFRED: (*Stunned*) You are widowed then?

COUNTESS: Since last autumn. Ere now I did not dare disclose my widowhood, for fear . . .

ALFRED: Of your uncle, the Prince? Of royalty's disapproval?

COUNTESS: Of you, of your love!

(*They embrace as both rise, kiss, and break suddenly away.*)

ALFRED: (*Pacing the room*) Even so, it cannot be. The Prince would never give his consent for one of such low birth to wed his niece. Ye gods, it can never be! And at dawn . . . My Countess, we have this single night left in all the world, this lone and paltry night and then — Good-by!

COUNTESS: Your king means everything?

ALFRED: I am a soldier. Still . . .

COUNTESS: My trunks are packed. There is a train for Paris in an hour.

ALFRED: Then you will renounce your title?

COUNTESS: Will you renounce your career?

ALFRED: Career? My career can go to blazes! (*Laughing*)

COUNTESS: I'll sell my jewels!

ALFRED: Who knows, perhaps I'll be a cobbler or a tinsmith, a tradesman in another country; but to have you to be my wife I would be servant to all the world.

COUNTESS: We must hurry before the Prince, my uncle, discovers us. I'll leave a note. (*Writes, reading aloud*) "I have gone to Paris to marry Alfred; do not look for me. Your niece, The Countess Nora."

ALFRED: My Countess! (*They kiss and exit arm in arm.*)

SERVANTWOMAN: (*Entering with feather-duster, finds note*)

What's this? The Countess gone? Countess? Eh? Ah! A note addressed to the Prince. (*Picks it up*) Oh, well. I'll deliver it to him in the morning. (*Turns, with a wink to audience*) For who knows, just now methinks I heard the tires of a fleeing carriage, and this note may well contain the news of my lady's runaway marriage!

(*Curtain: Finis.*)

12

THE candles about the altar were being lit. Two young acolytes, fair youths in their robes, performed the action which like rising curtains marked the beginning of a play; *"The beginning,"* Tom McCutcheon thought.

The end of Madam Shafer's play, the beginning of something else. Madam Shafer pushed a fecund pen, could quote Oscar Wilde, had written a letter to George Bernard Shaw. She could look at a man and make him feel guilty. She kissed Tom warmly on the stage and he returned the warmth of her kiss and found himself whispering to her behind the curtain before it rose. At home, before Adelicia, he feigned disgust for the role of Captain Alfred.

On the final night of the play, Madam Shafer consented to a secret meeting. Her terms were harsh: two in the morning in the harness room of her carriage house (not fifty paces from where her husband might or might not be sleeping).

He agreed to her terms, given the day before, and no sooner had he agreed than his conscience put him to torture.

Stretched thus on the rack, he saw that the former intrepid bachelor was now become a married coward. And finally, he went to the trysting place as to his death and there lit candles as she directed, two candles which his trembling hands could scarcely manage, small lights which lit the closet-like room in the carriage house, small lights which acted on his passion like a paralyzing gas; for he had depended on darkness. Still worse, she had also made him promise in advance, not to touch her, so that once inside the room, when his heart calmed, it dawned on him that he was risking everything for nothing in return! A blind, dumb anger at himself made him a little faint. He sat down on a milking stool. She sat on a bench against the wall and looked at him from eyes which the candlelight made fully as dark and mysterious as she had intended. Madam was dressed romantically, in a new gown, with a black lace shawl about her shoulders. In place of his Captain's uniform (scrounged from old military chests in Somerton's attics, in place of that stage garb which was, nonetheless, a splendorous collection when he donned it and mounted to the boards) he wore his coon-hunting clothes, which he realized only when the candles were lit, stank a little. To go coon hunting in the spring rain! Adelicia would not be fooled. It was sprinkling outside, muttering on the slate roof of the carriage house, making tinny rivulets down the gutters. The rain made just sound enough to muffle her husband's footsteps if he came; and there was only one door to the room she had chosen. Dressed in his coon-hunting clothes which, he now realized, smelled like wet hounds, having put the clothes on because to go coon hunting was the only excuse he could dredge up for being out at two in the morning, he recalled that he hadn't told Adelicia. Instead, fearing that she would wake, he had left a note beside her lamp to inform her that he had gone out coon hunting for a while. But she, being a Frick, was from too far back in the country, he realized, on reflection, to believe him if she woke and found what he had written. He shrugged off the old coat and threw his hat down on the floor. All Madam Shafer's husband had to do now was walk in (when he saw candle-light under the crack in the door) and shoot the wife-poacher off the milking stool. There wouldn't be any point in stand-ing up. So Tom sat waiting for the old man to come with his shotgun, and she sat calmly looking at him out of her dark, mysterious eyes. Madam Shafer. She frightened him almost to the point of insanity. The two candles, in brass holders, were placed on an overturned feed barrel. Looking from her to the candles, he wondered what had driven him so passionately to insist — nay, demand! — that she meet him. He smelled the burning tallow, smelled his wretched clothes, rubbed his palms foolishly over the droplets clinging to his oiled boots and looked about the walls. They were hung with body harness. Everything was coiled and set upon pegs. Two dusty English saddles racked by the wall to his left; bridle bits, whips, reins, halters, everything — and everything in order. But for his fouled clothes, the scents of old wax and linseed oil, of leather and mould and rust, would have lulled his senses. As it was he sat stinking and humbled before her, perched on the milk-ing stool, like a dunce. He looked at his shadow on the wall beside her.

"I've loved you always," he finally said, feeling stale, fear-ful, uneasy.

"Always? But *how* can that be? We met just a year ago," she said coquettishly, drawing the shawl closer.

"Our souls knew each other long before that," said he mechanically, wondering how far he would go, how much he would risk for fifteen minutes of her on a horse blanket, when, at any instant Doc Adam Shafer might appear all taken with an irresistible notion to decorate his harness room wall with brains; brains being, as Tom could understand, a favorite wall-splattering stuff with husbands for a thousand generations.

But in spite of all Tom McCutcheon feared, it was no great task to say to Madam what she wanted to hear. He found he could answer her mechanically, all the while wondering where old Doc Shafer might be, all the while imagining something rather soup-like splattered against the pine wall in front of him where his shadow wavered.

"Our souls? Do you really think we have souls?" Madam Shafer asked.

"We must have," he replied, "for my soul has spoken — no, whispered to me of its love . . . for you."

"You're sure it was not some baser urge, some lower voice? I couldn't bear to think of being a slave to one who did not respect me. Oh, I *am* your slave already," she muttered, drawing in a passionate breath to sigh it sweetly forth again.

He whispered, hoping she would do the same: "I'm the slave; slave to your beauty," he said, trying to think of a way to break off the interview and get away. She refused to whisper as he had hoped. He could picture the old man outside the door already, listening. Doc was bound to hear her if she spoke any louder.

"Oh, Tom. Tom, what's happening to us!" she cried. She

dropped the shawl and knelt, taking his hands. "What is it? Can it be love?"

"Love?" he whispered, trying to listen, to detect some outside sound of stealth above the rain noises.

"Why must you whisper, darling Tom? Speak, *speak* what's in your heart!"

"Confound it, do you want to wake the whole damned neighborhood!" he hissed, snatching his hands away.

"Wake *whom?*" she said.

"Well, your husband for one. He'd be enough!"

"Wake Adam? Darling, don't be silly." She turned away and took up the shawl, standing up with her back to him. "I gave him sleeping powders. He'll snore till noon tomorrow. What do you take me for, Tom? Do you have to come dressed as though you were visiting a . . . Negress?" She turned on him, twisting the shawl in her hands, breathing with slow erratic fury.

"I'm sorry," he said. "I . . ."

"Sorry! I'll say you *are* sorry, the sorriest sight I ever saw. Take *me* for a fool, will you?"

"Not a fool, an angel."

"Is that any way to dress for an angel? Well, is it? You look like a tramp!"

"I'm supposed to be coon hunting. These are my coon-hunting clothes."

"You fool! You told her *that?*"

"No. I left a note. Well, what am I *supposed* to tell her? Should I say I'm just dropping over to see you for a little private rehearsal at two o'clock in the morning? Eh?" The thought of the old man lying in the house drugged, asleep in his bed, made him feel immeasurably better. "Well?" he said loudly.

"Oh, I'm sorry, Tom. It's just that I'm risking so much. You will think of something better than coon hunting won't you?"

That she envisioned a permanent arrangement mollified him. He stood up and she put out her arms. "I promised I wouldn't touch you," he said stiffly.

"Oh, hang the promise!"

Going home in the rain, it came to him how more at ease she had been than he. "Can it be an old story to her?" He wondered.

He gripped the pistol butt, passing his fingers about it in a caress. There was a stir near the church altar. The candles all had been lit. Now the organist entered briefly, placed his music upon the rack, made some minor adjustment on the instrument, and went out again.

Even the milking stool had been there for a purpose; the smell of the burning tallow and the guttering of the candles, matching light with sound; the rough canvas breeches he wore, his hiking knees, the high boots; and the rough bench behind her, where she had been comfortably seated before, now occupied by the shawl alone, and thus he had tasted a new actor's role and stared for a time at their shadows moving on the wall, at their single, unseparating blot.

A tall woman sat down beside him wearing a dress the color of lilacs, the pews ahead filling, the ushers solemnly, self-consciously erect in the hollow echo of congregated sounds, thump of a heel against the wooden side of a pew, a whispered comment behind him, a bald-headed man seated three rows ahead of him, and the lance, the face, the horse, the armor of Saint George, still lit by the sun, its light tiding over into the shadowed side, sunnyside to the left, to the west where lay the flat, burnished brass surface of the river, sliding passively south; and where he faced, north and upstream, and altarward, the cross of gold stood, erected in his line of sight. It stood nakedly, its metal arms pointing in symmetrically opposed directions; pointing the way on one side to the river and on the other eastward where the sun must appear once more in a few hours, coming over the wild low hill and striking with tree-dessicated light the now-darkened panes at his right hand, commemorative of the life of a saint (but unvitiated by dragons, and therefore dull).

At five-thirty the music, at six the wedding ceremony, at ten minutes after six the swift thrust of the pistol, its pointed explosion, the pitched-forward corpse and the red dark blotting of blood into the white cloth aisle beneath. The blot would be one-inseparable with the cloth, and would have behind it no wavering, as did that blot long ago cast by two candles against the unplatonic (albeit cave-like) wall of a harness room.

And to the right, east under the westerly slanting rays of the sun, throstling in its humdrum plain, there was Somerton and all the scenes which time had laid there. To the east lay Somerton where Much Fentriss, lean of flank, had left the buggy seat and hopped through the air dead before his face met the road bed, so mercifully had he been relieved of his miserable life. Spence Frick took care of Much Fentriss and

Spence's daughter, Adelicia, took care of Tom McCutcheon. *To the east lay Somerton*. And his thoughts floated and drifted about its location and his location, and Adelicia's location, which must curl like a question mark, for whether she were alive or dead, he did not know. It was not knowing which had made precipitate his reduction, just as the same sort of uncertainty contributes to the reduction of the mother who gets word her son is missing in action. The thought, that perhaps he is alive somewhere, wears her away. It is a process, he thought, like water dripping upon stone. When he dreamed of finding Adelicia, he always reached for her slender throat. More than once he had felt its silken tissue beneath his hands only to wake to the incredible realization that he was an old man, and that Adelicia *was* gone and would never permit him to find her. He could not have hated her so much if he had not loved her; he could not, had he not loved her, have been so jealous of the man who had taken her away ". . . to find a new life in which I can forget I ever knew anyone as wicked and mean and horrid as Tom McCutcheon."

Yet she was the same Adelicia who, but a few years before, had brought a warming pan for his mother's feet, when she lay dying, the same Adelicia Frick his mother had made Tom McCutcheon promise he would cherish and care for, the same Adelicia who had sat swollen-bellied upon their high bed (the bed had been Mother's) and combed her hair and then brushed it one hundred strokes, wearing her high-necked gown, the brush crackling in her hair, as though she were a fiery daughter of Zeus, as though lightning from her father's thunderbolts lurked in those sweet tresses. Strange, to consider that even then, she had been plotting what she would do. Adelicia had chosen her pokeweed thicket, her ambush in the midst of the purple stalks and the poisonous berries. She brushed her hair and waited, and he, lean and strong had possessed in her belly before him the refutation of all which Luther, his father, had feared. The fear was refuted just as, by then, Madam Shafer had also refuted the notion that she and Doc were sterile. Madam's male infant was three months old. And she had named him Gratt Shafer. Gratt, for gratitude perhaps? Did she say thanks to God for his son, and therefore call him Gratt? Tom McCutcheon was well pleased. He was as much as gone home to dinner as Much Fentriss was before him, and as much in the dark about having offended anyone as Much Fentriss before him. Tom had gone through spells when he believed Adelicia suspected him. He had more than once thought during the early months of the affair that Adelicia had caught him. And then he had grown accustomed to the danger. And getting hardened to it, he had gone to the carriage house as much as three nights a month. He learned to be gone only a short while and to be back soon. Or, other times, he feigned coon hunting and stayed out almost until dawn. After six months, however, Madam Shafer had called a halt to their secret meetings, and there could be no doubt that Madam's child was Doc's, not Tom's.

Thus the affair ended. Besides he was getting tired of her. The relationship had lost its old illicit flavor and was a sin gone stale. By now Doc's child had changed Madam's outlook. She was inwardly becoming respectable. Perhaps she was getting old. Tom didn't know. At any rate he was glad the affair was over. And Adelicia had sat in the bed and brushed her hair. And he had thought (watching her) that nothing could be as sweet as a crime gotten away with undetected. What he thought he had gotten away with seemed like the refutation of the childhood ghost hovering in the past's background, showing again and again that God will not let wrongdoers go unpunished. Either Father or Mother or God saw to it that as a child he got his comeuppance. But now he saw the fallacious superstition for what, really, it was. A smart man took his pleasure where he found it, but went about it in a common sense way, cautiously. He had gotten through it scot-free! It was like realizing a profit. He had speculated with adultery, and he had won. The victory was as sweet as it was deadly. It made him prize Adelicia all the more. *She* was the profit.

And then she left him.

To the east lay Somerton, which had shriveled for him that afternoon like an orange peeling tossed on the coals of an open grate fire. It had happened in January.

(The music in the church began. He hardly noticed it.)

Remembering Adelicia he thought: "I loved her." He had not really paid much attention to the organist when he came out, seated himself, and began. Now the music was rolling forth. The church was filled by it. The guests were gathered.

He continued thinking of Adelicia; Adelicia hadn't given him a chance to argue, to explain, to beg. He had come home that terrible evening from the farm, getting back to Somerton a little later than usual, to find the baby in the hands of her Negro nurse, squalling, and the nurse in tears herself when she saw Tom was finally home. He hadn't been able to think for the noise. It had been like something buzzing in his brain. He tried to shake it off and listen. The Negress had handed him the note, a note hastily done because Adelicia Frick had left him in a hurry. The baby had cried so long that by then it was rasping hysterically. He couldn't think, just then, much less read. Something, he did know, was terribly wrong. But in order to keep first things first he took the baby and tried to soothe her, putting the note temporarily aside. There was need of organization and order. He brought both these conditions about before he opened the note. His hands were already cold, *they* knew. His feet likewise were cold, and the condition could not be blamed on the weather. He had put the farewell note aside to take the baby. He sang and talked until she stopped crying and the maid came back with a nursing bottle of warm milk. He had been saying over and again to the Negress: "Nothing can be *that* bad." By convincing her, he discovered, as he handed her back the soothed baby, he had *unconvinced* himself. But at least things were quiet. His head was throbbing. She took the baby and he sat down to eat. (He had told himself that no matter what, he must eat.) But even though it was January, the month and the weather were not the cause of his cold feet and hands. Now fear was back in him. Sin and punishment, the concept that is never so strong as when it undergoes its sudden reiteration in surprise, confronted him now. He was afraid. Sitting at the dinner table he unfolded the note beside his plate.

When you read this I will be gone and there will be no use trying to come after me. And I'm leaving Patricia Jose-

phine for you. I hired a man *who could, to take me away from here. You flattered yourself that you could deceive me, well, you couldn't. Now maybe you can raise this girl. I can't, because she is part of you and you can do something horrible. You can commit adultery. But you did not deceive me from the first, and I determined that if any man ever did me as you did, I would get back at him. So I have gotten back at you. And so good-by. I loved you. But now I have found and am joining someone* who truly loves me *and he is taking me to a new life in which I can forget I ever knew anyone as wicked and mean and horrid as Tom McCutcheon. You are the Devil Incarnate and I am*

> *Your former wife,*
> *Adelicia Frick*

He had crumpled the note in his fist and hung his head above the empty plate and thought how unfair of her, and said to himself over and again, *how unfair, how unfair,* and now with the music roaring in his ears he thought of it all again. How little regard she had shown him, how little respect! There had been no compassion in her. The organ shook the church. He had kept the note through the years and brooded over it. He had taken to the Bible like a runaway slave entering the woods. He had even prayed, and praying violated something, but pray he had. "If I had caught her!" he thought. For months he had sent money to one private detective and then another until he discovered there were frauds among them who would lead a man on indefinitely with bogus clues to get his money. "If I had caught her I would have had to kill her on the spot; perhaps it was a good thing after all that I wasn't able to track her down, for then I would have had the murder of Patricia's mother on my hands, and I wouldn't want that!" But yes, where he was concerned, Adelicia Frick McCutcheon, wherever she might be, could thank heaven he hadn't gotten his hands on her again. Longingly, he caressed the pistol beneath his coat.

To the east Somerton, to the west the river, and north, ahead of him, he saw the altar and now from that direction he heard the music rolling out.

13

G RATT SHAFER
With Camack Patterson he sat listening to the music.
"Well," he said, trying to shake off a feeling of subdued uneasiness.

"What are you thinking?" Camack Patterson asked.

"Oh, I was just wondering. I feel like walking out the back door. I just thought how it would be if I left now, while there's still time."

"And just kept walking?"

"Something like that. Camack, do you think I'm doing the right thing?"

"Of course. It is sort of permanent though, isn't it? I thought the same thing myself. Maybe I should have brought a flask." The lawyer smiled nervously.

"No, I don't think a drink would help," Gratt Shafer said. "That wouldn't help."

"You've just got the last-minute shakes. The groom always does, they say."

"This church, all those people out there . . ." Gratt Shafer said. His words seemed to increase the numbness. His mind seemed to be unfolding like a blank sheet. It was a fabric, suddenly woven whole, unfurled suddenly into doubt. Only now did he discover it. "Why didn't I think before?"

"You'll be all right," Camack Patterson said. "Think about Eleanor."

"Okay. I am thinking about her, though. How much longer?" Through the high window of the deacon's little office Gratt Shafer looked at the sky.

"Don't think about *that*," the lawyer said. "That's what I'm here for."

"I was just wondering about the time," Gratt Shafer said. "Damn waiting anyway. I never did enjoy waiting."

"Try to relax," Camack Patterson said. He got up suddenly from the chair where he had been sitting and began to pace, as though measuring the dimensions of the deacon's little office. "You'll be all right once we get started," he said. "I guess you know this is a great moment for me, Gratt. I hoped all along you'd marry her."

Gratt Shafer looked at him. The lawyer paced to the end of the room and turned about. He had done the same thing when they were rooming together at Vanderbilt. He would exercise that way while studying for final examinations. It seemed just the thing to do now, to pace back and forth. That was the charming thing about Camack, that he did everything with a measure of grace. Gratt Shafer had always admired him. It was apparent that he felt very proud for Gratt now.

"Well, thanks," Gratt Shafer said. "Thanks a lot."

"When we go out," the lawyer said, "let's try not to look

too serious. Just calm and pleased, that's how we want to look."

Tom McCutcheon

Ah sweet mystery, mound of Eve with life inside it, inside her, and that mound from whence we all come; for all men, he thought, are born of woman.

He remembered the slow sweet days, the slow sweet measures of Adelicia's breathing, the happiest hours of his whole existence, from the first day when she got dizzy and had to lie down, from that hour when he began to know the mystery of that swelling mound and all its labyrinths wrapt about the seed child, about life. *His* life had been in her through those plodding months. He sang about the house. Her time came, he held his child, Patricia Josephine McCutcheon. (In a few weeks Adelicia, the child's mother would be gone, but he had not known it then.) There lies the bitter mystery, he thought, it's in the future which always, must ultimately be bad. The end of everything is lurking there: The end of us all!

He sighed. How unfair she had been!

He left all alone to raise the child; motherless but having her mother's black, straight hair and Adelicia's smile to taunt him sometimes. He gave thought to marrying again, but there was no mortal woman fit to tie so much as a ribbon in the child's hair. He dressed Patsy Jo lovingly in little black patent leather slippers with a strap on her tiny instep. Before he knew it Patsy Jo was in high heels and had turned out just fine.

The marvel of it was she *had* turned out just fine. And

then Gratt Shafer had corrupted and seduced her, had turned her mind, had violated the sanctuary of her body.

Eleanor Fite

If I could lie down, she thought, and sleep for about a century and have a cool cloth to my head. Well, there's the music going again. A cool cloth and a dark quiet room and about six aspirin; but not on your wedding day, not on your life.

Mother said, "You look beautiful. Kiss me."

She came close, her soft weathered old skin, lips to flesh, head still throbbing. Mother gripped her arms above the elbows and looked into her eyes, past the pain. "My baby," Mother said. Then she went out. They would seat Mother in a moment. The mother of the groom was dead, so there was only one mother to be seated. Down the aisle she would go, dear old weather-beaten Mother, and take her front-row seat on the left like the queen dowager coming into court.

If I could lie down, Eleanor thought again.

"How are you feeling, dear cousin," Cousin Emma said, "still rotten?"

"Still rotten," Eleanor said, managing all the restraint she could muster. "Oh, Emma, what would we do without you?" Eleanor thought: You snide little pudgy-bottomed bitch.

"It's nearly time," Cousin Emma said. The buzzer sounded and they went outside and around the church along the walk, going slowly, the colored maids, slender Annie Bell and plump Janie, carrying her train. Outside it was bright but the air was fresh and the green trees were calm and the sun struck into the side of the church, into the warm brown stone of it beside where they passed on the walk, and finally they entered the dark vestibule and there waited. The ushers already were leaving to go to the altar. Through the door as it opened she had a glimpse of the church, well filled. The music poured out of the door and was then muted as the door sank shut again. The buzzer rang and another usher went through the door, letting through another great trump of music, a medieval march of some sort.

How like everything in life, being born, graduating, dying — with the others going before and finally it will be your turn to go. It was almost, comically, like a graduation.

But it gave her a little twinge of fear. The pain was still in her head, but she didn't notice it as much. Then the buzzer came again. Her bridesmaids were going down. And now she turned to her father, to Fletcher Fite at her elbow, and took his arm. His gloved hand closed on hers.

"Well, the moment's upon us, Eleanor," Daddy said.

"Yes," she said. She smiled at him and thought: *Now it will be legal.* And said: "Next time I'm going to run away and marry. To hell with *this* again."

He smiled. But she hadn't expected *him* to be nervous. The buzzer gave three rasps.

"That's us," she said. They went through the door to the aisle. At its foot she saw Gratt Shafer waiting and lowered her eyes. Look demure, she told herself, not hungover. Sweetly, the music pounded.

Gratt Shafer

The world's womb reduced to the lobby of the Peabody Hotel, the rabble bathed, combed, clothed and benched for the spectacle on the horizontal bleachers of religion known as pews because once the railed-off seats had doors to enter by and were assigned and you took Holy Communion in order — nobles first — by rank. And down Eleanor came, whom he had met in the lobby when she was ostensibly waiting for a "friend" from Mississippi who was driving up. She came on, blonde Eleanor Fite, dressed in a shining garb that, with the diffusion of late sun through stained windows, made her half golden and half silver. And she moved into the shade past the final window and came beside him, only then looking into his face, but not as he discovered, into his eyes, even then, but somewhere beyond them. He turned with her toward the little minister and the altar. The little minister, made large by his clerical robes, began:

"Dearly beloved . . ."

Tom McCutcheon

". . . we are gathered together," said the minister, "here in the sight of God, and in the face of his company, to join together this Man and this Woman in holy Matrimony; which . . ."

McCutcheon sat tight-lipped, listening. He brought his hand out away from the pistol butt, damping the sweat from his palm against the black hat brim.

He thought: Rapist, seducer, I would not give two bits for the difference.

". . . I require and charge you both, as ye will answer at the dreadful day of judgment when the secrets of all hearts shall be disclosed, that . . ."

And with these words from the minister it came to him suddenly that the root of his misery lay all with Adelicia Frick. If he had wronged her it did not mean that he did not love her, and if she had wronged him, even so he loved her still. Yet there was no hope between where he sat and where the final abyss of death lay, that he would ever again hold Adelicia in his arms, for no, he would never see her again. She was utterly lost and he was, from that day of her departure, a man utterly damned and miserable, for whom the world was merely a hell in which, for more than thirty years, he had contrived to build himself a nest of sorts.

For (oh, God, he thought) he had loved and did still love her and there would no explanation or reason suffice to tell why. No reason nor explanation, he thought, remembering her, the very scent of her breath, the overbroad tilt of her hips, teeth that were not quite straight, slim white ankles, her straight nose with the almost invisible scar across its bridge.

And there was a book on his library shelf which from time to time, over the years, he had rediscovered, with her unmistakably strong, feminine handwriting inside its cover:

"Thomas Gideon McCutcheon, Christmas, 1916." A brief phrase which his eyes passed over the first time idly only to pause and cross slowly over again, for the book was the last gift he had received from her. It was *The Poetical Works of Samuel Taylor Coleridge,* a 1905 edition published in London.

Gratt Shafer

Said the minister: "Gratt, wilt thou have this Woman to thy wedded wife, to live together after God's ordinance in the holy estate of Matrimony? Wilt thou love her, comfort her, honour, and keep her in sickness and in health; and, forsaking all others, keep thee only unto her, so long as ye both shall live?"

Said Gratt Shafer: "I will."

A movement beyond the organ caught his attention. He glanced that way and saw the florist, Mr. Lynch, fidgeting in the shadows.

Mr. Lynch reminded Gratt Shafer of the irrational and outraged parent who because of a warped mind or a checkered past, hides behind a smile, frozen into his very tissues, the fear, approaching certainty almost, that something will happen between the gymnasium and home to the daughter he grudgingly allowed to go to the high school prom; who interprets into that bygone world (once *his* world) the most depraved and bestial connotations, and later can recall none of its innocence, none of its tenderness, none of its self-conscious pain. The wedding was Mr. Lynch's child, and his white-faced trembling grin, fading to a smirk, told Gratt Shafer everything.

Eleanor Fite

" . . . Wilt thou love him, comfort him, honour, and keep him in sickness and in health . . ." Precisely, thought she, why I am here, to marry him.

". . . So long as ye both shall live?" The minister finished on a rising inflection and stood before her, waiting. He was waiting for something.

"I will," she answered, feeling a little flustered, and thought: I'd *better* pay attention.

Tom McCutcheon

Said the minister: "I, Gratt, take thee Eleanor . . ."

And Gratt Shafer, repeating: "I, Gratt, take thee Eleanor . . ."

The book, McCutcheon thought, 1905 edition. His
thoughts began racing, woven about the sound of the words,
minister and groom, groom and minister. Adelicia he thought,
Adelicia!

More than once he determined that every trace of her
must be destroyed, the books she had given him burned, the
pictures of her (hidden away deep in an old traveling trunk)
put on the fire after the books. But the resolution had always
found him unready, weak. For when the fire blazed in the
hearth and the child, Patsy Jo, lay asleep in her room, when
the books and letters and pictures were gathered on the rug
to be tossed in and destroyed, his strength always failed. Taking up a book, he would lay it aside. Opening a picture (hoping that the image of her would discover in him such a rage
that its furious energy would, of itself, consign the whole pile
of things to the red coals and yellow flames before him), he
would look once again on her face.

She had a straight nose, not unattractive, but made straight
because as a small child she had tilted a rocking chair over,
and, striking her nose on the floor had broken it. An almost
invisible scar on its bridge was the only reminder, he recalled,
but she had been sensitive about it.

Looking at her picture, he would always find it impossible
to imagine that she was capable of the crimes of which she
was accused by his imagination. The very immediacy of her
quenched the notion that she could have committed a crime

against him. The sight of her always served to rekindle rather than quench his love. She had left him to raise Patricia Josephine alone, and yet —

Recalling those days after she had left him, days in which he lay motionless on his bed, when Starkey Poe walked the whole way into town to bring him whiskey and see after the baby, to do what he could, and yet . . .

Even to tell himself that at this very instant Adelicia probably was lying in the carnal embrace of her lover, knowing all over again what pain could come from the examination of the little mound of papers on the rug, even so, still he put each card, picture, book and letter carefully into the chest again, and walking with it out of the fire's hot glow into his icy bedroom, stowing the chest away under his bed again by the brash yellow light of the ceiling lamp, then taking the books back to the shelves in his study, he was reminded. Over the creaking midnight floors he went, putting all away for a few years, until, accidentally, he would again find something and recognize with a groan that it was of her, *"Adelicia!"* She was the devil that could never be cast out of him and he knew that her loss had made him a madman, that conclusions more and more rushed in now before reasons and reasonings. For years — decades! — he had been helpless, had lain exposed to the crash of anger bursting against him like waves hitting a sea cliff. In quiet hours his world narrowed until it seemed like the sky viewed from a slit trench. He sank lower, sinking farther and farther away from the world, sinking into a murk of hell and fiends. Until, finally, he lay in the bowels of thoughts that began, of urges that began, of inner howls of horror that began, all beginning suddenly and as suddenly truncating themselves and falling back into the abyss like the half-formed, abortive things they were: falling, leaving him exploded, wrecked, and desolated on the floor of death-wished-for and kisses remembered, waking, finally, to see the carpet beneath his knees, to realize that he had been praying.

Praying, for he would never see her again, "Our Father," no hope of that? Between now and the final abyss of death, he would not hold her even once, not once, between here and hereafter? She was utterly, utterly lost and from the moment of her departure he was utterly, utterly damned, living merely in a brand of hell, nested up in his misery like a rat. *"Who art in heaven?* Who could love a murderer such as I?" Eyes wandering toward the cross, idle, staring. He touched the checkered grip of the pistol. The bride was pledging her troth.

"With this ring," said a voice, "I thee wed . . . in the name of the . . ."

The minister was blessing the ring. "Jesus Christ our Lord. Amen," he said. The *Amens* echoed about the church, and as he began the *"Our Father,"* McCutcheon bowed his head. "Our Father, who art in heaven . . ."

14

TOM McCUTCHEON
What had seemed far away even as recently as that morning when he had left Somerton and boarded the bus for Memphis, now was very close. The candles about the altar stood flame-steady, the company, lined on either side in white dresses and dark suits, and at the center, the bride stood by Gratt Shafer. The ceremony was ending. He slipped the pistol out from his belt and put it under his hat. The woman next to him did not notice. He looked away from her, back toward the altar. The nerves in his arm began to twitch. The church emerged with a clarity that was almost dazzling. The depth of the nave, the carved, fitted arches of stone, as smooth to the eye as glass, enchanted him. And still the words fell, like the last bits of grain being poured from an almost emptied sack. I must not faint, he thought.

O Eternal God, Creator . . .

O Almighty God, Creator . . .

O God, who has so consecrated the state of Matrimony . . .

They were running faster now, toward the end.

He looked again toward the altar. The pair knelt and the priest began — "God the Father, God the Son, God the Holy Ghost . . ." *I must not faint.*

The gentle movement in a congregation which signals that it is almost dismissed, that it is preparing for dismissal any instant, came in a collective sigh, a relaxed sound behind him which tightened the hackles of his neck. He glanced at the face of St. George in the window and let his eyes follow once again the slope of the lance, where it had pierced the dragon's hide. With his eye he measured the leak of dark blood, black where the shadows were turning. And there again he saw the enigmatic claw of the dragon, gripping the lance, but whether thrusting it away or plunging it deeper? *There is the question,* he thought.

With the final *Amen* the organ burst into a roar of music and the bridal pair rose. The bride looked down for an instant in confusion while her train was turned, and as she did so the unprepared for, unrehearsed happened, as right there before her feet and in the sight of all, the fat little pageboy bowed gracefully and began to vomit, spouting like a stone cupidon in a garden pool. The bride and groom drew back toward the altar and the congregation leaned out over the aisle to watch the wretched up-chucking little boy, who hadn't the presence of mind to remove himself, but stood heaving and gagging above the mess.

Gratt Shafer

The pageboy and what the page had done to the floor confronted them as they turned around, he with Eleanor's hand already on his arm. Looking at her, Gratt saw that she had already decided not to walk through the mess, and he held back with her. As he checked himself he looked out at the full church, wondering what they must do, wondering when someone would *do something* besides watch the wretched gagging lad, wondering if it would be up to him, Gratt Shafer, to do something. The guests in the pews sat thunderstruck. Some were craning their heads to see and others were smiling good-naturedly. Then, halfway up the aisle, Gratt saw a familiar face, the figure wearing black made a sudden contrast, a dark shade in the midst of pastels. Gratt looked back that way again to be sure. It was Tom McCutcheon, sitting by the aisle, and instantly Gratt knew. The old man had him. Instantly he knew that McCutcheon *had meant* what he had said, for otherwise he would not have come all this distance. But come the old man had, and there the old man sat. And the other guests were unaware of what was sitting in their midst. They were thinking only of the page and the mess he had made; they were only wondering how an awkward pause in the proceedings would be resolved. Gratt glanced at the space between the first pew and the altar, where, to the left, he had come out of the hallway leading from the deacon's little cell, coming out with Camack Patterson behind him. But looking back at the guests, he knew he could not leave that way, nor would Eleanor be dragged out that way. Gratt Shafer knew he would stand there with Eleanor on his arm waiting, and then, because he had to do it — for no other reason — he would smile and walk up that aisle and all but press his belly against the muzzle of the gun or the point of the knife, whichever one

McCutcheon might be carrying, because, now he realized at last, drawing a deep breath, that the old man had him. And Gratt thought: *Do something.* But nothing changed. Not even the faint, funereal odor of flowers.

There was nothing Gratt Shafer could do. And he looked at the pageboy and back again at McCutcheon. The old man sat calmly, like a gambler who has just won, a gambler who had figured it out all along that he *would* win. It was a *sure* calm, a *determined* calm. He had the grave look of someone holding a gun he is ready to use. While Gratt Shafer watched, McCutcheon calmly slipped on his glasses.

It came to Gratt what the old man, what McCutcheon would think, would be thinking now. Thinking: *"There Gratt Shafer is with the money he married and the society he married in place of Patsy Jo. There Shafer has it at his side and Shafer has to come up the aisle with it, just like I knew he would, Shafer has to come. So come ahead, you son of a bitch, and see now whether Tom McCutcheon meant it or not, meant what he said, come on now and see. Or show what a coward you really are, Shafer. Come or let us all see, all these big society folks you were so anxious to be among, to be one of yourself."*

Gratt swallowed hard. It was like swallowing the words. For he could almost hear them pouring out when he looked at McCutcheon, at the black suit and the battered glasses. They seemed to pour out at him, the words the old man must be thinking, pouring out like the organ music, rushing out. And he thought: *Do something.*

But the aisle was the only place to go. *He has me,* Gratt Shafer thought.

Mr. Lynch

"Ah!" the florist cried. "God damn it!" And, turning, he rushed back into the rear corridor behind the altar, finding it as dark there as a cave. He tried to yell loud enough to make his voice carry above the sound of the organ, but it was no use. No porter appeared. In desperation he burst into the choir's dressing room. Their robes hung supinely clean in an open fronted closet against the wall. He snatched one out, and still running, but no longer yelling, dashed past the organ and then braking suddenly, walked slowly out and majestically folded the robe down over the vomit. Now rising from his stooped-down position, he suddenly grabbed the boy and pulled him kicking and struggling out of sight, back into his alcove, past the organ, which by some miracle was still playing as though nothing had happened. Panting, he held the little brat, who continued to kick and fight. When Mr. Lynch could stand it no longer, he let his feelings go. "Little bastard!" Mr. Lynch whispered fiercely to himself: "Little bastard, little damned bastard!" He could have throt-tled the boy then and there. He leaned out to see the bride's train pass over the crimson choir robe, white above red. They were on their way up the aisle, no thanks to the page. It seemed to Lynch then that she slipped and fell. Then both were down, both bride *and* groom. A great, unaccountable cloud of smoke appeared in front of them. My God, what next! thought Mr. Lynch.

Tom McCutcheon

There was no way of clearly seeing through the smoke. The bride had been smiling. He had waited until he could see her fingers, clearly outlined on Gratt Shafer's coat sleeve where she held his arm. The organ had been roaring with a rapid and militant urgency. He had waited until he could see her white fingers clearly, thinking how much longer the aisle seemed than he originally thought when first he measured it with his eye. Gratt Shafer's face had been gray. Gratt Shafer had been wanly smiling, but even as McCutcheon raised the gun the smile vanished, disintegrating at the mouth and spreading in a paleness that extended into the very roots of his hair. Gratt Shafer had almost stopped. From the corner of his eye McCutcheon had seen the woman in lavender, on his left, recoiling, striking his hat as she did so. He grabbed after the hat and shot at the same time, and he thought he was able to see in the instant before the smoke rolled up, a small black stain where the bullet had struck the aisle cloth at Gratt Shafer's feet. He fired again, this time into the smoke and this time saw something fall (a whirl of white) and saw too that they were leaning out into the aisle again, again wondering what had happened. Vaguely, despairingly, he wondered if he could have missed his man entirely. They had been so close, had been on him, despite the greater length of the aisle, sooner than he had expected. There had been no time.

"No time," he said aloud, "no time to take careful aim." His hand had been cold, had pressed uncertainly on the trigger — he turned to leave — the gun had jerked unexpectedly in his hand, and then the second shot had been made through that cloud of smoke which he already smelled, pungent with sulphur. He had known the cloud would form; still it had confused him. He was into the aisle, waving the pistol in front of him, seeing them fall back away from him like a crowd of devils challenged with holy water. The cloud, he thought, seeking excuses; the cloud, the organ's tremor, the screams, the suddenness which the pistol had gone out of control. It left him confused, as it were, stumbling about in a mist. Still waving the guests back out of his way he began to run, going straight back through the inner doors and never pausing, flinging back the heavy outer doors and going down the stone steps and around the corner of the church to the right, making for the low wall and the wooded slope. He reached the wall and pulled himself over it, finding it higher than he had expected, and much wider across the top. He still held the hat, which he had snatched up from the floor, and he carried the pistol, carried both through the snatch of vines and the sting of briars in his face, fending his way with the hat as he tripped and fell across the ditch at the bottom of the slope and, half crawling, half running, measuring his direction by the slope of the grade, continued up hill. The thicket gave way to open spaces beneath the trees, carpeted with dry, brown leaves. He stopped, held his breath for an instant, and knelt to look behind him. There was a crash in the thicket below. He turned again and ran a few yards up the slope, stopping to listen, trying to hear above the ringing in his ears and the pounding of his heart. His pursuer came on through the thicket. Tom McCutcheon looked about him. Twenty paces up the slope a fallen tree made a rampart. He ran and flung himself down behind it. He cocked the pistol and laid it on top of his crushed hat. Now he drew out his handkerchief quickly and took off his glasses. He wiped them hurriedly and put them back on. And now he took up the pistol for a practice sighting down the slope. Just then the man who followed him came out of a thick grove of vine-woven saplings. It was the blond young man with the high forehead who had stood beside Gratt Shafer, who still wore his cutaway coat, who crouched, looking about him and had on his face a smear of dirt, perhaps where he had fallen coming over the wall.

Tom McCutcheon steadied the pistol with both hands, and aimed at the young man's heart. The sights wavered. He paused and held his breath, sighting the pistol again. Now he squeezed the trigger, and again the gun jerked in his hand and the smoke hung before him. The sound flattened out down the side of the slope and re-echoed loudly. He heard his pursuer running. Then there came a sound, a crash, as though the other man had fallen. Then silence. The smoke moved slowly upward and aside, thinning as it rose. He cocked the pistol and waited. The suddenness of the other's shout frightened him.

"McCutcheon? You missed me! You hear?"

He turned and crept slowly up the hill, trying not to make noise in the dry leaves. The other man moved too, scrambling recklessly up the slope, throwing himself behind one tree after the other, calling loudly. The voice taunted him.

"McCutcheon! You missed!"

McCutcheon stopped behind a tree. There was a sound, then a glimpse of movement. He fired again. Again the cry rose. "You missed, McCutcheon!"

From far below, as though suddenly released from the very earth's torpescence, there came a brawl of sirens. With the last of his strength he climbed toward the top of the ridge, where a low bluff of stone flattened out again to a shelf-like plot dominant with high trees. Tom McCutcheon knelt behind one of the largest of these, breathing heavily. His pursuer was making an animal of him, tracking him down, worrying at him from a distance like a hound scenting his quarry.

"McCutcheon!" The voice was much closer now.

"I'll kill you," McCutcheon gasped. "Stay away!" he shouted. He paused, shocked by the hoarse, inhuman timbre of his own voice.

The reply was clear, taunting. "That's four, four shots, McCutcheon! You have two left."

"I'm warning you!" McCutcheon cried. From behind the tree he looked down the slope. There was no one in sight. The sirens had come closer now, the vulgar caterwaul seemed to be in the very church yard itself. Shouts lofted from below. The sirens ceased, then started in the distance again, joined by others, now boiling like a pack in full cry. He shuddered. And the taunt came, again clear, again loud.

"How does it feel to be a murderer? How does it feel to shoot the wrong person, or did you *mean* to kill her? Huh, McCutcheon?"

He pondered. "A trick," he thought, "the same as knocking on the front door of the building and then running around to the back and grabbing the man as he tries to escape. Yet . . ."

"You shot the *bride*, the innocent, McCutcheon! You bungled!" the other said.

"You're lying!" McCutcheon screamed. "I killed Gratt Shafer!"

"No, you missed, missed him clean, like you missed me!"

"You're lying," Tom McCutcheon said. But the screams rang in memory's guilt. *Those shrieks,* he thought. And the truth snatched at him, struck in him like sharp hooks. He stood up and scanned the trees. He held the pistol cocked again. The other, the young man, broke from behind a tree and sprinted to a closer one. McCutcheon could hear him panting now. It had all been so clear, everything had seemed so plain. He tried to rearrange the logic of his thoughts: "Codes," he muttered, "his code and mine, in opposition, so that like two implacable forces . . . yes, exactly, that was it." He looked down at the pistol in his hand, remembering Luther, his father, the burst of smoke and the splintering snag, the slivers of wood. The pistol, was it at fault? But there could be no blaming the pistol, and it had been loaded just so . . . "Then what, then who," he asked himself, "who is to blame?"

"The innocent, McCutcheon, you bastard! You killed *her,*" the other man screamed. "I'm coming after you, McCutcheon!" At the sudden sound in the leaves Tom McCutcheon raised the pistol and fired at the running figure. Then he began to sob. The sounds came out of his constricted throat like wolfish groans. Somewhere there was Honor, shining in a white, a brilliant light . . . Somewhere. And somewhere heroes . . .

And somewhere heroes pushed forward recklessly, handsome and comely men, horsemen riding upon horses, in splendid attire . . . all of them desirable young men, captains and rulers, great lords and renowned, all of them riding upon horses. Dear God!

And she doted upon their paramours and oh, such re-

membrance — how to forget the lewdness of her youth, see them bruising her! her youth . . . and they defiled her and she was polluted and her mind alienated . . . And, oh, they set against thee now with buckler and shield and helmet round about. He despaired.

"My poor dear Alfred, my brave knight!"

He cocked the pistol.

15

CAMACK PATTERSON

He was running when Tom McCutcheon fired the fifth shot. It passed near his head like a whisper and he ducked, looking at the spurt of smoke hung like a plume beside the big tree up ahead, smelling the burnt and faintly sulphurous odor of the other shots riding over the sweet mustiness of the rotting leaves, and thought: *When you duck it's already too late, because by then if you're going to get hit you are already hit, yet still you duck anyway.* And he went forward flat on the leaves and rolled in behind a big beech tree, huddling up close to it, so close his cheek rested against the smooth silvery cool bark, and he cried out again: "Missed!"

He did not know why he had followed Tom McCutcheon. But in the church he had seen the smoke and wondered at it, running up the aisle to where Eleanor lay with Gratt Shafer kneeling over her, and the smell there was very strong and very acrid. He had to run then, and without thinking had dashed past the swirling smoke and seen the tall old man slashing out with the pistol while the guests fell back and over and behind each other out of his way, with no time for their faces to show terror, everything for them being the movements of bodies in a very businesslike and very determined jostling backwards, to get entirely out of Tom McCutcheon's way. The old man moved with almost unbelievable grace, bounding in long strides to the door, bursting heavily against it, never pausing, but bounding still in an unbroken stride, the door cracking back loudly like a mainsail jibed by accident in a high wind, whipped out with pure unshackled force, all unprepared for, and without warning. And following him, it was almost as if Camack Patterson were sucked forward in a backwash that allowed nothing, not time or thought or even realization's brief dawn at the swampy edge of the mind's horizons, nor anything but this swift, all but unwilling pursuit of a stronger will and a greater strength, drawing explosively away. Ahead of him the aisle constricted with people moving in confused directions, and he went through them brutally, muttering: "He must pay for this! He must pay for this!" Dashing out of the church, he had been barely in time to see the old man sprinting for the wall, going over it like a black cape snatched suddenly out of sight by an unseen hand, and his last impression was the quick memory of the akimbo runner with hat in one hand and pistol in the other, none other than Tom McCutcheon, who until then had existed for him only as a comic improvisation, a certain unlikelihood, a sure improbability. He was not so much angry at Tom McCutcheon as he was at the now palpable failure in himself, at the obvious and unaccountable error in his calculations. For here was the gambit he had dismissed in the beginning, yet it had not been successfully ignored out of existence. It was real, alive, destructive, and subject to no rules or laws or rulings, deaf to appeals and pleas, blind to all fear of punishment and inexplicable, totally without justice or logic, unpredictable as the wind itself; like a cockeyed man, aiming one place and striking another; like the chess player who cannot be beat; not because he is too brilliant, but because he is too stupid, lacking even the small intelligence required to lose. And it was this that he, Camack Patterson, had flattered himself he could organize and direct, like a simpleton proposing to organize forty farts into a crack drill platoon, in short, a stinking impossibility!

And only when the old man fired at him the first time, only then had he been frightened. He had flung himself down with a cry and lain shuddering behind a tree, for the first time glimpsing in himself the adumbral image of little death, and then knew the old man would kill him if he could. But even then he could not give up the pursuit. Something still drove him to his feet, although a little wiser now, a man more cautious, who crouched close to the fungous woods floor and smelled the turfy rot clutched up in his fingers as he sprinted and clawed forward, taunting as he went, driving the old man up the hillside ahead of him. And at last, when Tom Mc-Cutcheon answered, he heard anguish and knew, on that instant, that the old man, his quarry, was hopelessly rattled, and finally, that the old man was now all but defeated.

But if the smell of the fifth shot which reached Camack Patterson now — if the wretched sobs which he heard were those of a broken and defeated man, it was (he knew) none of it any winding sheet or death knell for what had created Tom McCutcheon, for to destroy this old man was not to destroy his improbable world, his inherited Creator.

He cupped his hands to his mouth and shouted. "You've got one more shot, McCutcheon!" The angry sobs continued, and prudently he wondered for an instant whether Eleanor Fite Shafer were really dead. Then ashamed, he pondered rashly, and saw her dead then, and felt her incredibly and horribly dead. The image turned his fear to his wished-for rage, turned it very coldly. "McCutcheon, I'm coming after you," he said.

He rose deliberately to his feet and leaning against the cool, smooth beech bark, leaning outward, measured the distance to the tree behind which the old man was hidden. A final effort would bring him to the tree — twenty-five paces perhaps. Then, methodically, he calculated: To reach the tree will require ten seconds . . . or less.

He paused to listen. The sobs had stopped. Crouching like a sprinter, Camack Patterson sprang forward, running. At the sound of the sixth shot he reached for the ground and rolled, and knew he was not hit, triumphantly thinking: His last shot . . .

And he was up again and running ready to grapple with the old man, to kill him. He reached the tree and leaped past it. Then suddenly he stopped, panting, and a second time saw what he had not expected. For Tom McCutheon lay stretched on the unkempt ground, the old pistol beside him, blood pooling from beneath his head into the leaves. He had put the last bullet in his brain. Camack Patterson sighed and taking out his handkerchief wiped his sweating face and then wiped his hands. He put the handkerchief away and leaned one hand against the scaly hickory tree. At its base were fresh cuttings, nut fragments dropped by a new generation of squirrels. There were no more sirens, no more pistol shots to explode the quietness. Birds once again shuffled in the leaves nearby. "You old fool," Camack Patterson said quietly, "you old crazy fool."

He turned, making his way back down the desolate slope, over the debris of rotting limbs and logs and finally to the thicket of vines at the wall. A little beyond it the crowd waited. He emerged in the face of its commotion, a sound that died as he hauled himself up over the wall and went slowly past them to the police, the reporters, the photographers — all of the solemn men, who now set out with him in a little band, followed at a little distance by the curious crowd, retracing his and McCutcheon's path into the woods. The trail was plain.

BOOK THREE
❧❧❧❧❧❧❧❧❧❧❧❧

16

AS LONG as I can, Toonker Burkette thought. He stood on the steps leading down in front of the hospital, where the big shots had just gone, watching, as long as he could, the big shots leave, thinking:

Dusk and street lamps coming on, just flashed on and their snappy driver holding the door open for them, closing the door and getting into the driver's seat now. And now they leave to go wherever it is that the big shots all go when their only daughter has been killed. They go home probably and the other big shots go piling over to see them and say how awfully sorry they are, because *awfully,* that's the only big word they have to know to make conversation. The liquor will flow with the tears.

So Toonker Burkette thought on the hospital steps in the dusk of that evening, the red glow of it, the rust glow of sunset when summer is starting and the kids are playing old man on the sidewalk and tree tag, yelling off somewhere under that red sky: I go back inside the hospital and find the phone booth and make the call collect, remembering even when I place the call and listen to long distance getting the McCutcheon house on the wire, remembering how it is to go to a snappy big-shot wedding and have the ringside seat two rows behind Tom McCutcheon, to honest-to-God *see* the old man stand up there and do the trick, first the smoke and then hearing the next shot and more smoke and the blood coming out of her like a fountain, a busted ram jet pump, Gratt Shafer laying on top of her without hands enough even if he was an octopus to stop the blood squirting out of her, the girl yelling and the big shot guests stampeding out of there like so much livestock making for the high ground. Gratt Shafer is like somebody trying to cap off an oil well with his fingers. That's what she is, an oil well that Shafer tries to save because he knows if he can't stop the blood there isn't anything in it for him, not a thin dime out of the Fletcher Fite vault will he get if he can't stop her from bleeding. Then at the hospital the surgeon couldn't stop it either, so that when I got there she was already dead and Gratt Shafer was already gone to his best man's house and only the big shots, Fletcher and Mildred, were there, Mr. and Mrs. Fite, and I says: "Well, I am awfully sorry about this whole terrible incident," and Mildred bursts out crying again and the surgeon keeps trying to explain out there in the corridor about this and that other thing which they had hoped might save her only when they got inside they saw it wasn't any use, that she had lost too much blood in the first place and was in shock and the old soft lead bullet had come apart inside of her, not like today if you get drilled with a copper-jacketed bullet which is nicer and cleaner. And Fletcher Fite keeps saying: "I understand. You did all you could do. I'm satisfied of that." All Mildred says: "I can't believe she is dead, I can't believe she is." And I says: "I am *awfully* sorry, *awfully* sorry about this terrible incident." And Fletcher Fite says:

"Doctor Burkette, Doctor Black. Doctor Black is Chief of Surgery." And I looked up at him, he was tall and shaggy-browed with big hands and a stoop in his young shoulders. I shook his hand and he shook his head just once, his eyes saying what he couldn't say about how bad this whole thing was, his eyes blue and young like his face and shoulders, one of the smart-aleck head-of-his-class types, that will get to be chief of surgery is what I think looking at Doctor Black. I go down to the corridor corner where Doctor Black shakes hands and says good-by to us and then down to the front entrance and outside where that sunset is burning the distance and Fletcher grabs my hands and says good-by and Mildred says how kind of me to come to the hospital. *As long as I can,* Toonker Burkette thought, *forever, I'll remember this day.*

And the phone rang and rang and finally it was Mattie French who answered it. Patsy Jo had answered the first time Toonker called, the time he called from the filling station across from the church to tell Patsy Jo her old man had blasted his brains out up in the woods and probably had killed the girl Gratt Shafer had just married, anyway she had been taken to the hospital and they had taken McCutcheon's body out of the woods, yes, that was right, her old man was dead and Gratt Shafer was all right and Eleanor Fite was probably dead or anyway dying if he knew anything about what ought to kill somebody.

Mattie answered and Toonker told her the body would be brought up in an ambulance, McCutcheon's *remains,* because it would have meant a delay if he, Toonker, had tried to put it on the train and Mattie said okay when would it get there and Toonker said well it would get there probably in the next three or four hours, however long it took to get it prepared, which he didn't know anything about. What he called to say in addition to the news about when Patsy Jo's old man would be coming back into Somerton, his *remains,* was that Eleanor Fite was dead, that the old man had made a good job of it even if he had missed Gratt Shafer. How was Patsy Jo taking it?

"As well as can be expected," Mattie said. Then she wanted to know when Eleanor died and Toonker told her the details, from the beginning of it in the church until Toonker, himself, walked out and went up the hill with the police to McCutcheon's body lying in about two gallons of blood, to when he called the first time and told Patsy Jo, to when he came to the hospital and missed seeing Gratt Shafer only by about five minutes, to when he talked to the big shots, to now, when he phoned. How was Patsy Jo taking it, he asked again, remembering when he did so that he had already asked once.

"She cries a while and then she is quiet a while. She's going to take a sedative," Mattie said. "The old man was all she had left in the world."

"Yeah, that's the truth," Toonker said. "He was all in the world she had left. Will you tell her the girl died?"

"I'll tell her. I'll wait till the right time."

"Maybe you ought to tell her now. I can hang on here if she wants to know anything else."

So Mattie French agreed and put the phone down. She came back in a few moments.

"She said to tell you thanks for calling to let her know the news," Mattie said.

"Anything else? How did she take it?" Toonker wanted to know.

"She stopped crying and looked at me, and then she said: 'I'm glad the bitch died.'"

"She said: 'I'm glad the bitch died?'" Toonker said.

"Those were the exact words," Mattie said. "She's glad the other woman is dead now. I think it helped her some to know the Fite girl died. The old man was all in the world she had left."

"That's true," Toonker said, seeing it all clearly now, seeing what really had happened and what, truly, he had seen in the church. "I don't know as I blame her for feeling like she does," Toonker said. "You tell her that for me."

"I'll tell her," Mattie French said, and then she said good-by and he said good-by and hung up the phone, coming out of the stale little booth and going on out of the hospital to the steps, where the sunset was almost faded to night.

All his life he had wanted to see something — a wreck with the dead lying freshly slain upon the highway would have sufficed — but what he had now seen outstripped Toonker Burkette's wildest dreams of the brutally exotic. Nothing touched it, unless a tale his Grandfather Burkette had been fond of telling could compare. It had been back when Grandfather Burkette was a young man. A wandering preacher had come to the Sligo County jail and converted a murderer being held there for execution. But in baptizing the criminal the preacher had been carried away by a feeling of loathing for the evil man he held submerged. The preacher had drowned the prisoner; and Grandfather Burkette, who had been part of a curious mob outside the jail, had rushed inside with the others just in time to see the killer's body being lifted from the wooden tub.

Not even the lights in the operating room or the green uniforms of the attendents or the smell of the place, the chemical odors, nor the weeping desire of her parents — none of this, Gratt Shafer knew, could prevent Eleanor's dying, for if the old man's aim had been faulty, it had at least been true where Eleanor was concerned, so true that she hardly knew what had happened from the moment she went down until the moment of her death, when the bright lights in the emergency operating room went out.

That was the signal that she was dead, when the lights went out, and there was nothing he could do or say to bring her back or to bring any comfort to those who mourned her. She was simply dead, and her murderer or executioner, whatever you wanted to call him, had run up into the woods and blown his own brains out. It was, in the final analysis, a crime which left no fugitive in its wake to be arrested, tried, and punished, which instead left Gratt Shafer himself feeling like the fugitive, feeling all a fugitive's guilt, but having nowhere to go, and no one to turn to for the punishment which now he felt should be forthcoming.

Camack Patterson was in the corridor. He had come quietly, and had waited, Gratt now realized. He had stayed to the very last. They turned and went out of the hospital together, to the lawyer's car, and then to the apartment on Carrington Place where they spent an hour in its alien rooms, Gratt wondering what he must do, Camack saying little or nothing.

Gratt Shafer fought inwardly now, looking at the chambers in which he and Eleanor would have lived. He fought back a sense of futility; he fought against fear. He tried, but could not rid himself of the terrible notion that if the old man's aim *had* been true it would be he who now would be lying dead and she, Eleanor, who might have come to this place where they were to have lived together.

"You don't mind if I say 'good-by' do you?" Gratt Shafer asked. He was taking a final look at the white furniture and the pastel rugs, at her portrait over the fireplace.

"Take all the time you need," his friend said.

"There's no comfort, not anywhere," Gratt said. He walked to the mantelpiece and looked up at the portrait. Where is she now? he wondered. Why did *she* have to be the one? She had put her arm about him when the portrait was hung there, a portrait painted when she was nineteen. She had worn the blue colors even then, making him think again of skies, flowers, and glacial ice. He saw all the cool composure of her features, hiding the real person, hiding the lonely girl who had put her arm about him and kissed him on the neck — impulsively, saying with the kiss: "We're going to live here!" And it came to him that he had murdered her, he, and no one else. No, not Tom McCutcheon. McCutcheon had only been the instrument, and McCutcheon himself was dead. What Patsy Jo had said of him, he thought, was true. He,

Gratt Shafer, had always been, in truth, an accident going somewhere to happen, a mistake that had been born and raised anyhow. Patsy Jo McCutcheon would be thinking what a fool she had been ever to become involved with him. For the first time he felt tears. They broke, and ran on his cheeks.

"I'm sorry. God, I'm so sorry." It was Camack Patterson, beside him now. "Gratt . . ."

"I'm all right," Gratt said. He gritted his teeth and wiped his eyes. "Let's go," he said. "I thought if I came here . . . I don't know what I thought."

They walked out, and he left the key in the lock. They went to Camack's house, and finally settled in the kitchen. Camack poured them each a drink and sat beside the kitchen table pulling the sticktights off his trouser legs and dropping them on the reddish tile floor. He told about McCutcheon again, how he had chased the old son of a bitch up through the woods, how he overtook him at last, and found him dead.

"And then I came to the hospital. It was pretty hard to face Mildred and Fletcher. I had to tell them about the old man, who he was."

"What else did you tell them?"

"What else could I tell them? It's hard to believe he really did it. It's something I keep trying to realize . . . Gratt, *why* did he do it?"

"Because he thought I was doing his own daughter a dirty trick, because he imagined things. I don't really know. Tom McCutcheon lived in another world. I don't suppose he ever entertained a single doubt in his whole life."

"You better have another drink," Camack said.

"No. No, thanks. I haven't anything to drink for, or to."

"Gratt, I hate it so . . . I'm so damned sorry about it, I'm so sick over it. Do you know what I'm trying to say?"

"You're trying to apologize for me, for my own futility. Maybe I could drink to that, to Failure. Why, I couldn't even walk out there this afternoon and get *shot*, not even that. Eleanor had to be the one."

"I'm not blaming you, nobody's going to blame you, Gratt, Nobody thinks of it as being *your* fault."

"But no matter what they think or say, it is, it was, it will always be my fault," Gratt Shafer said.

"It was the old man, *he* pulled the trigger."

"Tom McCutcheon?" Gratt turned and walked to the window. It was black dark outdoors. "McCutcheon knew whose fault it was. He even came and tried to tell me who was to blame, he even went that far, he even warned me, Camack."

"He was insane. You can't go by what a crazy man tells you. McCutcheon was an old nut, the common garden variety of nut. Nuts like he was shoot people down every day. They plant bombs in train stations. Eleanor was just unlucky."

"I think you've got him all wrong, Camack."

"Have I? That black suit and that black hat, those glasses? Don't tell me I don't know the type. I've seen that breed in the courtroom. We had a case here about two years ago where this old man killed his wife when he found out she drank beer, only from his point of view he was just *executing* her. All he did was play God. That's what your friend was up to this afternoon."

"Except that his aim was poor, except that he missed what he was shooting at . . ."

"I've been thinking about that too, since they carried him out of the woods," Camack broke in. Gratt turned to look at him where he sat pouring another drink out of the bottle. "I've thought of that too," the lawyer repeated, "and I'm not so sure he did miss what he was aiming at."

"You mean you think he shot Eleanor on purpose?"

"Of course we'll never *know*, but I have an idea the old man may have liked you, Gratt. Deep inside he may have had a feeling for you that he couldn't quite control in that last instant. Hell, a five-year-old child could have hit you at that range. It's just a thought, don't you see?"

But Gratt Shafer didn't see, nor did he see Tom McCutcheon as a fanatical old man. He was, after all, or had been, Patsy Jo's father. This, it was, that Gratt Shafer did see.

"Only a few places in your body where a bullet will actually kill you, a spot on your head, a spot on your heart, the narrow column of your spine," the lawyer went on, in a bemused tone of voice. "I spoke to the surgeon. He said Eleanor couldn't have been saved. The old guy shot her with soft lead slugs. They came apart inside of her."

While Camack Patterson was talking, Gratt Shafer looked down at the clothes he was wearing, and realized only then that he still wore the wedding clothes, stained now with Eleanor Fite's blood, the blood dry, the fabric stiff beneath his fingers. The realization brought with it a certain numbness. He wanted to be rid of the clothes, to be rid of everything that could remind him of what had happened, of what he, in a very real sense, was responsible for, had caused.

"I think I'll go up to my room," Gratt Shafer said.

"Look," the lawyer said. "You don't know it, but you're

not yourself." He stood up, Camack also wore the striped trousers and the cutaway coat, the gray vest . . . "Take it easy a minute. Have another drink. A drink will help, you'll see it will." He took Gratt Shafer's arm then and led him to a chair. "Sit down," he said. Gratt Shafer nodded. His friend was right. He sat down.

Gratt had two drinks with Camack, the two of them alone back in the kitchen. But the wedding party had gotten wind of where he was and their cars began rolling incessantly into the driveway. People were coming into the kitchen to find him. After two more drinks he excused himself to go up to his room and change clothes. When he showered the water made him dizzy and when he saw himself in the mirror, in order to shave, he realized that he was tight. He put on a dark suit, and it was laying the suit out on the bed with the rest of his clothes that did it. He had tied his wedding clothes up in a bundle and put them on the waste basket beside the desk at one end of the room, getting them permanently out of sight, even the shoes. But when he laid out fresh clothes on the bed, feeling a little tight and not too bad, feeling no pain, it came to him that the night before he had slept with Eleanor — slept here. The missing champagne cork, the one that had popped away in the darkness would be lying about somewhere, if the maid had not found it. The bed confronted him and he turned away. He could hear them downstairs. Their voices drifted up the service stairs from the kitchen. The cars were rolling in the driveway, passing beneath the porte-cochere. He walked to the dressing table where he had opened the last bottle of champagne. There were stains in the carpet beside his bare feet. I stood here, he thought, only last night.

He dressed and went back down the service stairs. Everywhere people were drinking and shaking their heads — the pity, the tragedy of it all was seeping into them with the liquor. The press was nibbling for information, by phone and in person. Camack was turning them all away. While Gratt was upstairs a doctor had come by and left a sedative. Camack handed him the little envelope. "Take two before you go to bed." Gratt put the envelope in his coat pocket. "The police may have some questions in the morning, but I got them to lay off tonight." Gratt fingered the little envelope inside his pocket. "What will the police want?" he asked. Camack handed him a fresh drink. "Just the most routine statement you can make, what you saw, any reason you might know as to why he did it. They have to file a report." Gratt took a swallow from his glass and shuddered a little. The drink was too strong. There had been no mention, no suggestion of food, not that he could have eaten anything. You get a fellow drunk and you figure his grief won't hit him so hard, he thought. And he said aloud, "McCutcheon was trying to kill me. He just loused up the job. There's the reason." Camack shook his head. "No, you don't know that. You don't want to say anything like that. All you want to say is that McCutcheon always was queer — full of queer notions and queer ideas, withdrawn, you know, the peculiar old man thing. Just say you think maybe he was crazy. That's all they want. You don't know that other business. You don't know it at all. I'll go along with you to the station if you like."

Rather than sleep in the bed he would have gone back to

Somerton. The last drink put him past grieving and he excused himself and went back upstairs, but when he looked at the bed this second time, not grief, but a goatish impulse instead, leaped inside him. He thought of Patsy Jo. But he remembered too that the police wanted his statement. He thought next of calling her long distance to convey his sympathy. He could let her know what he wished, felt, intended. That he wanted her beside him, with him now, tonight, that the urge he felt was blind to death — he could tell her that. His desire was insensitive to grief. I could tell her that, he thought.

He drew off his clothes and lay across the bed, dozing. Later, when the house was quiet, he got up wearily and turned off the light. When he lay back down he thought of the sleeping pills, still in his coat pocket, but he was too tired to get up and take them. Twice he woke, the last time just at dawn. He lay awake then, staring at the window's half light, watching the dawn slowly pale into day. He felt feverish and thirsty and he lay still, trying to re-image the strange, composite woman he had dreamed about. By waking up he seemed to have passed out of pleasant country, a place without worries. Her arms had been so real about his neck that when he first woke he could still feel them by closing his eyes again. He lay wondering what it was that lingered just beyond the ken of his thoughts, what little threat, what worry was there. Something was wrong, he could feel it, and then he remembered. "McCutcheon killed Eleanor." It fell on him like a weight. "But I'll call Patsy Jo," he muttered, remembering then that he had almost called her before he went to bed. But later, at breakfast, he decided against it.

At nine they drove to the police station. He felt light-headed. He kept looking at Camack to see if perhaps he felt the same way. He spoke slowly while the police clerk took his statement. The clerk wrote with a pen and stopped occasionally to take a drag from his cigarette. Gratt felt his ears stopping up as he spoke and he paused once to take a deep breath. The smoke annoyed him. The smell of the clerk's ash tray, a cupped bronze affair which had not been emptied that morning, gave him little twinges of nausea. *Hangover,* he told himself. "I would guess that Tom McCutcheon was crazy — insane," he said aloud. The clerk wrote the concluding line, took another drag on the cigarette, and left it in his mouth while he read the statement over. "I'll just get this typed up," he said, "and you can sign." He left them sitting by his desk. Camack smiled. He turned to Gratt. "That's all you need to say." Gratt moved his chair back from the desk. The clerk had stopped at the water cooler, now he went on out of the office.

All you need to say, Gratt Shafer thought.

17

BECAUSE the train left Memphis at midnight, there were not many passengers. The interior of the coaches was yellow. The few passengers Gratt Shafer saw had a tired look. The lights made them look like corpses, and the train went slowly, like a funeral train. The passengers were trying to sleep, sitting straight up in the plush seats, their eyes closed to the yellowish lights. The rattle of the wheels, the swaying motion of the train, and the brown daycoach odors of grease and cigarette smoke and stale, sweating bodies seemed not to bother them.

Nor did the stink inside the coach bother Gratt Shafer when he remembered the graveside scent of flowers, the nearly overpowering perfume of death which had sickened him earlier that day. He preferred to be where he was now. He had seen enough of death. He was going home now. But the swaying clatter of the train and the sleeping passengers scattered about in the other seats in the coach, set him wondering. His thoughts pushed through the night with the train and a groping, mysterious sensation of being all alone in the world came over him.

That same day, just ended a few minutes before at midnight, Thomas Gideon McCutcheon had been buried at Somerton. Like Eleanor Fite Shafer, McCutcheon had been laid out of sight. Living, McCutcheon and Eleanor had been citizens of two different worlds. Now dead, they had the world of death in common. The last difference between them had been the words spoken over their bodies, the difference in what the little Episcopalian minister had read from the Prayer Book for Eleanor and what the Reverend Bledsoe Worthington had undoubtedly said over the body of Tom McCutcheon. In essence, the Episcopalian had been unsure. His lack of conviction had seeped into his weary voice. The Baptist, on the other hand, *would* have been sure. Conviction would have been carried in Bledsoe Worthington's voice, and conveyed to all his listeners. The Somerton minister would have been sure that on Doomsday, when he inquired about Tom McCutcheon, he would be told that McCutcheon was in hell. He would not have said as much in preaching Tom McCutcheon's funeral sermon, but the conviction of what he felt would have been implicit in all he said. It must have been a sermon worth hearing.

The dead, he thought, closing his eyes. The past was over after all. What was done was done, as Camack Patterson had said on the way to the train station. In telling Gratt Shafer good-by the lawyer had seemed to be saying how sorry he was that things had turned out as they had. Yet he had never said he was sorry in so many words. His sentences had trailed away into hopeless gestures, a wave of his hand, a shake of his head, until, when Gratt Shafer shook hands with him before boarding the train, Camack had grown completely silent, as though to say what had happened was now lost, in the cold gray world of forever. Life was the world that must end, but death was the world without end. The dead must be dead forever, voiceless, as Camack Patterson had been, unable even to say "Good-by."

Gratt Shafer walked to the baggage room at Somerton to use the phone and presently he saw the taxi coming and heard its low-pressure tires bat over the tracks. The soft-jointed old automobile swung in toward the little station building. The train was gone by then and the unshaven taxi driver unsettled the cap he bought second hand on Beale Street in Memphis nine years ago, unsettling the cap as though it still didn't fit his head and settling it back again. Inside, the cab smelled like something that has sat up waiting all night for ten years and whatever it waited for never came; it smelled of one dead cigarette tamped out on another one. The driver steered with his right hand, taking more care to see that the ashes flew into the back seat than to mind where he was going. And, finally getting out of the cab, Gratt paid him thirty-five cents, dropping it into his hand after which, without a word, the man drove slowly away, heading for the Somerton bus terminal where he would have just time for a nap before the coach from Jackson chuffed its air brakes at the corner and geared down, waking its passengers for the stop, for Somerton, Sligo County, Tennessee.

Gratt found the house key in his pocket, and slipping it in the worn lock, he entered. The floors popped beneath him as he passed the parlor and started up the stairs. Finding his way straight to his room in the dark, he put on the overhead light. It was the room he had lived in all of his life, the room he had returned to from his Japanese imprisonment, the room that had been there waiting for him during the summers of his college years. He had wasted his life here, slept and dreamed it away, for dreaming, he now realized, had been the main business of his life up to now. There had been the ideal girl, not found; the ideal profession, not found; the ideal job, not found. In the instant before accepting anything that would have committed him to itself with any degree of permanence, he had always, in that last instant, turned aside. He had been willing to marry Eleanor only because it would not have been the demanding ordeal, which instinctively he knew, real marriage, by its very nature, must be.

He put his luggage down wearily against the wall and sat on the bed. He had brought Patsy Jo McCutcheon here, to this very room and this very bed. She had given herself to him for promises, gambling on the hope that someday . . .

But she could wait until tomorrow, he thought, consoling himself. Now he needed to lie down. A little time, a little rest, a day or two, and he would do the right thing. I will make a beginning, at least, he decided.

18

THE *truth was that Gratt Shafer had stood her up.* Patsy Jo waited for Gratt Shafer to come back and he didn't. She listened for the phone, but it didn't ring. She drove by his house and nothing happened, unless you wanted to count what happened inside of her, how her heart jumped when she saw his automobile and the house where he was. Her heart jumped and she drove on around the block to her house. She went in and had a Tom Collins and listened to the radio and had another Tom Collins and got back in her car and drove by his house again, just to see, and sure enough her heart jumped again when she went by, jumped like a little mouse. She had quit her job to wait for him. She had hustled her father into the ground so she would have everything out of the way when he came home. He would probably come after midnight at first, because he wouldn't want anybody in Somerton saying about how soon after his wife's death — all of that business — so he would come after midnight and leave before dawn. Which would have been all right. She got some books out of the library and sat up reading them. She kept herself awake with coffee, waiting for him to come, and it would have been all right with her. Only he didn't come. She sat down to write him. She started the letter: "Dear Gratt." She started over on a fresh sheet of paper: *"Dearest Gratt."* Sometimes she got almost three lines written. Then she threw all the wadded stationery in the waste basket. She had no more stationery left, only the envelopes, the unused, virginal, unlicked little lily-pink envelopes which she slammed in a drawer, out of sight out of mind. The phone. She would phone him tomorrow. Tomorrow came and she put off phoning him until the next day. Sometimes she even got the receiver in her hand, but it never came off the hook. It might as well have been glued to the phone. She ran out of gin and Mattie French went to Memphis and bought her some more, enough to last a month. Mattie was a dear. Mattie was the only one she could trust. Mattie was the only one who understood.

Mattie's heart wasn't made out of brass and Mattie knew you had to get your man, like the F.B.I. and the Texas Rangers, you had to get him. "Don't give up, Patsy Jo. Dear, don't give up," Mattie said. Like the Navy: "Don't give up the ship." Like the Army: "Hurry up and wait." Her daddy hustled off into the ground like she was sending him to catch a train for somewhere. Then getting her hair washed and set, getting a manicure and a pedicure, new bath salts and new dusting powder and perfume; getting out the negligee and washing it by hand, laying it close by — all for nothing. It was as though Gratt Shafer had evaporated, like nail polish remover, without leaving a trace except the smell of him, the godwonderful smell. When she woke she still smelled it for a moment, before it too evaporated, with the dream, and she saw the book lying face-down beside her and the cold coffee cup on the bedside table and the light burning wearily late. She would pick up her watch and look at it, the watch he had given her, and it would be three-thirty A.M., just the right hour, too early to get up and too late to feel like going to sleep again, like making the effort. So she would pick up the book. Or she would switch on the radio and listen to the station in Texas that sold mail order phonograph records and hearing aids and hernia trusses and dietary supplements and vitamins. All night the radio went sometimes, hymns and hillbilly music, Western jazz, and wonderful offers through the mail at ab-so-lute-ly no obligation, just send us your name and address on a post card. Sometimes she felt like doing it, like getting a post card and writing her name and address on it, like getting the one dozen rosebushes for a dollar plus C.O.D. postage, just to put herself on record, just to let some-one know she was still alive, that she was still waiting.

Then she started getting the phone calls. They came at all hours. "You know who this is, honey. You know what I want, honey. Don't tell me you don't like it, honey. Honey, I know you're living there all alone. Honey, I see you every day but you don't see me. I like the way it wobbles when you walk. I'm making you an offer, since you won't do it for love, I'm offering ten dollars. You better think it over, honey." She had the phone number changed and kept a secret. When the new phone book came out her name wasn't in it. But she couldn't forget the voice on the wire. It was like every man in Somer-ton had been rolled up into a pill to make that voice, begging her one minute and cursing her for a whore the next. With

her father dead and her man evaporated they knew she had
no protection. They knew she was living there alone, all that
stuff of hers going to waste. *The way it wobbles when you
walk.* She stayed off the streets. If she had to buy anything
she went to Jackson for it. One morning at three A.M. someone knocked on her window and then whoever it was went
around to the front porch and stood out there knocking on
the screen door. She phoned the police, but when the
policeman got there *whoever it was* had already gone. The
policeman swiveled his belly around and hiked up the little
pistol on his belt: "Don't you hesitate a minute, honey. Call
me — *anytime* — night or day." She got the message. She
made him think maybe she *would* call him sometime. That
got him out the door, sleek belly, little gun, and all. He
didn't want to go, but since she told him she had this awful
sinus headache, he did. She locked the door after him and
leaned against it, breathing through her mouth, her heart
fighting in her chest like a trapped frog. She went back to her
bed and lay down and stayed there with the radio off, listening. She stayed that way until daylight before she went back
to sleep.

She thought how she was thirty-four, but she didn't think
of Gratt Shafer. Because there wasn't any use thinking about
him. That didn't bring him back. And thinking about *him*
did something else, it threw her periods off — gave her one
this month and two the next and the next none at all. That's
how it had been before the wedding, his wedding, when she
decided he would be better off dead, that she would rather
bury him than lose him, and that's how it was when she

hustled her father off to shoot Gratt. Her periods were in tumult. It was like both the time she *thought* she was, and the time she *really* was pregnant. She was scared, but not because she thought she was pregnant now. She knew she wasn't. But her periods skipping that way reminded her of the other times, when she was nineteen, and the worst, when she was twenty and had to go to Memphis to have it fixed up.

But everyone had their man problems. As Mattie said: "Remember poor Flora, everything worked out all right for her." Mattie said this as though there were some similarity between what happened to Flora, her sister, and what was happening to Patsy Jo. Flora French *had* almost been an old maid. Mattie and Patsy Jo were ten years old when Flora's gentleman caller started coming to see her on Saturday evenings. Poor Flora's diarrhea started each Saturday morning. And because an old maid is a problem to her entire family, the entire family knew about Flora's diarrhea. The family knew about Flora's hand-sweat of anticipation. The family felt sorry for her, dehydrated and pale by nightfall from a day of trotting to the johnny. Did her gentleman guess? Patsy Jo wondered. Or did he take her little spasms of alarm for passion, her paleness for love-sickness? She remembered how poor old Flora had been persecuted by her coiling bowels, she remembered poor Flora's sharp nose, her rimless glasses, yellowish teeth and plain sexless figure. An amplitude of bosom or a round seductive belly would have helped her no end, but she possessed neither and her bad looks had kept her virginal despite an old and honored Somerton name. But at last a student mortician with a missing finger and a cock-eyed gaze had discerned the maiden, Flora, in her tower of aristocratic ugliness, and hoping to mix her somewhat bluer French blood with his own, had presumed to call. He came down from Nashville on Saturday after classes at the School of Mortuary closed, resplendent in a light blue double-breasted suit, he came full of mumbling hope, like a young, dignified bee preparing to assault an old flower. He proffered earnest plebeian pollination. He would transport her! Flora sighed. *He* was no butterfly dancing after milkweed. Still he was cautious, daring not rush nor risk rebuff, and in the long, hovering weeks of the interim poor Flora purged. The very mention of Mr. Peter Paul Clisby was enough — for then in her mind Flora saw Mr. Peter Paul Clisby's pale roadster coupe heading west from Nashville; she heard the rush of the wind past the coupe's windows and saw upon the wheel Mr. Peter Paul Clisby's hand with the missing finger, and she felt the unsure gaze of his glittering, irregular eyes upon the road. But the ending was happy for Flora French. Mr. Peter Paul Clisby made her his own and took her east in his pale coupe to a town with vast undertaking potential, and there he gave her a home and children, which calmed her bowels. Everybody had their man problems.

Gabe French, Senior, Mattie's own father, he had had his trouble. His trouble had been another woman, a dime-store clerk named Kitty Fay Felker. Gabe Senior had decided to leave his family for Kitty Fay. His children were all grown, his son, Gabe Junior, was in medical school and was married. Gabe Senior would soon be a grandfather if he didn't hurry and get out of Somerton and the notion of becoming a grandfather gave Gabe Senior a terrible fright. A grandfather didn't live much longer, and Gabe meant to *live*. He intended to start life anew, to begin all over with Kitty Fay Felker. So they left town together, intending to run away forever and live life all over again, from beginning to end, intending never again to be seen nor heard of in Somerton. But when they got well down into Alabama Gabe fell asleep at the wheel and there was a two-car collision. When Gabe woke up he was in a Birmingham hospital and the doctors were telling him he would never walk again. When he asked for Kitty Fay Felker they had to tell him she was dead and Gabe French, Senior, came back to Somerton living in a wheelchair. If he had come back walking it would have been different, for then he could have swaggered what had happened off, and lived it down. But you can't *swagger* in a wheelchair. So Gabe Senior wheeled himself off into a room where he wouldn't have to let his wife look at him, and he lived there like a prisoner, with Kitty Fay's picture turned face down on the table beside his bed. Mattie looked after him and Flora French Clisby wrote him from East Tennessee that she still loved and revered him.

Toonker Burkette was the only man in Somerton who had seen the shooting in the church *and* McCutcheon's body in the woods. It gave him a certain distinction around town and in a surprisingly short time he became an authority on what had happened and why. He wrote a special eye-witness account for the *Bugle-Gazette,* the Somerton weekly, and Patsy Jo had been told that the publicity had gotten him a good many more patients. It was said that now people came in to have Toonker work on their teeth so they could hear him tell about the wedding. Then they could go back home and tell the neighbors they had talked to Toonker Burkette, who saw the whole thing with his own eyes. It was said that Toonker told them just how Eleanor Fite fell and how she screamed, that he described just the way Tom McCutcheon was lying on the brown leaves. Toonker's theory was that Tom Mc-Cutcheon had *meant* to shoot the bride all along — not Gratt Shafer like he had said he was going to do. According to Toonker, McCutcheon had said he was going to shoot Gratt only to throw people off of his main purpose, his *real* purpose, which had been to shoot Eleanor Fite and thus send Gratt Shafer back to Patsy Jo. As Toonker saw it, therefore, the *real* son of a bitch was Gratt Cunningham Shafer, who had promised himself to one girl and then gone off and married another. Even if Shafer said he hadn't promised to marry Patsy Jo, Toonker discounted it; what was a lie to a guy like that? Toonker asked. Toonker was quoted as saying: "A guy who would deceive a girl like Patsy Jo would suck eggs." As Mattie French said, the only person Toonker made mad was Bo-jack, the old man that kept house for Gratt Shafer, and Bo-jack couldn't do anything about it. Even if he hadn't been a Negro he was down sick half the time and ninety if he was a day, so old his eyes had turned blue. Patsy Jo saw Bojack in the yard sometimes when she drove past Gratt Shafer's house. The old man would be killing dandelions, or mowing a little grass if he was able. But she could tell by looking at him, even from that distance, that he wasn't going to live much longer. It wasn't anything she could lay her finger on, as, for example, like the way he walked. It was more like a feeling she got before the weather turned cold in the fall. Even in hot weather she could feel cold weather coming. She had felt it ahead of time, that way, for as long as she could remember.

What she hadn't been able to feel ahead of time was what happened at the wedding. The day of it she had given up Gratt Shafer for dead. She had given up her memories of him, the way he smelled Sunday afternoons when he came by for her, of fresh dry cleaning and shaving lotion. And she had given up the memory of their nice clean affair — for that was what it had become — a clean adult affair that no one in Somerton resented because there was no one who wanted to deny a girl her man. She had felt no recriminations of conscience. In fact she wasn't even worried, even as late as her twenty-eighth birthday when he gave her the wrist watch, when their nice clean affair had been going on for eleven years and had survived the trip to Memphis where she had had *it* fixed up. She still had the watch Gratt had given her, and kept it by her bed so when she woke up at night with the light burning she could pick the watch up and see what time it was. The watch was six years old now and it still ran perfectly and kept good time. She had been sitting at home with a sick headache the day of the wedding and she had been in bed holding the watch when the hour for the ceremony came. Her father was gone and the gun was gone. His room still smelled like Hoppe's No. 9, for that was the pungent stuff he used to clean the gun with, or any gun for that matter. The orange box of Hoppe's No. 9 was on his dresser beside the open case in which the pistol was kept. That was how Tom McCutcheon let her know what he had really gone to do. He didn't need to leave her a note. No, for merely smelling the gun cleaner was enough, and that morning when she went into his room and saw the empty gun case and smelled the Hoppe's No. 9 she had phoned the Factory-to-You Store and told them the truth, that she had suddenly gotten a sick headache and that she wouldn't be in to work that day. She didn't know then that she would never go back to the Factory-to-You. She didn't know it when she went to bed that morning and didn't know it when she sat bolt upright that afternoon, holding the watch, imagining what was going on in Memphis just then, imagining Gratt Shafer being shot to death. For her idea then was that by working at the Factory-to-You, *afterwards,* she could forget there ever had been a Gratt Shafer. Afterwards. She sat there looking at the watch and gave him up. Tears blinded her once or twice, but she wiped them away using the edge of the bedsheet that was stretched over her knees. "I don't hate you, Gratt, but I want you dead. That's how much I still love you," she had whispered. She sat in bed, bolt upright, until she was sure the wedding was over, then shivering like a little animal, she had gone in and taken a shower with the water as hot as she could stand it. But she was still cold and trembling and it kept running through her head, from the instant she stepped into the bathtub, pulled the plastic curtain closed, and regulated the shower, that perhaps her father *hadn't* done it after all, that perhaps his nerve had failed. The notion didn't help her trembling any more than the hot water, but at least it bolstered her up. She let the water run for a long time, and when she stepped out of the tub she picked up the watch which she had left on the lavatory and looked at it. The wedding had been over twenty-five minutes. While she was drying off she wiped the steam off the mirror above the sink to look at her face. She found that it was holding up fine. It was maybe a little pinched-looking, but otherwise it was fine. She had almost finished drying off when the phone started ringing. By the length of the rings she had known before she answered that it was long distance, for long distance calls in Somerton came with rings that were easily a third longer — maybe more than that — than local calls. She let the towel fall and went into the hallway bare as the day she was born. "Gratt's dead," she had whispered, "and I'm free." Then she had reached for the phone and answered it. It had been Toonker Burkette calling collect to tell her Tom McCutcheon was dead. "What about Gratt Shafer?" she had asked. "He's alive. He's okay. Gratt's fine," Toonker had said, matter of factly.

When she hung up the phone it started ringing right away again but she let it ring and went back to her room and sat on the bed. She had fifteen more minutes to herself before the first person started knocking on the front door. She went back to the bathroom, past the incessant phone, and got the watch. She put it on first before anything, and then she dressed. "Well, I tried, anyway," she told herself. The simplest thing was to answer the front door first. She did, and Mattie came in, kissed her, and went back to the hall and answered the phone.

Of the others who came, some brought food. Why death and food were so interrelated was a mystery to her. "It's so awful to have to cook at such a time," said Betty Morgan French, Gabe Junior's wife, who brought a bowl of potato salad and three dozen stuffed eggs. "But *I* don't cook," Patsy Jo said to herself, "the *cook* cooks." It was the cook's afternoon off — Thursday. And aloud she said: "Why thank you, Betty Morgan, honey. How thoughtful you are. Here, let me carry the eggs." But Betty Morgan wouldn't hear to it. "Just show me to the kitchen, Patsy Jo, dear, and I'll slip these things into the ice box," she declared.

The kitchen had soon been jammed to overflowing with food. The refrigerator had a turkey and a boiled country ham in it. Cakes and pies were all over the kitchen table and the counters. They stretched out a sort of buffet in the dining room after nightfall and the women walked around the table and piled their plates high. There were plenty of pickles and preserves to select from, olives, cucumbers, watermelon rind, peaches, okra, strawberries, blackberries, apple butter. And there were at least a dozen deep dishes. The women ate eagerly, the men reluctantly, like they hadn't planned on eating, but arriving at the time they did and seeing how much there was on the table and having this and that one say she would be really offended if the men turned their back on her jam cake or her sweet slaw, they fell to and put away enough for a family of five and then ate a little piece of pie and a little cake. Betty Morgan and her boys were cranking a couple of freezers of ice cream out on the back porch, and when the men had let their dinner settle a little they went out and had a saucer of Betty Morgan's peach vanilla and declared they had never tasted anything better.

"At least *she's* out of the way," Mattie French had said when word came that Eleanor Fite had died in the hospital, when Toonker Burkette phoned the news "collect," from the hospital in Memphis.

Out of the way, Patsy Jo had been thinking when Mattie had said what she did about Eleanor. *Thank God,* Patsy Jo had thought, *thank God she went on and died like a good little girl.* Because Patsy Jo had been thinking it would be just her luck for Eleanor to live and keep Gratt all the rest of his life. And then there had been something else just then that arrived and had needed to be gotten out of the way, her father's body. Mattie told the funeral director to bring the remains on up to the house and set the casket up in front of the mantel. They could stand flowers and ferns on the hearth to hide the fireplace. So the funeral director came and helped arrange the flowers and about ten o'clock that night they had brought the casket up to the house and set it up, with the lid open, in front of the mantel. That cleared out the living room except for a few people at a time who came to see how nice Tom McCutcheon looked before they stepped through the doors to the dining room, now closed off from the rest of the house. The funeral director had arranged some lights on the mantel and had draped some fine netting, on the order of cheesecloth, over the whole thing. When she had looked straight in through the cheesecloth, at a certain angle, she had been able to see his face — very natural and lifelike — and no matter how hard she looked there was no sign of the place where her father had plugged himself in the head, even though she had been told right where the place was. The undertaker had a special wax he had explained, and it hid and restored nearly anything. Toonker had arrived from Memphis while they were setting the casket up in the living room and he had helped. He had said you could sure as hell appreciate what the undertaker did, what a hell of a fine job, when you had seen what he had to start out with, what a mess it all was. Patsy Jo had wanted to get the casket from in front of the mantelpiece and out of the way, so she had set the funeral for two o'clock the next afternoon even though it meant one of Tom McCutcheon's cousins from California didn't get there on time and had to console himself with going out to the cemetery and looking at the place where they had buried Tom McCutcheon. It was tough that he was a second cousin and had never seen Tom McCutcheon in the flesh. But she had shown him what pictures she had of her father and the second cousin had looked them over and, while he was at it, he had looked *her* over and said he thought he might stay around a few days to help straighten things up. Mattie's eyes met Patsy Jo's, for they had both looked up from the pictures when the cousin said it. "But I'm closing the house, Cousin Baxter," Patsy Jo said, "and I have plans. Everything *has* been taken care of already." Cousin Baxter had blushed and said, "But I thought if there was something I could straighten up for you — just offering." And Mattie had looked right at Patsy Jo and said: "Now isn't that *sweet* of him?" They had packed him off on the bus that afternoon. He had looked like an overgrown kid being packed off to reform school. "If you *ever* need me," he mourned, "just drop me a line and I'll be right here."

Cousin Baxter had been the last thing she had had to get out of the way, and it was all done before she heard Gratt had finally come home from Memphis. Then in August, after she had not seen Gratt even once in all that time, Toonker phoned her to say the cashier at the bank had told *him* that Gratt Shafer's check for twenty thousand dollars toward the Eleanor Fite Memorial Art Museum in Memphis had come through. "It's just like that son of a bitch to send his money out of Somerton, to send it out of his own home town down to Memphis," Toonker said. "All in the world he's trying to do is salve his conscience. Why don't you sue him for breach of promise? Long as he's tossing money around that way you might as well get your cut, right? Listen, he's buying Mildred and Fletcher off so *they* won't sue him. Isn't he?" There were a good many folks in Somerton who agreed Toonker was probably right, and as Mattie said, not one soul had told the dentist to his face that he was wrong. "I'd call it worth twenty thousand dollars just having *her* out of the way," Mattie had said, "otherwise . . ." And Mattie had looked at Patsy Jo and had not been able to finish. She hadn't needed to, because Patsy Jo finished it, *to herself*. "Otherwise your father would have died for nothing," she told herself.

Each time Patsy Jo realized her father was dead, each time the awful grief of losing him entered her, her thoughts turned backward to certain moments with him, to those times when she had needed him and found him always there to help her. He had been *there*. Now he was not *there*, and it was as though her father had been a wall protecting her from a terrible pit, as though he were a protector who had kept her from stumbling into a place of utter loss and utter terror. He had dried her tears, after all, her father had, even when he had not known why she was crying. His great strength, his belief, his moral fiber, more, even the smell of the cigarettes he smoked, his big hand which she sometimes kissed, his rough cheek, unshaven in the morning, the great pleasure in his eyes when he talked about her mother, followed by the pitiful dismay, like a dark cloak dropped about his shoulders, when he told how his wife had deserted him.

Desertion. It was, after all, the worst crime in his book, it inflicted, as he knew, the most anguish on the one deserted, imposing a penalty of life-long loneliness, setting the victim's spirit off wandering, never to return home again. Tom McCutcheon would not have *her* deserted, not even by a man he didn't approve of, not even by a man he didn't really want her to marry — with all his heart he hadn't wanted to see her marry Gratt Shafer. There was Gratt's Yankee father to think about, old Doc Shafer's queer mannerisms and queer ideas. And Gratt Shafer, besides, had never *done* anything with himself. Gratt Shafer would not be capable of *protecting* her, was how her father had put it, for a woman needed more than to be provided for — she required *protecting,* and there was where Gratt Shafer fell short, to her father's way of thinking. But really, he shrank, it had seemed to her, before the idea of her marrying at all, inwardly at least, perhaps because his own love and marriage have given him too much pain and loneliness, almost, to bear. When Adelicia deserted him, she had left her mark on him.

Patsy Jo wondered what her father might have been like had her mother not left him. It seemed to her now that he would have been gay and generous, a man who might have laughed a good deal and grown a little fat and red-faced as he got older, instead of growing into such a studiously grave person, into a man so taken up with issues of the mind and spirit, as to be always overly sensitive to insult.

She had loved her father, she now realized, despite the outward show of bitterness between them; she had loved him, even if, unwittingly, he had deserted *her;* she could not blame him. He had been trying to protect her, after all. He had taken his own life rather than subject her to the shame of his own trial and punishment. She saw his suicide, last thing he had done, as an unselfish act in her behalf. Let people shake their heads about him, question Tom McCutcheon's suicide how they would, but she respected and loved him still in her memory. She loved him. Her memories of him were full of pride.

My father, my wonderful headstrong father, she often thought lately, when her heart finally calmed down so she could realize what had happened. She bought black clothes then, hat, veil, gloves, stockings, dress. It was what he would have expected, that she would go into mourning. When there was an opportunity to say so she said: "My father was one of the most wonderful men who ever lived. That's the greatest and only consolation I have now. He was a very great and good man. And he loved *me* more than anything else in this world."

When she said it to someone, and she said it often, the other person seemed changed. The other person, it seemed to her, suddenly saw her father in a new light, as *she* saw him, as he really was, and not as he had appeared on the surface. She said it so fiercely sometimes that she could see the other person become truly sorry not to have the McCutcheon blood in his own veins. The McCutcheon blood was strong and loyal, fine blood, and now she was strongly proud of it. To be a McCutcheon counted for something. She realized that her father had not left her unprotected after all, for merely because she was his own child she *was* protected. He had left behind his courage and his spirit. These would protect her now, these would never be destroyed. They were her heritage, forming a protective wall between her and that awful, doom-felt pit, a wall she could touch when she wanted to, even lean against — a wall she could now put her back to and fight from when the time came. And the time was coming, she knew.

"I can wade up to my neck in blood," she told herself. "I can wade in blood and never cry. I can do it now."

Her father's death was a new dimension in her, her loneliness and her father's death grew close together inside of her, until the two were inseparable, loss of her father and aloneness. Together they made steel in her spine, a feeling of straightness and inflexibility which she had not felt before, a hardness in her eye which she had never recognized before. But now it was there. The black clothes she wore had finally done what nothing else could do, the black clothes and the steel — the feeling of stiffness in her spine — they took the eyes of men off her. And women, too, left her alone. She found her father's chair a better place to sit for reading than in bed. So she sat there through the long nights and read the books from his library. She read Gibbon, *The Decline and*

Fall of the Roman Empire, and began Ridpath, *History of the World.* She found when she showered that her bones were beginning to show. She was getting thin. In the mirror she could see that her cheekbones were higher, or seemed that way, and to avoid the beauty shop she drew her hair straight back and pinned it in a bun. So doing she saw a few strands of gray she had not noticed before. But it didn't matter. Nothing mattered but the new-found discipline in herself which could make her forego the world entirely if need be. She would not let herself think about Gratt Shafer any more. She would dry and shrivel inside before she would wonder about him again. She took the supply of gin Mattie had brought her from Memphis, and poured it all, every bottle, down the drain in the kitchen sink. When Mattie French came to see her and began to talk about men, about sleeping with them, about the overtures they made to her, Patsy Jo simply got up out of her father's chair and went into the hallway, slamming the door behind her and waiting quietly in her own room until she was sure Mattie French had left. Mattie was the last tie she had with the world, a world which Patsy Jo now told herself she was forever out of — forever. And finally Mattie left her alone.

Cleaning out her desk, she found a letter she had written to Gratt Shafer a few weeks before and had not mailed. Her first impulse was to burn it at once, as soon as she saw what it was she held in her hand, her lean hand with the closely trimmed fingernails which she did not paint or have painted any more. Because it would have been weak to burn the letter, because she sensed that it would have defeated every victory she had so far won against herself not to read it, she took it to her father's chair, sat down, and turned on the lamp:

Dearest Gratt:

Forgive me. I knew when Daddy left here what he was setting out to do — that he was going to kill you. When he didn't do it I was so relieved — Gratt, I was so relieved I cried. Then like a fool, after you came home, I waited for you to call me. I acted like a little girl when it was time I acted like a woman. Oh, Gratt, at least you lived through it. Now I hope you've found out something about yourself that I've known about me for a long time. I hope you'll come home to me now, because what I feel inside of me for you has never stopped. And it never will stop. You went on and married somebody else, but I know you did it only because you felt you had to — you had to because of my father and because I never grew up, because I wouldn't stop fooling around. But those other men were desperation. I tried to show you that you were going to lose me if you didn't marry me. I wanted you to know other guys wanted me — that you weren't the only fish in the pond, when the truth was that you always have been the only one. I died each time I was with another man, Gratt. You did what you did because you felt that I never grew up. But you didn't love her and she couldn't love you the way I love you. Because I love you so much I could kill you — that's as much as you can love anybody. Now you've broken my heart and I still love you and I don't want to lose you, I still want to kill you. Can you understand that I want to kill you with my love? Just a chance, that's all I ask of you. Just give me a chance. I'm not mad any more and I

*promise not to be jealous any more. That's how I drove you
away from me — being stubborn and jealous. That's why you
never would marry me — why you didn't ask me again. Well,
you don't have to ask me. I'm asking you to marry me. I haven't
got any more pride and this is my last chance and I've got to
fight for you. I'm ready to crawl down Main Street on my
hands and knees if it will do any good. You can't hide loving
someone. You just can't hide it, so don't blame me for not
being able to hide it, Gratt. And don't let me suffer like this
forever. Don't let me get old, Gratt, don't let me die not ever
having had the only thing in life that I really ever wanted. I
don't care if you don't love me. That doesn't matter any more
either. Just come back. Come back, Gratt Shafer. You know,
I get cold at night and I start to hurt all over. Sometimes I
dream you're here, but then I always have to wake up and
see this room and this house and this town, this rotten bastard
town and all its rotten bastard people looking at me —
always the same faces and the same looks. And I can't do
anything but look back at them. So I look at them and hate
them and they look at me and either hate me or lust after me
or both. I ought to be used to that by now, just as I ought to
be used to living without you. But as long as you are alive I'll
never reconcile myself to being without you, I never can, because I love you — and when I think that it could go on this
way until I die — do you see what I'm trying to tell you? That
I'm going to die one of these days and have behind me all the
years between the time you left me and then in which to
suffer for not having you. Don't you see why I don't have
any pride any more? Don't you know that if you love someone the way I love you, nothing else matters in the world?*

Not gold, not food, not drink, not precious jewels, not sex — they are just nothing, just hell, because no matter if you have everything else in the world and don't have that person you love, you can't be anything but a pain to yourself. And that's why I'm just a pain, Gratt, and that's all I am. My heart has taken over all my whole body, and it is aching in a way I hope you never feel an ache. I couldn't even be a decent whore, even though I think now that going through something like this is probably what makes a whore a whore. Not needing money, not just having the looks for it and needing the money, but loving the guy you can't have and loving him forever. Call it silly. I do myself. Call it what you want to and believe it or not. But in the final end it's love. And I love you, Gratt, so much I can't stand it, but I do stand it and you are killing me, just killing me or I couldn't have written this at all. Forgive me. Oh, please come back, please.

P.J.M.

She took the letter back to her desk. Her hand, she saw, was trembling. She had been afraid to mail it, why? Because, she decided, she had been so afraid Gratt Shafer still would not come. Fear had no place in her life, not any more. She took the letter back to her desk and addressed the envelope to Gratt Shafer. She folded the letter, slipped it inside and sealed it. There was a stamp left in the drawer, a single stamp that she had put on the original envelope in which she had intended to mail the letter when she wrote it. But before, after putting the stamp on the addressed envelope and sealing it, she had become afraid. She had torn the letter out of the envelope and lifted off the stamp with her fingernail, throwing the envelope away and saving the letter and the final stamp, until now.

The stamp needed glue. Going back to the kitchen, she took an egg from the refrigerator, tapped the end of it gently with a table knife, and used a bit of the oozing white of the egg to wet the stamp. Then she put the egg back in the refrigerator and put the stamp carefully on the envelope. It stuck. She went then to the porch and put the letter in the mailbox for the postman. It gave her a quiet, elated feeling to realize that now she didn't care what effect the letter might have on Gratt Shafer. Now that she had posted it, she felt that she was more free than ever before in her life. She cautioned herself to forget the letter, and taking up her book, she sat down and began to read. She was into Volume 4 of *History of the World*. "It has been said that the new Caliph Waled, whose youth had been passed in Damascus," she read, "was in his manners and tastes more Greek than Arabian. Certain it is that he was indolent in habit and voluptuous in disposition . . ."

She heard the postman's step on the porch, the sound of the mailbox, opened and shut. Then the postman was gone. She looked back at the page, hunting her place, ". . . the new Caliph Waled, whose youth had been passed in Damascus," she read again. But her mind could not somehow settle into the sense of the words. Putting the book aside, she went to the window. It was raining outdoors, a mild rain pouring from a dreary sky, Main Street black and glistening with it, the automobiles passing, windshield wipers rocking back and forth. She counted the months on her fingers. August was over now. It was September. *September, September!*

She looked at the postman's wet footprints on the porch. *September,* she thought again. The very name of the month bit into her vitals. She stiffened suddenly, and, going back to the chair, she resolutely took up the book again.

19

IT WAS his policy, on awaking each morning, to kneel down beside his narrow bed and address a prayer to the Jesus calendar on the wall. Bojack Markam knelt and folded his hands comfortably together. The Christ was black, a Negro in flowing robes, feeding the multitudes — a black Jesus calendar distributed by the Lord Byron Jones Funeral Parlour for Colored, where Bojack carried his burial insurance. He looked at the face of the black Christ. "Save me in the end," he said. "You can do it; I know you can do it. You got all the power it take." His mind swept backward over the sins of a long lifetime. Women and drunkenness were there, especially during the years he had shined shoes in the Somerton Barbershop on Main Street, his *middle years,* as he thought of them now. He had stayed with a lot of women and drunk many a half pint of white whiskey from a bottle kept in the back of the barbershop. "You can do it," he repeated aloud. "You got the power."

Outdoors it was raining, the second day of rain, falling steadily, a bad thing for cotton at this time of year, he thought. A bad thing he had done before the barber fired him from his job, stealing three quarters out of the cash drawer. And *that* time the barber had a trap laid and caught him red-handed, taking him into the back of the shop and beating him like a dog, whipping him with a broom handle the way Bojack himself had whipped mules on the farm before he had run away from it, whipping him until he went down on his knees, whipping him until he wondered if the barber meant to kill him. He still felt the pain of the beating in his joints, in his legs and in his back. That's when Doc Shafer had hired him to help out at the Mountains of Gilead, to unearth bones and arrow points and broken bits of pottery. It was the only work he could get, for the barber had told it on him, that he, Bojack Markam, was a thief. But the barber was dead, and most of the heads the barber had cut were buried too. If they gave haircuts in hell, Bojack thought, the barber would be busy. He looked intently at the majestic black Jesus. "You can save me," he said. "Amen."

Slowly he got up off his knees and dressed himself. He went out the back door to the carriage house and washed up in the bathroom Doc Shafer had built for him there, coming back through the rain to the kitchen, putting the kettle on to boil while he mopped the floor, wringing the mop out in the sink, and working slowly, trying to come awake *right*. For he had found that if he could come awake *right*, in a certain easy way, then the day could be made the same way, could be made easy. So he went slowly with the mop, working out the stiffness of his sleep, the pain in his legs and his back. The kettle boiled and he put coffee in the pot and poured the boiling water into it. Then he went out through the rain again, to the carriage house, for a pan of grain which he threw to his chickens, throwing the corn high over the fence into the little yard behind the carriage house. Returning to the kitchen, he washed the mop out and hung it on the back porch. Then he set a pan of bacon on to fry and put buttered bread in the oven for toast. While he fried the bacon he drank a cup of coffee and began to feel better. It would be time to wake Gratt Shafer soon. Putting the cup down, he went into the dining room and set the single place. Then he took the bacon off, laying it on a brown paper sack to drain, and went out into the hallway to the foot of the stairs to call Gratt Shafer.

"It's time!" he yelled up the stairway. Gratt would be down by the time his eggs were fried. Bojack went to the front porch and got the newspaper and the mail, putting both beside Gratt's breakfast plate. He was in the kitchen frying the eggs when he heard Gratt come down the stairs. With the toast, bacon, and two eggs on one platter, and the coffee-pot in his other hand, Bojack went back to the dining room and put Gratt Shafer's breakfast down before him. Then he poured the coffee. Gratt already had the letter open, he saw, and was reading it.

"You feeling okay this morning, sonny?" Bojack said.

"Fine," Gratt Shafer said, automatically. He put the letter down. "Fine," he said again.

"Just one letter this morning," Bojack said.

Gratt Shafer picked up the envelope and looked at it closely. "The postmark says yesterday," he said. "But she didn't write it yesterday."

"Who is the letter from, Gratt?"

"It's from Patsy Jo."

"She wants you back, don't she?"

"Yes. She wants me back."

"Didn't I tell you she did? You've frittered all this time away worrying about it, but I was right all along. Didn't I tell you?"

"Yes, you told me."

"But you couldn't listen to me," Bojack said triumphantly. "You couldn't listen at an old man, could you, sonny boy?" Gratt Shafer shook his head, holding the letter and staring straight ahead at the wall. "Well, now's the time to go back if you plan to go, like you said. Ain't it?"

"Yes," Gratt Shafer said. "Now's the time."

"You're going, ain't you?" Bojack asked.

"Yes, I'm going," Gratt Shafer said. "I'm going back to her."

Bojack took the coffeepot back and put it on the stove. Then he went back to his own room and went down on his knees before the bed again, before the calendar. He hadn't thought Gratt Shafer would go back to Patsy Jo McCutcheon, even though he had asked for it to happen when her father was killed. Now Gratt *was* going back to her. He looked at the calendar steadfastly, not knowing what to say, distracted now by the rain, and what it must do to the cotton, coming so late, when a dry fall of the year was what the countryside needed. He, Bojack Markam, old and broken down with his sins, his joints sore from the wet weather, the memory of the beating the barber had given him even now clouding into his brain. He closed his eyes. "Much oblige," he said after a moment, and opened his eyes again. "If . . ."

he began a little gruffly. "If they have a baby, I wouldn't mind getting a look at it. I ain't begging for no promises, understand, but if it take a little extra living time, maybe you wouldn't mind to let me see it, okay?" He gripped his hands together tightly. "Much oblige. Amen." Getting up, it came to him that he had come awake *right*. Now he could make the day easy. Now he could do it. Since it was raining, he decided he would clean the stove and polish some silver, and spend the afternoon waxing floors. Yes, Lord.

He took the coffeepot off the stove and carried it to the dining room, but Gratt Shafer was gone. Only the toast was broken in two and half a piece of it gone, with the coffee. Gratt Shafer had abandoned the rest of his breakfast, leaving behind the empty envelope, propped against his water glass, beside the still-folded newspaper.

20

H E TOLD himself over and over that he had been a fool, driving up to Main Street, the rain coming steadily down, pelting at the wing vent beside his left arm and spattering his face with tiny droplets. Gratt Shafer held the folded letter in his left hand. He swung left into Main Street and parked the car in front of her house. Getting out and running up the steps and up the walk to the long front porch, he realized that the rain robbed him of his dignity, making him run at a moment when he would have preferred to walk slowly and think about what he must say and do. Standing on the porch, he looked down and saw that the ink on the letter was running. He thrust it into the coat pocket of the dark suit he wore, and rang the bell. He had not worn a hat nor a raincoat, in his haste, and his hair felt uncomfortably wet, as though water would run out of it and over his face at any instant. The damp air gave him a steamy sensation, as he waited for the door to open. When it did finally open, he was not prepared, for he was listening to the rain scatter through the leaves of the two magnolia trees on either side of the walk behind him, hearing the drops break against the hard, slick leaves. And then the door was standing open and Patsy Jo McCutcheon was standing on the other side of the screen, her face pale, more pale than he had ever seen it, and gaunt, the black dress making her look strange, almost like another person. He stood silent.

"So it's you," she said. "So you finally came after all."

"Yes."

"Was it because of the letter? Because if it was . . ."

"It wasn't the letter." He interrupted her. "It was something inside me that was always there, so close always that perhaps I was never able to see it, for that very reason." He knew he was lying, and discovered that his hand had unconsciously slipped back into his coat pocket, and was clutching the letter now, as though to make sure it was still there.

"Well, come in," she said in a flat, even voice. "It's been a long wait."

"I don't know what to say," he said, opening the screen door and following her into the living room. He saw her father's chair, the lamp, and the book folded face down on the table beside it. It was as though the old man had just left the room for an instant, and would soon return. With a sudden sense of shock he realized that until now he had not seen her since her father's death. "I've been a terrible fool," he said, groping for what he wished to say.

She sat down in her father's chair. "It doesn't make any difference, Gratt. Either you were going to come back or you weren't. A woman can resign herself to anything after a while. You see I found that out, don't you see? You might have called me first, you might have let me know you were coming. I could have dressed up for you."

"But you look fine — you're looking well," he said.

"In *these* clothes? When did *you* get so polite? I look like hell, and you know I do."

"Look here," he said. "I want to make all of that up to you — the entire past. I'm asking you to marry me. I'm sorry for everything, the whole rotten everything that's happened. It was all a great mistake, don't you see? I *know* that now, and I'm asking you — will you marry me? Patsy Jo, will you marry me?"

"You know God-damned well I'll marry you. You've known I'd marry you for years. I don't want to think of how many years you've known I'd marry you, Gratt Shafer. My answer's yes, I will marry you, but I'm not going to wait another year, hear me?"

"We'll be married anytime you say," he said. "I've tried to say I'm sorry." She came out of the chair to where he stood and he put his arms out, drawing her into him. "I'm sorry as hell," he whispered.

"Never mind," she said. She took his face in her hands and began to kiss him, drawing back to look at him between kisses. "I'll just change clothes and we'll go get married," she said.

"Anything you say."

"To Mississippi, we'll drive down to Mississippi. You don't have to wait in Mississippi."

"I'll go buy you some flowers while you change clothes," he said.

"No, you'll stay right here. You'll sit right in this chair and look at this book. It's your turn to wait for me now." She pushed him around and back into the chair and sat in his lap. "It's your turn to wait for me, understand?"

"Yes," he said. "I thought flowers would be nice . . ."

"No flowers. You wouldn't come back. This would be a dream and I would wake up. Do you know how many times I've dreamed of this? You wouldn't think of leaving if you knew."

She went back to her room then, leaving him sitting where, so many times in the past, he had seen Tom McCutcheon sit. She kept shouting to him from her bedroom. It was a terrifying moment for him too, he realized — an unreal moment for them both. She came back wearing a white dress and red shoes, carrying a red purse and a red hat. They went out, across the porch and through the rain, scarcely conscious of the wet. She said the same word over and over again, until it echoed in forgotten chambers of his memory. "Hurry," she said as they turned south, passing the Mountains of Gilead. "Hurry!" she cried.

She didn't want to stay in Mississippi, to drive south to the Gulf Coast after they were married, as he had thought they might do. And they had no luggage besides, and the only places to stay in North Mississippi would have been the motels strung out from the hamlets along the way, and she would not consent to a motel. He pulled into one before she had said anything, a place with a bird bath on its front lawn and funny rustic chairs about the bird bath, chairs that probably no one ever had sat in, a bird bath that probably no bird ever had bathed in, because, like the rest of the motel, the chairs and the bird bath had an untended look. It was as though someone had dreamed of building a beautiful motel in North Mississippi where people would stop and sit sedately in the chairs, where birds would bathe, but the reality of the place had not, somehow, fulfilled the dream.

"No motels," she had said. She spoke quietly, and he spun the wheel and drove the car rapidly back onto the highway, leaving the long whitewashed building behind, with its row of shuttered windows and white doors and its neon sign blinking in the daylight, announcing a vacancy.

"Then where do we go?" he asked. They had driven out of the rain coming south, but rain had fallen on the road only recently. The highway was steaming. Far off, on the flat horizon, more clouds jutted into the sky. The land all about was pastureland, and cattle grazed in the deep grass.

"Let's go home," she said, after a time. And he turned the car around, cutting into a narrow country lane and backing out on the highway, and they were heading north, over the way they had come. They went back towards Corinth, where they had gotten married before a preacher who charged ten dollars a marriage, and did the thing quickly. They passed through Guntown and Baldwyn and Booneville, and a little town called Rienzi, before they reached Corinth. Outside of Corinth, going north, they saw a young couple in a car. "Just Married" was painted on the rear in tall letters with what looked like white shoe polish. The car had a Mississippi tag.

"They're probably going to the mountains," Patsy Jo said, "to the Smokies."

"Would you like to go there?" Gratt Shafer asked.

They passed the car. The young bride was pressed close against her callow groom. He had a crew cut and they both looked very young and very happy.

"I can just imagine them planning to spend their honeymoon in the Smokies where it's cool," Patsy Jo said. "When you live all your life in hot, flat country like this, the mountains have a special meaning. But I don't want to go there. I just want us to be home."

"Then you don't want to take a wedding trip?" he asked.

"No, I'd feel out of place. It's too late for trips."

"What makes you say that?"

"It just is too late. And I don't want to talk about it, if you don't mind. I . . . I think I'm resentful, and I don't want to be like this. I didn't plan to be this way."

"It's all right," he said. "You'll get over it."

"I may try to punish you for the way you've hurt me. And I don't want to, Gratt, I don't want to punish you. I love you too much for that. But it's the way I'm made, it's so awful, it's such a terrible feeling, here inside me. Do you know what I'm trying to tell you?"

"Yes," he said. "You have a right to feel that way."

"No," she said. "I don't. I don't have any right at all to feel this way. But I'm going to get over it. I can't stand to feel this way."

"Is that why you don't want to take a wedding trip?"

She was quiet a moment. "It's just the idea of having to live in rooms, the way we did before, because I don't like to remember that. I want to forget those years, Gratt, even though parts of them were beautiful. I have half of my life that I want to forget. I'm afraid I'm pretty wretched."

"You'll get over that feeling," he said.

"There's no saving the good parts, you have to forget the good with the bad," she said. "My father took me to the Smokies once when I was a little girl. I was ten years old, and it was summertime and we went walking by a stream that came tumbling out of the mountains. It was full of big white boulders, and I put my hand in the water, it was icy cold. It was all so beautiful, and I thought then that when I married I'd have my husband take me to the mountains, and just as . . . as my father and I had done on that day, I'd . . . I'd put my hand in the water." She began to cry.

"You mustn't cry," he said. He took a handkerchief from the breast pocket of his coat and handed it to her without taking his eyes off the road.

"Oh," she said. "I . . . I can't help it. When I think of my life, oh, hell, of what I wanted and of how long I've had to wait for everything . . . everything." She tried to stop crying, to control herself. "I thought I'd never cry again," she said. "I thought nothing could ever make me cry again."

He put out his hand, to touch her shoulder, but she pushed his hand away. "Don't," she said. "Don't touch me. God, I haven't any right to hate you. Not this way, Gratt. How can you hate somebody and love them?"

"I don't know," he said. "You're upset. Look, I'm going to make all the bad times up to you. We'll be together, I'll do things . . . some sort of job — I'll work at something now, you'll see."

"That would be silly. I don't want that for you, Gratt. I just want us to be together, and do what we like. That's enough."

"I'll make it all up to you," he said. "We have the future now."

"No," she said. "Don't say that any more. Don't say you'll make it up to me, because you *can't* make it up to me. God damn you, Gratt, *nobody* can ever make it up to anyone else. Can't you see that now? Can't you?"

"Then I'll try," he said. "You'll see . . ."

"But I don't want you to try. I don't want pity, damn it! Pity would come between us, just as trying to make the past up to me would come between us. Can I make things up to you? Do you think I can go back and unhave Tom, Dick and Harry? Or do you think if you have me twice to their once it's all made up, all hunky dory? Do you think you can bring my father and that bitch he killed right up out of the grave? Gratt, don't try to make it up to me. If you're saying you're sorry, I'm saying let's forget it."

"All right," he said.

"You're a simple guy, Gratt. When you touch me, it's going to be as though you never touched me before. And later, maybe then you *can* take me to the mountains. But not now."

"Not now then," he said, after a pause.

"What — what bothers you?" she said.

"Somerton," he said. "Seeing people. Going home."

"But isn't Somerton where the beginning was, where it still is? We've always lived there. We have to go back. Because it's no good to run away, Gratt. That's why I want to go home now. We're going to look them all, every last one of them, straight in the eye."

"If you say so," he said. "Still I've wondered a long time,

nearly all my life I guess . . . I've wondered if the world were really worth a try. Maybe you're right, maybe it is. I think . . ." he struggled for the words ". . . sometimes I think of the day the Marines marched out of Shanghai, I was marching and the people all around, both sides of the street, yelling and cheering. The regimental band was playing. We, marching, and they, the ones cheering, believed something — that there really was truth and bravery and love, and that fighting for any one of these . . . these things was worth it, that risking it all, which is only your life, that risking everything was sensible."

"For my money the world is just as much Somerton as it is Shanghai. I wouldn't know of course, but my blood tells me it is, Gratt. And my blood, oh God it makes me hate sometimes. To hate and love — I was born knowing that's all there is. Is that what you finally found out in Shanghai, Gratt? Is that what happened? You've never talked about what happened," she said. "What did happen?"

"I haven't really liked to think about it. I've never wanted to talk about the ugly difference in what I expected and what finally was. I don't know what I expected, maybe I thought it would be like knowing about Santa Claus and the Stork, but for one thing I didn't expect to be captured. Killed, perhaps, yes. Maybe I thought we would fight down to the last man. I don't know. But we kept losing. It went on and on. It didn't seem possible. And, after the surrender, after Bataan fell, instead of trying to escape I did just like I was told. I . . . I was so damned sick and afraid that when they shot another American or beat him to death, I . . . I didn't feel *anything* — least of all anger. I only felt *glad,* glad it was someone else and not me. I got to know a coward — me. The thought of you even kept me going when I had run out on you. It was anything to live, anything at all."

"Gratt, you don't have to tell me," she said.

"No, let me finish. You see I felt smart at first because I thought I *had* found something to believe, that day in Shanghai, when we left. But after the surrender, no matter how deep down inside myself I went, there was nothing, nothing. It was a case of nothing at all, of having brought home just what I left with, no more no less. When things were at their worst, I thought of you, of those things you say you want to forget. Well, I don't blame you. And when I came back, after they liberated us, when I went to the veterans' hospital in Memphis for the final check-up before they discharged me, they asked if I needed a job, what I was going to do. And it gave me a sick feeling. I was reminded of it just now, by what you said. I could tell they were trying to make it up to *me,* without knowing just what it was that had happened. Somehow they knew it was more than just malnutrition and scars, more than war neurosis and nightmares, of waking up to think you're in that Jap barracks, and that you'll go back down into the mines at dawn, wearing a lamp on your cap — that you'll be doing that same thing every dawn until your last one. But the poor bastards didn't know just what. So they offered to get me a job. And when I got so I could speak, after the dizziness passed, I finally got calm enough to say no thanks, I was going home to get married, and they said fine, good luck, and if I needed them, a job or anything . . . to let them know. They were relieved. A former war prisoner was a tough case because he was a freed slave. And I could see they had already seen two or three others like me."

"You were tired, Gratt. But, well, it's over."

"Yes. Thank God, yes," he said. "It's over."

They ran into the rain again, a sodden steaming rain from puff-bellied clouds. They crossed the Tennessee State Line in the rain. At dusk they reached Somerton and Gratt Shafer phoned Bojack from the McCutcheon house to tell him they were married, then he handed the phone to Patsy Jo. The old voice sounded very far off to her. "Just want to say I hope a lot of happiness for you," he said. "The right thing has been done, and I hope you luck."

"Thank you," she said. "We're . . . happy." She said good-by to Bojack and hung up the phone. "I think you can touch me, now," she said. "I think I want you to."

They went to her room, a place so familiar to her that she long since had ceased to notice anything about it. But now, with Gratt Shafer sharing it, she saw the old furnishings with a stranger's eye — the high canopy bed that had been her mother's, the washstand with its porcelain pitcher and bowl, the stern chairs, and the tall, narrow windows. "Turn your back," she said. She didn't want him to see how thin she had become. He must not see her sallow breasts. She put her clothes quickly on a chair and climbed into the high bed, pulling the cover up over her. "Please put out the light," she said, and turned away on her side.

The darkness created a distance between them. She lay there shivering, more alone than at any other time she could remember. His touch was alien. "Are you all right?" he asked.

She clenched her teeth and made her hands into fists, but her sorrow would not be held back. It could not be denied, and finally it came out in a low cry, a sound so strange and forlorn, so hopeless and lonely that she felt a sickening weight. It seemed to sink from inside her chest into her belly. "I'm sorry," she cried.

His arms came about her tenderly and she turned against him. "I'm sorry," she said. They lay still for a long time. She pressed close to him in the protection of his arms while it seemed that beyond that circle of bone and flesh hell's eternity howled for the loss of her. She did not know when she stopped sobbing. She only realized, at last, by the sound of his breathing, that Gratt Shafer was asleep. He turned after a time, but she clung to him, pressing close against the warm wall of his back, holding him, she thought, holding him forever. And then she fell asleep.

She rose then, from the deep sleep of exhaustion, to the quick and silent intensity of daylight, to the room filled with it, and to the consciousness which comes from being watched. Gratt Shafer's eyes were so clear, so blue and innocent, and his face sun-tinted, so calm and rested after sleep; her memory swept back to the lad of seventeen, to the impish carefree youth so long buried in this solemn man.

"I was thinking what our baby will look like," he suddenly said.

And she stopped breathing an instant, tense, so very tense again. "No," she said. "No children. I'm sorry, Gratt."

"But you can't mean it," he said.

"Can't you see it's too late for children? We're not kids any more, it's all over . . ."

"It isn't," he said. He was disappointed. He was hurt. She saw that. She had hurt him and she was sorry, but there was nothing she could do.

"No," she said. There was no place in her for life, for the quickening of life. There was nothing but the weight inside her, the leaden despair which left no room for anything else. "You're enough, Gratt," she said quietly. "Just you. Nothing more."

He reached for her now, not pulling her close, but only touching her, with a slow touch that made her eyes close, that calmed the panic somehow and let her sink away toward the center of herself, living only in the slow movement of his hand, feeling her flesh resistant at first, fearful, but by slow degrees blushing and warm, bringing a heaviness to her cheeks. What had been despair somehow melted, as though fired through the slow touch of her body's secret places, as though life somehow had been raised within her from a dead tomb she had imagined must be empty forever. The cold breath of fear, the lonely despair which had encased her heart, seemed by tiny droplets to begin flowing out of her and to want him in its place. There had not been room for him, until now, but his touch prepared the way until she was like dry earth, hungry for rain, for all the gentleness she had forgotten. There was no thought or memory of the intervening instant, for it was as though his hand had slowly shaped the rest of him, into and over and about her, in the blind blackness beyond her closed lids. She had always been this, the earth and sea, white clouds in a drifting sky, trees shimmering in the sunlight of a strange August blended from July in a surge of memories, nameless as a rose trellis, its vines and flowers twining back into the tangle of years, and only a smell of leaves and rain, so quick and sure, to remind life that all of it is you, in a small, sweet instant of time.

21

THE days began to get short and cold. In February they drove out to the Mountains of Gilead and walked over the frozen ground on the coldest days of that winter month. The mounds were clearly visible then, with the leaves gone from the trees that covered the Indian mountains, the trees now brown and bare-limbed. They climbed the mounds, pulling themselves up, holding to the rough bark of the trees, tasting the cold wind and looking out, when at last they had reached the top, looking over the patchwork fields of picked-over cotton and beaten-down corn. They kept to themselves through the winter and spring. Gratt Shafer followed the news from the war in Korea, and they played gin rummy in the evenings, and they read books. There was pleasure for them, simply in being together, in looking up from a book to see the other there.

It was 1951, and when the strawberry festival came they watched the parades together, and stood together in the grandstand to see Starkey Poe's parachute leap. Patsy Jo was pregnant, feeling heavy and full, and before the old man jumped from the balloon, she became dizzy from standing and had to sit down, but even so, she saw the parachute open.

At night she pressed her swollen belly against his back, and slept while Gratt Shafer lay awake and felt the movement of their child, feeling the child kick him, a quick and mysterious thing turning about fish-like in the watery bowl of her womb, lashing out again and again with those waterbound pummelings against his back — *his child*, kicking.

They continued to live on Main Street in the McCutcheon house, while Bojack kept the Shafer place as he had always done. As Patsy Jo's term neared, Mattie French came to spend the final days in the house, and Gratt Shafer frequently went back to the old Shafer house in the evenings, not to go indoors, but to sit on the back steps with Bojack. Having Mattie French in the house displeased him, for Gratt Shafer jealously wanted to be alone with Patsy Jo.

As they sat on the back steps Bojack Markam consoled him. "Don't worry, sonny," the Negro said. "A woman gets to feel a certain way about this time, and she *needs* some other woman. Now you already done the man part, ain't that right?"

"Yes."

"So your part is done, so you stay quiet and lie low. See what I mean?"

"It has to be that way, I guess."

"It has to be, that's right."

Bojack held the mouth organ in his hands. It was worn down to the brass on the sides, the chrome plating gone from its being handled so many years. But it would still play.

And the mouth organ reminded Gratt Shafer of his boy-hood, when he and Bojack had sat on the steps, hearing Madam behind them in the kitchen. She had had a way of humming, a sound of contentment that could enter your heart, a sound which Doc, off in his study, could also hear. Madam had been the life of the house, the pulse and breath of it, and sitting beside Bojack, Gratt Shafer could feel Madam there once again. And feeling her there, he could feel Doc's presence, and remember how many times, sitting thus, he had heard his mother's footsteps in the kitchen; how he had heard Doc, for the old man had been in the habit of yawning when he got tired working in his study. It was a stretch and a yawn all in one. Doc's yawn was a sort of yell, a sound of strength and happiness that derived from his con-tentment to be living so close to the Mountains of Gilead. His yell seemed to say: "I am here and the world is all right." It had been Doc's way of letting the house know what he felt and what he dreamed, and the sound came almost every hour after supper was over and cleared away, until it was heard the last time, just after midnight, for Doc had worked hard, and with all of himself.

Bojack put the French harp to his mouth and played "the baby." He played it differently each time, but always Gratt heard in the tune the moment of conception and all the months of life in the womb, heard it born and then growing, from infancy to boyhood to manhood. Sitting in the darkness, Gratt Shafer heard Bojack play how the baby finally must become an old, old man, how he must be punished by the world through all of this, and discover, out of himself, what parts were strong, and what parts weak, the good and the bad, the brave and the cowardly. The baby's discovery could come only through the world's cruel process, through living. Pain would show him the way, and the world must finally crush him down, in the end, to death. But even in death the baby had his triumph, for *death* was one last high, single note on the mouth organ, the most beautiful note of all, even though tremulous and fading. *Death.*

Bojack wiped the mouth organ off on his sleeve. "You know how to prevent yourself from mistreating a man?" he said. "The way to do it is before you mistreat him, as you set out in your mind to do it, right then, to think to yourself that he was once a baby. And that will stop you. For every *man* will always love a baby. A *man* will love the idea even. And if you love the child, then you got to love the man. You got to do it. See what I'm trying to tell you?"

"I see, yes."

"Don't ever mistreat a fellow man. Because man was not born to be struck down, was he?"

"I suppose man was born to rise. I've always heard it that way," Gratt Shafer said. "But I wonder sometimes."

"That's God. He *wants* you to wonder. He wants all of us to wonder."

"Well, what is God?"

"You mean who is He?"

"I said *what.* You're old enough to have sense, so tell me. *What* is he?"

"What is God?" the old man said, his voice gone reverently quiet. "Well, it's hard to say . . . but if I *had* to say I *would* say that God is a voice inside of every man, a voice speaking *so softly* that you just can't ignore Him."

A month after their child, Adam Gideon Shafer, was born, Bojack Markam died. He died during the cotton season, in September, waking sick one morning and dying on his bed that afternoon, when his heart completely failed. Gratt Shafer waited in the kitchen of the house for the undertaker to come for the old man's body. It was shortly after three o'clock. He heard a tractor pass in the street. It would be hauling a trailer-load of cotton to the gin. In the adjoining room Bojack Markam lay dead. At home Patsy Jo was nursing the baby, Adam. The child had seemed to draw out of her all the bitterness she had felt over the past.

The past. It reminded him that there was no need for the house any more, an old barn of a house with the last person who had cared for it now gone, now lying a corpse; the house in which Gratt Shafer had grown up, the house in which he had been born. But the place was meaningless without the people — with the people dead, the house too died. It, too, must decay. Sitting on the stool beside the kitchen sink, where Bojack had sat so much of the time, peeling potatoes and shelling peas, Gratt Shafer felt the house as a great dead hulk, a burden which he no longer cared to support. For the house cost two thousand dollars to paint and five thousand dollars to roof, something the man who had built it one hundred years before had never considered, since slaves had built it, and slaves had painted it and repaired its roof. Caring for the old place required a slavish devotion, and now, Bojack Markam, in a sense its last slave, lay dead. Leaving the kitchen, Gratt Shafer wandered through the high-ceilinged rooms, down the dank and cool and catacomb-like hallway, into the formal parlor with the piano Madam used to play, the old fringed lamps, Madam's picture as a young woman.

The house had appealed to her. For the story was that Forrest's men had fired on Yankee soldiers from the roof, and for years Gratt Shafer had imagined the soldiers must have been on the roof of the sleeping porch, since that roof was flat, but Doc had disabused him of the notion. For it had been Doc who had added the sleeping porch, that high, screened-in place, where, when the fancy struck him, Doc had slept in a featherbed on winter nights. Standing in the parlor, it came to Gratt Shafer how seldom he had been inside the house at all since he had moved his clothes to the McCutcheon house and hung them in the closet there. The removal had been without emotion. He had not even thought of the old place until now.

He had, instead, pushed to the back of his consciousness the impending truth that Bojack had not had long to live, that Bojack must die, and that Bojack was his, Gratt Shafer's, last remaining link with that fallen generation to which his father, Doc, belonged. What remained of Bojack's handi-work were the waxed floors inside and the trimmed lawn outside, ephemeral monuments at best.

Turning out of the room, he went back through the kitchen and out into the back yard, wondering when Lord Byron Jones would come and take Bojack's corpse. It was a nice day outside, with sunlight and a breeze and a clear blue sky. The pickers would be at work in the fields, laughing and talking. The work and the excitement of cotton season would last now until December. The money would jingle briefly, and the money would be gone. And the house behind him must be

closed, and it must either finally burn or be razed, or simply
rot away for lack of roof and paint, rot down on its unkept
lawn until little boys broke out its windows, taking the re-
venge which boys always take on the old abandoned places,
seeming to know somehow that the enemies of boys, the old
and the dead, have once lived there, and that those dead
deserve some form of desecration, if nothing more than a
tossed stone through an already broken window.

But there would be *tomorrow* to think of all this, to decide
things and attend to what must be attended to, for it seemed
enough, just then, to have lived now more than a year, spending that time with Patsy Jo, having her to touch and know,
and love, to have held in his arms the child, Adam, his own
flesh, and to have taken each day as it came, since the afternoon Tom McCutcheon had aimed and fired a pistol at him,
and missed. Nothing, he knew it now, nothing endured, short
of man's own faith, short of man's faith and his monuments
to faith. No man living knew why the Mountains of Gilead
had been built there, nor what exact purpose they had served,
except to know that men had built them. And yet they stood,
and would stand. And they would, he knew, be there still
— they would still be there when the world burned and the
sun exploded — they would be standing at Doomsday to
assert the magnificence, the tears and the comedy, the inde-
structable resolve of humankind to rise and conquer death
even if the means to it had to be one basket of earth at a
time.

*An old man digging for arrow points, an old man playing a
harmonica, an old man firing a pistol.* He heard the hearse
enter the driveway, and he stepped into the carriage house to

be quickly out of sight, afraid now that if he spoke to Lord Byron Jones he might lose control of his feelings and break down before him.

Lord Byron himself was driving. He stepped out of the hearse, followed by his assistant. The two black-suited Negroes mounted the back steps, both of them splendidly tall men. Lord Byron knocked on the back door, and then quickly entered, finding the screen door unlatched.

Gratt Shafer could hear their voices. Lord Byron called his name: "Mister Shafer?" They came out again and looked about. They took the little body cart from the back of the hearse and up the steps into the house. Lord Byron's assistant came back out alone, carrying Bojack's best suit, a shirt, tie, and a pair of shoes. He put these burial things in the hearse and went back in the house. Both men came out next, carrying Bojack's body, covered with a blanket. They rolled the cart from the foot of the back steps to the hearse, and then, one standing on either side, lifted it gently but briskly up, and loaded it inside. The assistant closed the door and Lord Byron looked about as though faintly conscious, perhaps, that he was being watched.

"Mr. Shafer seems not to be anywhere about," he said.

"His car's here," said the other man.

"But I don't believe he's here," Lord Byron Jones said. "You're looking at an old house," he said after a pause, as though he too realized what the fate of the place must be, now that Bojack Markam was dead.

"Yeah?" said the assistant.

"Built many, many years ago," Lord Byron said. "Somerton grew around it."

"Well, say. It *must* be old. And the old man, this old gentleman, he worked here," the assistant ventured.

"He worked here in this place," Lord Byron Jones said. "He worked here."

They got back in the hearse slowly. The engine started and it moved away. When he could no longer hear the engine Gratt Shafer left the carriage house and mounted the back steps. He pulled the back door shut and locked it and got into his own car. But he didn't feel like going home to Patsy Jo just yet. He drove instead out to the Mountains of Gilead, and stopped the car, parking it just off the road. Cotton pickers were at work in the fields about the base of the nearest mound. They were a good distance off, and bent over at their work. He sat in the car several minutes, until the feeling finally passed. And then he drove home, to the McCutcheon house, to Patsy Jo, and to love, grateful at last, at long last, perhaps, content.

22

"LIVE and learn," said Lord Byron Jones, "die and forget it all."

"Amen," said his assistant, Benny, a long-footed, jack-kneed Negro with gold caps on his front teeth. Benny served as a hired mourner for funerals. His main job was to sit on a folding chair close to the casket and weep through the entire preaching service. He could use up a stack of white handkerchiefs every time. And although some people might laugh at the notion, still, a hired mourner helped, for when the service was over the bereaved ones had truly mourned. They had known, Lord Byron thought, the depth of everything the world had lost when one they loved passed on, on into the mystery, and beyond.

"No more pain and sorrow," said Lord Byron Jones, pulling off his rubber gloves.

"Amen," said Benny.

"His body was the temple of his soul, so that's why we handle him gently. The old gentleman is gone from us."

"He gone from us," Benny repeated. He had stood back to

watch Lord Byron work. The work was now done, the work of the old, old craft to which he was apprenticed. Now, at last, the remains were ready.

"You watch him a while," Lord Byron said.

He went outside for fresh air and a smoke, to put the sloping table with its steel headclamp out of sight, to forget for a time the buzzing of the fluorescent tubes overhead. Stepping out on the side stoop he pulled the heavy door shut after him and watched the traffic pass in the street and the children playing in the dusty yard beyond it. He lit a fresh cigarette and held to the iron railing, watching the children play baseball. They used an old slat and a rock wrapped in rags. On the porch behind the children, leaning against one of the unpainted supports, a pregnant girl in a blue dress watched the game enviously. Like the children she was bare-footed, and her baby rode high in her belly under the tight dress. Behind her inside the house, a small naked light bulb, visible through the open door, hung suspended from a thin cord. The bulb lit the inside of the house and Lord Byron Jones could see a bed and a chair. The girl lifted her eyes, looking at the glow from the fluorescent lights against the high frosted windows of the embalming chamber over Lord Byron's left shoulder. It was almost twilight. Lord Byron smoked slowly, enjoying the warm, humid air, feeling how more relaxed it was here than in the clammy air-conditioned room behind him. The outside air had a rich smell. Cooking fires were being lit for suppertime. The slat cracked against the rock. The dust rose and the children shouted. The girl smiled, her high tight belly swelling proudly under the blue cotton print.

Reluctantly, after a final puff, Lord Byron flipped the cigarette into the street and released his hold on the iron rail, retying the sash on his half-length sleeves. He paused an instant more, wiping his glasses on the tail of the smock, and finally wiped his face with his handkerchief, before putting the glasses back on his nose. Then at last, he stepped back inside, slamming the heavy door and crossing the thin carpet on the vestibule floor. He re-entered the tile embalming chamber, stepping beneath the light from the fluorescent tubes, and was immersed in his craft once more.

He had read it somewhere, at some time, how the ancient Greeks sometimes tossed the bodies of plague victims into some city their soldiers were trying to capture. The people inside the city would take sick. Lord Byron was half a mind to mention it to Benny, but a glance at the mourner sufficed to make him dismiss the notion. No, Benny wouldn't appreciate it, Lord Byron thought. Benny was just good for mourning, for wetting a handkerchief with tears and snot. It only remained now to paint the old gentleman's face. Lord Byron turned to the little glass cabinet containing the paints and powders. First he pulled on the gloves. Then he washed a camel's-hair brush under the sink faucet before putting his paints out on the counter. "You got the clothes?" Lord Byron asked.

"Here," said Benny softly. They were hanging on a costumer in the corner. When the shirt was on Lord Byron carefully knotted the tie, standing back an instant to see how the old man's dignity was being restored. He was always glad to reach this point. It gave him a sense of elation, a sense of rising out of some great depth and gloom. It was an awareness which had stayed with him all his life, a feeling of ceremony, of ritual. Each time, at the beginning, he felt his spirit lost in darkness. It was the dismay of his calling, but this point signaled the return of dignity, and it was his reward. Benny tucked the shirt neatly into the trousers and adjusted the suspenders. He got the black coat.

"Now the paint," said Lord Byron. Benny handed him the camel's-hair brush. Taking up a paint jar, Lord Byron dipped the bristles three times until they were full and swollen. Then draining the brush a little against the rim of the jar, he leaned down and began on the face, working down from the hairline. Where the paint covered it the old man's skin began to appear warm. What had been a sick hue, a drained pallor, and hard lines, now disappeared. For the eyelids and lips he used a lighter shade. While he finished, Benny went out and wheeled in the casket on a table cart. Lord Byron washed out the brush and when he came back Benny put the paint away. Lord Byron puffed just a final bit of powder over the dried paint, and the old man's face sunk into a restful expression. It was the expression of repose, of rest and dreaming. Now, Lord Byron thought, it shows the truth.

Raising the casket lid they put the old man carefully inside. "He's asleep now," Lord Byron said. He closed the lid and Benny rolled the cart away, leaving Lord Byron alone. Untying the smock, he turned to the sink and pulled off his gloves. He washed his hands until they felt clean and then he dried them thoughtfully. Outside he heard tractors passing in the street. They were hauling cotton to the gin. He drew out his watch and looked at it. Nearly eight o'clock. Benny would be arranging the casket in the big parlor. He would train a light on the old gentleman's face. Finally Benny would drape a scrim of cloth over the entire casket, and then, at last, he would unlock the doors for the public.

Lord Byron stepped into the vestibule and phoned Gratt Shafer. "Mr. Shafer? I just called to say we got him lying in state. I must say he looks very nice."

Gratt Shafer seemed satisfied. Lord Byron knew where to send the bill. Yes, Lord Byron replied, he knew.

After the phone call he spent a while longer straightening up the embalming chamber. He liked having it orderly. He was relaxed now, still rising, leaving *his* sorrow, at least, behind. There would be the funeral, and after that a day, perhaps two, of rest — but no more. The dead were like children in that respect. Children came, were born, in flocks. And people left, they passed on to death, the same way, in little flocks.

When he was through in the room he turned out the overhead lights and stepped across the hall to see how Benny was doing. Quietly he slid the hall doors apart and saw at first only the dead man, only Bojack Markam, wrapped in that certain stillness which he had come to know, the stillness which only the white satin lining of a casket can effect. Yes, there was dignity about the old man now, with the furze of white hair just powdering his head, and the frugal sanctity of the black suit and the white boiled shirt. Benny had already set up his mourner's chair with the white handkerchiefs on the floor beside it. Glancing toward the foot of the casket, Lord Byron had a shock of surprise. There, beside the barbaric array of greenery and floral sprays, stood Gratt Shafer. Lord Byron recovered his composure, and sliding the doors shut behind him, he approached the casket. "He was certainly a fine old gentleman, Mr. Shafer. I want to say I'm sorry for your grief."

Gratt Shafer took Lord Byron's hand. "Thank you," he said.

"One of the last of his kind," Lord Byron said, after they had shaken hands, thinking how suprisingly hard Gratt Shafer's hand was, how quick, and firm, and hard. "How long did he work for your family, Mr. Shafer?"

"Over thirty years."

"Over thirty years," Lord Byron Jones repeated. "More than three decades." He shook his head. "How is your family?"

"Fine," Gratt Shafer said.

"And your little child, how is your baby?"

"Adam is fine."

"Didn't you call him Adam Gideon?"

"Yes."

"I thought you did, Mr. Shafer. You know I thought to myself at the time. I thought *Adam,* that's the name of the first man God ever made. And Gideon, he put the Midianites to rout with blowing horns and breaking pitchers on the stony ground. I said, 'That's a good combination.' I said, 'Adam he lived nine hundred and thirty years and Gideon, he ruled over Israel for forty years.' So it's a good combination, Adam Gideon."

"I'd never thought of the name that way," Gratt Shafer said. "Gideon was his McCutcheon grandfather's middle name and Adam was my father's name."

"I see," Lord Byron Jones said politely. "I see," he repeated.

Gratt Shafer turned toward the corpse, a little bent with grief. He stood the way a man will when it hits him inside for the first time that somebody he loves is really gone. Lord Byron had seen the stance before. He brought a chair for Gratt Shafer and watched him sit down gratefully. Then he signaled to Benny, a high sign, and Benny left the room.

Grief bent a man just that way, and when he saw a very old man, bent like some very old men are bent, it came to Lord Byron Jones that grief and not age had done it, that the old man had undergone so much sorrow until finally it had weighed him down. Grief and not age, Lord Byron thought, for the grief will do it. He got a paper cup of water from the cooler and took it to Gratt Shafer. "Thank you," Gratt Shafer said. Lord Byron went out then, leaving the room closed, leaving Gratt Shafer alone with the body for a little while.

Coming into the hallway and closing the door, Lord Byron felt a second surge of suprise. He had seen Patsy Jo McCutcheon many times. He had known her father, in fact, and had respected him. And it was she, standing in the hallway, holding a sleeping baby in her arms. But she was, he saw, somehow changed, somehow vastly changed from the way he last remembered her, from the brittle pretty girl who had clerked in a Jewish dry goods store.

"Hello, Lord Byron," she said.

"How do you do?" he said. "I didn't know you were here with Mr. Shafer. Do you want to go in and view the remains?"

"I think it's better for Gratt to say his good-by alone," she said. It was her face, he decided. So much suffering had changed her. Her beauty went deeper now, and the old brittleness was gone, scoured away, leaving great strength in its place, and a sort of fierce majesty which left him awed.

"I understand," he said politely. "You have your child, Adam Gideon."

She turned so he could see the baby's face. "He's sleeping," she said.

He saw the McCutcheon features. The child had dark hair, and it gladdened him. "He's pretty," Lord Byron Jones said.

"Thank you," she replied, looking down at the baby. "I waited for him, I waited a long time to get him."

"Children are life," Lord Byron said.

Patsy Jo McCutcheon (for he could think of her as no one else, no *Shafer* could ever be connected to *her* name) nodded. "Yes," she said. "He's going to look like my father. I thank God every day for him . . . every single day that passes."

"Your father was a fine gentleman."

"The finest," she said. "The very finest."

Lord Byron saw in her a woman of character and courage, full of fight and will. She was toughened now, and she would be all right. She would prevail. For she knew how to hold up her head and dare the world. It was a little frightening to see so plainly what capacity she had for hate and love. She was a person who lived in every fiber, who lived fiercely. Life rippled from her like electricity, he thought, a destructive force, reptilian and mysterious, that could easily destroy a man — the McCutcheon blood and the Frick blood. So proud, he thought, so beautiful. "Your father was always kind to me," he said, at last.

Gratt Shafer sat alone beside the casket, tired and grieving. He sat with his legs crossed and his hands clasped together on his knee, trying to push away the memory of Bojack, of how he played *the baby*, when Adam was as yet unborn, Gratt Shafer's and Patsy Jo's baby — but it was a memory that could not be forced away, and it crushed him with grief to hear those sounds in retrospect. He looked up at the casket, and finally stood. He looked inside it one last time, hoping to find comfort. But it was not Bojack Markam lying before him. Bojack was gone, and a million miles and a million years would not bring him back. Turning away, he stumbled against the folding chair. He wanted to be away now, to be outside.

He pushed open the sliding door and saw Patsy Jo standing with Lord Byron in the hallway. She came to him, holding the child, and he put his arm about her waist. Lord Byron Jones opened the door to the street and they stepped out to the sidewalk. The door closed behind them.

"I just want to stand here a minute, before we go," he said. With his arm about her he stood breathing deeply.

"I love you, you don't know how I love you," she said. She laid her head against him.

The lights at the cotton gin were brightly burning. Looking up the street, at the gin, he could see the suck operators standing on top of the cotton, swinging the big tubes back and forth under the yellow lights. The locks of cotton were being sucked by the thousands out of the truck and trailer beds and hurled into the roaring gin. More trucks were lined up to go on the scales; and it would be that way far into the night. It would be that way clear on up into the cold weather when the pickers finally put on gloves and pulled the cotton one last, bitter time, before the gins fell silent. But now the ginning sounds reached everywhere, in the still, warm night. Now if a person sat outside his house in the evening he could hear the trucks coming in from all the outlying roads. If he looked at the gutter he could see the lint rolled up there. And if he went outside of town along any road he could see cotton scrapping the roadsides in brush and weeds, a lonely white fringe, like the whiskers of a million old graybeard men, clipped off and cast away forever.

"I think I'm ready now," Gratt Shafer said. "I'm ready to go home."